Ferocious Fire!

▼

The huge, gaping maw was rushing down at him. Cabe pushed Gwen aside and jumped back, barely clearing the massive head. Grunting, the dragon pulled back.

The powers were twisted as Cabe's towering adversary unleashed his strength. Golden the reptile might be, but his sorcery was of the darkest kind. As he fended off a crushing wall of pure force, the warlock realized that everyone had underestimated the Dragon Emperor.

The Lady joined him, melding her power with his. The great leviathan was forced back onto his throne. He roared and let loose with a sea of flame. Cabe shielded them both, but the heat was nearly unbearable. They lost the momentum they had just gained. The dragon moved in once again, adding physical threat to his magical attack.

Claws raked at both humans ...

► ◄

AN AUTHORS GUILD BACKINPRINT.COM EDITION

Firedrake

AN AUTHORS GUILD BACKINPRINT.COM EDITION

Published by iUniverse.com, Inc.

For information address:
iUniverse.com, Inc.
620 North 48th Street, Suite 201
Lincoln, NE 68504-3467
www.iuniverse.com

Originally published by Warner Books

ISBN: 0-595-09214-4

Printed in the United States of America

This book is dedicated to M.W., T.H., and P.M.

It is also dedicated to the English/ Rhetoric Department at the University of Illinois in Champaign–Urbara, the folks who finally gave me a degree.

I

Below, toward the great Tyber Mountains, they came. Some in pairs, some alone. Fierce dragonhelms hid all but the eyes; eyes that, in most cases, burned bloodred in the coming darkness. Each was armored in scaled leather, but anyone testing that protection would find it stronger than the best of mail. Flowing cloaks, like wild specters of the night, made the riders appear as if they were flying, and, in truth, any onlooker would have believed such were possible for these men.

If men they were.

Eleven they numbered, gradually coming together in one group. There were no words of acknowledgment or, for that matter, the simple nod of a head. They were known to each other, and they had traveled this way countless times for countless years. Sometimes their numbers were different, but the path had always been the same. Though each counted the others as his brethren, feuding was common among them. There was also little love lost among many of them. They thus rode silently for the entire journey, ahead of them the Tyber Mountains, stretching to the heavens, beckoning.

At long last, they reached the first of the mountains. Here appeared to be an end to their travels. No path wound through the mountains; rather, the road ended abruptly at the base of one of the largest of the leviathans. Nevertheless, the riders made no attempt to slow. They seemed intent on charging into the very earth itself. The mounts did not question their masters, but merely pursued their course as they had always done.

As if bowing to their defiance, the mountain seemed to melt and shift. The impregnable barrier of nature disappeared, and a vast path now led through. The riders, ignoring this fantastic act, continued on at their hellish pace. The horses snorted smoke as they passed the barrier, but showed no sign of fatigue. This journey was nothing to their kind.

Through twisting and turning road they moved. Icy trails and treacherous ravines did not slow the group. Again, though things not of man's world hid and watched, the riders were not hindered. Few creatures would be so foolish as to confront them, especially knowing the travelers' nature.

Quickly looming up was the great sentinel of the Tyber Mountains, Kivan Grath. Few humans had ever seen it up close, and fewer still had ever attempted to climb it. None had ever returned. Here the path led. Here the riders came. They slowed their animals as they neared the great Seeker of Gods, as its name translated. At its base, they stopped and dismounted. They had reached their goal.

Buried in the mountain was a great gate of bronze that seemed as ageless as the land. It towered over the onlookers, and on the face were carvings ancient and undescribable. One of the riders walked up to it. Beneath his helm were eyes like frost. What little of his face that was visible was also white. Grimly, he raised his left arm, fist clenched, and pointed it at the gate. With a groan, the huge, bronze door slowly opened. The pale warrior returned to his companions. The riders led their mounts inside.

Torches provided the only light inside the cave. Much of the cavern was natural, but the work in expanding it would have left even the hill dwarves overwhelmed. It made little difference to the riders; they had long stopped paying attention to their surroundings. Even the sentries, only shadows, but ever present, were ignored.

Something dark and scaled and only barely humanoid crawled up to the riders, its clawed, misshaped hand outstretched. Each of the cloaked travelers turned his horse over to the servant.

The riders entered the main cavern.

Like some resplendent but ancient temple, the citadel of their host gave forth a feeling of tremendous power. Effigies of human and inhuman form stood here and there. All were long dead, and even history had forgotten their kind. Here, at last, did the riders show some measure of respect. Each knelt, one at a time, before the great figure seated before them. When all had done so, they formed a half-circle, with their·host before them.

The serpentine neck arced. Gleaming eyes surveyed the group. A bloodred tongue lashed out momentarily in satisfaction, the tremendous, membraned wings stretching out in full glory. Despite the dim light, the gold sheen of the dragon's scaled body completed a picture of pure majesty, befitting the king of his kind. Yet there was just the slightest note of something akin to insecurity. Whether the others noted it or not was hidden in their own thoughts.

In a voice that was a hiss, yet caused the very room itself to vibrate slightly, the Gold Dragon spoke.

"Welcome, brethren! Welcome and make this home yours!"

Far spread apart, each of the riders became blurred, as if they had become nothing more than illusion. Yet they did not disappear. Rather, they grew; their bodies became like quicksilver, their shapes twisting. Wings and tails sprouted, and arms and legs became clawed, leathery appendages. The helms melted into the faces of their wearers until they had, in actuality, become the faces. Mouths spread back into maws, rows of long, sharp teeth glistening in the dim light. All traces of humanity disappeared in the space of a minute.

The Council of the Dragon Kings came to order.

The Gold Dragon nodded. As emperor, King of Kings, he was pleased to see that the others had followed his command so readily. He spoke again, and this time smoke issued out as he did.

"I am pleased that you could make it. I feared that some of you might have let emotions overrule you." He stared momentarily at the Black Dragon, monarch of the sinister and deadly Gray Mists.

The Black Dragon did not speak, but his eyes blazed.

The Emperor of the Dragon Kings turned his attention to

the nearest of his brethren. The Blue Dragon, more sea serpent than land creature, bowed his head in respect.

"The council has been called due to the request of the master of Irillian by the Sea. He notes strange happenings and wishes to discover if such events exist in the lands of his brothers. Speak."

Sleeker than most of his kind, the Blue Dragon resembled a race animal, his movements fluid, as was appropriate for a being who spent much of his life in the seas of the east. The smell of salt and fish filled the room as he spoke. A dusty, tan dragon, Brown, wrinkled his nose. He did not share his brother's fondness for the sea.

"My liege. Brethren." He studied all around him, especially the Black Dragon. "In the years gone by, my domain has been very placid. The humans have remained quiet and my clans have had good hatchings."

This time there was a grunt from the Brown Dragon, who was lord of the Barren Lands in the southwest. Since the end of the wars with the Dragon Masters, he had seen his clans decrease. Most claimed it was the work of the self-styled Masters themselves, but no one was sure what sorcery the warlocks had used in their attempt to defeat the Kings. They had caused the Barren Lands, but whether they had caused the loss of fertility in the Brown clans was open to speculation in private. Brown was still the fiercest of fighters.

The master of Irillian by the Sea ignored the slight outburst and continued. "Recently, however, things have changed. There is unrest—no, that implies too much. There is . . . a feeling. That is all I can call it. Not just among the humans. It appears to affect others, even the wyverns and minor drakes."

"Ha!"

The remark was followed by a wave of bone-numbing cold. A slight frost settled wherever the Ice Dragon's breath had reached. The Gold Dragon stared disapprovingly at him. Gaunt to the point of being cadaverous, the king of the Northern Wastes laughed again. Of all the dragons, he was one of the least seen and the least loved.

"You are becoming an old dame, brother! Subjects always

become unsettled. One merely places a restraining claw on a few and crushes such thoughts."

"Speaks the monarch of a land more empty than that of Brown."

"Speaks the monarch who knows how to rule!" A blizzard threatened to erupt from within the Ice Dragon.

"Silence!"

The thundering roar of the Gold Dragon overwhelmed all else. The Ice Dragon fell back, his snow-colored eyes averted from the brilliance of his emperor. When the King of Kings became angered, his body glowed.

"Such infighting near brought calamity on us once! Have you forgotten that so soon?"

All held their heads low, save for the Black Dragon. On his massive mouth was just the barest hint of pleasure. The Gold Dragon looked at him sharply but did not reprimand. In this instance, the king of the Gray Mists was justified.

Drawing himself to his full height, the Emperor of Dragons towered above the others. "For nearly five human years did we fight that war—and nearly faced defeat! Our brother Brown still feels the aftereffects as he watches his clans dwindle! His problem is the most evident; yet we all have scars from the Dragon Masters!"

"The Dragon Masters are dead! Nathan Bedlam was the last, and he has long since perished!" bellowed the Red Dragon, who ruled the volcanic lands called the Hell Plains.

"Taking the Purple King with him!" Black could restrain himself no more. His eyes became like beacons in the night.

The emperor nodded. "Yes, taking our brother with him. Bedlam was the last and deadliest of the Masters. With his final act, he crippled us. Penacles is the city of knowledge, and Purple was its master, he who planned our strategy." The last was said almost reluctantly, for Gold did not care to remind his brothers who had really led in those days.

"And now his lands have been usurped by the Gryphon! How much longer must we wait before we strike? Generations of man have since come and gone!" Black shook his head in anger.

"There is no successor. You know the covenant. Thirteen Kingdoms, thirteen kings. Five and twenty dukedoms, five

and twenty dukes. No one must break the covenant . . ."
For now, the emperor added to himself.

"While we wait for a successor, Lord Gryphon plots. Remember, he was known to the Masters."

"His time will come. Perhaps soon."

Black eyed his lord warily. "What does that mean?"

"As custom, I've taken Purple's dams as mine. The first hatchings produced only minor drakes, most of whom were put to death, of course. This hatching, however, looks more promising."

The other kings leaned forward. Hatchings were of the utmost importance. A few bad hatchings could threaten any of their clans with extinction.

"Only a handful of the clutch turned out to be minor drake eggs. The majority were firedrakes. However, four eggs contain the speckled band!"

"Four!" The single word was like a cry of exultation. The speckled band, this was the sign of Kings. Such eggs were to be guarded, for successors of Dragon Kings were extremely rare.

"It will be weeks before hatching takes place. The dam guards against unruly minor drakes, not to mention scavengers of all forms. If luck holds, they will all break free."

Black smiled, and a dragon's smile was something sinister. "Then will we crush this Lord Gryphon!"

"Mayhap."

All turned to he who would dampen their rejoicing. Once again, the master of Irillian by the Sea stared at them, his eyes challenging each of them to speak. When none would protest, he shook his maned head sadly.

"None of you will listen! Must I speak again? Do not misunderstand me. This news brings great happiness to me. Perhaps my fears are unjustified. Nevertheless, I must speak, or I will always have regrets."

"Then speak and be done with it! I grow weary of this prattling on!"

Ignoring Black, the king of the Eastern Seas continued. "I have felt such a stirring of uneasiness only once before. That last time, it foreshadowed the coming of the Dragon Masters."

There was a hiss of anger—and, perhaps, fear—from more than one of the great lords.

Black was now smiling. "In truth, brother Blue, I must apologize for myself. You have brought up the very point that I wished to discuss."

The emperor shook his head. "This land is old. The Dragon Kings have ruled for ages, but our reign is young compared to that of some of the earlier races. Even now, traces of ancient powers turn up. This stirring of our subjects' feelings may very well be magical in nature. Still," he paused and studied the cavern, "we have tried to weed out those who might possess some sort of attunement to those ancient ways. I know of few humans now living who are a threat."

"There is one that may threaten us." The words were quiet but firm. Without looking, all knew that Black had spoken out again.

"And who may that be?"

The Dweller of the Gray Mists spread his wings in confidence. The audience was his. "We know his family well. Very well. He is young, untrained, but his name is Cabe Bedlam."

As one, the Dragon Kings, even Gold, backed slightly, as if just bitten. "Bedlam!" was whispered by more than one voice.

The emperor fairly shrieked. "Why have we not known of this human? Where is this hatchling of a demon-warlock?"

"In the lands now held by the Gryphon. Nathan Bedlam placed the child, who is his grandson, in Mito Pica. Since the region is known for the spawning of warlocks and their like, I have sometimes sent spies forth. It was one of them who discovered the human."

Red growled. "You crossed two borders at least, brother! I wonder how many spies you have."

"We all have our ears and eyes. Besides, this human had to be watched!"

"Why did you not have him killed?" the Green Dragon asked. "This is most unlike you, Black. When have you become hesitant in pursuing your goals?"

Bowing his head subserviently to the emperor, Black replied, "I would not do so without permission from my lord."

Gold snorted. "There is a first for everything, apparently."

"Do I have your permission?"

"No."

There was silence.

"With the hatchings only a short time away, I will not permit a conflict that may draw the Gryphon in against us. He is cunning; he knows the importance we place on the speckled-band eggs. His agents could cause us harm in that respect. As long as the Bedlam whelp remains where he is and knows not his danger, we will leave him alone."

"If we wait much longer, this youngling could take up the mantle of his accursed ancestor!"

"Nevertheless, we must wait. When the hatchlings are strong enough, this last of the Bedlams will die."

He settled back. "This council is over."

The emperor leaned back and closed his eyes as if to sleep, pointedly ignoring his brethren from this point on. Wordlessly, the Dragon Kings spread themselves apart. Their bodies quivered and shrank. The great reptilian faces pulled away until they were once again dragonhelms covering near-inhuman faces. Wings shriveled and tails ceased to exist. Forelegs became arms while the hind ones straightened.

When all was done, the riders saluted their lord and departed from the chamber. Gold did not watch them leave.

The dark thing that had taken the reins of each horse waited as the travelers took their mounts, and then shambled back into the vast, eternal night of the caves.

Out of the bronze gate the Dragon Kings rode. Some in pairs, others single, all following the one path through the mountains. A wyvern, just waking, accidentally stuck its head out in their path, and sighting the riders, pulled itself to one side and cowered. It did not move again until they were long by.

At the end of the Tyber Mountains, the group split apart, each one going his separate way, knowing that mortal men would pay little attention to a single rider. Those who dared impede them would only be leaping into death.

A single rider, heading to the south, slowed as his fellows disappeared from sight. Ahead of him was a small grove of trees, and it was here he finally halted. Staring into the darkness, he settled down to wait.

His wait was short. Within minutes, he was joined by another of the Dragon Kings. Wordlessly, they acknowledged one another's presence. There was no friendship in their actions; they merely had a common goal and sought to accomplish it through the easiest means possible.

The newcomer pulled a great sword from its sheath and held it out, point first, to the other. His companion reached forward and placed a gauntleted hand on the tip. His eyes glowed brightly as power emanated from him. It flowed through his arm, through his hand, and finally into the weapon itself.

When they were finished, the sword glowed and pulsated. Slowly, the light dimmed, as if the power were being absorbed by the object itself. After a moment, the sword had returned to its former state, save for a slight vibrating. The other rider replaced it into the sheath.

The two stared at each other, communication taking place on a level far different from those of men. They nodded. What was to be done was necessary. Then the newcomer kicked his mount and rode off. He was not headed in the direction of his kingdom; rather, his destination appeared to be south.

The remaining rider watched until his comrade was out of sight. His gaze turned momentarily to the overwhelming mountain range and to Kivan Grath in particular. Then, turning away, he rode off in silence.

The floodgates had been opened.

II

"Where's my ale?"

The Wyvern's Head Tavern was known for its diversity of customers, some human, many not. One such nonhuman was the ogre that now banged down his meaty fist, breaking off a good portion of a table. His demeanor matched his face—cruel and ugly.

His eyes sought a black-haired human in his twenties who even now was hurriedly filling a mug with ale and cursing the slowness with which it poured from the spigot. To the ogre, his features were as ugly and incomplete as any other human's, but by human standards, they were regular. His face was not the face of heroes, but the strong chin, slightly turned nose, and attentive eyes gave him a rough sort of handsomeness.

Customers standing nearby formed an unintentional barrier that hid him from the thirsty creature's sight, but the human knew it was only a matter of time before the ogre came searching for him.

Cabe rushed forward, nervous, but forced to confront the ogre because he was a serving man of the tavern. Quickly, he dropped the heavy mug on the table and almost blanched when a drop nearly hit the ogre in the face. He waited for his rather dull life to flash before him.

The creature eyed him murderously, but decided the ale was more important. Tossing a coin to Cabe, the ogre picked up the mug and drank with a gusto that would have outdone most men. Cabe made a quick retreat to the kitchen.

"Cabe! Brought Deidra a present, did you?" A deft, slender hand relieved him of the coin and a well-endowed form wrapped itself around his body. Deidra gave him a long, moist kiss and then artfully deposited the coin into her blouse, a piece of clothing that did very little to conceal her generous attributes.

She flung back dirty-blond hair and smiled as she saw him staring at her ample chest. "Like a view, do you? Maybe later." It was always later for Cabe, never now.

Deidra turned, wiggled her backside, and carried a tray out into the tavern. Cabe watched until she was out of sight and then remembered the coin he had lost. It might've been worth it—later on, anyway.

He knew that Deidra liked men with money, but she still seemed attracted to him—somewhat. Admittedly, he was not ugly, and while he was not the stuff of heroes, he was still capable of handling himself in a fight . . . providing that he stayed long enough. For some reason, Cabe almost always backed away if a fight seemed close. That was why he was working in a tavern and not making his way in the world, like his father, who was a huntsman for the King of Mito Pica. Although Cabe had been useless on the hunts, his father had never seemed too upset about it. He even seemed pleased when his son told him that he had managed to find work at a two-bit tavern and inn. Rather odd behavior for a warrior, but Cabe loved him.

He pushed back a lock of black hair, knowing that somewhere under his touch was a wisp of silver that he constantly kept covered or colored. Silver streaks were supposed to be the sign of warlocks and necromancers. Cabe did not want to be killed by a mob just because he had hair like a sorceror. The trouble was, it appeared to be spreading.

"Cabe! Get yourself out here, basilisk dung!"

The summons by his employer was one that Cabe would have obeyed even if he had not been employed here. Cyrus was a mountain of a man, and beside him, even the ogre looked small.

He rushed out. "Yes, Cyrus?"

The owner, who looked more like a bear than a man, pointed to a table far away in a dark corner. "I think I saw a customer back there! See what he's up to and if he plans on buying something!"

Cabe made his way to the spot Cyrus had pointed out, slipping around the various tables and customers. It was strangely dim, but he could see that no one was there. What had Cyrus—

He blinked and looked again. There *was* someone there! How he had failed to see him the first time was beyond him. Hastily, he moved to the table.

A cloak. That was all the man, if it was a man, appeared to be. A hand, the left one, slipped into sight and placed a coin on the table, and from beneath the hood of the cloak, a strong but unreal voice spoke.

"An ale. No food."

Cabe stood for a moment and then realized that he should be getting the customer's order. With a mumbled apology, he made his way back toward the bar.

The ale was handed to him by Cyrus almost immediately, but as Cabe started back through the crowd, he was caught up by a large hand.

The ogre dragged him over and stuffed a coin into Cabe's hand. "When you're done there, bring me another ale! Keep it in the tankard this time!"

Reaching the table, he placed the ale down carefully. As he did so, the gloved hand reached out and grabbed him by the wrist.

"Sit, Cabe."

Cabe tried to loosen the grip, but it was as if the hand were stiffened in death and would never let go. Resignedly, he sat down on the opposite end of the table. As he did so, the hand released him.

He tried to look at the face under the hood. Either the light of the tavern had become dimmer or there was no face beneath the cowl. Cabe jerked back in fear. What sort of man had no face? Worse yet, what would such a creature want with someone as insignificant as he? As if amused, the stranger turned his head for better inspection.

But there was a face. It was slightly out of focus and always in half-shadow. He caught a glimpse of silver hair amidst a field of brown.

Warlock!

"Who are you?" It was all he could get out.

"You may call me Simon. This time."

"This time?" The words made no sense to Cabe.

"You are very much in danger, Cabe Bedlam."

"Danger? What—Bedlam? I'm not—"

"Cabe Bedlam. Can you deny it?"

He started to speak, and then thought. Regardless of what he thought, Cabe could not make himself deny the bizarre accusations of this warlock. No one had ever called him by that name, nor had he ever thought of it. . . . But for some reason, it sounded right.

The face of the stranger sported a small smile. Maybe. It was so hard to tell. "You cannot deny it. Good."

"But my father—"

"—is your stepfather. He has served his purpose. He knew what had to be done."

"What do you want of me? I mean— Oh, no!" Cabe remembered what sort of tales surrounded the name. It was a name of legend . . . certainly not one suited for a serving man in a tavern. Cabe was not, did not want to be, a warlock. He shook his head frantically, trying to force the reality away in much the same way he tried to deny the silver streak in his hair.

"Yes, because your name is Bedlam."

Cabe wrenched himself away from the table. "But I'm not a warlock! Get away from me!" Quickly realizing his outburst, Cabe looked around the tavern. The customers were drinking as if nothing had happened. How could they have missed that shouting, even with the noise of the crowd? He turned back to the warlock—

—only to find that no one was there.

Frowning, he searched under the table, half expecting the shadowy form to be there. There was nothing . . . except a coin, perhaps left by the warlock. Cabe was uncertain about taking money from a necromancer, but finally decided that the coin appeared normal enough. Besides, he needed it.

With one final, uncertain glance, he hurried away. The crowd was barely noticeable to him. Only the words of the warlock demanded his attention. He was a Bedlam. He could not deny it, even though he had never known it before.

New thoughts issued forth. A warlock was a person of power. Why had his ability not manifested itself? Who was this stranger who called himself Simon—"this time"?

Cabe broke out of his reverie as someone grabbed him by the shirt. He found himself staring at the grotesque features of the ogre, its hot, fetid breath wrapping over his face in waves. Cabe felt like throwing up.

"Where's my ale?"

The ale. Cabe had taken the ogre's coin and had forgotten the drink.

"Try to run off with my coin, eh? Thought I'd be too drunk to notice, did you?" The creature held up his other meaty fist and prepared to swing. "You need a lesson!"

Cabe shut his eyes and prayed the blow would not break his jaw. He waited, expecting it to fall any second.

And waited.

And waited.

Opening one eye a slight crack—and then both wide—Cabe saw the crumpled body of his attacker. The ogre's companion, a heavyset thug, was trying to revive him by throwing water on his face.

Those in the crowd that had seen the incident appeared awed.

"Did you see?"

"I never saw a man move so fast!"

"One punch! Igrim never went down from just one punch!"

"Igrim never went down before!"

The thug helped a still-groggy ogre out the door. Cabe had a dark suspicion that he had not seen the last of the creature. Most likely, he and his friend would be waiting in some dark alley.

Some customers congratulated him while others merely watched warily. Cyrus, far in back, was nodding in what could only be described as confused satisfaction. Cabe wondered exactly what it was he had done. As far as he was concerned, he had been motionless.

Gradually, the crowd returned to normal. Cabe went about his duties, but his mind was on other things. Occasionally, he would turn his attention to the table in the shadows, and once or twice he thought he saw something, but when he looked again, the spot was empty. Oddly enough, none of the new customers chose to sit there.

Dark was falling, and with it came the first signs of storm. Most of the customers had disappeared for some reason or another.

He did not hear the rider enter, but he could feel his presence. So could those around him. The silence that came so suddenly spoke much for the power of this newcomer. Cabe dared a glance and immediately wished he hadn't, for that short glimpse revealed to him an armored figure whose very presence caused those customers near the door to scurry out in a hurry. Each step taken by the newcomer was arrogant, threatening in its precision. The warrior, whoever he was, scanned the interior of the inn as he walked toward the back-most booths, and every being who had not yet left secretly prayed that they were not what the silent visitor sought.

As the armored figure sat down, most of the remaining customers departed. The eyes of the armored figure watched each and every person leave and then began to study the various employees of the inn. Cabe tried to find other things to do, but knew he could not avoid the newcomer for long. Cyrus came over and whispered to him.

"Quickly, man! Serve him whatever he wishes, and don't, for Hirack's sake, ask for payment!" He gave him a shove in the general direction of the stranger. Cyrus only called upon Hirack, the local god of merchants, when he was extremely nervous.

What, Cabe wondered, had happened to the peaceful existence he'd once maintained? Slowly, he made his way through the now-empty tavern and finally stopped in front of the stranger's table.

The helmeted head turned to him. With a start, Cabe realized that the man's eyes were bright red. Little of his face was visible, and the skin seemed clay-brown and as dry as parchment.

"C-can I get you something, sir?"

The eyes appraised him. Cabe now noticed the sinister dragonhelm the traveler was wearing.

"I want none of your poor ale." The voice was nearly little more than a hiss.

"Food?"

The unblinking eyes continued to appraise him. Cabe shuddered, remembering he had just asked if the stranger wanted food. He had not intended to offer himself in that respect.

"Your name is Cabe."

"Yes."

"So simple." The words were not intended for Cabe, but were merely a comment.

"I am going to leave now. When I leave, you will come with me. It is of the utmost importance."

"But I can't leave! My employer—"

The figure paid little attention to this. "He will not prevent you. Go and ask him. I will wait outside."

Cabe backed away as the other stood up. Even considering

the elaborate dragonhelm, the stranger still towered over him. There was little doubt in Cabe's mind that this was one of the Dragon Kings. He shuddered. When a Dragon King summoned, even the highest of men obeyed.

The rider left without another word. Cabe hurried back to the others, most of whom had hidden in the kitchen.

"What happened? What does he want?" Cyrus no longer acted like the bear Cabe remembered. Fear covered him.

"He's waiting outside. He wants me."

More than one pair of eyes widened. Cyrus looked at him closely. Cabe might as well have been a leper. "You? What have you done to incur the wrath of the Dragon Kings? It has to be something horrible for one of their own to come amongst us!"

The others, including Deidra, backed away. Cyrus continued to rant and rave. "Go! Quickly! Go before he chooses to destroy my tavern! I'll not protect you!"

Cabe tried to defend himself. "I've done nothing! Someone! Tell Lord Gryphon's agent here!"

One of the cooks, with his arm around Deidra, picked up a cleaver and waved it in his direction. "We're too far away from Penacles for the lionbird's protection! Get out before we throw you out!"

Reluctantly, Cabe backed out of the kitchen. The sound of thunder warned of the storm coming. He grabbed a cloak and reluctantly made his way to the front entrance. There was no chance of escape. If he attempted to hide or run away, the Dragon King would surely have him hunted down. Few would try to protect him.

It was raining outside. Cabe put the hood of his cloak up over his head.

A horse snorted. Cabe turned and found himself gazing up at the rider. The mount was a fiery, unnatural animal. Beside it, nervous, was a smaller, normal horse. It was the reins of this mount that were thrown to him.

"We ride! Hurry!"

Cabe climbed up. The Dragon King waited until he was settled and then started off. The serving man hurried after him, half wondering why he did so and knowing what might happen if he did not.

High above, the storm screamed unnaturally.

* * *

In the city of Penacles, in the midst of its bazaar, was the tent of Bhyram the fruit peddler. It was a stormy night, and Bhyram was cursing because he was having to put all of his merchandise in the tent by himself. With every sack, he cursed his assistant, a young man with great thirst.

An odd voice came to him from outside. "How much for two srevos?"

Srevos were sweet fruits that usually brought four coppers. Bhyram automatically said eight.

There was a clink of coins on the ground. The merchant turned around and rushed outside the tent. It was raining hard, but he could tell that none of his fruit had been stolen.

He could also tell that no one could have been nearby. Muttering an old saying to ward off sorcery, he cautiously picked up the eight coppers.

After all, he was still a businessman.

On and on they rode. The dark rider seemed untroubled by the storm, and Cabe had long since given up fighting it. Even when the rain ceased to fall, neither noticed it.

They were heading west, and in the deep recesses of his mind, Cabe vaguely recalled that these were the lands ruled by the Brown Dragon, the aptly named Barren Lands. Dry mud and occasional weeds made up most of the Barren Lands. It was not the most hospitable of places . . . and they were heading into the heart of it.

Reason told Cabe to run. Reason told Cabe that his end was surely in sight. Reason, however, could not overcome the fear that Cabe felt when he dared a glance at his unholy companion. Fear—and something else.

A duty for him to perform?

It seemed so muddled in his head. He frowned. His head had not felt straight ever since the . . . since the . . .

He could not think about that time. Something was blocking all such thoughts, protecting him.

Protecting him from the Dragon King.

They were now well into the Barren Lands. Despite the heavy rain, the ground beneath their mounts' hooves was dry and brittle. Such was the curse, for no matter how much water poured into the Barren Lands, none of it was absorbed. Instead, it just disappeared. Cabe knew that the Dragon Masters had been responsible for this.

They had seen. They had known. The firedrakes of Brown were the deadliest of fighters. Only because of this waste had their power been checked—but to no purpose. The Dragon Kings still ruled, and the warlocks and witches who had fought against them were no more.

Cabe looked up. The clouds above the Barren Lands were breaking up; yet the storm still raged elsewhere. Even the giver of rain dared not stay long. If there was a land cursed, it was this one.

"Stop."

The hissing voice of the Dragon King pierced through his mind. The helmed figure was staring at the ground as if searching for something. After a moment, he dismounted and ordered Cabe to do the same.

"Wait here."

The lord of firedrakes stalked off into the wastes. Cabe waited, knowing that flight was foolish. Perhaps, he thought, the Dragon King merely wished him to perform some task. Somehow, though, that did not ring true. The Kings had more than enough servants capable of handling anything Cabe could do.

It was not long before the other returned. His hands were empty. With great purpose, he walked up to Cabe and, with one sweeping motion, pushed him to the ground. The great sword that had hung in its scabbard was now out and pointing at the hapless human.

The Dragon King was a figure terrible to behold. The eyes burned—yes, burned—bright, fiery red. The dragonhelm seemed to smile the smile of a predator, and Cabe realized that he was seeing the true face behind the human form. In the pale light, the scales of the Dragon King's armor glistened brown. The sword, held in his left hand, did not shine. Rather, it seemed as black as an abyss.

The hiss that was not quite a voice reached Cabe's ears. "These were once my lands. They were not barren. Once, they were the most bountiful of grasslands and forests." He glared at the shivering human with total hate. "Until the time of the Dragon Masters!"

The point of the sword brushed back Cabe's hood. The eyes of the King widened. "A warlock! The final proof!"

The silver streak in his hair was evidently visible. Cabe wished that he really had all those powers that were supposed to be at the beck and call of a sorceror. At least he would have stood a chance of escaping. Why had he come with him? All along, some part of him knew that the Dragon King meant to kill him.

The dark figure raised the sword as if to swing. "By the blood of firedrakes killed with his own hand, Nathan Bedlam destroyed the life of my clans! By the blood of his own kin, I will bring that life back!" The edge of the sword came screaming down at Cabe.

The point of a gleaming shaft came through the front of the Dragon King's chest, the blade of his sword stopping short of Cabe's head.

Transfixed by the sight, the human could only watch as the reptilian monarch stared at the arrow that had pierced his body completely. A look of incomprehension passed over what little was visible of his face. He touched the point gingerly.

And fell forward.

Cabe only barely managed to roll out of the path of the Dragon King's body. The corpse hit the ground with a dull thud. The black blade slipped from the grasp of the limp left hand and clattered to one side.

Slowly, unbelievingly, Cabe stood up. No one came forth to claim the shaft. No one. He stared at his feet, and the enormity of the situation hit him for the first time. He was alone in the midst of the Barren Lands, and at his feet was the lord of those lands.

Dead.

A trio of firedrake dams, in human forms, scratched and clawed at an emerald-colored piece of amber in which stood a human form. They had scratched and clawed at it in one form or another for several decades, but had never made so much as a single mark in it.

* * *

A furred hand moved an ivory piece on a game board, and leaned back, looking for a comment from the opposing player whose mastery of the game made each move a lesson.

"Brown appears to be in a weak position," was all his companion had to say.

Cabe gingerly picked up the dark blade and hung it in his belt. It made him feel only slightly better to be armed. He debated on what to do with the body. If he left it where it was, the dead Dragon King's subjects might consider this an act of disgrace and hunt him down. If he buried it, he might not give it the proper ceremonies. Again, the subjects might seek him out.

He left it where it was.

There was no sign of the Dragon King's mount. That had seemingly disappeared at some moment after its owner's death. Cabe's own mount was still where he had left it. He climbed on and considered his next action.

He could not return to his village. That would be suicidal. Where, then? The city of Zuu? No, Zuu was too well controlled by the Green Dragon and was too close to the Barren Lands. Though the master of the Dagora Forest rarely interfered, it was just too much of a chance to take.

Penacles? The Gryphon ruled there. He had taken over the City of Knowledge after the death of the Purple Dragon. Most claimed it was for the better. Everyone knew that the Gryphon was an enemy of the Dragon Kings.

That was it. It would mean several days extra, but it was the only safe place for him to travel. If he survived the journey.

He took one last look at the form on the ground. The strange, gleaming shaft protruded from the backside. Somewhere, there appeared to be an ally, but where? Nervously, he looked around and then rode off at full gallop.

Hours passed.

Riders came. They were seemingly without substance, mere shadows of men. Yet they bore some semblance to the Dragon King who lay at their mounts' hooves. They paused, uncertain of what actions to take. Finally, one stepped down and touched the body. He noted the wound that went clear through, but saw no sign of the projectile. Gingerly, he turned the limp form over. At sight of the helmed face, there arose a muttering from the group, of which there were five.

Two more riders climbed down and helped the first. The body was placed with one of the mounted horsemen. When that was done, the others remounted their own animals.

The riders turned and headed off at full pace. They did not move toward the direction they had come from. Rather, they now faced north. There was fear in their movements. It was so rare in their kind that it became that much more noticeable.

Above them, the two moons traveled on, oblivious to the happenings of human and inhuman. Below them, however, at the site at which the Dragon King had fallen, a few small, daring blades of grass had shot up.

They were soon to be followed by others of their kind.

III

With the black blade clattering against his leg, Cabe rode through the wilderness. The Barren Lands had long ago given way to grassy plains, which had soon given way to woods. Nevertheless, he was not fooled by the beauty around him. Wyverns often made such trails their hunting grounds. Though the small dragons had only a minute amount of intelligence compared to the Kings, they were still more than cunning enough to fool a man.

The sun was bright overhead. By Cabe's estimate, he was nearly halfway to Penacles. That he had encountered no obstacles so far had sped up the trip, but he was sure his luck wouldn't hold.

The basilisk rose in front of him. Such creatures had an acute sense of hearing, because in order to make his presence unknown, a basilisk had to keep its eyes closed or else it would leave a large pile of statues wherever it went.

Cabe caught sight of the creature just before it tried to catch sight of him. The horse was not so fortunate; even as Cabe jumped, the basilisk saw it. The stone animal tipped over and fell to the ground, nearly catching its rider as it toppled.

Rolling into the woods around him, Cabe fought to pull out the sword. Somewhere off to the side, he could hear the basilisk moving slowly in his general direction. Giving up on the weapon momentarily, he picked up a piece of wood and threw it as far as he could in another direction. There was a pause and then the sound of the basilisk pushing through the brush toward the noise.

Pulling the sword free, Cabe made his way back toward the trail. Moving through the woods would alert the creature. The trail, while it would leave him in the open, promised him better speed and quieter steps.

He could hear the basilisk searching the area for him. With any luck, the monster would keep heading away. If it didn't . . .

Cabe did not care to complete such thoughts.

The trail was soft. That was good. Cabe padded along quietly, the sword ready. He doubted that he would stand much of a chance if he came face-to-face with the basilisk, but it still made him feel a little better. He stepped over the frozen form of the horse. That loss would make his journey three times as long.

A crashing noise erupted from the forest to his rear. Cabe tore off on a dead run. His only chance—and he knew it was a slim one—was to outrace the creature. Judging by the closer and closer sounds, even slim seemed to overrate his chances.

He stumbled. The blade nearly flew out of his grasp, but somehow he held on. The trampling of the basilisk was so loud that the monster had to be nearly on him. Completely in reflex, Cabe turned around to confront the lizard, not realizing how foolish that would have been for any other man.

The basilisk leaped out in front of him and stared.

Cabe's first reaction was his surprise at not being turned to stone. His surprise was mirrored by the basilisk; it had never failed to freeze a victim before. The beast stood rock-still, almost as if it had been petrified like its countless victims.

Brandishing the dark blade, Cabe took advantage of his newfound immunity and stood up. The basilisk looked at the sword and shrank back. Cabe took a step forward, and the creature cowered. Putting on a grim face, the man waved his weapon only an arm's span from the monster and screamed.

The basilisk turned tail and fled.

Watching the beast run off, Cabe breathed a sigh of relief. Now that it was over, his body felt akin to a crushed piece of fruit. Fear, however, cautioned him not to stand around marveling at his luck; other, more daring beasts might come along.

Slowly, he trudged down the trail. It was always possible that he might come across a village on his route, but the odds of it were greatly against him. The lands around here were known to be fairly unpopulated, at least by humans.

He was still pondering the implications of his immunity to the basilisk when he saw the hooded figure. It was sitting near the side of the trail, a horse grazing next to it. The traveler appeared to have little fear concerning the creatures of the woods. Cabe recognized the figure and knew why.

The blurred face of the wizard smiled—or seemed to smile—at him. Cabe stopped, the sword pointed in the general direction of the shadowy form.

"Greetings, Cabe Bedlam."

"You're the one in the tavern, aren't you? The one who called himself Simon."

The necromancer nodded. "Yes. I see you've traveled since last we met."

"Traveled? I was nearly killed by one of the Dragon Kings, only someone killed him first!"

"So I've heard."

"He was going to use this!" Cabe held up the black sword.

Simon frowned. "A thrice-damned blade. If things were otherwise, I would tell you to throw it away and be rid of it. Unfortunately, it may be the only thing between you and death . . . that is, until your powers manifest themselves properly."

"Manifest properly?"

"As in the tavern. You remember your bout with the ogre."

Cabe's eyes widened. "That was me?"

The half-shadowed face may have smiled slightly. "You let yourself go. When the power is released like that, it can strike with potency."

The hood slid partly back. Cabe caught a glimpse of the great streak of silver in the other's hair. Unconsciously, he touched his own hair.

Simon nodded. "Yes, the silver has spread. My confrontation with you was the catalyst. Warlocks always react to other warlocks. Brown, the Dragon King who sought your death, also contributed, although by then your true nature was already very evident."

Cabe remembered the words of the reptilian monarch. Now there appeared to be no turning back. If everyone was determined to call him sorceror, Cabe was going to have to learn to use his power. As he came to this decision, he saw his companion nod again.

"It is the only path left for you. Without you, without your power, this land will remain under the dominion of the Dragon Kings."

"How could that be?" Such a prospect made Cabe shudder.

"There exists in you . . . power, for lack of a better word. Great potential. More than most men, even Nathan, have ever achieved—and you are untrained, which makes it all the more unusual. That power turned into skill is what we need. Since the Dragon Masters, the drakes have taken to seeking out humans with dangerous potential. You are one of the very few they have missed, which is why you are so valuable. Without you, we lack the power to withstand a concentrated struggle with the Dragon Kings."

"Then why have they never overwhelmed us? Why let us grow to be so dangerous?"

The hooded figure shrugged. "Two reasons, perhaps. We outnumber the major drakes, the intelligent ones, by a vast margin. Even in defeat, we stand a chance of turning them toward extinction. Their clans are too small. The second reason is related to the first. Their culture has become too intertwined with ours. We are too efficient a subject race. We do so much they no longer care to do, and we do it because we need to. Why disturb what worked so well?"

Cabe thought back to his own life. He could not say it had been too difficult. "Why do we need to fight, then? Don't we have everything? Can't we do everything?"

Though Simon's face was unreadable, the tone of his voice was not. "The illusion of freedom is always that, Cabe. An illusion. As long as the Dragon Kings rule, we will never rise further. We will stagnate and die with them."

An overwhelming sense of duty swelled within Cabe. His grandfather had given his life for this belief, and Cabe, understanding that belief at least a little, could at least help—especially with his own life at stake. "What should I do? Will you teach me?"

"Later, perhaps. For now, however, you should continue on your journey. The Lord Gryphon awaits your arrival."

"He awaits? How does he know about me?"

The warlock chuckled. "One does not kill a Dragon King without gaining a quick notoriety."

"But I didn't kill him! There was a glowing shaft! It pierced his body!"

The warlock's eyes became a deep crimson. The hands gestured in his direction. At first, Cabe believed that the shadowy figure was about to destroy him. He held up the sword, hoping it would protect him.

Simon lowered his hands. "You have nothing to fear, my friend. I was merely checking your story. It is true, what you have said. Brown, master of the Barren Lands, died by the power of a Sunlancer's shaft. These are strange times indeed."

Cabe lowered the sword. "What is a Sunlancer? I feel I know that title."

"You should. It is most likely a part of your power. Sunlancers were Dragon Master elites. Nathan was their leader. They could draw the light of Kylus and control it with their bows."

Slowly, Cabe looked up to the sun. If he could control a part of that! It was beyond belief. Yet something was not right. . . .

"The Dragon King died under the Twins. He had chosen that time for my death."

"Hmm. It is possible that the blood of one such as you would revitalize the dead lands. The meeting of the Twins is a time well known to those with the power. It increases the potency of any spell that involves sacrifice. Still, the Sunlancers required day. To create such a weapon at night, one would have to use the Twins, and they are not noted for their generosity. They demand payment. I must investigate. Perhaps, by the time you arrive in Penacles, I will have an answer for you."

"You're leaving me? But I'll never make it on foot!"

The blurred face may have actually revealed a fleeting glimpse of surprise. "On foot? No. You will ride this horse. I brought it the moment I realized your plight." Despite his gloves, the warlock snapped his fingers. His mount walked over to Cabe and nuzzled the startled wanderer.

Cabe stroked the horse, somewhat awed by the abilities of his companion. He had lost his mount only some minutes before.

"I thank you for the steed, but what will you do?"

"I have no need of it."

Frowning, Cabe gazed at the horse. It was strong. Stronger than his other. He turned his attention back to the warlock—

—only to discover that Simon was gone.

He did not question the disappearance. The cloaked and hooded form had helped him. It would be best to make use of that assistance. The sooner he arrived in the Penacles, the better.

Sheathing the dark sword, he mounted. A quick scan of the area revealed no other path then the one he was on. The woods were too dangerous. Not that the path had proven to be simple.

Keeping his grip on the hilt of the sword, he rode off again.

Nightfall was coming. To Cabe, it seemed as if the day had been shortened by half. He had hoped to reach the end of the forest before this, but the path twisted frequently. A small portion of his mind suggested that sorcery might be involved, for no human would have designed such a winding trail.

Something strayed into his path. Cabe glimpsed a very feminine form. A woman screamed. He pulled his horse to a stop, barely missing the body in front of him.

Recently developed reflexes caused him to reach for the sword.

"Good sir, stay your hand! We mean you no harm!"

Cabe jerked his head toward the voice and caught sight of two women. Not ordinary women. Of that he was sure. They were clad in thin but ornate gowns. All the color of the forest. In fact, even their skin—and much of it was visible—had a slight greenish tinge.

The tallest of the three stepped up to him. She could have been elfin, with her narrow face and wheat-colored eyes. Her smile dared to chase away the coming darkness. "Hail to you, oh gentleman!"

Gentleman! Cabe held back a laugh. She had certainly overrated his status. "Who are you?"

"I am Camilla. This is Magda." She indicated a smaller but more voluptuous woman who smiled shyly and curtsied. Her face was almost a copy of her sister's, for such they had to be. Cabe stammered out a greeting.

Camilla turned to the woman whom Cabe had nearly run over. "This one here is our younger sister, Tegan, who, it seems, must learn to watch her path more closely."

Tegan was barely into womanhood, but there was a grace about her that seemed to argue years of experience. Like Magda, she was also nearly a double of her eldest sister. As she curtsied, her long, golden hair fell from her shoulders.

"And what, may I ask, are three fair ladies doing out here? Surely, a land filled with hazards, such as the wyverns, is no place for the trio of you to live. Where are your men?"

The eldest became quiet. "Alas, my husband is dead. As for my sisters, they never had the chance to marry. We do not fear the creatures of the forest, however, for they stay away from our home. My late lord believed that it was possible that some enchantment protects the area."

Cabe nodded. He had heard of such places. Some were said to be the former homes of sorcerors. Others appeared to be the work of spirits, benign or otherwise. These women were fortunate; some areas meant instant death for those who trespassed. For every oasis, there was also a trap.

The youngest came up to his horse and tried to pet it. The animal shied back, as if bitten. Cabe saw that it was breathing fast.

Camilla eyed his mount. "Your horse is obviously tired. Perhaps you would allow us the pleasure of your company. It is high time we had a guest in our house again. Such a handsome one makes the idea seem even more pleasant."

Unaccustomed to compliments that didn't end in sarcasm, Cabe nearly reddened. "It would be an honor for me to accompany you."

"Then come. It is only a short distance off the path."

He motioned his mount to step off the trail, but the animal refused. A second and third attempt failed to make the horse do more than shift back and forth nervously. Realizing the futility of his situation, Cabe climbed off.

"It seems I must walk, but I have no place to keep my horse in the meantime."

Tegan stepped up and gently took the reins from his hands. Up close, she took on an air of seductiveness that Cabe had not noticed earlier. Her voice was like the call of a Siren.

"Go with my sisters, Cabe. I will attend to your animal's needs and return shortly. Have no fear, he will be safe in my hands."

Few, if any, men could resist a voice and face such as hers. He nodded and thanked her for her kindness. Camilla and Magda each took him by an arm.

"You shall escort us as my husband once did. Today, we are again ladies of the manor." Camilla smiled, and Cabe had a deep wish to lose himself in that smile.

They led him into the forest, the man lost in his dreams. Behind him, strangely unnoticed, were the sounds of a horse both enraged and worried.

A moment later, the hiss of a larger, more sinister creature joined in, but by then Cabe was out of earshot.

Much could be said about the diversities of taste in the Dragonrealms. Both humans and inhumans differed greatly from their nearest brothers, and these tastes were greatly evident in the type of dwellings that each respective member of each respective race chose to live within.

Such was the case with the manor of the three ladies, Cabe decided.

Great stone walls intermingled with barriers cut out of the earth itself. Parts of the house were cut wood, but the right side appeared to be formed from a massive tree. Plants of fanciful and bizarre appearance filled the areas around it. High above, like the symbol of the manor, a fierce-looking avian prepared to swoop down on all comers. Despite its being formed from metal, Cabe had to stare at it twice before he allowed himself to be led inside.

The interior of the manor was even more unreal than the exterior. While the floor was polished marble, here and there were spots where trees grew. Some went through the ceiling and beyond. Vines traced their ways along the walls, pillars, stairway, and, of course, the trees. It was strange to think that anyone could live here. He wanted to question his enchanting hostesses about its history, but decided to wait until the moment seemed right.

Camilla released his arm, allowing Magda to lead him to an elaborate chair. Cabe sat down cautiously, for the chair seemed so ancient that it would most likely collapse. He was surprised to find that it was actually very sturdy and quite soft. Unused to such luxury, he allowed himself to sink in deeply. The two women exchanged glances, as if quite amused by his fascination with an everyday object.

Magda leaned down, giving Cabe a splendid view of her womanhood. She smiled, and the smile was so much like her sisters'. "Are you pleased?"

It took him a moment to realize that she meant the chair. Red-faced, he nodded. "It's been a long time since I've sat in anything so comfortable."

"Good! We want you to be happy. Would you like to remove your sword? It must be terribly uncomfortable to wear!"

Cabe, for no reason that he could think of, felt a great desire to keep the blade with him. He shook his head and turned the conversation to other things. "This is a most unusual place. Who built it?"

"My sister Camilla's husband. He was a . . . a man of

the forests. He could not do without the presence of the lands. We have come to love it."

"I meant no discourtesy."

She leaned even closer. "None was taken."

"Magda!"

At the sound of Camilla's voice, the woman pulled away quickly. She looked at her sister with eyes of fire. The eldest met her with an equally fiery stare.

"What is it, my dear sister?"

Camilla pointed at the door. "See to Tegan. Make sure that she is all right."

Her sister laughed. "That one? No creature—"

"See to it now!"

The younger one frowned and departed. Cabe watched her leave and turned to Camilla. "If Tegan is in danger, then perhaps I should help."

The woman took a goblet from a tray that she had placed nearby. "Be not overly concerned, Sir Cabe. I only meant that she might possibly have had trouble with your steed. It was a strong and spirited steed." She handed him the goblet. "Enough of this! My sisters together will have more than enough skill to take care of your horse. In the meanwhile, I shall do what I can for you."

Cabe nearly choked on the wine. Never had he met such hot-blooded women! Perhaps it was because of their isolation from other people. It was difficult to resist their charms, and he wondered why he was doing so at all. Most likely, he was afraid of what the other two might do if he showed any favor to one. Beautiful they might be, but they acted like a pack of wild dogs, each trying to claim a kill.

It had not escaped his notice that his hostess was dressed differently. She was now in a gown that very definitely failed to do what most clothing was designed for—covering one's form. If Cabe concentrated . . .

He need not have bothered to try. Camilla, with surprising speed, sat down in his lap, nearly causing him to spill his wine. Her arms were around him, and she spoke only when her lips were less than a finger's width away from his own.

"My sisters will take some time. They know that it is my right, as eldest, to be first. Why not remove that sword and belt? Come, now, am I unattractive?"

He managed to choke out, "No, my lady."

She smiled like a predator about to sink her teeth into her prey. The gown made it easy for Cabe to feel the warmth of her body against his. In fact, it was hard to tell if he was sweating from her nearness or from the heat she seemed to emit. Hot-blooded indeed!

The front door burst open. Camilla pulled away from Cabe, rage making her face decidedly ugly. She stopped short as she saw Magda helping an injured Tegan in.

"What happened?"

The youngest was only half conscious. Cabe watched her and squinted. She appeared slightly out of focus. He looked at his wine and hastily put the goblet down.

Camilla was giving quick instructions. "Magda! Not here! Bring her to—to her room!"

"Darkhorse! Darkhorse . . ." Tegan mumbled incoherently after that.

"He comes!" The words were Magda's.

There was a thrashing from the woods nearest to the trail. Cabe reached for the sword.

"No!" Camilla stopped him before his hand had touched the hilt.

"There's something coming!"

"It cannot enter here! We are safe!"

The crashing continued. Whatever it was, it was coming closer and doing so with great speed. Cabe wondered how safe they really were. He did not put much stock in his ability with a sword.

The two sisters helped Tegan into another room. Cabe stood by the open door, shaking, and looked out. Something was out there, but it appeared to have stopped a short distance from sight. Cabe put his hand on the hilt and took a tentative step out.

Something shifted in the woods. He caught a quick glimpse of a shape like a horse but not quite real. Two strange urges pulled at him. One was to step out into the forest and confront the creature; the second was to call the creature to him. Neither seemed very sensible, so Cabe fought both ideas as best he could. The beast snorted in irritation.

"What are you doing?"

Cabe spun around, his hand still on the hilt of his sword.

It was Camilla, but she appeared different. She was still beautiful, but that beauty had now taken on a somewhat reptilian aspect. Cabe's grip on the sword became much tighter.

She calmed herself and moved closer to him. She was still very much the enchantress. "Calm yourself, Cabe. The creature cannot enter. We may ignore it."

He did not relax. "What is that thing? Tegan mentioned 'Darkhorse'. That sounds familiar, but I can't—"

Camilla put a hand to his mouth. "Hush. My sister was distraught. You need not worry about her. She will be fine by morning."

The thing outside created more noise but sounded no closer.

The woman so near to him was becoming less and less human, though she apparently had not noticed any change. When the snout stretched forth from her face, Cabe was struck by sudden realization.

He pushed Camilla away with his free hand and pulled out the dark blade with the other.

"Firedrake!" he roared

The whole demeanor of his hostess had changed. With an inhuman roar, she altered completely. Wings sprouted from her back. The beautiful face stretched out until much of it had became gaping jaws with great, sharp teeth. The slender arms and legs became scaled legs that tried to claw at the man.

Cabe had walked into a trap. He had heard tales from adventurers who told of firedrake dams who enchanted and then devoured unwary male travelers. They were more successful in their shapeshifting than the males. A male firedrake, even the Dragon Kings, could not make his form into a perfect copy of a man. That was why the males always appeared in the guise of armored warriors.

The females, however, could not only make themselves appear human, but could even improve on the image. Hence their ability to seduce unwary victims.

Somehow he had been freed from whatever spell had been laid on him. Maybe it was the sword in his hand. It had come from a Dragon King. Perhaps, he thought, it had more advantages than he had believed.

All of this had gone through Cabe's mind in a fraction of a second. Fear can be a great motivator. With nowhere to go, save toward the creature in the forest, he held the point of the sword in the direction of the dragon and prayed.

The thing that had been Camilla, about to lunge, stopped abruptly. It seemed to shrink into itself. Heartened, Cabe took a step forward and pretended to attack. It had worked against the basilisk. The firedrake backed away, its tail between its legs.

The creature spoke. "Have mercy, man of the Horned Blade! I will not attack you!"

Cabe paused. "Do you swear to that?"

"By the emperor, the Horned Blade, and the Dragonrealms! Please!"

The dark sword, which now had a name—and an ominous one—throbbed in his hand. There was power there. Power to do anything! Power that could meld with his own! Give him mastery over beast and man!

There was the neighing of a great war-horse. Cabe blinked and realized that he had fallen under the influence of the blade. Small wonder that Simon had called it thrice-cursed!

The firedrake had nearly dug itself into the floor in its fear. Cabe found himself disgusted. "Change back, blast you! I'd rather you looked human!"

"As you wish!"

The form melted, and the entire process began to reverse itself. Soon he found himself watching the beautiful, but distraught, Camilla. It was something to note; the sword had allowed her to regain her human disguise.

"That's better. Call in your sisters!"

She did so. Magda came in, the injured Tegan leaning on her. They moved to their sister.

Camilla looked at them. "He knows. He also bears the Horned Blade."

Magda's eyes widened, and Tegan let out a small gasp. Despite its evil nature, Cabe knew that he had better keep his hand on the sword or risk an attack.

"What would you want of us?"

He snorted. "Not what you had in mind, that's for sure! You were playing with me like a cat with its dinner!"

"We needed food. Our duke was out of favor with the Green Dragon and is now dead. Even we cannot face the glare of the basilisk. That power is reserved for the Dragon Kings alone. That is why we have been reduced to this!"

Cabe did not feel inclined to mention his own encounter with the monster. Any secrets he kept from the dams would be to his advantage.

"The sword kept you away." He phrased the thought as a statement of fact, not a question. It would not do for them to know that he was working by guess.

"Yes. The Horned Blade was created by a sorceror. It is a bane to both our kind and yours. Beware, human, it is treacherous. It might very well bring about all of our deaths."

"Yours will be first if I think I see a trick."

She raised a hand. "I will do nothing."

Little things were starting to come back to him. "You called me Cabe, yet I never told you my name. How did you know?"

Camilla became silent.

"If you do not tell me, I'll use this. Or—or I'll make you go out and face that thing." Any creature that preyed on the firedrakes could not be all bad.

That broke her resolve. "The Lady of the Amber told us of your coming."

Lady of the Amber? Cabe felt a light touch in his memory. There was something about her. He did not know what it was, but he knew that he had to see her.

"Lead me to her."

"Will you release us when we have?" Even defeated, Camilla still sought to bargain.

"We shall see."

The thing in the woods bellowed and crashed about. Cabe still felt the urge to call or go to it, but he fought it down. Such an action would most likely end in his death.

The eldest sister took the lead. Cabe made the others follow after her. Despite their frail appearances, he did not want these women behind his back. They moved slowly, since Tegan still needed the assistance of her sister.

He knew, even as they stepped into the garden in the back, that the firedrakes had taken over this manor from someone else. Someone who had not been quite human, yet was much more so than any of the great reptiles could ever claim to be. In fact, Cabe could almost feel a kinship with the former tenant as he followed his captives.

The garden was similar to the manor in that plants intermingled with the structures. Vines wrapped around arches, and flowers sprouted out from areas in the floor. It should have looked like anarchy; instead, there was an order that was so subtle that one almost took it for granted that it should be that way.

"Behold, man, the Lady of the Amber!"

They were on it so abruptly that Cabe had at first thought it was part of the garden's design. The large honey-colored crystal rested on a platform of marble. Here and there, creepers had grown around it. It was transparent. Also, the longer one looked, the more noticeable it was that it was glowing slightly from within. A greenish glow.

In that glow, the center of the crystal, was a woman.

IV

The Council of the Dragon Kings had been called hastily. With the exception of Black, only the nearest of the emperor's brethren had been able to attend. Yet the rumors of why the Council had been called together was enough so that those who could not be there were nonetheless making preparations for possible battle.

Silver was there. Green and Red sat on opposite sides, eyeing one another suspiciously. Iron, great and massive, second in power only to the emperor, had made one of his rare appearances.

Gold scanned over them. Even Iron was forced back by the stare. When the emperor acted in such a manner, things were ill indeed.

"I am sorry that the rest have not arrived—especially Ice, who is so close—but this number will have to do."

He paused, as if awaiting some comment.

"Fate, master of the game, has dealt the card once again. The Dragonrealms threaten to escape our rule once more."

The flatness of the statement served only to emphasize its importance. Only once before had their power been challenged. That enemy had come close to defeating them.

As if speaking what was in the mind of all, Iron roared, "The Dragon Masters are dead! None can challenge us!"

"The Masters may be gone, but their legacy lives on."

Red spat in disgust. The stain burned its way into the earth. "This sounds too much like the last Council."

"It will continue to sound like the last Council."

The despot of the Hell Plains gave an almost human look of curiosity. "What do you mean, my lord?"

Instead of answering his brother, Gold lifted his massive head, spread his wings, and bellowed toward the shadows, "You may enter!"

They came slowly. Two of them. There was much in their appearances that told of the close relationship between all in the chamber. Dragonhelmed, they might have pretended to be Kings, but the others knew better. In accordance to custom, they kneeled, their heads down.

Iron blinked. "Whose dukes are these?"

"They are Brown's."

"He sends his underlings and does not deign to come himself? Sire, let me take my legions and teach our arrogant brother hisss place!"

"I fear a lesson now would do little good." Gold turned to the two. "Summon those who carry the body."

"Body?" The single word issued from more than one mouth. There was consternation. And fear.

The newcomers stood up, bowed, and left silently. A short time passed, as if those who must enter feared to do so. The Dragon Kings shifted impatiently.

At long last, five figures, including a third warrior of the Brown Dragon's clans and two of the Gold Dragon's own warriors, returned. On a platform borne by four lay a shrouded form. One of the reptilian monarchs hissed as he recognized what that form truly was.

"Brown! They bear Brown!"

Unaccustomed to the power that had gathered in that room, the dukes fell to their knees, still bearing the platform between them. Though powerful, they feared for their very lives. To their monarchs, though, they were invisible. The Dragon Kings were too concerned with the death of one of their own.

"Who has done this?"

"He wears his man-form!"

"Someone must have struck him down soon after he left us!"

Gold noticed that Black was strangely silent. He called for order and received it. "Brown is dead! There is a wound, going through his chest, but I see no weapon, and the servants of our brother claim none was to be found! Even in a human form, we are nearly invincible. How, then, was this crime done? Who is responsible?"

Even as he spoke, his eyes turned to the keeper of the Gray Mists. Black smiled, but it was a smile that Death might have painted on, so grim it was. "Well? You seem strangely pleased by this! What have you to say, brother?"

Black inclined his head. "Respected brother, it is as I said. The blood of the Masters still exists. I suspect that there are others, too. We could never be absolutely sure. It was, after all, Purple's strategy, and he died facing the last and greatest of our enemies."

"Then you blame this on the grandson of Nathan Bedlam. I had ordered that this one should be watched! Where are my spies!"

Something flitted out of the darkness of the upper level of the chamber. It had no mundane counterpart, and even the emperor knew little about the history of its kind. The spy served, and that was all that mattered in the long run.

Something had happened to their intended target. The dark servants of the emperor had arrived, only to discover that he had vanished. Ordered out by one of the Magnificent Ones, it claimed. Both had ridden off into the Barren Lands. The servants had returned here, to the Most Magnificent's dwelling, but had feared to tell him.

"So." Gold dismissed the spy. It flew back up to its black roost and disappeared. "Brown chose to disobey. He sought to kill the Bedlam-hatchling by himself! His disobedience cost him dearly."

Most of the others kept quiet. Gold was generally a calm and reasoning leader. His knowledge was almost as great as that of the late master of the City of Knowledge. Purple, however, had turned down the power of emperor. This fact had always surrounded Gold. To him, such blatant disobedience indicated a lack of faith in him as ruler. It was one of his few weak points. No one dared to mention it.

The emperor calmed slightly. "Our brother was found in one of the most desolate—if one can use the term without sounding very repetitious—parts of the Barren Lands. It is thought that he died under the eyes of the Twins."

The reaction he received at these words did not disappoint him. The Twins' hunger for sacrifice was well known. In return, they would do much to increase the strength of one's spell. Brown had obviously intended to use the human to bring back his lush fields. That he had died instead left much to speculation.

"We must prepare." Gold's voice was dead. This was to be a command that must be obeyed in full. "We must mass together our legions once more. If a second rising of men is imminent, we must locate it while it is still in its birth stages."

Though he paused, they knew to what he was leading. Black was smiling, but Gold did not reprimand him.

"We must take Penacles. We must return to our power the City of Knowledge."

Iron roared his approval. "Yesss! I will take my Beast hordes down and crush the Gryphon! Then I shall collect the—"

"No! I will take charge of the defeat and sacking of Penacles!"

The emperor's words silenced all. While Gold's legions were superior to all others, they seldom saw action such as this. The real reason for this sudden switch was evident enough: to the Dragon Kings, knowledge was power. The King of Kings had no intention of letting any of his brethren take control of that power, lest they become a threat to him.

"Sire! To do so might threaten the life of your august self!"

The others nodded agreement. Silver looked to his master with worry. The emperor frowned as best a dragon might. Silver was loyal to him, but unfortunately that meant that the lord of Mines was unconsciously taking the position of the other side. Gold sighed ever so slightly. A compromise would have to be made.

"Very well. Black, you will bring your forces together. Iron, I appoint you to gather up what remains of brother Brown's and add it to your own. You will strike from the west. The master of the Hell Plains and myself will stand in reserve and then strike. Toma will lead my Imperial legions."

There was agreement here. Toma, hatchling of Gold, but only a firedrake, was still a well-trained battle leader.

"I shall remain here, issuing such commands as are needed." And playing dam to a pile of eggs, he thought. Still, it would keep the others on guard. Toma could protect himself. Though lacking the genes that would have made him an Imperial successor, his mind was the equal, if not the superior, of many in this chamber.

Damn the fickleness of the egg patterns!

"All servants are to watch for the Bedlam whelp! If he can be dispatched, then they are to do so. If not, they are to report to you immediately."

"The battle, sire. Are the rest of us to sit idle?"

Gold looked at them. "You and the others must police your lands. We may have missed something. I will want to hear from all of you." He stretched himself out to his full height. "This Council is at an end. You have your duties. Perform them."

The corpse of the Brown Dragon King was carried away. After that, the Dragon Kings departed. They did not speak. Their duties had been explained, and it would be shame if they failed to carry out those duties.

Watching them go, the emperor was grim. We have changed considerably, he decided. More and more, our thoughts become like those of the humans. Some who leave tonight may shirk their duties before this situation is resolved . . . if it is resolved.

We are meant to rule, but to rule, we must be united. I will crush the Gryphon and then use the knowledge to make an end to my other . . . concerns.

Satisfied, Gold curled himself up and drifted off to sleep.

She was beautiful, breathtaking. A thousand words could not describe her well enough to suit Cabe's tastes.

"Who was she?"

Camilla frowned. "We know not. It has been hazarded that she created this house. We do know that she is a powerful witch."

"You speak as if she is still alive."

"Look at her, manling! Can you not see that still she breathes? She is merely imprisoned!"

He looked closer. It was true! She did breathe. Cabe waved the black sword at the three firedrakes. "Release her!"

Tegan let out a very human squeal. "We did not imprison her! She was like this when we first came here!"

Camilla nodded quickly. "True! We have tried for countless seasons to remove her from her prison, but we cannot!"

Cabe glanced at the figure inside. Long, flowing tresses of a fiery red fought with the emerald green of her thin dress. A shock of silver added to a startling contrast. Her lips were nearly the color of the hair, while her eyes matched more with the clothing. Her face was perfect; Cabe found himself unable to think of any other description for it. A goddess of the Dragonrealms, he finally half decided.

He was at a loss, for these creatures before him, even with their formidable powers, had been unable to even scratch the surface of the stone. What could he possibly do?

As if mocking him, the thing lurking in the woods cried out. Cabe shuddered and wondered why he still felt a desire to call the thing to him. Thankfully, whatever it was, it could not overcome the spell that protected the manor and the grounds.

Camilla looked at him expectantly, interrupting his thoughts. "We have brought you to her. Will you leave us in peace now?"

Something in her words added menace where there should have been none. Cabe eyed the female reptiles. "I don't know what to do yet. Tell me what you've done to try to release her."

Disgruntled, they told of using claws, strength, and branches to shatter the casement. With the description of each of their failures, Cabe's spirits sank further. How could he succeed where all others had been defeated? He finally swung the dark blade at the crystal, though he had little hope it would even make a scratch.

It was like metal scraping against metal. Green sparks flashed about as the two artifacts made contact, and the screech caused by the blade as it sank deep into the crystalline prison made Cabe shiver. The progress of the blade came to an abrupt halt, though, and he lost his grip on the weapon as well as his balance. As he fell, the firedrake dams let out a triumphant yell and began to alter their forms. The sword remained buried in the crystal.

Tumbling, Cabe was able to survive the first attack. Camilla, only half human now, made a leap for him. Even as she landed where he had previously been, her last vestiges of humanity disappeared. He was now confronting a full-grown firedrake, and to make matters worse, the other two sisters had now finished transforming and were about to join the eldest for what appeared to be an easy victory.

There was no way that he could reach the sword. He dodged as the creature that had been Camilla tried to rip his chest open, barely missing and taking off most off most of his shirt.

The thing in the forest bellowed in such a strange tone that Cabe almost believed that it was pleading with him to allow it to enter.

All three of the firedrakes were on him now. Cabe got just a glimpse of the slowly melting prison. Not only would they kill him, but he'd given them access to the Lady.

The pleading from the forest increased tenfold. Cabe had no choice and gave in. The thing would probably make short work of him, but also might put an end to the firedrakes. The words slipped out of his mouth automatically, and he understood nothing of their meaning.

"Enter freely, child of the Void!"

A triumphant cry answered his command. The three dams

stopped in their tracks. The one that had been Tegan turned and fled, while the other two paused, measuring their chances.

It tore through the manor, the sound of its hooves on the marble like a sword striking rock. It cleared the inside of the building in record time and crashed through the back. With another cry, it landed between Cabe and the monsters.

It was blacker than anything he had ever seen. Its general outline was that of a horse, but it was much, much more than that. It pawed the ground, digging small ditches where there should have been none, its eyes not crimson red, as one might think, but icy blue, and colder than one would think possible.

The cry turned to a mocking laugh as it stalked the two retreating firedrakes. Even more shocking were the words that issued from its mouth. Bold and echoing, masterful!

"Come, my darlings! Are you so afraid to embrace a loved one? Have you forgotten so soon that Darkhorse finds you always? Come! Will neither of you be first?"

Both reptiles realized that the creature called Darkhorse would catch them if they ran. In desperation, they lunged simultaneously, hoping one of them would make a mortal strike. Darkhorse jumped nimbly aside and even managed to kick one of the monsters as it landed. The firedrake fell hard, stunned by the blow.

The other rose to attack.

Darkhorse laughed again. "Now, that's more like it, darling! Show a little teeth and claw!"

Even as the firedrake slashed, its opponent reared up and kicked it soundly on the jaw. Something cracked. The dragon fell, its mouth bent strangely out of shape.

Darkhorse laughed.

Unseen, the other had come to its senses and had attempted to claw the underside of the steed. Huge and sharp, the claws merely slid off the skin. Darkhorse, still on his hind legs, came down hard on the head of the firedrake. This time, the cracking of bone was unmistakable. The dragon grunted and went lifeless.

Blood dripping from its broken jaw, the other tried to run, but Darkhorse moved so quickly that Cabe could not believe it. Almost immediately, it was in front of the reptile, which could not slow its momentum and dove straight into the horse . . . literally.

As Cabe watched, the hapless monster fell into the emptiness that was Darkhorse, and, with a scream, it kept falling, getting smaller and smaller. In moments, it had disappeared completely.

The steed cried out triumphantly. Then, with blinding speed, it tore off in pursuit of the third firedrake. Cabe made no attempt to call it back. If it went far away, that would suit him just fine. He did not know exactly what Darkhorse was, but he knew that the name was familiar to him. He also knew that, more often than not, the creature brought death.

The events finally caught up with him. Free from the threat of the firedrakes, Cabe sank to the ground and lost consciousness.

From far off came the triumphant bellow of Darkhorse.

High above the Barren Lands, a large, predatory creature circled. It was not scaled, as most of the nearest inhabitants were, but was nevertheless related. An avian. A bird, yet like no bird that had ever been seen, for it was more manlike. Silently, it landed near a large patch of grass.

The Seeker folded its massive wings and bent down. One feathered hand touched the long green blades. Hawk eyes watched carefully as dust nearby turned to rich soil and then became populated with small shoots. In all directions, especially those leading into the deepest parts of the Barren Lands, the field spread. In death, Brown had succeeded beyond his wildest dreams.

A horse, yet not a horse, snorted. The Seeker pointed one of its sharp claws in the direction of the sound. A moment later, a single rider appeared. His dragonhelm proclaimed him a firedrake, one of the late King's liegemen.

The reptilian warrior rode directly to the other, but despite this, the avian did not move. It stared at the firedrake with what appeared to be only mild interest. The warrior, oblivious to the form in front of him, slowly turned to the right. He bypassed both field and Seeker as if they were no longer there.

When the firedrake had left, the Seeker once again put its

hand to the grass. The pointed claws ran lightly along, learning all, and, when it was satisfied, the creature stood up once more, turned this way and that, and scanned the lands around it. Within days, everything in sight would be green with life.

The massive wings spread once more. Into the sky it rose. The Seeker circled once and then flew off.

Below it, the field continued to spread.

Another hand, this one furred, although sometimes it was feathered, depending on mood, of course. The hand belonged to the Gryphon, or Lord Gryphon as he was often called, and was running slowly over a smooth piece of glass shaped like an egg.

If one knew how, one could see pictures. Many did not make sense. Some were of the past. Others, the future. The rest were unidentifiable.

The Gryphon was most interested in these.

"I see a dragon, larger than any, mottled in color. Every color. Do you know it?" The Gryphon's voice was the proud rumble of a lion, though his eaglelike face would never have made that fact evident.

The one who called himself Simon nodded slowly, his sluggish response possibly indicating some worry. "The Dragon of the Depths. They say he lived in the deepest part of the seas, where water and molten earth meet. It is believed he died long before the coming of men."

"Believed?"

"One never knows about legends."

"No. What of this?" The furred hand indicated a new picture, one that showed a shattered skull.

"I do not recognize it, though I feel I should."

With the wave of a hand, the picture was dismissed. Yet another took its place.

The Gryphon stroked the large crystalline ovoid, his eye into the past, present, and, most important, the future. "Yalak's Egg is showing off today."

Simon nodded. "As peril draws closer, the crystal becomes more attuned with the multiverse."

"I recognize this. It is the chamber of Gold, King of Kings, greatest of the Dragon Kings."

"He appears to sleep."

The Gryphon nodded, his mane fluttering slightly. "His features have softened. I suspect that most of the others are the same."

"They have dared to take the treacherous path leading to humanity. It is reflected in their forms and actions."

"For our sakes, let us hope not."

The warlock indicated the device known as Yalak's Egg. "Change the picture once more."

"Very well."

Once again, the Gryphon dissolved the image, but this time, however, instead of another picture, only fog could be seen. The Gryphon looked up at his companion.

"Are you interfering with the Egg?"

"Yes. I am attempting to focus on a particular person in the present."

"I had no idea that you could do this. You've not told me everything about yourself, after all."

"I do not know myself very well. You know that."

"Indeed. My apologies."

Simon ignored him. Something was happening. "I've done it. Look quickly."

"I see a jewel with some sort of figurine inside."

"That isn't a figurine. That is an actual person."

The Gryphon glanced up. "Her?"

"Yes. The amber. Does it look unusual?"

"It appears to be melting."

Something unusual infiltrated the warlock's voice. It appeared to be pleasure. "He's done it! He's freed her!"

The image faded.

He fell back. "I'm sorry. I couldn't hold the image any longer."

"Say nothing." And with that, the lord of Penacles snapped his fingers. A servitor, not quite human, appeared from nowhere. "Serve my guest some refreshment."

Within moments, Simon was presented with a goblet of wine. The warlock drank the contents with one gulp, his host eyeing him with amusement, for the sorceror was not known for his drinking abilities.

Simon put down the goblet and nodded thanks. "When I

learned of this Cabe Bedlam, I came to believe that he might be able to release the Lady Gwen. My faith has been justified."

"And how, may I ask, did he come across her? That was not his original path."

The warlock may have smiled. "I engaged the services of . . . an old friend. He took a different path, though Bedlam did not realize it."

"This . . . friend. I don't think I'd care to meet him, if he is the one I believe he is."

"Few would. That is why he and I have become so close."

The Gryphon shuddered, something he did rarely. Few things frightened him. Darkhorse, being what it was, did. He chose a different subject. "The Lady. How long has she been trapped?"

"Since just before Nathan Bedlam's death."

"Then the power has been building all this time. She was strong, I believe."

"The only woman capable of enchanting the greatest of the Dragon Masters. That alone makes her formidable, and love conquers all, they say."

"You are getting away from my question. What about the release of power?"

Simon leaned forward. He appeared to be lost in thought. Finally, he answered. "It will be as formidable as the Lady."

"What might it do?"

A long pause. "It might very well destroy the entire area, including Cabe Bedlam."

It was terribly, terribly hot.

No. It was freezing cold.

A dog with hands was playing the flute.

The skull kept laughing.

Cabe woke up. He shuddered. The dreams had been so incredibly real. He stood up, brushing the stardust from his body. A tentacled bird landed on a branch nearby and howled. Cabe's mind cleared enough to tell him that the dreams were no dreams. Madness, perhaps, but not dreams.

Strange, gnarled plant-creatures hurried along, complaining about the drought. A bullfrog flew by, only to be snatched up by the perched octupoid-avian. Cabe realized that all the creatures were coming from the Lady. To be precise, they were issuing full-grown from the crack in her prison.

It took little imagination to realize that a tremendous amount of power was escaping. It also was obvious that the crack was spreading, and when it had spread far enough . . .

The dark blade was still caught in the amber. The wisest choice would be to flee . . . but could he run far enough?

A small piece of the outer shell crumbled. As larger chunks slowly cracked away, releasing greater amounts of power, Cabe was astonished that he had not been affected so far. Part of his heritage, or just luck? It was senseless to run, he realized. Power such as this would overwhelm him no matter how hard he ran.

A great series of cracks developed all over the crystal. Shards began to fly off. This was it. Cabe fell to the ground and found himself wondering just how large an area the power would flatten. Miles probably.

The shell collapsed.

Cabe ducked his head, and the world became chaos.

V

Cabe opened his eyes and, to his surprise, the world still existed.

"I've not had a day like this in an eternity, my friend! This promises to be interesting indeed!"

Cautiously, he raised his head and looked to the voice. Infinity, in the shape of a stallion, greeted him with the twinkle of an ice-blue eye. The creature called Darkhorse was standing between Cabe and the Lady, and the great flood of raw power had washed over it with little more effect than a summer sprinkle. The creature seemed in a very good mood, in fact, something that nonetheless did not lower Cabe's level of anxiety.

"Come, come! One of your ability shouldn't grovel in the dirt! Get up! I mean you no harm!" Darkhorse chuckled.

More out of fear than anything else, Cabe rose. Even at full height, he was still dwarfed by the creature.

"That's better!"

His eyes glancing here and there for the sword, Cabe asked, "Who are you?"

The cold, cold eyes stared through his very being. "I am Darkhorse, of course!"

"Are you a demon?" Cabe found it difficult to look at Darkhorse for very long, for to do so made him feel a dizziness that threatened to pull him toward the endlessness of the steed's inner body.

The creature snorted. "To demons I may be a demon! To most others, I am he who brings an end to all time!"

That sounded suspiciously close to death, Cabe thought. Small wonder the firedrakes had had no chance, even with there being three of them. "I thank you for your help, Lord Darkhorse."

Laughter rocked the manor grounds. "Lord! Darkhorse a lord? You do me great honor, Master Bedlam! Darkhorse can never be lord, for such was not written into the multiverse!"

Cabe covered his ears. The other's voice threatened to shatter his eardrums. Accidentally, he glanced toward the broken prison. Lying on the ground, apparently unhurt, was the unconscious form of the Lady.

The gaze of Darkhorse followed his. "You'd best see to her, my friend! I fear she won't take too kindly to my interference, even if I mean her only good!"

Cautiously skirting his unreal companion, Cabe moved over and bent down to examine the woman in green. He was again struck by her beauty. He was almost afraid to touch her, as if that touch would taint the perfection of her form. Fortunately, reason took over and he lifted her up and placed her on softer ground.

She stirred.

Cabe found himself staring into eyes that pulled at him as emotionally as Darkhorse's infernal form pulled at him physically. When she whispered something too softly for him to hear, he put his ear closer.

"Nathan." She smiled and lapsed into unconsciousness once more.

Darkhorse trotted up for a better look. "She has not changed . . . which is all the more reason for me to leave you for a time! You and the Lady Gwen may have to find some sort of transportation to Penacles if I do not return in time!"

"I have a horse—"

"Master Bedlam! I was your noble steed! I had to play the part of the fearful mount so that the dams would allow you to enter. A demon I am not, but my nature is much like theirs, and so stronger barrier spells affect me as they would them! Without someone willing to summon me, I cannot enter areas that are well secured by such enchantments! Especially when the spell was cast by a power like the Lady herself!"

The creature wandered away and studied the lands of the manor. It seemed somewhat annoyed. "When I leave this area, you will have to give me permission to enter when I return! If that woman awakes before I come back, do it quietly. She will never allow me in willingly! Ha!"

With a sudden leap, Darkhorse disappeared into the forest. Cabe felt a pulling, as if something were resealing itself. When he looked around, he discovered that, for all practical purposes, he and the Lady were alone.

Alone? Something else seemed to tug for his attention. Cabe used one hand to shift what remained of the amber prison. Uncovering the hilt of a sword, he pulled his hand away. It would not do to touch that blade. Not now, anyway.

With little else to do, he tried to rest. The creature called Darkhorse seemed confident of the woman's ability to survive. Cabe had no training in healing and knew that it would be impossible to locate anyone in this area. For that matter, any stranger could very well turn out to be another firedrake or some other sinister terror.

Reluctantly, he allowed himself to drift off into sleep.

"We should not be so close to the Tyber Mountains, Twann."

Twann, a burly, very ugly man with more scars on him

than many an army veteran, grunted at his equally ugly companion. "It couldn't a been helped, Rolf. The city guards back in Talak had all the southern roads watched. I know! I scouted 'em while you went off on a drunk after we hit that merchant!"

Rolf scratched his balding head. "I suppose you're right. I just don't like riding close to this area. You know what's supposed to go on here."

"Pfah! Legends! What do the Dragon Kings care about us, anyway? We're just two hardworkin' fellows. Like bugs to them."

"Bugs get squashed."

Annoyed, Twann turned on his companion. "Perhaps you would rather try riding through the Dagora Forest? At least here, we can't be surprised. We can see for miles and miles. Anything coming from the mountains will be so high up that we'll easily reach cover."

The other said nothing. It was futile to argue with Twann, and Rolf had no better ideas.

They rode on, now and then discussing plans for the future. Mito Pica seemed the most likely spot to head for. It was a city large enough to hide them easily, and it was located in the general center of the Dragonrealm. All they needed to do was head east for a short time and then turn southward. If Mito Pica proved unsatisfactory, they would head east from there to Wenslis.

They traveled near the base of a particularly large mountain. Something seemed unreal about it. Rolf slowed his horse and squinted at it. It was almost as if the mountain was not quite there. He grabbed at Twann's filthy shirt and attracted his attention to the great leviathan.

"Look close. Somethin' looks funny!"

In the dim light of the moons, Twann's tired eyes could see nothing. "You're beat! We'll ride another hour and then stop."

"I'm tellin' you that the mountain ain't there! Take another look!"

Twann sighed and humored his companion. The sight chilled him. Wordlessly, he pointed a finger. Rolf smiled, satisfied that his fool of a partner had seen what he had. He turned his head toward the mountain.

The dragons came out in great numbers.

Most were minor drakes, barely intelligent animals useful to their brothers only as shock troops because of their great numbers. Most lacked the vestigial wings and therefore ran or crawled or hopped. Firedrakes, in their true forms, flew overhead, keeping the masses under control. Scaled abominations and things that could not be described by words followed. It had to be an advance party ordered out at the last moment by Gold's commander.

The two thugs were in their path.

Rolf's horse panicked, threw him, and ran off, ignoring the man's shouts. Rolf looked at the advancing monsters and turned to his partner for help.

Twann, quickly measuring the shrinking distance between the dragons and himself, shouted, "To hell with you!"

The other man watched him ride off, the horror dawning on him. He tried to run, but the first of the minor drakes was already upon him. It was more serpent than lizard, and it half slithered as it moved. Gaping jaws clamped on to him. A scream of surprise and pain, then silence.

Ahead, Twann could hear the scream. He had only momentary regrets and then concentrated on increasing the speed of his mount. He had little to worry about on that aspect; the animal was doing its best to save its own life. Nevertheless, the distance was still decreasing. Minor drakes were the steeds of the ruling class. When Dragon Kings and their liegemen traveled in the forms of humans, minor drakes were enchanted to appear as horses. This allowed the dragons to travel through the lands without attracting attention. Though they ruled over nearly all of the realm, the Dragon Kings and their relations were, for the most part, solitary and private creatures.

Even with only the dim light of the moons, Twann was able to notice the dark shadow that passed over him. He looked up in panic. A huge firedrake, eyes glowing, came swooping down. The thug pulled out his sword, knowing full well how futile that would be.

The great claws closed upon him.

The horde raced on. Talak was their first destination.

When Cabe awoke, darkness was all that met his eyes. He did not know if he had slept minutes, hours, or days. Darkhorse had not returned. He shuddered, and almost wished the fantastic being was here.

There was a slight fluttering. Cabe stood up abruptly. The trees blocked most of the light from the Twins. Styx was barely visible at all. Cabe was not sure whether all of the strange creations of released magic had vanished. He began to grope for the sword. Now he was willing to hold it.

Something fluttered nearby. Cabe recalled the barrier to Darkhorse. Suppose his bizarre ally had tried to come, but had been prevented. He may have finally given up and left. That would leave him all alone to face—what?

That the barrier did not prevent all creatures from entering was evidenced by the dams. They had lived here for countless seasons. What else might have found its way here?

The sword. It should have been near him, but he could not find it in the darkness. He began to dig frantically. It had to be here! For a brief second, he felt something like the pommel. His search, though, was interrupted by the sudden sound of great, beating wings coming from behind him. He whirled about.

Something landed in front of him. He could not make out much of its features, but it did not appear to be a firedrake. . . . No, it seemed more birdlike, or manlike, he thought as two clawed arms reached for him. He ducked away, barely avoiding its touch.

The avian moved after him with such accuracy that Cabe suspected it had night vision. There would be no rescue this time. Whatever happened would depend upon his actions.

In the darkness, he nearly stumbled over something. It was long and hard, possibly a branch. He quickly reached down and picked it up. It was not much, but it felt better than being totally unarmed. At any rate, the bird-creature had now become more cautious in its attack.

Desperation set in. Cabe swung the branch at his opponent. The wings flapped, lifting the avian away from the piece of wood. It landed a short distance away and waited for the man to make his next move. Cabe started toward it, remembered his precious burden, and backed up. He would defend the Lady at whatever cost.

The avian fluttered up into the air until it was up more than four times Cabe's height. It flew toward him, hovered out of reach, and then flew around him. Cabe spun around, ready for the attack, but the bird-creature merely continued circling him. Its pace had increased, and the man found it hard to keep his eyes on the thing without becoming too dizzy.

Around and around it flew, never within striking distance. Cabe threw the branch at it, but missed. It was a foolish act, but he was quickly becoming disoriented and needed to do something.

Cabe paused to clear his head. That was the moment the avian had been waiting for. Swooping down, it landed behind him. Clawed hands reached out and grabbed hold of his head. Cabe jerked as his mind suddenly left the present.

He found himself traveling backward. The Seeker—the name came to him, though he knew not how—had found what it had sought.

It was dark, but not the dark of night. Rather, it was the darkness of nothing. A void.

Something of importance was lacking.

Cabe came screaming into existence, but he was not himself. Unborn, he was older than his mother and father.

Pain.

Memory of pain.

A bright light, quickly coming; he had to get away. He had to. Had to.

The one who called himself Simon was alone. The Lord Gryphon had had other things to attend to, and the warlock wished to be alone anyway, for only in privacy could he find any hope at all.

A great voice shattered his thoughts. "As morbid as always!"

The warlock lifted his head and may have blinked. "Darkhorse. I wasn't expecting you yet."

The creature of eternity laughed. "Rubbish! You expect everything! I know you too well!"

Simon nodded. "More than anyone else could."

Darkhorse trotted closer. Despite his form, not one object was knocked out of place. Darkhorse moved only what he wished to move. "I come to tell you that young Bedlam has succeeded in freeing the Lady, with the Horned Blade, as you predicted and no doubt knew already, of course."

"Was there trouble?"

"The dams? They will seduce no man ever again."

"I meant with the power buildup. The Lady has waited a long time."

The creature snorted. "I absorbed everything! Wild energy is of little concern to me! If it had not been controlled . . . Ha! Why imagine disasters that did not happen? Now, as for those two, the only thing they need to worry about is rest."

The warlock said nothing. Instead, he picked up the Egg and held it up to his unearthly companion. Darkhorse shook his head in irritation and fixed a cold blue eye on the warlock. Any other man would have shrank back, but he who called himself Simon did not.

"Look into the Egg."

"You know that I cannot! The Egg is useless to me. All I see is mist!"

"Try."

Something in the warlock's voice made the creature obey. Few others could do such a thing, but Darkhorse knew who and what it was he faced. Simon was beyond his powers, his fate in the hands of another. That may have been why the creature could call him friend. Eternity had been lonely.

An almost human sigh. "I will try."

Darkhorse stared into Yalak's Egg. Simon may have watched the mist closely. It swirled, like a beast of Chaos tearing at its chains, the darkness becoming deeper and deeper. The mist vanished, leaving a void so vast that it threatened to pull even Darkhorse into it.

The great steed pulled his gaze away quickly. "No more! I will look no more!"

"What was it?" Though the warlock asked a question, his tone was that of someone seeking confirmation of a fact already known.

The eye fixed on him. "It is where we two may not go. It is where I have sent countless others. It is the place from which none may return."

The blurred features of Simon may have added a deeper

frown. "Then what does it mean? I am not like the Gryphon. I believe that anything the Egg shows us must have meaning."

"Perhaps, but then again, you may be wrong."

"No. I feel that there is some significance as far as Cabe is concerned. If I could see it again . . ."

"I will not go through that again!"

The warlock shook his head. "I would not ask you to."

Darkhorse changed the subject abruptly. "The Lady will soon wake. I do not relish returning there and confronting her. Though she cannot kill me, she has the power to exile me for a long time."

"She will care for you even less when she learns that I am the one who summoned you."

The spectral horse nodded. "You, I think, would face worse than exile."

The face beneath the hood was unusually distinct. There was an impression of a young man with eyes that seemed as eternal as his companion. "I already do. I do not fear her hatred."

There was silence. Darkhorse felt strangely mortal. He shook off the feeling. "I will return to Bedlam and the Lady."

"Safe journey, my friend."

Darkhorse started to laugh, thought about it, and sobered. With a roar, he opened up The Path Which Men May Travel Only Once and disappeared. There were sounds in the wake of his going. Unreal sounds that his companion knew all too well. *Damned souls* was the closest description he could find.

Thoughtfully, he who called himself Simon sat stroking the Egg.

The contact was broken.

He was back at the manor. The avian flew from him, shrieking in anger. Though it was dark, a strange light illuminated the nearby area.

"Wake up! The Seeker will try again!"

Cabe blinked. What had happened to him? Why had all the details of his life become so realistic yet so sketchy?

There was another shriek. He looked up and immediately regretted that action. Above him, almost hovering, was the huge bird-creature. It had arms and legs similar to a man's, save that the knees were reversed, like a real bird's, and all four limbs ended in great, clawed digits. It was musty gray, and the hawklike features of its face gave every indication of a predator. And it was starting to swoop down on him again.

A great ball of light burst in front of it. The avian stopped in midair, blinking rapidly and flying slightly wobbly. When another flash burst, the creature took flight into the cover of night.

Now that the threat was gone, Cabe whirled around to see his savior.

The Lady faced him. Though she had saved him from the Seeker, she did not seem to trust him. Cabe couldn't blame her. It would be hard to trust anybody after being trapped for such a long time. He decided that the safest thing to do would be to let her make the first move, providing that she did not destroy him outright.

"Who are you?"

The voice had a musical quality to it, and Cabe would have found it quite wonderful at any other time. Now, however, he could hear the menace in it.

"My name's Cabe. I—I freed you."

The expression on her face indicated that she found his story more than a little difficult to believe. "How were you able to free me? The spell that formed the prison was one of the most powerful ever used. No ordinary man could break it!" She glanced at his hair and saw the silver. "Warlock! I was right! No ordinary man could break Azran's spell!"

Something fluttered in the shadows behind the Lady. Cabe squinted. With shocking speed, the avian attacked.

"Look out!"

The sorceress turned, but had no time to defend herself. One of the Seeker's clawed feet struck her, and she tumbled to the ground. Cabe's frustration grew; he longed for the power to lash out. The bird-creature shrieked and came for him. Involuntarily, he thrust both arms straight out, the tips of his fingers aimed at the Seeker.

A line of force burst from his hands. The avian, unsuspecting, felt the full brunt of the attack, and was thrown back by a force much stronger than that used by the Lady.

It tumbled into the nearest trees, striking one awkwardly with an arm. There was a crack, and the Seeker shrieked, this time in pain.

Flapping very ungracefully, the avian flew off. This time, however, it was obvious the creature had no intention of coming back. Cabe watched it disappear into the dark and then sat down on the ground in relief. It took him a moment to remember his companion. When he turned to check her condition, he saw that she was staring at him closely.

"Your actions are unskilled, but your power is potent." Her hands were once again prepared for attack. "Who did you say you are?"

Cabe groaned inwardly. "Cabe—Cabe Bedlam, if I believe what's been said."

The Lady's eyes widened. There was shock and . . . some emotion that could not really be given a label. She studied his face for several moments and then, much to Cabe's relief, relaxed.

"I should have seen it in your face. Power that great comes along only now and then. The coincidence is too much. What—" she paused to wipe away a tear "—is your relation to Nathan?"

"I've been told I'm his grandson. I found out only recently. One of the Dragon Kings—"

"Dragon Kings!" The hatred in the Lady's voice was so fierce that Cabe shrank back. "I had forgotten those cursed lizards! They still rule!"

She slumped. For a moment, Cabe thought she had fainted, but she slowly looked up again. "Nathan—is he alive?"

He could not bring himself to say it. He shook his head.

"Nathan!" She looked up to the heavens. Suddenly, she was not the Lady, but merely a woman named Gwen. Cabe had forgotten the name, so awed was he by her earlier.

"Azran!" This time, it was the Lady speaking. The hatred was as intense as that for the Dragon Kings. "By his son betrayed!"

Cabe had lost track of what she was saying, but did

not dare interrupt. The Lady Gwen finally looked at him again.

"I knew your grandfather well. Loved him. I was on my way to help him when Azran imprisoned me. I suppose Nathan died in the struggle against the Dragon Kings."

"He took the Purple Dragon with him. Everyone knows that."

That made her smile. "Nathan! Even in the end he did his part! Who now rules in Penacles?"

"The Gryphon."

"We must go to him. I must learn everything I can before I face those reptiles again. And Azran." The smile turned grim. "You'd best come with me."

"I was going there anyway." The trials of the last few days started spilling out. "If the body of the Dragon King is found, they're sure to—"

"Dead? Which one?"

"I think it was the Brown Dragon. We were in the Barren Lands."

She nodded. "That would be Brown. So . . . they know about you too. You are in great danger. Every firedrake will hunt you in the hopes of gaining glory from their masters."

"I have a sword that frightens them. I used it on a basilisk and the firedrakes. I think it's called the Horned Blade."

The Lady shivered. "An evil sword. It will save you from one enemy, but draw the other to you. Azran had it cast —when he believed he could conquer both Kings and Masters—but lost it. Lost it only after he had murdered several times! He will want it, and you. I know not which he will desire more."

"Who is Azran?"

She pursed her lips. "Azran is one of the most powerful warlocks alive. His power rivaled that of Nathan's. Not surprising, really." Gwen paused. "Azran was his son." She watched Cabe's expression turn to shock.

"Your father, Cabe Bedlam."

VI

Azran was furious.

The ancient seer paced the length of his dim abode. Things of the dark chittered around him, waiting for commands but receiving only silence. None had the power to re-create the skull of Yalak, master of foresight. That was what Azran wished.

He snorted. Foresight. It had not saved Yalak from dying nor had it prevented his skull from being ensorcelled by Azran. The warlock had used the skull many times since. Never had it spoken of its own will. Something was amiss.

A dark shadow fluttered outside. Azran stopped his pacing and moved with great determination to his balcony. His tired legs screamed out their annoyance at such abuse.

It was waiting for him. Though the Seeker would have easily torn him to pieces, it could not. It was his. They all were. More ancient than the Dragon Kings themselves, the avians were still no match for the warlock's power. His slaves, they were his eyes and ears in the outside world.

The Seeker knelt. Azran put one hand gently on its head. This was no sign of affection. The old necromancer cared for no one. Not his late wife, his deceased brother, his son, or—most of all—his father. No, there was no affection in his touch. The contact served only to relay information from the mind of the bird-creature to himself.

A picture formed, that of the Tyber Mountains. This, Azran realized, was the spy he had sent to watch the Dragon Kings. For a brief moment, he wondered what had happened to the other. He shook his head. His mind must be clear for contact. He forgot all else and concentrated on the images.

The words of the reptiles were heard as the Seeker had

heard them. The warlock nodded. As he had suspected, the Kings were on the move.

Azran briefly remembered kicking the pieces of the shattered skull as they lay scattered over the floor. Everything in this business had to be so mystifying. Why couldn't someone just come out and say what they meant? Where was it written that the dark arts had to be mystifying? Complex, yes. Otherwise, any fool could lay waste to the Dragonrealm. Mystery, however, tended only to irritate him.

He realized that he had broken contact, but the Seeker apparently had already told him all he needed to know. Now the avian awaited his next command. Azran pondered his next move. It would have been easier if the other had returned, but he knew that the creature would not fly back until it had completed its mission. Therefore, he would have to plan without the knowledge it might carry.

Penacles seemed to be an important factor in the coming crisis. Azran had always meant to wrest the city from the Gryphon, but the thought that the lionbird might have the knowledge to destroy him had always prevented such an act. It was well known that the Purple Dragon had been the real power of the Dragon Kings. Gold was strong, but he had ruled only because his brother had had no desire.

Still, his father had destroyed the reptile. Azran had to acknowledge that fact. Without a weapon like the Horned Blade, too. The old warlock was no fool; in his younger days, he would have never gone up against a Dragon King unarmed. Cursing, he remembered the loss of his sword. Who would have suspected that one of the Kings would be nearby when Azran had slain Yalak? Brown, his lands dying rapidly from the Masters' spell, had needed a weapon. To him, the young warlock was only an annoyance. Azran was just completing his spell to control Yalak's skull when the Dragon King had ridden by and grabbed the dark blade.

A sword meant to kill dragons in the hands of one. It was almost funny. Almost.

Nevertheless, Azran had felt something recently. The Horned Blade was making its way toward Penacles. It had also tasted Dragon King blood. Only such could have reanimated the life-force that existed in the sword. Someone else had the blade, and that someone had great power. It was too much of a coincidence. Azran would have to send a spy to the City of Knowledge.

He motioned for the Seeker to stand. It did so, never taking its predatory eyes off him. He wondered what it would do if he ever released it from his power. Probably would rend him to ribbons. It was no secret to him that the avians hated him. It didn't matter; they also feared him too much.

His orders to the creature were short and simple. It was to watch for a traveler carrying the black blade. Whether the sword was hidden would not matter; the Seeker would recognize its presence. In the meantime, the avian must listen for whatever information it could find concerning the Gryphon's movements. There was no doubt that the ruler of Penacles would already be preparing for conflict. To underestimate the Gryphon was to invite disaster, for he was almost as devious as Azran.

The Seeker squawked once to acknowledge its understanding and spread its wings. Azran stepped back as the great creature flew off. He hated sending it away without knowing more about who had the sword. He scratched his chin. There was something else. The path of the Horned Blade would take it near . . .

Azran whirled and stalked over to his charts of the Dragonrealm. Selecting the one that interested him, he studied what he assumed would be the most logical path. After a moment, he nodded. The manor was a bit out of the way, but he had a strong suspicion that it had been a stopping point regardless. There were firedrakes there, but anyone with even the slightest ability would be able to hold them off with the sword.

Yes, he thought, *she is free*.

He knew that he should have destroyed her, but envy had prevented him. The Lady had preferred his father. The ultimate insult. Well, he'd taught her, trapped her so no one else could have her, especially him. The trouble was, he had always been the type to lust, but not the type to do something about it. Besides, the Lady intimidated him.

A wizened hand scratched a bald and wrinkled head. There was a third reason. The necromancer's time had been taken up by something far more important. So important, in fact, that he had forgone even casting spells of youth. Soon, though, he would be young again. Soon his masterpiece would be finished. That thought held him like a drug did an addict.

He chuckled. Casting a minor spell, he opened the passage to his most private of workshops. Only he could step through the gate; anyone else trying would find themselves randomly teleported to one of a number of hellish locations. Azran would allow no disruptions where his prize was concerned.

This was his true inner sanctum. Let them tear apart his castle; they would find only minor spells in comparison. But should they dare to attempt invasion of this place, they would suffer the consequences.

It was simple, a principle applied to his masterpiece as well. Each time he entered, Azran would leave a small portion of his power. Each time, then, the enchantment would grow. It drained him for a time, but it was well worth it. Especially if one knew of the results.

A thing not of any true world crawled toward him. Azran dismissed it back to the unnameable regions. A second spell dismissed the horrendous odor it had left behind. The warlock's nose wrinkled; sometimes it was almost not worth dealing with the things. The least they could do is learn to be clean.

Slowly, almost reverently, he turned his attention to a long, black casket in the center of the laboratory. It might have been the final resting place of a serpent—if Azran had ever had any pets—for its length. The width of it was slightly longer than his hand, as was the height. He caressed the lid in a loving fashion, for what it contained was truly part of him. He had poured more of his power into the contents of the box than he had into a hundred other potent spells. He took off the lid cautiously. This would be his glory and his triumph. This would lay the Dragonrealm at his feet.

Carefully, majestically, he reached in and grasped the hilt of the Nameless.

Talak was a city somewhat secluded. Its closest neighbor was Mito Pica, but that city was more than two weeks' journey to the southeast. Not that it really bothered the inhabitants too much, for they produced nearly everything they needed and their army was considered one of the best in the lands. Besides, they had always tried to maintain peace with the Dragon Kings. The ruins of a sister city, some miles to the east, was a great incentive.

Rennek IV was now ruler of Talak. He was well into his fifties, plump and gray-haired. Once, he had been a powerful warrior, but today, some whispered that it would be better if his son, Melicard, sat on the throne. No one, of course, said it too loudly, for Rennek still had occasional outbursts of ability, especially when angered.

He was angered now. Something was persisting in dragging him from his dreams. He tried in vain to ignore the din, but it seemed only to increase the more he covered his head. Swearing by his three earlier namesakes, the ruler of Talak lifted his form from the bed, put on one of the royal robes, and burst into the hallway screaming.

"Hazar! Where are you? Come to me quickly or I will have a new prime minister!"

He looked around. Even the guards were nowhere to be seen. Ignoring his rather unroyal appearance, Rennek marched through the castle in the hopes of finding someone to lash out at. He caught a frightened servant who was crouching in a corner and pulled the man to his feet. The servant was quivering.

"Basil! What is going on? What is that noise? Where is Hazar?"

"They—they're here, milord! At the gates!"

King Rennek shook the man. "Who, blast you? Who? Where's Hazar?"

"At the gate!"

Cursing, he released the servant. Before looking for Hazar, he would first get a glimpse of this army. The story did not quite ring true; if there was an army at the gates, then why was there no sound of a clash of arms? If there was no army, then why were his servants so frightened?

He located the nearest window opening to the front and leaned out. It was still dark, but he could make out several forms, none of which seemed human. The sounds that had awakened him were those of animals, not men at war. Unfortunately, the night would show him little else, and he could not wait for the approaching dawn. He would have to go down now.

With no servants to attend him, Rennek was forced to dress himself. He was only partially successful; the years of the crown had made him lazier. When he was finally satisfied, he hurried quickly through the castle, slowing only when frightened servants or guards spotted him. He must seem in control, he knew, even if he really was not.

Coming down the stairs, he heard what sounded like the voice of his prime minister, Hazar Aran. The high-pitched tones indicated that Hazar was doing his best to please someone. Another voice interrupted, and King Rennek shivered at the sound of it. It was almost like listening to a snake.

Snake?

He walked majestically into the main hall. Hazar was not his usual sly self. He appeared actually pleased to see his lord. Rennek immediately knew why, and suddenly he wished he had followed the wishes of his people and allowed his son to take over.

The dragonhelm turned to face him. Half hidden by the enclosing darkness of the helm were a pair of red, glowing eyes. The helm itself was only slightly ornate. This was not one of the Dragon Kings, but one of their dukes, a firedrake in human form. As Rennek watched the massive warrior stalk toward him, the king knew he would have to treat this duke as if he were one of the Kings themselves.

"You are King Rennek?" The words were breathed, not spoken.

"I am." The monarch tried to look impressive.

"I am Kyrg. My force has come from the Tyber Mountains."

The Tyber Mountains. These were some of the hellish forces of the emperor. The Gold Dragon. To disobey would mean instant retribution. To make even a small mistake would mean the same conclusion.

"What is it your august majesty wishes with my city? We will, of course, help you in any way we can." He hoped he sounded formal enough.

Kyrg laughed, and it was the laugh of a mass murderer sizing up his prey. "Your city? You may rule the people here, but this city belongs to the King of Kings! You will assist us because you are commanded to!"

Rennek felt his reserve slip away. "Uh . . . yes. Of course."

The infernal duke nodded. "Good. Now, then, we have a great journey ahead of us. We require food for that journey."

The sweetness of the reptile's words served only to make him more frightening. Rennek had horrifying visions of what sort of food the duke might want for his inhuman army. It would not have been the first time; such tales had been spread through the generations.

Kyrg seemed to read his thoughts. "We will take only livestock this time. Should you ever seek to betray us or should you fail us in some capacity, then we will come for other meats, starting with the leadership of this city. Do you understand me?"

Both king and prime minister paled.

Rennek managed a nod.

"Excellent." The duke motioned to his aides. One of them disappeared through the open entrance of the castle. Kyrg pulled out a piece of parchment.

"Can you read?" The voice dripped of sarcasm and contempt.

"Of course! One of the first thi—"

"Numbers?"

The king shrugged. "Fairly well."

The shapeshifter handed him the parchment. Rennek unrolled it.

"This will tell you exactly how much we require. You will gather it in four hours." The duke held up one of his gloved hands to emphasize the time. There were only three fingers and a thumb. Humanoid the firedrakes might appear, but human they were not.

The king of Talak glance down at the list. While the numbers themselves were a little difficult to comprehend, the enormousness of the task did not escape him. "It will take us at least a day."

"Fourrr hoursss." Kyrg's voice had lost almost all traces

of humanity it might have possessed before. "If you do not complete the task in the time period specified, we will take what we need. Indiscriminately."

Rennek shoved the parchment into the hands of his prime minister. The thin man looked at it as if it would devour him. The king looked at his adviser nervously.

"Get on with it, man! Hurry!"

Hazar stumbled away quickly. Rennek glanced at his unholy guest and caught just a shadow of a smile beneath the sinister dragonhelm. "Will there be anything else?"

Kyrg glanced around the room. "Yesss. I have not eaten recently. Nor have my officers. While your people gather up the necessary food, we will dine in your hall. You will have your butchers prepare two of your finest animals for us. You will join us. I wish to learn what I can of the lands to the south."

"Of course. Just let me instruct my cooks as to your pref—"

"The butchers will be sufficient. We prefer our meat very rare. Raw, in fact."

The king felt his stomach turn. This time, he could definitely see the smile on the firedrake's half-hidden face. The duke bowed to him in mock respect.

"Lead the way, Your Majesty."

Dawn came to the manor, and with it came the flood of memories. Cabe tried to keep his eyes shut, but the sound of another finally forced him up.

The couch was now surprisingly uncomfortable. Cabe had been too exhausted and had simply chosen the first soft place to fall down on. The Lady Gwen had been slightly more discerning; she had created a bed of air. Even the sight of a woman floating three feet above ground had not been enough to prevent Cabe from collapsing. The unusual was just not so unusual anymore.

Dangerous, yes; unusual, no.

The Lady was wandering around the manor, apparently reliving memories. To Cabe, she was more beautiful than when he had seen her last. There was, however, a sadness in her movements. A hand would gently touch an object and then quickly pull away. Eyes would stare off into realms of the past, only to immediately lower and return to the present.

Cabe remained quiet in the fear of disturbing her, but she finally turned her attention to him.

"We should be moving on. I wish to speak with the Gryphon as soon as possible. As it is, it will take days to reach him."

"Can't you teleport? I've known of sorcerors who do."

"To teleport, one must know one's destination. I've never been to Penacles. Besides, I really don't feel well enough. We'd best ride. You have a horse, don't you?"

It was a difficult question to answer, especially when Cabe remembered Darkhorse's remarks concerning the Lady's enmity toward the creature. "Sort of."

The frown of her face did not detract from its beauty. "Sort of? What answer is that?"

Cabe's response was prevented by a crashing noise in the forest. Gwen turned at the sound and stared, as if trying to see through both manor and woods.

"What is that?"

"My . . . horse."

"Your horse? How unusual an animal it must be. I think I'd like to have a closer look at it." She waved her left hand and with it drew two circles, the latter reversed from the former. There was a slight shuddering in the air, and then the eerie form of Darkhorse leaped into sight.

"At last! I thought I'd never get someone's attention!"

"Darkhorse! Demon!" The Lady pointed both hands in the direction of the steed. A wave of force erupted, aimed straight for the center of the darkling creature.

Her target merely stood there, taking the power as one might take a drink of water. Darkhorse laughed. "Raw power is not the answer, Lady Gwen! It never was! Besides, I come in peace!"

The Lady's face was a mask of rage. "Knowing you and those you deal with, I find little to believe in your statements!"

Darkhorse sighed. "Call me Prince of Darkness, Lucifer, Thanatos, Death—if you wish! You know my nature, but not my mind! If I am different, it is because one must be so when eternal! Otherwise, madness would've taken me long ago!"

Cabe felt forced to intervene. "He helped, Lady Gwen. The firedrake dams would have taken me."

She looked at him with eyes that burned. He knew that she was capable of leaning either way. She could possibly cast out Darkhorse, but Cabe was a target that had no such immunity. He tried desperately to hide his nervousness.

Finally, though, she lowered her hands. Cabe breathed only slightly more easily; the hands were still tensed. A wrong word or movement could quickly change things.

The fire-tressed sorceress spoke slowly. "Very well. I will trust you for now, Mount of the Infinite Journey. However, even the slightest of false moves will win you a long exile. You know I have the power. Be thankful my head was still muddled or I would have never tried so futile an act as using brute force."

The chilling eyes stared into her. "I will not play false, Lady Gwen. These events concern me as well as you."

Cabe chose to change the subject. "We were going to try and reach Penacles. The Lady wishes to confer with the Lord Gryphon."

"And he with her. The Dragon Kings are stirring. Something has done this, and events can now only be stalled, not prevented." Darkhorse nodded his head to the sorceress, who did not bother to respond. "You will be needed. We must also assure that Cabe reaches the city as well. He may be our trump card. He may be our one hope."

A deep chill passed through Cabe. If the dark steed's words were true, he would most likely find himself in the center of the worst situations. It was not a comforting thought, to say the least. He did not, however, say as much to his companions. It might lower him in their eyes, especially the Lady Gwen's.

Darkhorse lifted his head to the sky, his great, black mane falling back as he did so. "I cannot travel so swiftly in the light, but even that would not be safe for the two of you. We would also find ourselves easy targets for the Dragon Kings or others. I do not relish exile—for any length of time—and the options for you two are even dimmer. We must travel as most mortals do. We will attract fewer eyes."

"We have already attracted more than enough." It was the Lady Gwen who was speaking. "During the night, a Seeker attacked. Fortunately, it sought information more than anything else."

"Then Azran will know, being master over those ancients. He will also feel the presence of the Horned Blade."

She nodded. "We must hurry."

"I daresay. Azran is the sort who might even dare to slay me, if that is at all possible."

Cabe, remembering that they now stood in the center of the manor, thought of food. It had been a long time since he had eaten. He mentioned the idea to Gwen.

"I heartily agree, Cabe. I haven't had a decent meal in . . . several generations, I guess."

"Will there be anything left? I'm not sure I want to touch any food left by the firedrakes."

"We'll see. I kept most of my food in a hidden cellar. The place is sealed with a preservation spell. If it still holds, there will be plenty for us to eat."

A quick check by the Lady revealed that the cellar was not only still intact, but the preservation spell was also still in place. With Cabe's assistance, she gathered up a large amount of exotic foods. The would-be warlock's eyes feasted on the sight. Most of the items were unknown to him, but everything looked delicious.

The emerald enchantress then formed a second pile of much more ordinary foods. These, she indicated, were their supplies for the journey. Cabe nodded, mentally reminding himself to eat as much as possible before they left.

The two humans ate with a passion. Darkhorse commented on the sin of gluttony, but was interrupted by Cabe, who tossed a large, juicy piece of fruit to him. The eternal ceased his remarks and absorbed the food slowly into his form. Although having no need for sustenance, he apparently enjoyed the tastes.

When the meal was over and various other activities had been taken care of, the great steed reassumed his earlier form of an actual horse and allowed the two to mount. Cabe offered his assistance to the Lady, who seemed unsure about whether to sit on the back of a creature she hated. Assuring himself that the Horned Blade was secure in its sheath, Cabe climbed on in front of his companion.

There were reins, but no saddle. Gwen held on to Cabe. Darkhorse turned his head as best he could.

"Are you ready?"

Cabe looked at the Lady. "What about the manor?"

She stared at it wistfully. "I've strengthened the spells. This time, nothing will get in unless I allow it."

He nodded and turned back to the horse. "We're ready."

"Hang on! I will push us as fast as a horse can possibly go!"

With a laugh, Darkhorse reared. Both riders held on tighter as he raced out of the manor and into the forest. With such transportation, they would have no trouble reaching Penacles.

Barring unexpected incidents, of course.

VII

The Gryphon admired his chess set.

"Things just aren't made the way they used to be, wouldn't you agree?"

The one who called himself Simon shrugged. "My memory is patchy, you know that."

The lord of Penacles picked up a single piece that was shaped like a dragon in flight. Its detail was striking. If anyone looked closely enough, they could see that even the smallest of the monster's scales had been carved in. While this was fascinating in itself, it was the Gryphon's opinion that this chess set was for more than just games. Then again, it may have been designed specifically for certain games—of godlike proportions.

The warlock interrupted his train of thought. "They are on their way."

"How soon?"

"Two days. Maybe three. Darkhorse must be cautious. He cannot die, I think, but he may be exiled for some time. Add to that that his passengers are still mortal."

The feathered hand placed the dragon back on the board. "And does she know that you will be here?"

"I thought it wise to have nothing said about my presence here."

"Just so long as the two of you do not destroy the city. I recall the stories about Sika. She may too."

Something that might have been a frown may have played across the other's face. "I have tried to make up for Sika. As I have for Detraq, Coona Falls, and a dozen other cities through the ages. Until I can put an end to myself, I will continue to try and make up for my sins."

"While you add new ones."

"Perhaps. I can only try, though."

The Gryphon walked over and put a clawed hand on Simon's shoulder. The warlock stiffened momentarily and then allowed himself to relax. It was obvious that the touch of the other disturbed him.

"Forgive me, my friend. I spoke without thinking."

The warlock shook his head. "You spoke the truth. I have lived long enough to know that. I am completely accountable for my actions."

"Let us change the subject. What news have we of the Dragon Kings?"

"Forces led by the firedrake known as Kyrg have stopped at Talak. There they demanded a vast quantity of meat."

"And received it, no doubt."

"Of course. They are now heading toward Mito Pica, and from there, the destination becomes obvious."

Nodding, the Gryphon walked thoughtfully over to his chess set. He picked up another piece, this time an armored knight, and fingered it as he spoke. "So. After all this time, the Dragon Kings move to regain the City of Knowledge. This time, though, there are no Masters to help us."

"We have the Lady. We also have Cabe. His powers alone could make the difference."

"Could. I would prefer something more concrete. If only we had Nathan himself."

For the briefest of moments, both were suddenly bathed in sharp, searing gusts of icy wind. The wind disappeared without trace and the room returned to normal. The two looked at one another.

"You felt that, warlock?"

Simon stood up and walked to a window. Only after he had scanned the surrounding areas did he speak. "An unusual breeze for this time of year."

The lionbird grunted. "Unusual for any time of year. It chilled more than the bones. I felt it in my mind. What was it?"

"Difficult to say. Perhaps the city has the answer."

"An interesting thought. I believe it might be best if we investigated at once."

Replacing the knight on his proper spot, the Gryphon moved over to a huge tapestry that covered one of the walls. On the tapestry was a representation of the City of Knowledge. Though the figurines had been very detailed, they paled in comparison to the picture now before him. Every building, every street, every wall; nothing was left out and nothing was incomplete. Even the eye could not have viewed a city so thoroughly.

The tapestry was the only sure way of locating the legendary libraries of Penacles. They moved, though no one knew how or why save their long-dead creators. Without the tapestry for guidance, one might seek libraries forever.

The warlock came over beside him. "Where is it this time?"

"There. See the small scroll design in the window of that house? The libraries will be under there." The Gryphon pointed to a small home on the outskirts. The scroll in the window was barely visible, and only a trained eye would have found it so quickly.

"Ready?"

Simon nodded. The Gryphon put one finger to the spot marked by the scroll and began to rub it gently. As he did so, the room around them blurred. Neither figure paid the change any attention. They had seen it several times before.

Slowly, the Gryphon's chamber vanished. The two of them were now standing in the middle of a strange sort of limbo, the only real object other than themselves being the tapestry. As the ruler of Penacles continued to rub, a new room began to take shape. At first it was as out of focus as the original, but gradually things became more distinct. Walls filled with books appeared around them, save for one long corridor.

A bright light with no discernible source illuminated the libraries. The floors were polished marble and the shelves were of some substance similar to but obviously not wood. The libraries were ancient; any wood would have rotted, crumbled, or petrified by now. Yet the shelves looked as if they had been set up only a few days before.

The shadowy face turned to him. "Where?"

"I have no idea. We shall require the uses of a librarian."

No sooner were the words spoken than a small, incredibly ancient figure stepped into sight. There was something not quite human about him, for his legs were much too short, the arms nearly touched the ground, and not one strand of hair could be seen on the egg-shaped head.

This was a gnome, one of the learned kind. There were very few of them; solitary, they cared more for their books than the companionship of other creatures. They ate very little and lived far longer than most other beings. They were, however, perfect librarians. In all the years the Gryphon had ruled, the gnomes had always been there.

"How may I help the present lord of Penacles and his companion this time?" The voice was cracked and seemed to emphasize the age of the gnome.

The Gryphon took no slight from the use of the word *present*. "We wish to know about winds. Cold, unusually numbing winds that appear out of nowhere and vanish almost instantly."

"A wind spell. Is that all?" The little librarian's disappointment was quite evident.

"It may be a wind spell. It may be something else. Whatever the case may be, I want to find out what I can about it."

The gnome, whose name no one knew, sighed and nodded. "Very well. Follow me. It isn't far."

It never was. Some had speculated that the libraries had an intelligence of their own and did what they could to speed up any search. Adding fuel to this speculation was the fact that the rows of books were not always the same color. Last time, for example, the countless volumes had all been blue. This particular visit, they were a bright orange. The Gryphon began to wonder if he was even talking to the same gnome or whether there were numerous little librarians hidden away in each area. It was something to ponder on in quieter times.

The gnome moved swiftly for a being of his type. He who called himself Simon had barely enough time to glance at some of the books as the three walked down the corridors. Oddly free of any dust, they might have contained the sum knowledge of the multiverse. Sadly, though, that was not the case. For all its information, Penacles lacked, so far as he knew, that which would release the warlock from his curse.

For some reason, the walk was taking longer than anticipated. The gnome muttered something and seemed almost worried. The Gryphon said nothing, but he could not recall ever having to walk this far to find the information he wanted.

"Ah!" The gnome pointed a bony finger at a new corridor. "This is the one. About time!"

With the little man leading, they turned. The librarian was the first to notice, and he screamed as if someone had torn his arms from their sockets. The Gryphon cursed, and his furred hands suddenly revealed long, sharp claws. The warlock merely nodded, as if he had suspected such earlier.

Before them, where the volumes they sought should have been, was a great, charred space.

In the fog-shrouded land known as the Gray Mists, ghostly figures dressed in coal-black armor slowly marched their way west. There was a look in their eyes that would have caused most men to turn away.

From the dark city of Lochivar, in the land of the Black Dragon, they came.

Azran lay on his bed, as still as if he had died. The spell always took a tremendous toll on his system, and it would be hours before he was well enough to stand. Nevertheless, he was pleased. Very pleased. His crowning glory was nearly completed, for soon he would have the weapon that would break all others before it. Soon—

A great rush of wings alerted him to the presence of one of the Seekers. There was something odd about the sound of its landing. Azran suspected that that creature had run into trouble. Hard trouble, judging from its difficulties. He waited, knowing that the avian would come to him when it could.

When it appeared, it looked even worse than he had imagined. It had obviously been flash-burned, and that meant sorcery. One arm was twisted at an odd angle, and the ancient mage suspected it was useless. What, he wondered, had happened to his servant?

The Seeker stared down at him with its predatory eyes. Even as weak as the sorceror was, the creature could not attack him. Azran's spells had assured that. Wobbling, the Seeker kneeled at the foot of his bed and moved close enough so that his master could touch the crested head.

The images came again. First, there were the Barren Lands. Oddly, they were now not so barren. Azran's eyes widened as he saw the patch of grass that was spreading rapidly toward the center of the Brown Dragon's domain. Tremendous power would have been required for overcoming the curse laid down by the Dragon Masters. It was one of their most potent, designed to crush the strength of one of the more lethal of the Kings, and it had succeeded well. Brown's clans were now fewer than two dozen groups. Only a fraction of what they had once been.

That it had been performed under Styx and his pale sister was apparent. That the blood used was Dragon King blood was shocking. Azran almost lost contact as his hand jerked. So, that was the fate of Brown. Quite likely, the Dragon King had been intent on sacrificing someone else and had fallen prey to some attack. Yet two things bothered the warlock.

The Brown Dragon had possessed the Horned Blade.

To succeed with such a spell, the victim had to be a being of power. Who had Brown's intended victim been? The sword's present carrier, obviously, but that did not tell Azran names. There were very few people of Master status in the Dragonrealms; the Dragon Kings had seen to that. He knew of the Lady, the Gryphon, and the cursed, blurred warlock best called Shade, although his first names had been many. There were others, but none were worth calling a threat.

This new warlock was an enigma.

There was more to view, much more. Through the gleaming eyes of the Seeker, Azran viewed the passing of the firedrakes. There was no danger from such as these; other than the Kings, few of the reptiles could master more than the most minor of spells. He mentally ordered the avian to advance to the next memory.

The manor.

He had dreamed of mastering the woman who had lived there. Only dreamed, of course. That stung him more than anything else. Now it was too late. If he understood some of what had taken place, the Lady Gwen was undoubtedly itching to repay him for past indignities.

There was a slight jarring. The Seeker had passed through a spell of Shunning. Azran supposed that the spell had weakened somewhat since being placed on the Lady's dwelling. It was either that or the avian was stronger than it appeared.

The creature had quickly flown over the manor itself. As it reached the back, the crumbled ruins of the amber prison could easily be seen. That did not interest the old mage as much as the two figures near it. One was most definitely the Lady Gwen, apparently asleep or unconscious. But the other . . .

The Seeker was swooping in on the unsuspecting male. Azran had just a glimpse of a young, startled, and hauntingly familiar face before the image gave way to something else entirely.

It took him only a second to realize that the avian had pulled the stranger into a memory lock. Well versed in the Seeker's methods, Azran easily picked his way through the rambling thoughts, occasionally picking out bits and pieces that might be of importance to him. It was only when he started through the most recent memories that he called for more thorough play-through.

A large, blank spot greeted him at one point. Someone, of obviously powerful nature, had blocked all attempts by the creature to record a particular scene at young Cabe's—at least he had learned the name of his new enemy—place of employment. He contemplated kidnapping and questioning the owner, but shrugged it off. Whoever had cast the spell was no amateur; the inn's owner would probably also have a block, as well as anyone else who had happened to be there. Still, it did no more than delay, something the caster no doubt knew as well.

The scene that replaced the blankness proved more interesting. There was no doubt as to the identity of the demonic warrior seated at the table. It was indeed the Brown Dragon. Sheathed at his side was a presence all too familiar to Azran. The lord of the Barren Lands had carried the Horned Blade with him on this journey. It was to be the tool by which the Dragon King would have sacrificed this new, unsuspecting warlock to the Twins.

He laughed slightly. Even the lizards were fools at times.

Azran skipped ahead to the moment of decision. Brown had unsheathed the Horned Blade, and the warlock was pleased to see that his first sword had not lost any of its power in the time since its theft. The Dragon King was saying something. The blade rose in the air—

The memory was cut short. Azran cursed by several of his more unsavory deities. He was back to the scene at the manor, and it was apparent that the Lady had just attacked. The Seeker's view became distorted as it turned its head this way and that. Frustration set it. The sorceror still had no idea of what his adversary's face looked like and who he really was. There were bits and pieces that could be formed into assumptions, but . . .

Then, as he watched the fight, even to the point where the stranger unleashed his power, he could not believe it. He stared at the face again and again, knowing by the look and the feel that what he saw was true. He had never seen the child, never really known the mother, except as his servant. His father had seen to that.

My son, he thought bitterly. *My son is alive*.

He would have trained the boy carefully, making him strong but obedient. His father had been a fool where Azran's upbringing had been concerned, caring only for Dayn, the eldest of the two. Leaving the teaching to amateurs was a mistake that had cost him. Azran had secretly turned to the more desirable forces of magic, the so-called dark powers. Once entranced, he had never wished to be free.

Releasing the Seeker from his touch, Azran ordered the

creature away. The taint of Nathan was evident on Cabe; the boy might very well have to be destroyed. To allow him to train with the Lady or the Gryphon would be suicidal. He, Azran, would be the first target. Against Gwen or the Gryphon, he would be victor.

Cabe, however, was family. That made him more dangerous than the Dragon Kings.

Yes, his son must be captured, and there were only two who could do it. It would be difficult summoning them. Azran would have to rest another day. Though they were forced to obey, they still had the will to resist somewhat. They would do so, knowing that they would weaken him and possibly cause him to commit some fatal error.

The dead never made things easy.

Deep below the Tyber Mountains, in the midst of the flow of magma, lay the eggs. Most were ordinary—wyverns, weak-minded beasts barely fit to be called dragons. A smaller group, glistening in the fiery light, were those that would hatch into firedrakes.

There remained two other groups. One consisted of only two eggs. The misfits. Mutants. Whether they hatched or not mattered little to the Dragon Kings. They were allowed to grow only so long as they did not harm the others. If they were unfit to live, they would be killed, as many of the smaller drakes would be.

The fourth and final group consisted of a handful of colorful, banded, and speckled eggs. They were much larger than the others and were carefully watched over by the strongest and wisest of the dams. These were to be the hope of the future. New Kings to replace those who had died or might soon.

The first of the eggs began to crack open.

Riding had never been so painful. It was not that they had been jostled; in fact, Darkhorse nearly flew across the land. The problem was in dealing with the speed and the length of time. The Lady was determined to reach Penacles as soon as possible and had bade the steed to run as quickly as safety would permit. Cabe was under the impression that his idea of safe speeds greatly differed from his two companions'.

It was Gwen, however, who was finally forced to call a halt. She was still unused to the needs of her system, and nearly fainted, almost causing both riders to fall off their mount. Only the eternal's maneuvering kept both humans on. Slowing to a trot, he gave Cabe the opportunity to assist the Lady. Her decision was made almost the moment she opened her eyes.

They were now on an open road, one of the few in the Dragonlands. Darkhorse turned off and trotted over to a small grove of oaks. Once down, the Lady opened up her pack and removed some food. Cabe grabbed one of the waterskins. The two of them sat down under one of the trees while their transportation pretended to graze nearby.

Gwen leaned back. "What a fool I am! Even a novice knows when their body can take only so much!"

Cabe nodded. "Every point on mine aches."

They divided the food. Cabe bit into a biscuit and discovered that, while lacking much in the way of taste, it filled him up and revived his tired muscles. He asked her what it was.

"It's elfin bread. Eat it enough and you might want to take on the Dragon Emperor's armies single-handed."

Cabe was tempted to spit out the piece in his mouth.

She laughed. A smile appeared momentarily. The Lady looked around at the grove.

"Nathan and I used to go on picnics now and then. It made us feel like ordinary people, not high-level sorcerors. Still, I wonder how many ordinary people could protect their picnics from dragons. Or ants, for that matter."

"What was my grandfather like?" He hesitated as he saw her face. "If you don't mind telling me, that is."

She smiled at him, and Cabe was once more in awe over her beauty. It dawned on him that this woman was old enough to be at least his grandmother, and almost had been.

"I met Nathan when I was only an apprentice. My teacher was an old wood witch. She and Nathan's wife, Lady Asrilla of Mito Pica, had been good friends. Tica, the witch, had even acted as midwife at Azran's birth." Her face clouded over. "He killed his mother with his birth. Nathan should have realized then that his second son was first in evil."

Cabe said nothing, but his thoughts were on this new family

of his. It was not one in which loyalty played an important part. Father against son. Would this be repeated?

Gwen did not notice his faraway look. "I was awed by the power inherent in Nathan. The colors glowed more brightly than any I had ever seen. Colors, which I will teach you to see, are the true aspect of any magic-user's character. Until trained, they are generally bland. Whether one chooses the dark power or the light determines the final rainbow. Azran's became a bleak combination of blacks and grays."

Darkhorse let out a snort, but said nothing.

"Tica could teach me no more, but she knew I had tremendous potential. Therefore, she asked help from this great warlock. He was an imposing sight in his blue robes and hood, stern face staring at this young, gangling girl. I think I first started to love him then. His elder son, Dayn, was just finishing his apprenticeship, and his younger was being tutored elsewhere. Out of friendship, he accepted me. I did my best to live up to the standards I thought he expected. I nearly killed myself doing it. Progress came rapidly, but it was at great cost."

The food was long forgotten. Cabe sat there, taking in everything.

"One day, while I was berating myself for fouling up a fairly simple spell, Nathan came to my room. There was a sadness in his face, and I thought that he was about to dismiss me from his home. Instead, he merely sat down in a chair and talked to me. Talked to me about his wife, his dreams, the Dragon Kings, and . . . my future. Before my eyes, he conjured up the image of a woman." She smiled. "At the time, I thought her the most beautiful woman I had ever seen. I told him this, expecting it to be the form of his late wife. It wasn't. Nathan said that he was showing me a picture of myself, once my powers were fully realized. I was shocked. Tica had never had this much power. My awe increased. It was at that point that he bent down and kissed me. That was all. Just kissed me. He said nothing else. I watched him walk out wordlessly."

The Lady looked deeply into Cabe's eyes. "Only later did I discover that he had just received the news that Azran had murdered his own brother."

Cabe was at a loss. "What—what did Nathan do?"

"What did he do? He tried to forgive him. Tried to bring him back into the light. Tried and failed. Azran had delved too deeply. He'd even made slaves out of his tutors. Worse yet, he sought out and found the Seekers. Found them and made them his slaves too."

"The Seekers. That bird-creature. You said it was a Seeker."

She nodded. "No one knows the history of the Seekers. They are said to be older than the Dragon Kings. Much older. They live in dark rookeries somewhere near the Hell Plains. Few men find the Seekers, and fewer still survive."

"What are they?"

"They once ruled this land. Now they search. Constantly. Always seeking information. No one knows why, even Azran, I suspect. He may have enslaved them, but he could not have dominated them completely. They are a tool that must be watched."

Remembering the stealth and strength of the creature, Cabe could only nod in agreement.

The Lady resumed her story. "I understood after that meeting that I had been pushing myself too hard. Nathan allowed me to ease things. Strangely, my lessons seemed to become simple. I followed his word to the letter, ignoring any mistakes. The mistakes became fewer and fewer. I soon came to realize that I was now as one with my powers. Instead of rushing out in spurts, it now flowed smoothly. Three years later, I was the image I had seen. It was then that Nathan told me how much he really loved me."

Her eyes stared absently as she remembered memories of what might have been yesterday. She had even forgotten the presence of Darkhorse. The infernal steed was still pretending to graze, though Cabe realized that the creature was very silent. After a minute, she blinked, wiped away a single tear, and pretended as if she had never stopped talking.

"The Masters were Nathan's idea. His and Yalak's. They were determined to destroy the Dragon Kings, who had ruled for as long as men could remember. This lot is the worst. They crushed all resistance and any advances men made beyond our present level. All servants were ordered to specifically seek out warlocks and such and to kill them. Fortunately, their servants often lacked the power. The Masters grew in strength and numbers until they were prepared to challenge. Thus, the Turning War began."

Turning War. Few people Cabe knew ever mentioned it by that name. Whole lands had been set into disarray; upheavals were everywhere. It was a stalemate. Lesser mages died, but scores of firedrakes did also. The war had finally turned to the City of Knowledge.

It was well known that much of the Dragon Kings' strategy came not from the emperor, but from the Purple Dragon, he who ruled Penacles. Knowing that, the Masters planned the final offensive. Yalak led a group to the Barren Lands, the site of the Masters' only true victory. He was to prevent the coming of Brown and his remaining clans. Lochivar, the city of the Gray Mists, would hold back the tide of Black. Nathan Bedlam would lead the rest on an all-out assault of the city.

"They were betrayed from the start. Lochivar, long in the Gray Mists, turned traitor. Instead of holding back the dragons, they led the march toward Penacles. If not for the Gryphon, they would have made it. We had never seen his like before, yet he met the betrayers with a small mercenary army and pushed them back. It was because of this that he became the new lord of Penacles."

More and more, Cabe longed to reach the city before anything else happened. As things stood, it was their only real hope for safety.

"Yalak was also betrayed. By Azran. That thing Nathan called a son struck him from behind with the Horned Blade. Yalak never even knew he was there. For once, his future-sight had failed him."

"How did the Dragon Kings gain control of the sword?"

Gwen smirked. "Even Azran is not all-knowing. Brown, seeing his enemies in confusion, sought to crush them. The lord of the Barren Lands had chosen to fight in his human form, but his weapon was broken. Seeing the Horned Blade and knowing it for what it was, he struck down Azran and stole the weapon. Would that he had killed him! It was at that point that I fled, seeking to join Nathan and secure the city before all was lost. Brown, though he finally defeated the Masters, could not give chase. His clans were perilously close to extinction."

The words of the Dragon King filled Cabe's mind. The hatred had been so overwhelming. Cabe could feel little compassion for the reptilian tyrant. Brown had created his own destruction.

The Lady was looking at him with amusement. "I'd heard there was a babe. Your mother was dead, and Nathan must've stolen you from your father rather than see you fall to the darkness. I—"

"Wait!" Something had finally dawned on Cabe. "You saw me?"

"Yes, but—"

The idea seemed impossible. "You have been asleep for years, decades!"

The insinuations were not lost on her. "Yes. I see what you mean, but I cannot explain it."

"I am only only in the midst of my third ten-year! Yet your claim makes me an ancient!"

Darkhorse had stopped his grazing. Though he still wore the form of a real horse, the intelligence in the icy-blue eyes was unmistakable. The ears were at attention. He, too, realized the implications.

The sorceress began to cast a simple spell. Her fingers moved quickly as she spoke. "You remember only a normal life?"

"Only that. No one ever commented on my growth."

"Strange. I see that some spell has been cast over your form, but it is now so much a part of you that I cannot read it. I can tell, however, that it was beneficial to you, if anything."

"What do I do?"

She removed the spell. Cabe felt as if small tendrils had gently detached from his body. "I don't know." She turned to Darkhorse. "I am open to suggestions from you."

The dark steed snorted. "How magnanimous! For the lad, however, I can make only two suggestions! The first is that the spell was most likely the work of Nathan Bedlam and may be the reason for Cabe's strange childhood. You said it appeared to be beneficial. The second suggestion is that we put this problem aside until we reach Penacles. We may receive more information there."

"Do you think that the libraries would know something of this?"

Darkhorse uncharacteristically pawed at the ground. "I was thinking of another."

Her face darkened. "Who?"

Cabe, not realizing the change of mood, suddenly recalled. "Of course! Simon!"

Gwen turned back to him. "Simon?"

He nodded. "He brought Darkhorse to me. He said he would be at Penacles."

"Describe him." Her voice was cold.

"Tall. Wears a cloak and hood. I can't describe his face. It always seemed a blur—"

"Shade!" The scream was akin to the one Gwen had emitted at knowing of Darkhorse. "You accept help from one more cursed than Azran! Fool!"

"Lady Gwen, you know Shade's curse as well as I!" Darkhorse shouted even more loudly than the Lady. Cabe was glad that the road was empty.

"I will kill him!"

"Ha! You would do more damage to this land! He has shifted the balance once again, Lady Gwen!"

She calmed somewhat. "He works with the Gryphon?"

"Until his destruction! You know that!"

"If times continue the way they are, that may be soon."

At a loss, Cabe looked from one to the other. Their words were meaningless.

The Lady stood up. "We have wasted enough time. Now that I know who else awaits us at the City of Knowledge, I am even more eager to be there."

Not waiting for Cabe, she walked over to Darkhorse and mounted. Cabe followed quickly, still wanting to know the reason for her behavior. She was obviously an emotional woman.

As he positioned himself on the dark steed, he spoke to his companion. "Who is Shade? How will he figure in all of this?"

She looked at him, and her words were both blunt and

puzzling. "He is perhaps the only warlock comparable to Nathan. He is also the most hated. Before this is over, he may be both savior and destroyer of us all. It is part of his dual nature."

Darkhorse reared before starting anew his run. This time, there was no laughter.

VIII

They were nearing Penacles. They knew that from the tides that passed them or moved with them. Many seemed agitated. Some groups, heading in opposite directions, argued with each other. Cabe could not make out their words, but he suspected he knew the cause.

Gwen was also watching the lines of humanity. "Some believe Penacles is the safest place to be since it's so well fortified. Others believe that nothing can stand the onslaught of the Dragon Kings."

"Is there war already?"

She shook her head. "I have increased my range of hearing. What I hear has been mentioned several times. Firedrakes, wyverns, and creatures so foul that they have no name. All move south of the Tyber Mountains, and each bears the mark of the Dragon Emperor himself. I have also learned that the Gray Mists have spread toward Penacles from the east."

He tried to see if the city was visible from this distance, but succeeded only in spotting more humanity. "Can the city hold out?"

"The Gryphon has the knowledge from the libraries as well as his own unique abilities. It may well be a long fight."

A column of riders rode past them, choosing to avoid the crowds by traveling well off to the side. They were all dressed in leather, and each one had the look that could only come from years of experience in the art of war. Their small, metal helms failed to cover unruly, blond locks. By their faces, Cabe would have been tempted to believe that they were all brothers.

"Soldiers from Zuu. The Gryphon must have been preparing for this and sent for reinforcements."

"Won't that leave their own city defenseless?"

She shrugged. "Probably not. The Barren Lands are to their south. To the north lies the Dagora Forest, where the Green Dragon rules quietly and seldom interferes with the other races. Even during the Turning War. That was one reason that we never attacked him." There was a strange tone to her voice, as if there was really more to say.

Suddenly, Darkhorse became agitated and signaled that he wished to turn off and converse with the two. Cabe made as if he were pulling the reins, but it was the mount that made the actual decision.

When they had ridden far enough from the road, Darkhorse halted. He waited a moment before speaking.

"I feel something. Large forms, perhaps firedrakes. They appear headed this way."

"Do you think they're coming for us?" Cabe nervously scanned the heavens.

Darkhorse laughed. "Would it matter? If anything happens, we will most definitely be in the middle of it anyway!"

The Lady looked at the beast with distaste. "I find your humor somewhat difficult to understand. How many would you say?"

"Two. Both swift."

She nodded. "Scouts. How soon?"

"I daresay that they will be in sight just after we return to the road. Providing that we go back now, that is."

Cabe was looking at something in the direction of the City of Knowledge. "Something is disrupting travel up ahead."

All three looked. Darkhorse focused one gleaming eye on the area that Cabe had mentioned. "My apologies! I have obviously miscalculated! Two drakes flying quickly down the road! They appear to be harassing travelers at random points along the way!"

The sorceress was grim. "Hurry! We must destroy them!"

That made Darkhorse laugh again. "You accuse me of being bloodthirsty!"

Before she could reply, they were on their way back to the road. The drakes were swooping down here and there, taking great pleasure in what they were doing. As yet, they had merely confined themselves to frightening the humans, but it would not be long before the dragons began to play more seriously.

Darkhorse was almost to the road. "I suggest you dismount. Otherwise, we present ourselves as an obvious target once the fighting begins!"

The drakes were becoming more daring. They were seldom allowed to roam far from their masters and were now reveling in their freedom. One spotted the two travelers and their horse and roared. It soared toward them.

Cabe was on the ground, the Horned Blade out. Gwen dismounted just before the dragon came into range. Darkhorse backed up.

As the monster drew nearer, Cabe turned quickly to the steed. "Can you take him as you did the dams?"

"No! The air is not my element! If you can get him to land—"

The Lady's fingers were moving in swift patterns. "I hardly think that he'll be very happy to oblige us!"

Her spell went off. The drake suddenly found itself bombarded by small bursts of energy. They were going off constantly. The creature tried to fly around them, but they merely moved with him.

"Fireworks, Lady Gwen? This is no holiday!"

The other drake joined its companion. Prepared for sorcery, it flew in an erratic pattern, confounding the Lady's spell-casting. As it moved closer, its great jaws opened wide. However, instead of fire, a strange mist shot forth. Gwen was just able to dissipate the mist before it reached them.

"What was that?" Cabe had never seen a dragon use such a defense.

"Airdrakes don't breathe out fire! They breathe out poisonous fumes!"

The first, totally disoriented by the continual blasts, fell to the ground with a thud. Its partner, though, flew in once again, this time to totally crush its opponents. It moved in toward Cabe, using the same sort of confusing pattern it had earlier. Cabe knew it would not come within striking distance. Oddly, he found he did not care.

Darkhorse moved to cover him. "I will try to absorb the mist if the Lady fails to stop it!"

"No!" Cabe felt strange, as if something was swelling up inside of him. "Both of you, stand away!"

The authority in his voice was such that neither argued. The bizarre but comforting feeling filled him. The drake roared, sensing victory. Cabe remained steadfast.

When it was little more than fifty yards away, the dragon seemed to shrink. The closer it flew, the smaller it became. It was no longer in control; they could see it struggling to alter its course. At twenty yards, it was no larger than a dog. At ten, a small bird.

Three feet from Cabe, the drake ceased to exist.

There was only silence from his two companions. Still filled with power, Cabe turned his attention to the other drake. The creature continued to struggle, albeit much more feebly, against the bursts of energy. The warlock's eyes glowed. The dragon disappeared.

It was the Lady Gwen who first spoke to him. "What did you do?"

"I sent the drake to Penacles. One of their holding cells for wild beasts." Cabe's voice sounded alien to him.

"I meant the other."

A smile played on his face, though he had nothing to do with it. The Lady—and even Darkhorse—seemed taken aback. "Its ego was too great; I merely reduced both to a more appropriate size."

She was shuddering. The single word she spoke was barely even a whisper. "Nathan."

Cabe's head felt funny. He put one hand to it and promptly fell to the ground. Gwen was by him immediately. He opened his eyes and found her staring at him with new wonder. The moment was extremely pleasant, but it was suddenly interrupted by the arrival of several men on horseback. The soldiers from Zuu, to be precise.

The leader, a longtime veteran with jagged scars all over

his face, frowned as he looked around. "What happened to the airdrakes?"

Gwen answered. "Gone."

"We saw them attack you. They ignored us. Too much manpower for the lizards, especially since we all carry bows as well." Each of the soldiers had a longbow. It would have been folly for the drakes.

"You are from Zuu?"

"Aye, milady. We have come on the Lord Gryphon's request."

She nodded. "Then perhaps you could escort us to the city. The Lord Gryphon is expecting us as well."

The commander grinned, his mouth revealing a fairly bad set of teeth. "Oh? And who might you be?"

"I am Lady Gwen of the Green Manor. This is my companion, Cabe."

"The Lady of the Amber!" The man was visibly impressed. He stared at Cabe. "A warlock, too! So that's what happened to the drakes! The Gryphon is going all out!"

The manner of the entire group changed. The commander, Blane, promised to give them the best honor guard possible. He would personally escort them to the Gryphon's lair. It was obvious that the addition of sorcerors to the city's defense was a great boost in morale. Especially when one of them was the Lady Gwen.

They mounted Darkhorse. Blane, seeing the horse closely, stared at it with expert eyes. "I've seen many a fine animal, but I sure as damned wouldn't race any of 'em against that! What is it?"

Smiling, the Lady pretended to pat the head. "A rare breed. Very strong and swift, but lacking much in intelligence."

Darkhorse snorted and threatened to throw both of them off. Blane shook his head.

"Seems pretty smart to me. I wouldn't go insulting an animal like that. Might throw me good if I did."

The dark steed snorted in agreement. The commander turned his horse back in the direction of the city. Darkhorse brought his companions even with the soldier. They started off, the troops following close behind.

The tides of humanity continued to flow back and forth.

* * *

In the lands of the hill dwarves, where iron is mined and shaped for trade through the Dragonrealm, there was a stirring. The dwarves, busy at their tasks, paused. Many muttered to themselves, for they knew only one reason for such shaking.

From mines long played out, a scaly head appeared. It was the very color of the metal so precious to the hill dwarves. It roared, causing the little people to scurry to their caves. A long, sinewy neck, followed by a strong, muscular body, completed the form of one of the dragons of the Iron clans.

No sooner was the creature out than another appeared. The first watched the area as his fellow made his way to the open. When that dragon was done, yet a third revealed himself. The first two kept watch, one looking to and fro. The original looked to only one direction. It was not southeast, where the city of Penacles lay, but rather east.

The Tyber Mountains.

The City of Knowledge might easily have also been dubbed the City of Beauty. Barring Mito Pica, there was no other city like it. Great towers overwhelmed all other buildings. Pointed spires topped many. Below, more on a level with men, gardens dotted the city's streets. The original creators of Penacles did not fight nature to build their metropolis; they worked with it.

Thousands wandered the streets, especially those around and within the city's bazaar. The travelers, escorted by Blane's troops, easily moved through the crowds. Their movement was slow enough so that they could enjoy the sights. Cabe, never having seen a city so large, spent most of his time staring at the throngs with an open mouth. Gwen looked at him and laughed lightly.

"You'd best close that great gap before someone takes you for a dragon! Besides, it ill befits a warlock to be seen looking like some young boy from the outlands."

Cabe held back from commenting that that was exactly the way he felt. He turned his attention back to the city, but found new thoughts reshaping his view of the inhabitants. The Lady had mentioned dragons. As this thought lodged itself, he saw the fear and wonder in the faces. Many people were muttering or glancing this way and that, and especially at the column and its two sorcerors. He saw more than one person point at him, marking the way the streak had extended itself through his hair. They would be expecting miracles from him, he knew, but he had none to give them. Merely bursts of power at one time or another.

He prayed that the Lord Gryphon would be better prepared.

At long last, they reached the palace, though palace was perhaps a colorful term for the building. It was, Cabe decided, definitely a fortress. The walls were all gray stone, and the only entrance was a large iron gate. No decorative columns, no statues—save one of a real gryphon in flight—no decorations of any kind.

Something else was missing. There were absolutely no reminders of the reign of the Purple Dragon. The Gryphon had cleansed the city—and especially the palace—of any signs of the creature. To show his feel for the common people, he had erected few of his own.

The immense iron gate opened as they neared. They were expected. Blane ordered his men to head to the barracks. He was to accompany the two travelers; the commander's orders had been to report directly to the lord of Penacles himself.

To Cabe, the hardest part of their journey up to this point had to be the steps which they had just begun to climb. He estimated that there had to be at least a hundred. Surely, this had to be some sort of defensive measure. No doubt a charging army would soon find itself lying exhausted some two-thirds of the way up, easy prey for defenders.

When they finally reached the top, he looked down. Darkhorse was gone. The guard at the base, one hand clutching the reins of the commander's horse, seemed oblivious to the fact that his other charge had disappeared. Cabe knew his unearthly companion would meet them later.

A servant led them in. The inside of the palace proved almost as spartan as the outside. Their host had little time for luxuries, it seemed. Here and there, some strange artifact hung on the wall or stood nearby, but all of these seemed to pulsate with a life of their own. Cabe glanced at Gwen, and she nodded. Blane was ignorant of anything out of the ordinary and merely looked straight ahead.

Eventually, they reached an elaborately decorated door

guarded by two beings who were only somewhat human. Both stared with sightless eyes and had skins the color of iron. They did not move at first, causing the three to believe them only statues. That belief was shattered by the servant, a small, wiry man who walked up to the one on the left and spoke to it.

"I come with three visitors of importance to the Lord Gryphon."

To their shock, the head tilted to look at the servant. Each movement was accompanied by the sound of metal hinges in sore need of oil. It peered at the man for several seconds, never blinking, and then turned to look at the three.

"The commander from Zuu will enter first and alone." The mouth had not opened, almost causing them to believe someone else had spoken.

The voice was melodious and totally the opposite of what they would have suspected. Blane moved slowly toward the doorway, his hand on the hilt of his weapon. He was no coward, but like most ordinary men, he tolerated magic when it was with him and distrusted it when there was even the slightest chance it wasn't. The commander turned his head from one guard to the other until he was through the doorway. The door closed behind him.

The servant made his apologies and left Cabe and his companion alone. The guard on the left continued to stare at them with sightless eyes, and Cabe had an urge to find some hiding place, preferably outside the city.

Gwen whispered in his ear. "Iron golems! I'd thought the forming of such creatures had been lost to the ages!"

"I wish it had been. Does that thing have to keep looking at us like that?"

"He's not looking at us. He has no eyes as we know them. The only reason he acts like that is that he wears a human shape."

He glanced at the two guards. "I wouldn't exactly say 'human.' If he can't see, how does he know if something happens?"

"I didn't say he can't see; I said that he has no eyes, at least as we know them. He sees by other means. Unfortunately, I don't know how."

Her voice trailed off. Despite her knowledge, the iron golems still made her nervous too. She knew little of their limits, attacks, and defenses. The fact that the Gryphon entrusted his life to them made them all the more dangerous. The monarch of Penacles rarely placed his faith in anything unless he knew it would not fail him.

After several minutes, the door opened and the commander from Zuu stepped out. He was pale and sweating, but there was a look of respect on his face. He nodded to them.

"The Lord Gryphon awaits you."

As he passed them, Cabe whispered quickly to his companion. "Have you met the Gryphon?"

She shook her head. "No. I'm sure we have something to look forward to, though."

They walked through the open doorway, Cabe watching the golems as he went. Neither moved. Any unsuspecting person would have taken them for statues.

"Welcome, my friends."

Cabe turned. He stopped, no more taken aback, though, than the Lady.

Tall and regal, the Lord Gryphon was every bit the monarch. The aura of power and wisdom was unmistakable. Yet it was not this that so astonished the pair. For the Gryphon was more than man. Though his form was near-human, his features were not.

His face was that of a bird of prey, a proud eagle with eyes that saw all. The Gryphon walked toward them, and the great, golden mane that trailed down past his shoulders shook as he did. He extended his hand, and they saw that it was covered with fur but had claws much more avian. Though they should have felt repulsed by this picture, they did not. Rather, they felt the urge to kneel before the grand majesty of this man-beast. The Dragon Kings reigned through terror. The Gryphon, however, reigned through intelligence and understanding.

Cabe took the offered hand, feeling extremely clumsy in every movement. The monarch of Penacles did not move so much as flow. Every action was precise.

"Greetings to you, Cabe Bedlam, grandson of Nathan. I am honored."

He turned to the Lady and took her hand. As he did, his face altered. The lionbird was gone. In its place was a man of hawklike visage who could have easily stolen many a woman's heart. Gwen smiled as he kissed her hand.

He straightened and looked at both. "The Lady is known to me by reputation. You, friend Cabe, are known to me only through a mutual acquaintance."

The Gryphon indicated a figure, unnoticed until now, seated on a couch behind him. The hood and cloak were enough to identify him, but the blurred face clinched the matter for all.

"Simon!"

"Shade!" Gwen's face was a sea of hatreds.

The warlock may have smiled sarcastically. "I am pleased to see you too. Especially you, Amber Lady."

She swung around to face the Gryphon once more. "How can you deal with someone like him? Even if he claims to be on our side? His mixed past condemns him beyond all justification!"

The lord of the city frowned at her. The stern look was such that she was forced to back away. "Simon pays for his sins with every moment of life, Lady Gwen. He will do what he can for us."

"Until next time!"

Throughout this exchange, the hooded warlock kept silent. Cabe could not read his face, but there seemed to be a great sadness prevalent in his movements. Sadness—and guilt. Tremendous guilt.

The Gryphon finally calmed the lady down by offering her a look at the libraries. The thought of that knowledge thrilled her. Cabe was also invited, but he declined. Something inside urged him to talk to the shadowy sorceror.

When they were alone, Cabe walked over to the man who called himself Simon. The other looked at him expectantly; but before Cabe could speak, they were both interrupted by the sound of thundering hooves.

"Couldn't someone at least tell me when it's safe to come up here? I remained in hiding so I wouldn't spook that fine commander from Zuu!"

Shade chuckled, his depression momentarily lifting. "Fine commander? He must have complimented you, my friend."

"Merely gave me the respect that some are rather reluctant to give."

"I have only the greatest respect for you."

Darkhorse snorted. "I was referring to the woman! I assume you were treated in similar fashion!"

Almost as quickly as it had gone, Simon's depression returned. "The Lady does not forgive easily. . . . Nor should she have to. I take full responsibility for my curse."

The warlock stood up abruptly. "If you will excuse me, I have some preparations to make. Keep the lad company, old friend."

Shade vanished.

Cabe looked to the dark steed. "What did he do? Why does the Lady carry so much hatred for him?"

A sigh. "Sit down, friend Cabe. This will take some time."

He did as Darkhorse suggested. The phantom mount stood before him. Cabe tried to imagine what it would be like if someone walked in and found him talking to a sleek black horse. Then again, it would only take a minute to realize that this creature was no true animal. The aura of eternity was quite evident to anyone who looked.

A cold eye was fixed on him. "Once there was a warlock of tremendous power. Shade. A man possessed with one goal. The greatest goal men have ever sought for." A pause. "That goal was immortality."

Immortality. The word alone seemed to breathe magic.

Cabe remembered stories of countless individuals who had sought for the treasure that was greater than gold. The mere possibility would be enough to send whole nations to war, either with one another or against themselves. It never mattered.

"Did—did he find it?"

Darkhorse ignored the question completely. "Shade was a man of two minds, both hotly contesting with one another for supremacy. He walked the thin, gray line between white and black. At times he would teeter in one direction or the other, but never was he completely ensnared. As the years passed, he gained tremendous knowledge of both powers, and it was this combination of knowledge that led him to what he believed was the solution." He snorted. "In such a way have men's egos and greed brought them to disasters unparalleled."

Cabe said nothing. It was an age-old story.

"Shade invoked powers from both sides, strong powers unknown to men today. He failed to consider one thing, however. Where light meets dark, there is always conflict. His very nature proved that. Shade found himself caught amidst the fury of the two sides. Lesser men would have died. Shade, being what he was, faced a far more terrible fate."

There was a sadness in the creature's voice. Darkhorse had few friends, and none more important to him than the shadowy warlock.

"In their collective fury, the powers overcame his protections. He who would have been immortal instead found himself a puppet at the mercy of several masters! He was twisted, changed, melted, torn. Each power strove to make him their tool. Each only partially succeeded, and when it was over, the forces returned to their planes of existence. Of the warlock Shade, there remained only a battered corpse."

Cabe uttered a gasp.

The demonic horse nodded. "A corpse, yes. For a week, it lay where it had fallen. No one, of course, entered a sorceror's lair if they could help it. Besides, it was not uncommon for Shade to remain inside for weeks. On the eighth day, the body dissolved, leaving no trace of the warlock. At the same time, in the midst of the Hell Plains, a figure rose from the magma pits. It was unharmed by the elements and reeked of evil. Shade's dark side had apparently triumphed, for it was he."

"Then the Lady was right about him?" Cabe's eyes darted here and there, looking for someplace to hide.

"Have no fear! The story is far from over!"

Darkhorse watched the boy relax slightly. "That's better! Where was I? This Shade, who gave himself the name Belrac, soon created terror that rivaled that of the Dragon Kings. He was now confident of his immortality and made reckless attacks. By sheer audacity alone, he won many of his battles.

Yet, for all his seeming invulnerability, Belrac found that he was far from perfect. First, he had lost much of his memory from his former life. It was as if he were actually a son and not the real warlock. The second and far more important point he discovered was that he could be killed. He found out the hard way, when Illian of the Birds drove an enchanted staff through his form. Belrac crumpled to the ground and watched his life fluids spill out. Illian had his body burned in order to prevent a reoccurrence of the nightmare, but it was not enough. Three days later, in the Dagora Forest, he stepped out from the trees. This time he named himself Jelrath."

"Why the names?"

"I'm coming to that. Jelrath remembered only small fragments of his past lives, but enough to know who he was. Filled with remorse for his evil deeds, he dedicated his life to righting his wrongs and helping the people. There was no evil in his system; he was a servant of the light. He knew then that immortality was his, but it was perverted. The two sides of his personality had been torn asunder. Both dark and light claimed him; both dark and light controlled him. He was cursed to live an infinity of lives, alternating between good and evil. With one hand, he healed; with the other, he crushed all in his path. Each death brought forth the opposing personality. The names? It may be to hide his past. If he kept the same name, someone would eventually hunt him down. Shade does not die easily, but he can suffer as much as any man. Another possibility is the one I believe. Though all the lives are Shade, they are only portions. Incomplete. In their desire to be whole individuals, choosing a name would be the first place to start." Darkhorse lowered his voice. "Sometimes I think that they all believe the curse ends with them."

"How—how long has this been going on?"

"Ha! I stopped trying to remember the names centuries ago! You want a list, check any legend! Odds are that many will be him. If you know what to look for, that is."

Cabe studied the walls. He could really think of nothing to say at this point. How does one comprehend the pain and sadness of a thousand lifetimes? The Lady had a good point; there was no telling when Shade might suddenly be their most dangerous enemy. Yet he was now one of their few real hopes.

Could they pass up such a chance?

Did they dare take the chance?

The Gryphon brought Lady Gwen to a room remarkably similar to the one they had left. Like the first room, this one was guarded by two iron golems. She asked about their creation.

He smiled. "No doubt you are wondering where the information came from."

"I would assume it was the libraries."

"True, but the actual spells and items listed are from the days of the Harkonens."

"The Harkonens? But that means—"

He nodded. "Yes, the libraries contain many surprises." The Gryphon frowned. "Too many. It took me twenty years to understand just that one spell."

They passed through the doorway. The lord of Penacles led her to a tapestry hanging on the far wall. Gwen inspected it.

"Transporter?"

"Yes. The libraries move randomly. By what means, I don't know. This allows us to reach them, and, as far as I know, there are no other entrances."

"How did the Purple Dragon build this?"

As he started to rub the picture, this time a small shop, he looked at her strangely. "The Purple Dragon didn't build this. This was here long before the Dragon Kings gained control."

She would have asked more, but the room had begun to fade. Gwen watched in fascination. This was a mode of teleportation that she had heard of but never experienced. Within moments, the two of them were standing in one of the corridors of the libraries. Row upon row of books lined the walls, and the sorceress noticed that they were all the same.

A small gnome, who may or may not have been one of many librarians, was waiting for them. The Gryphon had mentioned him earlier, but he still came as a surprise. The little man said nothing; he would not move until he received word from the present lord of the City of Knowledge.

Somewhere along the way, the Gryphon's features had reverted to the lionbird. Gwen also noticed that the hands were now feathered with claws akin to those of a large cat. She wondered exactly what the limits were to her host's shapeshifting. In many ways, it was even more versatile than that of the Dragon Kings.

The monarch of Penacles spoke. "Lead us to the same location as before."

The gnome blinked. After a moment, he nodded, turned around, and started to shuffle away. They followed him. While they traversed the corridors, the Gryphon began to explain.

"As I mentioned, I know of no other way to enter. The librarian will back me up. However, something has happened to make me wonder if the libraries, and therefore Penacles, are truly safe."

"What do you mean?"

They turned a corridor. "What do we know about the knowledge in these hallways?" He indicated the endless walls of books. "Much of it contains ideas and spells we might never even think of but would be willing to do anything for. With these libraries, one could potentially rule the Dragonrealm and beyond."

"Why not have scholars start reading the books?"

He laughed, and the sight made Gwen smile. "Even if it were possible to gather enough scholars—trustworthy ones, mind you—and set them to work, they wouldn't get very far. Look."

The Gryphon paused to pull one of the large, imposing, leather-bound tomes out. There was no dust on it. He handed the book to her. She opened it up to one of the first pages. Her eyes widened.

The pages were blank.

She thumbed through the book. Every page was blank. Gwen searched for some spell, but she felt nothing. Looking up, she saw that the Gryphon was smiling as best as his animal face would allow him.

"Every one of these books is the same. I know; I looked

through more than a hundred in various spots and had others do the same. Nothing."

"What about him?" She pointed at the gnome. The small, bent man was standing nearby, patiently awaiting his charges.

"Apparently, he can only read what someone requests. He does know, however, where to find something when I ask for it. He feels its presence."

"How long has he been here?"

The Gryphon turned to the librarian. "How long have you been here?"

The gnome closed his eyes momentarily. When he opened them, his answer was quick and short. "I have always been here."

"You see?" The Gryphon shrugged. Replacing the book, he turned back to the gnome. "Lead on."

They turned down a final corridor. The squat librarian stood to one side. The Gryphon watched his guest. The Lady gasped.

"That shelf! The books have been destroyed!"

He nodded, a grim look on his face. "Yes. It was like that when Shade and I came to investigate the cause of the icy wind."

"What wind?"

"Only a small breeze, but one that chilled the soul as well as the body. We came here seeking an answer. Instead, we found this."

"Who—"

The master of Penacles slammed his fist against a shelf. "Does it matter? The libraries have been invaded! Damaged! Whether it was Azran, the Dragon Kings, or some other evil, our most secure area is in danger!"

The Lady stared at the burnt area. The Gryphon continued to speak.

"I fear we may have been beaten before we have even begun the struggle!"

IX

Bronze and Iron.

Colors of war. Strength.

The drakes swarmed into the Tyber Mountains. A flash of iron. A swarm of bronze. They came with one purpose. They came with one cause.

They came for betrayal.

Great Iron, surveying his legions, nodded in satisfaction. He was atop one of the larger mountains, commanding his clans. Small drakes, his messengers, fluttered around him. They were his contact with his commanders. They were also his contact with his ally, Bronze. Between the two of them, they would crush the emperor while his legions marched to Penacles. Iron would lead, with Bronze as a strong addition to his power. The Dragon Kings would regain their momentum. Gold was weak, and should never have been made emperor.

There were a few pockets of resistance. A number of wyverns and basilisks died as unidentified creatures of darkness attacked. The deaths did not disturb him. There were always too many of the lessers. Besides, the defenders had eventually been overrun and killed. Dragon blood flowed easily this night.

In the distance, the war cries of the Bronze clans rose to a triumphant high. His ally had broken through. Now was the time for the final push. Soon, Iron would put his jaws around his brother's neck and end his reign.

As his legions poured into the cavern that was Gold's home, Iron climbed down from the mountain. He would be there when the final defenses were crushed. It would prove his cause.

They met in the chamber where the Dragon Kings held council. Bronze was already there. He had ordered his commanders away and waited for his brother alone.

Iron surveyed the vast chamber. "Where is he? Where is our weakling brother?"

"I have searched high and low. He appears to have escaped to the underground. Perhaps the hatchery."

The Iron Dragon stepped toward a tunnel to the rear of the chamber. As he neared it, he altered his shape. Gone was the beast, in form but not in spirit. The helmed figure of the Dragon King stepped up to the entrance of the tunnel.

"He has gone this way. To do so, he must be in a like form. Change and follow me!"

Bronze was skeptical. "Are you sure this is wise?"

"He is alone, save for the dam who guards. She will not sacrifice the eggs. If we choose to kill the emperor, she will not intrude. Come!"

Two armored warriors, they stalked down the dark cavern. The lack of light had little effect on them; their eyes were still those of the great reptiles. Iron led the way; Bronze guarded their rear. They were not fools. Though beaten, their brother might still have defenses of some sort.

The heat generated in the hatchery spread toward them in wave after wave. They ignored it. A thing of the dark detached itself from the ceiling of the tunnel and flew to meet them. Iron killed it with one stroke of his blade. He laughed as he did, for he enjoyed the destruction of foes.

They came to the hatchery, and Iron stepped inside. The old dam, a creature of unbelievable size even for a dragon, watched him cautiously. So long as he did not touch her charges, she would leave him in peace. It did not matter whether he was a king or not; her decision would be based on his actions.

The other joined him. "Is he here?"

"Are you a fool? Does it look as if he is here? We have no business in the hatchery! He must be farther on!"

They departed from the hatchery, not without some relief, and climbed deeper into the depths of the mountain. Much time passed. These were unfamiliar areas to the two conquerors. They were now in Gold's private domain. Both moved closer to each other, and Bronze cursed inwardly for not bringing some of his legion with him.

"I dislike the closeness of this tunnel, Iron! We cannot shift out of these human shapes!"

"Neither can the emperor! He may know these caverns, but it will not save him."

"At least let me call forth some of my clans!" Bronze was one of the few Dragon Kings able to master any sort of telepathy. The only other two were Iron and the very emperor they sought to overthrow.

Iron growled impatiently. "Very well! They had best arrive soon, though! I hunger for death!"

His eyes blank, the other summoned his warriors. He blinked. Iron watched him curiously. Something was obviously amiss.

"Well?"

Bronze turned to him. "I receive no answer to my summons!"

"The walls—"

"No!" Bronze was surprised by his own anxiety. "I would know that! They—they don't answer! As if we are alone!"

Frowning, Iron sought to summon his own clans. He felt only a great void, as if all had ceased to exist. He stood straight.

"This bears investigating! We must return to the chamber!"

"What about—"

"If there is indeed trickery involved, our brother will be close by. In the chamber, we may revert to our full forms."

Sword in hand, Iron marched angrily away. Bronze paused only momentarily and then followed quickly behind.

Nothing obstructed their path. They ignored the hatchery, knowing that the guardian of the eggs would never permit sorcery near her charges. The walk seemed to be both quicker and slower, and with each step, Iron's anger increased.

They stepped back into the council chamber.

Once out, their human forms melted. They stretched their wings nervously and surveyed the area. Nothing had changed.

"I still receive no word from my clans," Bronze muttered.

Something shrieked in the night.

Dragons fear little. The Dragon Kings feared almost nothing. Until this moment. The scream chilled their very marrow, yet, shocked as they were, they were still fighters. Angrily,

Iron roared his challenge, and Bronze joined him. What could defeat two of the mightiest of the Dragon Kings?

"I have awaited you." There was mockery in the tone. Both knew who spoke.

"Brother Gold! Show yourself!" Iron glanced here and there, waiting for a chance to strike.

"Here." Out of a small hole stepped the emperor. Bronze laughed. Their brother was in human form and made no attempt to shift. His death would be quick.

The thing shrieked from behind them.

Bronze turned his great head in dismay. Iron, knowing that they had been tricked, tried to wrap his jaws around the small form in front of him. Both burst into flames. Nothing else in the room was touched.

Gold watched their tattered remains burn away. The thing wobbled up to him and placed its leathery head near his feet. The Dragon Emperor petted it softly on the head. The thing crooned happily. Gold continued to stare at the burning, smelling masses. He knew with satisfaction that the same scene had been repeated countless times outside.

The smile that played across his half-hidden face was neither dragon nor man, but the worst of both.

"Good-bye."

Azran faced the pit that opened to the Plane of the Dead. The smell of decay and rotting flesh bothered him, even though he had cast his strongest spells to keep the odor away. Death was something that just could not be ignored, apparently.

The pit bubble and oozed. Azran waited for something to emerge from the muck. It had taken him much longer to recover than expected. There was little doubt in his mind that his son and that witch had arrived in Penacles. The Seeker had not returned yet. He was forced to go blindly again.

The hand shot out of the ooze. The old seer nodded in satisfaction. A guardian of the dead rose to meet him, ooze dripping from its putrid flesh. Like a mixture of every dead creature, it stood a foot taller than Azran. The stench it brought with it overwhelmed the earlier smells. The warlock nearly gagged, but managed to hold on to his composure and the contents of his stomach.

"Whom do you seek?" The voice was raspy. Now and then, it changed completely.

He stiffened. "They know who I seek! They are bound to me until I release them!"

"Or die."

Azran tried to hide his discomfort. "Send them to me at once!"

"They are coming." The guardian sank into the mire almost as soon as it spoke. When its head disappeared, Azran was greatly relieved.

He waited patiently now. Once commanded, the dead had to obey.

A form broke through the murky surface. Another joined it. Unlike the guardian, neither dripped of the slime out of which they had come. Both stared at him with the blank eyes of their kind.

"We are here, Azran." Despite its being dead, there were hints of hatred in the form's voice.

The ancient warlock had noticed it too. He allowed himself a smile. "So I see. I also see that you have tremendous spirit for one who should not. How about you, Tyr? Do you also have this spirit?"

The other figure, clad in what was once a robe of dark blue, said nothing, but the hands curled into fists.

"I see. Good! That should help you put more effort in your work! Now, then, Basil and Tyr, are you ready for your orders?"

The same tones. Basil, armored and wearing a leather cloak. "We will listen."

"You still know where Penacles is?"

"Yes."

"Good! I was afraid your brain might have rotted in all this time. Anyway, I want you to kidnap someone there."

Basil gave a ghost of a smile. "For this you need us? It is your brain that must have rotted."

Azran glared. "I think not. Hmm. You two are pretty active for undead! Maybe I should leave this to others."

"Fine! Then we may return to our rest and—"

"You'll go nowhere! It would take too much time to summon others. Besides, despite your unusual animation, you are bound by the powers to obey me until I release you."

"Or die," the ghostly Basil added with great desire.

"It takes a lot to kill me. Now, then, as to the kidnapping. His name is Cabe; he is a warlock. Do not underestimate him. He is my son."

He watched with satisfaction the looks on the faces of the undead.

"This Cabe is a Bedlam?"

"Have your eardrums fallen into the space where your brain used to be? He is my son, stolen from me by my damned father! I want him here! If he proves impossible to take, kill him! In fact, kill anyone who gets in the way! That witch, the Lady Gwen, will be there. So will the Gryphon and possibly others."

Tyr spoke, and his voice was like a tomb opened after generations of decay. "Why not send us to do battle with the Three Lords of the Dead? We stand as much chance if so many powers are there."

"First of all, my decrepit friend, the boy is untrained. Second, the Lady's powers are least effective against the dead. She may banish you at best. Between the two of you, you should be able to handle this."

Tyr turned away. There was disgust in his voice. "Do not make us do this."

"Why not? Who better to strike against a new rising of Dragon Masters than the old ones themselves?" Azran laughed.

"I give you full use of your powers for this mission! Listen and I will now explain in detail what you will do!"

He made them kneel, just for spite.

The dark of night was upon them, but something disturbed them too much for sleep to come. Darkhorse had no use for sleep anyway, and no one had ever seen Shade even doze. The Gryphon was on a balcony and staring out at the heavens and the lands beyond.

"Do you sense something?"

The lord of Penacles turned to face Shade. "I not only sense something, I feel almost on the verge of being overwhelmed by them. Events are on the move this night. We must be prepared for anything."

"Such as stars that vanish?"

The Gryphon nodded uneasily. "You've noticed. The Gray Mists seek to enshroud us. I fear that Black has stirred up his traitorous fanatics. Judging by the close proximity of the fog, they can be no more than two days from us."

"Two days? How is that possible?"

A sigh. "When I met them in battle, I knew only a little about them. One thing that I did discover immediately was that they seldom rest. They will march day and night for weeks, fight a battle for days, and then march home again. All without sleep. They eat as they march. Some say it is because they live within the Gray Mists."

The left hand rested on a marble rail. He who called himself Simon noticed that there were now deep gouges in the marble. He said nothing to his friend.

"Something else. I have heard that the Dragon Kings war against themselves this night."

Shade nodded. "Both good and bad. It lessens our enemies, but makes the few bolder."

He suddenly took hold of the Gryphon's arm and started to lead him inside. "I have something to show you."

They stepped into the room. The Gryphon started to speak, but his companion hushed him. Shade said nothing until they were far from the balcony. When he did speak, it was a whisper.

"Something watches and listens from above!"

"What? I felt no one!"

"It cloaks itself well. Fortunately, it was not expecting one of my abilities."

"What is it?"

"I suspect it is one of Azran's spies. A Seeker."

The Gryphon started for the door, intending to summon his golems. Shade stopped him, still whispering. "Hold!"

"Why? If he's been here for more than a day, he knows of the danger to the libraries and the presence of Cabe and the Lady! The gods know what else!"

"The golems will not be able to catch him. The Seekers are of the oldest magic. Only one versed in such stands a chance of stealth. I will go."

There was little room for argument. The Gryphon knew

the warlock was correct. Simon told him to behave as normal. After a few moments of waiting, he then bid the Gryphon a good night and left the room as if intending to return to his quarters. The monarch of Penacles stared at the doorway.

The Seeker would notice a spell of teleportation. Shade would be forced to climb the stairs and then pull himself up to the roof. He hoped the avian would be turned the other way. The old spell of Shunning that the warlock was using would most likely work, but Shade had never really faced one of the creatures before.

He also had little knowledge of the Seeker's limits. It could not kill him, he believed, but it might be strong enough to hurt him. He sought death, for a good cause, not pain. Pain had a way of lingering that death did not.

Shade had reached the end of the stairs. His only option now was to climb through the window and pray that the ancient roof edge would hold him. He began a memory check of all flight spells that could be used at very short notice. He also hoped he would be conscious if such a spell was needed.

Summoning the strength of several centuries, he pulled himself up to the roof. Nothing attempted to push him into empty space. The warlock crouched down and studied his surroundings.

The Seeker was there, its back to him, its powerful wings folded behind it. At present, it appeared to be concerned with whatever movements the Gryphon made. He knew, however, that the creature's duties might change at any moment. Shielding his presence as subtly as possible, Shade made his way toward the Seeker.

Magic would blank out any sounds he made, but it would not do so for the roof itself. Thus it was that a crumbling piece of the roof alerted the avian to its danger. The warlock was just short of effective range for the spell he was preparing to cast, when, with a silence more frightening than any cry, the Seeker launched itself at him.

What he had originally chosen to cast was now useless. Shade was forced to throw a bright burst of light in the hopes that it would blind the creature. The Seeker easily bypassed it, but the spell gave the warlock much-needed time. He rolled away and started a new offense. His birdlike opponent turned with amazing speed and came in for a second attack.

This time, he was ready. Bright red bands, two feet in diameter, formed around the avian. The creature whirled to escape them, but the bands merely became tighter. Unfortunately, the wings were not included in the trap. The Seeker reversed directions and then shot up into the night.

Shade sought for his adversary, the powers adding to his night vision. Despite this, the Seeker was nowhere to be seen. He became worried that the avian had flown off to its master. If that happened . . .

He was suddenly struck violently from behind. Unable to control himself or his thoughts, Shade nearly rolled off the roof. Only a last-minute hold saved him from going over. He cleared his senses just in time to see the avian speeding toward him, arms free and claws bared. It was going for the kill.

Wrapping his cloak around him, the warlock disappeared. The Seeker was momentarily at a loss, and that was all that Shade needed. Materializing behind his foe, he leaped on the back of the flying creature and tried to force it down. The avian hit the roof—

—and was immediately off again. Shade found himself clinging to the avian as it soared off into the night. It could not free itself from him, but it was assuring itself of the advantage. The warlock was having difficulty holding on. If he lost hold, the creature would not allow him the time to cast a spell of flight.

He received unexpected assistance from the Seeker. In trying to pry him from it, it succeeded only in pulling him higher. Now they were both locked together in a struggle where Shade found he had an advantage in skill, and so started the one spell that might destroy his opponent. Like the warlock, the Seekers could be injured, but they were very difficult to kill. Shade needed this one dead. No word could be allowed to reach Azran.

The spell was nearly complete when he discovered that his adversary was also casting.

For all practical purposes, both spells were the same. Each had recognized the danger the other represented. The Gryphon, watching the sky for some sign, was the only one who actually saw the burst. The others only heard the explosion.

One second, both were lit up. The next instant, the flash

of light that ripped through the heavens caused many to believe daylight had come. Of the two combatants, nothing could be seen. It was as if they had ceased to exist.

Angrily, the Gryphon spun away from the balcony and summoned his commanders. There was hope, some hope, that they might find the necromancer alive. The lionbird tried hard not to think about how little chance there really was.

It was the flash, not the explosion, that woke Cabe. Not that he had been able to sleep well. There were so many questions running through his head. They were all forgotten the instant the light flooded his room. The blast itself nearly threw him from the bed.

He ran to a window and peered outside. There was nothing but darkness in the heavens. Cabe failed to notice the gathering mists as his gazing was suddenly interrupted by the many voices echoing his confusion. He looked for something to throw on, only to discover that he was wearing his clothes. Before retiring, he had definitely removed them.

Shrugging off the incident in the heat of the present situation, Cabe departed from his room. His first intention was to find the Lady or one of his other friends. That proved to be more difficult than he thought. With people running this way and that, it was hard to tell who was who. Fortunately, it was Gwen who found him.

"Cabe!" She was clad in a tight, emerald-green hunting outfit, short skirt and feathered cap completing the picture.

"What's going on?"

"I don't know, but I feel it has something to do with your friend, Shade."

Her tone indicated that she still did not trust the other warlock. Cabe felt need to defend the man, but was not given the opportunity. Instead, he found himself being led by his companion to the main chamber of the Gryphon's palace.

The Gryphon was there when they arrived. He was issuing orders to commanders and scouts. They could not make out what was being said, but several of them seemed to revolve around the shadowy warlock. Gwen gave Cabe a look. He turned his eyes away, refusing to believe as she did.

Their host finally turned his attention to them. "I'm sorry I was unable to speak with you any sooner! Things have gone terribly, terribly bad!"

The Lady nodded. "I'm sure we all saw and heard the same thing. Was it Shade?"

"Partially. He was locked in struggle with one of Azran's Seekers. It was spying on us and had to be destroyed."

Cabe was elated that his faith in the sorceror was justified. The Lady seemed to ignore this and asked the Gryphon some questions. When he described the blast, she shook her head.

"Power overflow. Rare, but deadly."

Both looked at her blankly.

She continued. "They both tried to use the same spell at the same time. Oh, maybe there were slight variations in each, but to the powers, they were identical. Instead of two separate attacks, there was one general spell of four times the strength. Most likely, it destroyed them instantly."

The Gryphon agreed. "Nevertheless, I intend on having the grounds searched. Thoroughly, I might add."

He did not say what was now on everybody's mind. That the Simon personality of Shade was gone. If that was true, then a new threat had been unleashed.

Cabe had an idea. "Where's Darkhorse? He should know what's happened to Shade!"

"If that demon was anywhere near here, he's failed to appear! I have no time to go searching for him!"

A scout came in. Begging his lord's pardon, he started to report on new movements by the hordes from Lochivar. The Gryphon turned his attention to this matter completely. Lady Gwen and Cabe excused themselves. Once outside of the room, they began to talk.

"What happens to me now?" Cabe was not terribly thrilled with the thought of taking on Dragon Kings. Especially with two of their strongest allies missing, one presumed dead—and quite possibly soon to be a new threat.

"I don't know. First the library, now this. We're on the defensive. We should take the offensive before it's too late!"

"Simon—Shade took the offensive; look at what happened to him!"

"That worries me little compared to what we face should

he have perished out there. The legends of his evil side would chill the soul of even the strongest of men!''

They both paused, pondering the unpleasant possibilities. It was at that point that Blane appeared. The commander was obviously anxious about something, but he paused to talk to them before heading on to the Gryphon.

''I see that this hellish night has everyone up! My father always told me to beware times when both Twins are full!''

Cabe studied the man's uniform. It was grimy and wet. Blane caught the look.

''I've been scouting near the Gray Mists since darkness. I always like to know what I'm up against.''

''Isn't that dangerous? What would happen if you were captured or killed?''

He laughed. ''I'd kill myself through sheer will if captured! We're trained for that. Studied under a Shizzaran priest. If killed, my men know which of them is to take over. Actually, any of them are capable, but don't let them hear that. I'll have myself an army of leaders!''

Gwen was far more interested in the Gray Mists. ''What did you discover?''

Blane's face hardened. ''It's expanding. They'll be here in no time. Ever seen one of those zombies? No? I have! So doped up from living in the mists that they're hardly human! Gaunt, skeletal men who fight even if they lose both arms and both legs!''

Frowning, Cabe asked, ''What could they do then?''

''Bite you, man! Their teeth are sharpened to a point. They've been know to play dead and then get a soldier in the ankle as he passes. Don't know what they have for blood, but most people bitten die fast. Any soldier with smarts knows that he better steer clear or lop off the head.''

And these horrors were marching toward Penacles, Cabe thought despairingly. I'm to blame for most of it. Men will die—

''Stop that!'' Gwen was looking deep into his eyes. ''I know what you're thinking! This would have happened whether you existed or not! The Black Dragon has always coveted the City of Knowledge. He merely waited for the chance!''

Logic has little to do with love. At that moment, Cabe was willing to believe anything the Lady said. He was even willing to lay down his life for her, should the occasion arise. She now owned him heart and soul, though she may not have realized it. It did not matter to him that she had once loved his grandfather.

Though the enchantress did not recognize the look, being herself too caught up in all matters at all times, Blane did. The soldier, a good, honest man, had left more than his share of broken hearts and had seen his own men turn soft at the sight of some woman. He decided to remove himself.

"Excuse me. The Lord Gryphon will want to know everything I've uncovered." With that, he was off.

"We've got to think this out," Gwen was saying. "We have to strike back! Waiting for disaster will only get us killed!"

"Whatever you say," Cabe replied absently.

She blinked. "Maybe we're just tired. Get some sleep. There's nothing we can do right now. I'll see you in the morning."

"Right."

The sorceress raised an eyebrow in mild curiosity and then departed. Cabe watched her leave, amazed at the wonders nature could produce. So amazed was he that he failed to notice powers coming into play.

A bright light formed behind him. In that light, a golden bow, gleaming like the sun, floated purposely. A single shaft, aimed toward the ceiling, was ready to be fired. Cabe ignored all and, in fact, seemed almost asleep.

The arrow was released. Silent but swift, the gold shaft flew to the ceiling, finding its way to a dark corner. Its target had no time to utter a sound, if it were capable of doing so. With the shaft protruding through its neck, the creature of darkness fell to the ground.

Neither arrow nor victim touched the floor. Both vanished into nothing only halfway down. The bow and the light surrounding it dissipated.

Stirring, the young warlock stumbled off to bed, his thoughts focused on the fire-haired enchantress.

X

Three riders.

A dragon patrol.

The firedrakes dismounted from their lesser cousins. They were both awed and suspicious at the sight before them. The Barren Lands had produced many bizarre things, but this—this was not the work of the dying land.

Rather, the Barren Lands were giving way to a new, greater power. The small patch of grass had become a lush, green field that stretched as far as the eye could see. Trees of all kinds dotted the area. Birds, the first immigrants to this splendid wonder, had already started their nests.

One of the firedrakes cursed. He was young, and had never known the Lands to be other than what their name implied. This was wizard's work, the work of soft humans, warm-bloods. He pulled out a gleaming longsword, stalked over to the nearest green, and hacked away.

The first slices were made easily. The fourth was much more difficult; the grass seemed to swarm over and wrap around his weapon. He pulled it loose, ignoring the jibes of his comrades. They warned him to beware of his obviously dangerous foe. He could not pull his sword free.

New grass blades had sprouted under his feet. With stunning growth, they soon stood as tall as their fellows. The firedrake tried to step back, but his boots were entangled in the plants. It was almost as if they had grabbed hold of him. Unable to free his sword, he pulled out a small knife and tried to cut the trapping grass. Not only did his small blade fail, but both the knife and his hand were now caught as well. He was no longer angered; fear had taken root as strongly as the green around him.

The lesser drakes became nervous, one even emitting a very unhorselike hiss. One of the other firedrakes came forward to free his companion. He stopped abruptly; the grass was growing quickly toward him. He jumped back. The one trapped in the field was now half covered with strangling tendrils that threatened to pull him to the ground.

In desperation, the firedrake metamorphed. Gone was the warrior; in his place was a strong, tall dragon that rippled with muscle. A creature of power. A creature who still found itself unable to escape.

The other two had backed away from the tide that seemed intent on adding them to its collection. Since the entrapment of the first, the growth had sped up several factors. The two free warriors were forced to make a dash for their mounts, the grass close behind.

Fearful and enraged, the struggling firedrake let loose with a fierce rush of flame. The wave of fire and heat washed over the nearest of the greenery. For several moments, it seemed to burn uncontrollably; then, almost abruptly, it died out, revealing little more damage than a few singed tips.

His companions had reached their mounts. They were counting on their cousins' superior speed. One leaped up and kicked his agitated mount. Rider and animal rushed off.

The other was not so lucky. His mount, seeing his brother go and already panicked by the sinister growth, bolted. The dragon warrior fell to the ground and hit his head. It took only moments for his mind to clear, and his first thoughts were to take the lesser drake belonging to his hapless companion. He tried to rise, but found himself held fast. The mount he had intended on taking screeched nearby. He struggled to reach his swords, but the ever-present grass continued to envelop him. The tendrils wrapped around his throat. He succumbed to the lush field even while his companion still fought.

The young firedrake had exhausted himself. Failure to burn the field had sapped him of all hope. Even as the life went out of his mount, which had been trapped at the same time as the other warrior, he slipped. Plant life swarmed over the huge, dying form.

Moments later, there was nothing to indicate that anyone had passed this way.

The single rider pushed to the fastest pace possible. He received no objections from his mount. His destination was not the caves of his clan. Instead, he intended to reach the Dagora Forest and eventually make his way to the Tyber Mountains.

Small animals wandered into the field for the first time in its existence. A small burrower nibbled on a blade of grass. The birds above sang. The sea of greenery did nothing. Unlike the dragons, these creatures were welcome.

At Penacles, there was no sun.

The mists enshrouded the land almost as well as the night. Firewood had been quickly gathered, enough for two months. Soldiers watched warily from the walls of the city for some sign of the enemy. They could see little in the all-encompassing fog.

No one traveled the roads anymore. The Lord Gryphon had ordered all traffic halted. That kept people in. Why no wagons arrived at the city was anyone's guess. It was hoped that the mere sight of the mists would turn back the unwary travelers. If not . . .

Food would be no problem. The Gryphon, knowing his many enemies, had long ago ordered the storage of grain, water, and other food items. Workers were also trained to keep out rodents and other small pests. On the whole, they tended to succeed.

Cabe studied his reflection in the mirror. There was no doubt in his mind that what he saw was real; the silver streak in his hair now covered nearly half of his head. What that meant, he had no idea. It frightened him, though. It had something to do with his birthright. Coming from the family he did, it could only mean trouble.

Someone knocked on the door. Cabe walked over and opened it. It was the Lord Gryphon, standing patiently and without any fanfare. He nodded to the young warlock and then noticed the change in his hair. An expression passed over the inhuman face so quickly that Cabe was unsure exactly what it was.

"Excuse me for interrupting you, but I was wondering if you would step up to the nearest watchtower with me."

Curious, Cabe agreed. They left his room, the Gryphon leading the way. The ruler of Penacles was silent the entire time. Cabe thought of a hundred reasons for this walk, but discarded all of them. He would have to remain unsatisfied until his host told him

They reached the top of the tower only after a breathtaking climb. Cabe paused, but the lionbird appeared not in the least winded. When he had regained his breath, he looked out to where the Gryphon was now pointing. At first, all that he saw was more mist; it was heady stuff, and Cabe longed to go back down into the palace proper. Then he noticed a dark movement far off in the distance. That did not seem right. What could make itself noticeable in such fog from that distance?

The answer came to him. His stomach wanted to curl.

"Yes, my friend, that is the army of Lochivar. Do you know why their darkness cuts through the mists itself? I do not. Normally, they should be invisible. The Gray Mists are their home; they know how to shape it to their will even as it has bent their minds. Why, then, does it betray them now?"

"Someone is interfering?"

The Gryphon looked at him sharply. "You are correct. I thought that perhaps Shade did not die. Or he did this before his death. Darkhorse! It might have been that creature! Or an enemy who brooks no interference from others."

"Azran?"

"Yes, it could be. He would covet the City of Knowledge. Good thinking."

Disturbed, Cabe watched the swelling mass. "How soon will they attack?"

"How soon? As soon as they can! Fortunately, we have been able to prepare a little surprise for them."

Even as the Gryphon spoke, the sounds of men rushing back and forth and moving large objects could be heard. Cabe wanted to ask for details, but it was obvious that his host wanted this to be a surprise for him as well as for the Lochivarites.

The Lady joined them. Cabe felt a wave of emotion wash over him, but he managed to hold it in check. After all, to this woman he was probably little more than a child. She smiled at him, looked back down the steps leading to the top, and faced the Gryphon.

"You two would be in the tallest tower. How goes it? I could sense the stench of those wyvern bastards even in my sleep!"

The Lord Gryphon chuckled, a strange action for one with a face like his. "I imagine so. You're just in time to see the opening shot. Come."

They stood and watched, Cabe and Gwen curious, the lionbird smiling grimly now. Below, most sounds of movement had stilled. The defenders of the city were ready and waiting for the word. The Gryphon stared at the swelling, dark mass for another minute and then dropped something over the edge. He turned to his two companions.

"They will spread out as soon as they are able to. Right now, though, they still think themselves safe enough. Their master does not realize the range of my new weapons."

As if on cue, a series of noises went off. To Cabe, they seemed akin to someone snapping a piece of wood in two. Large projectiles appeared briefly in the thick fog in front of them. Within seconds, they disappeared in the direction of the oncoming enemy.

"Catapults. Nothing new about them, save their range."

"Wait, my Lady. Watch."

The missiles took some time reaching their targets. When the first one did, though, the two humans backed away, shock all over their faces.

"By Havak!" the sorceress shouted. "What was that?"

A cold gleam was in the lionbird's eyes. "Final justice!"

Great bursts of green flame rushed out wherever the projectiles landed. A few missed, but most found some part of the enemy. The light from the fires caused the Gray Mists to take on a slightly different color for a change. There were obviously men on fire everywhere, but the dark shape of the army continued to advance with amazing speed.

Cabe watched in horrid fascination. "What was that?"

"Something I discovered in the libraries. Two potions, separated, placed in compartments of the missile. When the missile hits the ground, the violent action causes the inner containers to break and mixes the two liquids. That is the result. It is quite effective. One of the few items from the libraries that I've managed to make use of."

The Lady watched the advance of the legions. "Not good enough. They're still coming through. It seems like an endless line."

"I didn't expect this to stop them. It will, however, soften them up and lessen the odds. We shall deal with the survivors when we have to."

More projectiles flew up. It was obvious by their accuracy that the men had been training for this for some time. Cabe commented on this and received an approving nod from the Gryphon.

"Only a fool trusts the ghouls of Lochivar. We knew this day would come, and we estimated their most probable route."

"The Black Dragon would have thought of that. He must not care how many he loses."

"Unfortunately, he has many more warriors to lose than we do. He hopes to take us with sheer numbers. He may do it, especially if the forces of the Dragon Emperor join him." The Gryphon watched another volley. "Confidentially, I believe Black wants the city for his own. That is in our favor."

After the first few strikes, it was more than obvious to the invaders that their cover was gone. Quickly, efficiently, the armies of Lochivar spread themselves along the hills and fields. Successful shots became rare; only a few men would be hit, if any. The Gryphon called for a cease-fire.

Cabe grew uneasy. "What happens now?"

"That would depend on our visitors. I daresay they might return the favor we just gave them."

Sure enough, it was only moments before dark shapes began separating from the bulk of the forces. Larger than a man, they flew up into the air. That they were dragons of some kind was soon obvious. Whether they were airdrakes or firedrakes was uncertain. The lord of Penacles paced back and forth, waiting.

They neared the city in two formations. A hundred yards from the walls, they split up, one group going left, the other right. The Gryphon signaled his archers. The first of the dragons moved in to attack.

The front set of archers let loose. The sky was filled with arrows, but even as the shafts sought their targets, more dragons entered the battle. The second line fired. The drakes in front suffered heavy casualties, and a number fell to the ground in rapid succession. Still, the next group came closer. The Gryphon's third and final line of archers fired. More dragons died. The first set barely finished reloading before they were forced to fire. The strategy was obvious; Black was sacrificing numbers so that his airborne killers could get close enough for a deadly assault. Meanwhile, the Lochivarites moved ever nearer.

A drake flew swiftly over the battlements and unleashed a powerful smoke that turned the Gray Mists yellow. Those nearest to the smoke fell to the floor or over the wall. They screamed and tried to wipe the foul gas from their eyes. One killed himself rather than continue suffering. A few ran madly from the walls, only to plummet to their deaths in the city itself. The three onlookers watched in horror.

The Lady was the first to react. Cabe sensed rather than felt the first stirrings of the wind that formed around her. It was not strong enough to push the airdrake away, but it made his deadly weapon useless. In fact, the wind was carrying it in the direction of the advancing forces.

"I don't know whether I can keep it floating long enough, but that's not the point! Someone's got to stop the dragons!"

More drakes had made it past the archers. One set a catapult on fire, causing one of the chemical missiles to explode. The crew manning the catapult died instantly. Fires raged all over the area of the explosion. Two other war machines went up in flames before the men below could contain the fires.

The archers could not stem the tide of dragons. For every one shot down, two were making it into the city. If this were only a small portion of the enemy's strength, Penacles would stand little chance of survival.

The Gryphon had been silent for some time. Now he pulled something from an inner pocket. Cabe saw that it was a ring on which hung three small whistles. The ruler of the City of Knowledge chose one of the whistles. His face contorted as it assumed the more human appearance that was necessary for proper use of the instrument. The tiny metal pipe was placed to his lips and blown.

No sound came from the whistle, but something replied almost immediately. There was a challenging shriek, as if the intruding dragons had dared to enter into personal territories. From out of buildings, trees, and places invisible in the fog came a rushing of wings. Cries of a thousand different species formed into one. The deadly wave of lizards paused in confusion.

Birds covered the darkened skies.

The drakes, despite their speed, appeared almost motionless compared to the birds. From the tiniest of the plant feeders to the largest of the predators, countless feathered creatures clawed and bit at the invading reptiles. Hundreds died from flame and gas, but each helped cut the dragons' numbers down rapidly. The drakes snapped and grabbed for their adversaries, somtimes colliding with each other in the process. One firedrake thoroughly scorched his nearest neighbor, who happened to be an airdrake. The airdrake exploded, taking all within the immediate area with him.

The most surprising part of this bizarre battle in the sky was the way in which the birds herded the monsters out of the city before finishing them off. Few dragons actually died in Penacles itself. Those that did landed in the outskirts of the city proper. The loss of life was small compared to what it might have been.

At some point, retreat was called. Only a handful of the original force remained, and most of these were injured in some way. Even as they departed, more than one suddenly wobbled violently and fell to the ground. The birds continued to harass them until they were far away. When the last of the drakes had returned to the enemy lines, the feathered victors turned back to the city. Most never made it. Released from whatever spell had summoned them, the various birds returned to their normal ways of life, flying this way and that way. The few who reached the walls of Penacles merely continued on to their roosts.

It was as if they had never taken part in the war.

It had happened so quickly that none of the defenders could believe it was over. The entire battle had lasted only minutes. Calm now prevailed. The Lady ceased her spell, and then both she and Cabe waited for an explanation from their host.

The Gryphon's face had reverted to the one of legend. He

held up the whistle to them. They could both see that it was rusting before their very eyes. Within seconds, it was dust.

Gwen smirked. "Another one of the surprises from your bag of tricks? What was that?"

"A gift to me from someone long dead. Call it part of my heritage and leave it at that."

"What about the other two whistles? What do they summon?"

The lionbird put the ring back into his pocket. "If the time comes, you will see."

He refused to say anything more on the subject.

The invaders had slowed down. Now that they knew some of the resistance they would encounter, the commanders would replot their strategy. For the moment, there was a lull. This was fine for the defenders. Enough men would be kept busy clearing away the wounded and dying, not to mention putting out the numerous fires that had been started by the dragons.

The Gryphon suggested they return to the main floor of the palace. The trip took them several minutes. When they reached the bottom, they were met by Blane and the general of the army of Penacles, a foxlike man by the name of Toos. The fiery-red hair on his head and face was almost a match for the Lady's, and there was also an ominous streak of silver that covered a good quarter of the right side.

When the general was introduced, Gwen commented on his appearance immediately. "I have seen many warlocks in battle, but I've known few who commanded armies personally."

The smile on the face of Toos served only to make him look even more like a fox. "My skills in sorcery are far too meager. They serve only to accentuate my ability to command and plan."

"What damage has been done?" the Gryphon asked, concerned about his subjects.

Blane's face grew dark. "The northeast wall was hit hardest. Thirty men dead there, most from the initial encounter with the airdrake. Gods! What man can fight the very air around him?"

The lord of Penacles nodded. "Yes, that is a problem. I

shall have to consult the libraries soon. I'm sure there will be something—if I can understand it."

Cabe looked from one man to the other. "I don't understand. Shouldn't you be able to find what you need to win this war? I'd think that one long search in those libraries would tell you everything you wanted to know."

His host tugged at the fur below his beak as a man might tug on his beard. "You don't understand the libraries, Cabe. They give us what we need to know, with one exception. No page of any book is written straightforward. All are either riddles or verses. It is up to the reader to translate this into real information. In my own opinion, they were written by minds with a very warped sense of humor."

Toos cleared his throat. "There is something else you should know, sire. We estimate that the advance group of the Dragon Emperor is no more than three days away. The main bulk, under Toma, follows about a week—maybe ten days—behind. We will be hard-pressed to stave off both armies."

"Who of noteworthiness travels with the advance group?"

"A duke named Kyrg leads them. I have heard ill things about him—"

The Gryphon held up a hand. "You need not tell me of Duke Kyrg. I know the drake. A brilliant sadist. One I'd hoped was dead."

He looked from one person to another. The looks on their faces did not give much indication of confidence. Even the Lady, well known for her strength, appeared to be unsure of the days ahead. Only Cabe appeared to have anything remotely resembling hope. The others had seen too much destruction in the past. The Gryphon, therefore, fixed on the young warlock.

"You, young friend, are the key to this thing. In you is the blood of the greatest line of sorcerors. Nathan was the best—"

"—and Azran the worst!" Gwen interjected.

Ignoring her, the lord of Penacles continued. "The mark of the powers is the silver in the hair. Generally, the more silver, the greater the power. There are exceptions. Toos has little in the way of practical power. Shade—Shade was an enigma. The silver in his hair varied every time one looked."

The Gryphon turned to the Lady. "Train him. Train him quickly. I suspect that everything we hold dear depends on his ability to harness the powers properly and soon!"

It was nearly finished.

With movements that would have left him gasping for breath only hours earlier, Azran cleared away the various pieces of equipment from his room. The Nameless required only one more burst of power, one very minor burst of power. Already, it blazed with a fury. The box where it lay might as well have been transparent; power from the sword cut through it like air.

He snapped his fingers. A spirit, one of those not-born that Azran had summoned from the depths of the Other, flittered to him. He ordered a full meal. Meat usually was bad for his system, but there was no need to worry about that. Now he could eat and do as he wished. The spirit departed to fulfill his command. Azran summoned another and ordered it to bring a mirror. A full-sized one.

The mirror came first. He ordered the dark servant to place it against a wall. When that was done, he straightened his clothes, freshly created for this occasion, and stood in front of the mirror admiring himself.

It was good to be young again.

All those years of hard labor were about to pay off. He studied himself critically in the mirror. The black of his outfit, more like a uniform than anything else, was complemented by the navy blue band around his collar and his wrists. Azran paused and then added an emblem to his chest, a dragon impaled on a sword. Good touch, he decided. Let them know he was their master. The new Dragon Master!

His head was covered half by black and half by silver. Another indication of his power. The face resembled too much that of his father, but that was also a plus in its own way. The Dragon Kings and their servants would remember the past and tremble.

A beard. He hadn't worn a beard in decades. It would be

the finishing touch. A short, trim one. That would do it. He gestured, making the seconds turn into weeks.

Azran blinked. Like the hair on the top of his head, the beard was half silver. It was a bizarre sight. Almost ominous.

He decided to keep it.

Boots, hip-length in the front, and gloves completed the picture. To an opponent, the clothing would appear as show. Try to cut it with a weapon and it would be revealed to be stronger than chain. Much lighter, though.

Smiling at his reflection, Azran walked out onto his balcony. No one would have ever suspected that he lived in the midst of the Hell Plains. It was far too close to the Tyber Mountains and was also ruled by the Red Dragon, one of the more bloodthirsty of the Kings. He laughed. His castle stood in the very center of the most naturally violent of lands. A volcano stood no more than two miles away. Yet nothing could harm this place. It was older than the Dragon Kings and invisible to the outside world. Azran had discovered it only by chance. He never did learn who had built it, and no longer cared. It was now his, and it served him well.

A shriek came from above. The Seekers were angry, perhaps frightened. The one sent to spy on Penacles had still not returned. The warlock suspected that it no longer existed. That was two attacks in the recent past. Events were rushing to a head. He had to ensure that he would control the flow.

His food was brought to him. It was a sumptuous feast. Azran planned on making up for years of corn mush and bread. Now, with new teeth, he would bite into all those delights he knew only from memory.

From within its casket, the Nameless pulsated. With each bite Azran took, the pulsating increased.

Cabe and the Lady were walking to his room.

"We will begin your training with basics. I'll teach you some simple defensive spells first. Just in case. I—we don't want you dead before you have a chance to fight."

"Neither do I."

She smiled. "So much like Nathan. Still, even Nathan never had the head of silver. The Gryphon may be right. You could be more powerful than anyone."

They reached his room. Cabe opened the door for his companion, who stepped through. He followed immediately, closing the door as he entered. They were alone, he realized. Perhaps, he thought, he could tell her how he felt. Now, while no other living soul was around.

There were indeed no living souls around . . .

. . . but they were not alone.

The Lady was encased in a glow. The glow solidified, and, with a start, Cabe recognized it as the same sort of prison that had held her captive for so many years. He pulled out the Horned Blade, feeling its power embrace him. He did not, however, have a chance to use it.

A hand touched him on the temple. Cabe felt his body quiver. Though he remained armed, the weapon was useless. His limbs were as solid as the marble columns of the palace. Frozen in time, he could only watch as the dark blade was wrenched from his grasp. His eyes widened at what he could only momentarily see.

"So simple." The voice was dry and curiously sad in tone.

The sword was tossed to the ground. He could hear footsteps behind him. Suddenly, he was floating. Gwen remained where she was, once more trapped in amber. They were after him, no one else. He drifted like a feather, randomly turning this way and that. During one of those turns, he caught sight of his captors.

The eyes that met his were eyes no more. Blank, upturned whites. Whites set in decaying, parchment skin.

He was a prisoner of the undead. One started to speak, then checked himself. His companion gestured. A great hole opened up in the middle of the room's reality. Cabe found himself floating into it. When he touched it, all conscious thought faded away.

Tyr turned to look at the Lady, trapped in the amber, and then at the Horned Blade. His companion put a hand on his shoulder.

"We must go."

They stepped into the portal. Undead and hole disappeared.

XI

The explosion rocked the palace.

At first, the Gryphon feared some sort of attack by the Lochivarites. This fear was laid to rest by Blane, who reported that there had been no movement by the forces from the Gray Mists. The lionbird then thought of Azran and suddenly remembered where his guests were being quartered. Summoning his golems, he rushed to Cabe's room.

The door, what was left of it, lay in the hallway. Small fragments of some crystalline substance, vaguely familiar, dotted the area. The Gryphon ordered the two golems forward. They would form a shield for him. He hoped the two creatures would prove sufficient. He was unsure of their limits.

Nothing stirred in the room as the three entered. Dust obscured most of his vision, but he did see the Honored Blade lying on the floor nearby. He left it where it was; nothing would be gained by possessing the accursed sword at this time.

Someone moaned. The dust was settling, and the Gryphon could finally make out a form lying near the bed. He ordered the two golems to stay and investigated cautiously. It might have been a trap, but he doubted it.

The figure on the ground turned out to be the Lady Gwen. She was half conscious and strangely untouched by the dust that filled the room. In fact, whenever she moved, the dust that had settled around her shifted away so as not to be near. There were no marks on her body. Exhaustion seemed to be her worst problem. Assured that she would recover, the Gryphon had his two unliving bodyguards carry her to her room. They picked her up with a gentleness that was surprising for such strong creatures. As they carried her out, the Gryphon took one last look around the room.

Cabe Bedlam was nowhere to be seen. The Horned Blade, left behind, was the only indication that he had ever been there.

Dark thoughts racing through his mind, the lord of Penacles stalked out of the room. He hoped that the lady would be well enough to answer some questions. He already knew most of the answers, but there was always the hope that he might be mistaken.

The two golems flanked the door of her room. They were becoming surprisingly competent servants. Lady Gwen was lying on her bed, awake. She looked up as her host entered the room. The expression on her face said everything he feared it would, but he was determined to ask despite that.

"What happened?"

"We were struck from behind. Shadow people! Do you understand what I'm saying? Shadow people!"

He nodded grimly. Shadow people. The undead. Those who were forced to obey a master until granted release. They could not truly rest until then. He did not know whether to hate or pity the kidnappers.

"They almost caught me by surprise! It's fortunate that I've become somewhat paranoid. I swore I'd never be trapped like I was. Only that saved me from another amber prison!"

"They used the same spell?"

She nodded. "Yes. Weaker, though. Not that they didn't have the power. They were strong. I just don't think they really wanted to do it."

"How many were there?"

"Just two. This time I was able to keep consciousness. One struck me while the other froze Cabe in place. Gryphon, they took him! They took him from under my nose, and I couldn't do a thing to stop them!" Tears threatened to fall.

The Gryphon noted her tremendous anxiety but said nothing of it. This was not the time or the place. "How did they get in? Where did they go? I received no reports from my sentries."

"Blink hole. They needed it so that they could pass his body through." Her eyes regained a bit of their fire. "I might be able to trace it! Sometimes they leave afterimages. We could follow them to Azran's castle!"

"Where he will no doubt be waiting for us. I think not. Besides, would he be that foolish? Rest now. You've expended far too much energy to go charging into the hidden fortress of Azran."

"But Cabe—"

He stopped her. "You believe you failed Nathan and now you will fail his grandson. I tell you that this is unfounded. Nathan did what Nathan had to do. He would not have done any differently if you had been there. As for Cabe, he was kidnapped, not killed. That means that Azran wants him alive. I think he's curious about his son. Cabe will be all right."

She was only half listening, but that was as much as the Gryphon could have expected. She put her head down and closed her eyes. The lionbird quietly departed. Her concern for the young warlock was great, far greater than it would have been for any other person.

The Gryphon was also concerned, but he had different priorities. Penacles and its people came first. There would be no chance to rescue Cabe if the city fell. If they were to act against Azran, Penacles must be cared for in the meantime.

There were still no attacks. This in itself was unusual. It could mean only that control of the army was in the hands —or claws—of the Black Dragon's firedrakes. The Lochivarites never would have waited so long. They had little interest in saving their necks; death in battle was one of the few things important to those drug-filled fanatics.

He remembered the first time he had faced the hordes from the Gray Mists. No one knew their real loyalties then. It was assumed that they would fight for man just as most other cities would. There were always traitors, of course, but never on this scale.

Thousands of men had died that day. Many others would never be whole. The remnants of that Lochivarite army had drawn back into the shadowy lands from which they had come. Only a fraction of the original force had remained.

In taking control of the City of Knowledge, the Gryphon had been forced to recruit more mercenaries and outsiders.

His original group had been almost totally wiped out. Building up to his former strength had taken several years and tremendous amounts of money. Yet the Lochivarites, with little in the way of enticements, somehow rebuilt their invasion force from scratch. Granted, generations had gone by, but even an increased birthrate could not account for the numbers.

Lochivarites, Dragon Kings, and Azrans.

There were always too many enemies.

He summoned Toos, Blane, and the rest of his commanders to him. Cabe was important; he could not ignore this fact. But he could not desert Penacles. The people were looking to him

A chilling thought occurred to him. Would Azran be able to corrupt Cabe? The idea of a warlock of his potential being controlled by such a fiend shook him almost as much as the thought of possibly having to fight off Shade. Even the Dragon Kings would think twice.

His war council was complete. Grimly, the ruler of the City of Knowledge put on a mask of confidence and determination. Inside, he cursed himself almost constantly.

Into the den of the Beast.

He was no longer frozen. Not that it mattered. The bonds around his wrists, legs, and waist held him as securely as the spell. They were not, needless to say, normal restraints. Each glowed; each glowed brighter if he struggled to free himself. When they grew brighter, they burned him. Not outwardly, but in his very mind. That was why Cabe remained motionless. The first attempt had been sufficient to teach him.

His kidnappers had left him. That was fine with Cabe; the undead made very poor company. Especially these two. They had spent most of their time staring at him with the whites that were their eyes. To make matters more uncomfortable, they seemed sad and ashamed about something. He had the annoying feeling that it had something to do with him and who he was.

A shadow flittered. He blinked. This was not one of the nameless things that lurked in the shadows of the room. This was something much more physical, yet also more powerful.

In the dim light of the room, he could make out only its outline, but that was enough to tell him he was being studied by one of the Seekers. Was this his captor? Probably not. More likely, it was just another one of the servants. Deep down, he already knew who was in charge. It could be none other than Azran, his father.

There was little he could do at the moment. He was the helpless prisoner of a madman. The Seeker, still watching him intently, let out a low squawk. It almost sounded sympathetic. The Seeker did not, however, make any move toward removing the bonds.

Azran faced his two decaying slaves. The blank eyes glared at him, more so now that he was young once again. He did not have them kneel this time. He wished to look at them face-to-face, despite their odor of rot and their peeling skin. He wanted them to see his face, his hair of silver and black, to feel his vitality and life. To feel his power.

"I must commend you both," he said dryly. "I see you were able to carry out my plan in record time. Your fears were, of course, unfounded. The Lady never had a chance, and my son, strong though he may be, had no skill. Yes, overall, I am pleased."

"Are we free to return to our rest?" Basil's face revealed no emotion, but his voice was sullen. He was disgusted with his own actions.

"No, not quite yet. I may still need you. Besides, you and the boy haven't been formally introduced!" He laughed at that and laughed even harder when he saw Tyr's fists clench in rage that his face could no longer reveal.

Basil longed for the ability to spit in his tormentor's face. "You are black, Azran. Black as the darkest of the powers."

"Thank you. I try. Shall we go?"

Against their will, the two corpses shambled ahead of their master. Azran made Basil play butler, even nodding to him as he walked by. In what was left of his mind, the undead warlock cursed, but he was unable to break free of the servile position he had been forced to assume.

Cabe turned wide-eyed as the trio entered. The zombies

he had seen before, and, though they still frightened him, they were dismissed from his mind at the first sight of the sinister figure with them. Even despite the two-toned hair covering the face, he could see the family resemblance. Father and son faced each other at last.

The dark mage turned his head momentarily to one of the windows. There had been—what? Nothing was at the window. Nothing. He turned his attention back to his son, who now looked only a few years younger than he did. The brilliant head of silver, covering more than three quarters, made him blink. By all rights, this Cabe would be a very powerful warlock. Even more than Azran himself.

The boy must be corrupted or die. Those were the only two choices.

He greeted Cabe affably. "So, you are my son!"

"Azran?"

"Of course! Who else could I be?"

"What do you want with me?" There was fear in Cabe's voice, but there was something else: defiance.

"You're my son! Every man likes to see his son once or twice. I thought you died at birth. You have no idea how much your life means to me, son!"

Cabe shuddered.

Azran's eyes narrowed, and the humor was gone from his voice. "I saw your small, limp form. Nathan tricked me! You were very much alive. He'd spirited you away in a futile attempt, no doubt, to raise you as a tool against me!"

The black warlock smiled. "Now, however, I have you back. I look forward to teaching you about the dark powers, my son. You have great potential. Nathan saw it. I will use it. Together, we will make the Dragonrealms ours!"

He broke off suddenly, his eyes focused on Cabe's side. Azran whirled around to face Basil. He said nothing, but the undead knew what was on his mind.

"He was not wearing the Horned Blade when we captured him. It was not in his room. There was little time to search for it. The Lord Gryphon is known for his promptness when danger arises."

"Damn you, Basil—"

"We are already damned."

"You were supposed to bring me the Horned Blade, too! You failed!"

Cabe looked from one to the other. He had carried the sword; one of the kidnappers had taken it and tossed it to the side. Why was this creature lying?

The other, Tyr, chose the outburst to look toward the captive. Cabe watched as the animated corpse waggled a finger in his direction. Cabe understood. Azran did not have the power over his servants that he believed he had. There was hope yet.

Calming himself, Azran turned back to his son. "Never trust the undead, my son. They are highly inept. Especially these two. Untrustworthy, also."

He waved his hand. His unearthly servants stepped forward. "An object lesson, Cabe. Before you, you see two shambling wrecks that were once full of life and in command of their own existences. This bear of a man was called Basil. Basil of the Eye. He could freeze a person solid in a prison of amber or merely paralyze with a touch. His friends called him Basil Basilisk. I borrowed his powers to take care of the Lady Gwen. Pity it didn't hold. His angry friend here was named Tyr. Just that. Don't let his priestly garments fool you. He was known to go into berserker rages that doubled his abilities. Both were Dragon Masters under my unlamented father, your grandfather, Nathan Bedlam. Both, despite their so-called prowess, fell easily at my hand."

Cabe choked.

"They didn't protect themselves too well. Overconfidence, Basil?"

The voice sounded of dirt and death. It was also filled with vast hatred. "Yesss!"

The dark sorceror smiled grandly. "Poor Dragon Masters! They are now forced to obey me until I release them."

"Or die!" Tyr's voice was just loud enough to be heard.

"Enough of that! You may return to your rest until summoned again. This time, come swiftly!"

The two decaying figures shambled out of the room. Cabe caught just a glimpse of Tyr's face as the ghastly warlock turned his head to look back at him. It was the face of the damned. Cabe swore then and there that he would find some way to release them.

Azran gestured. An elaborate chair, more a throne, appeared just behind him. With great satisfaction, he sat down. Another spell removed the bonds holding his captive.

"There! That should be more comfortable. I would, however, not recommend trying something foolish. The area around and including your seat has been set up as a sort of warning system. Do something disruptive, or even get up, and you will find yourself in for a big shock. Literally."

"What happens now?"

"Now? Now I give you your first lesson in how the world of magic really works. Especially where the powers come in."

Cabe could not hide his interest. His father smiled approvingly.

"To begin with, the titles warlock, sorceror, necromancer, enchanter, their female counterparts, and any term I've forgotten are used fairly interchangeably these days. Once, they each meant something specific. No more. Once the key to colors became obvious, anyone with the ability to control the powers could raise themselves to the levels of masters. This nonsense about good and evil powers is just that: nonsense! Some merely choose different colors of the spectrum. I found the darker shades much more efficient. Nathan could never understand that."

Understand? Cabe felt that his grandfather had understood very well. There was no doubt in his mind that choosing the dark side of the spectrum was the same as falling under the seduction of evil. Azran, being one who had succumbed, could no more see the truth than any addict.

Azran mistook his thoughtful expression as a sign that Cabe was being won over. He pushed on. "The Dragon Kings also have magic. Thus, most of their names are colors. Even their skins take on the color they have chosen to use." He paused. "You may think that Iron, Ice, Crystal, and Storm differ from their brethren, but they do not. Have you ever studied the appearance of iron, the metal? It has a color all its own. Not quite blue, not quite gray, not quite anything. Crystal diffuses the essences of the spectrum and, therefore, uses many fine fractions of each. Storm takes his power from lightning, and what is that but light itself? Ice posed an enigma; he seemed not to use the spectrum in any way. This was false. Ice is similar to Crystal; both diffuse the colors. Crystal takes the pure. Ice, the impure. By standards, this makes him more evil than his fellow Kings."

He smiled knowingly at Cabe, who shifted uneasily on the treacherous chair.

"Where have you been all these years?"

The change in direction totally disarmed Cabe. "What?"

"I am, perhaps, the only one who would've noticed the discrepancy immediately—if I hadn't assumed you were dead, that is. I know it takes a long time to grow up, but really . . ."

Cabe shook his head. "I don't know. I don't remember anything strange or unusual about my childhood."

"Well, we'll have to come back to that some other time. Are you hungry?"

Another abrupt change in direction. Azran was no doubt mad as well as evil. Cabe did not answer.

Azran appeared uncomfortable. "No? I am. I must say, ever since I rejuvenated myself, I've had an appetite like one of the Dragon Kings! Sure you won't join me? Roast vin-beast!"

Cabe shook his head numbly. Better to eat with the Gold Dragon himself!

"Then I shall leave you for a time. If you change your mind, speak out. One of my servants"—he indicated a thing flitting in and out of the darkness—"will tell me. Good-bye, Cabe."

With a flourish, chair and sorceror vanished. A faint smell of brimstone drifted near the hapless young warlock. He sneezed.

There was nothing else to do but sit. Sit and think. Not that the latter would probably do much good. Cabe was finding himself too dependent on others. He was supposed to have powers, but with no one to teach him properly, he was helpless.

Something fluttered near one of the windows. To no surprise, it was a Seeker. He was not sure if it was the same one and realized that it didn't matter. The creature swooped through the window and landed soundlessly on the stone floor.

Several shapes detached themselves from the dark corners of the room. They flew toward the Seeker. The avian waved a clawed hand in their direction. The servants stopped in midair, remained there a moment, and then returned to their nests—backward! It was as if time had been reversed for Azran's pets.

With incredible grace, the Seeker moved to Cabe, who was nearly tempted to test the power of his father's trap. Something, though, kept him where he was. It was not fear, he discovered, but the need to know. To know what it was that this servant who was not a servant wanted. It was not, obviously, Cabe's death. That could have been accomplished easily enough already.

The Seeker reached out for the top of the other's head. Cabe stiffened, but the touch was gentle. It was not the pulling that had been used the other time. Rather, the avian was communicating. Communicating in such a way so that Azran would not discover.

Words did not form as he had half expected. Rather, images appeared. The Hell Plains, a path leading southwest to Penacles, a sword, and then Azran. The intention was obvious: the Seeker wished to free Cabe. In return, Cabe would reclaim the Horned Blade and use it to kill his father. It did not bother him to fight Azran—the man was his parent only by nature; there was no love—but the odds were not very much in the young warlock's favor. Azran had years of experience. He had none. There had to be another way.

The avian shook itself, a gesture indicating its irritation. Withdrawing contact, it stared at the prisoner. The eyes were ancient and arrogant. Humans were a lesser form to it. That Azran forced the Seekers to do his bidding was an insult beyond all, as far as the creature was concerned. All this was as evident as if the images had been shown to Cabe.

Returning to the window, the creature looked at the prisoner one more time. The head was cocked to one side, emphasizing the Seeker's nature. When Cabe made no sign of agreement, the winged enigma flew out the window. The would-be warlock was left to himself again, this time his hopes even dimmer. If there had been any hope of assistance by the Seekers, Cabe's lack of confidence had destroyed it.

Silver, Red, and Storm were the only ones summoned. They were the only ones trusted.

Ice cared only for himself. The Dragonrealms could sink into the seas for all he cared. Green allowed his humans too much freedom; soldiers from Zuu had added to the strength of the Gryphon's army. Crystal was an unknown and, therefore, not to be included. As for Black, the Dragon Emperor had suspicions concerning the master of the Gray Mists.

They did not meet in their natural forms. Instead, four armored warriors conferred in the great chamber. Though they dressed alike, it was simple to tell which ruled over his companions.

"Treachery! Bronze and Iron have paid for their folly! Let this be a lesson to those who would usurp my power! I shall be obeyed!"

Gold stood. The others, seated before him, nodded agreement. Each knew that a new distribution of the kingdoms was imminent; there were too many dead rulers, and the royal hatchlings would take far too long to grow to adulthood. Add to that the knowledge that Gold contemplated taking the lands of Blue and Green, and each of his servants who remained loyal would be rewarded well.

Red, most of all, awaited the change. Gold would no doubt split the kingdoms of Iron and Bronze between himself and Silver. That would leave Irillian by the Sea for Storm, and, most important, the thick, lush Dagora Forest would belong to Red himself. It would make a welcome change from the Hell Plains. That such alterations in the ruling structure meant the downfall of his brothers did not bother him in the least.

There was a fifth figure in the chamber, hidden by both the shadows and his or hers or, quite possibly, its voluminous hood and robe. That it was not a firedrake was the only thing any of Gold's companions knew as fact. It was something that they could feel. The spectral visitor had spoken only to the emperor, and it was partially for this the three had been summoned.

Curiosity was not limited to the human race.

Through his helm, Gold studied those with him. He knew very well what thoughts were going on in their minds. They were his. They would serve him well. Greed was a perfect motivating tool.

"We find ourselves in a new war. The Gryphon seeks to re-create the Masters. Our own brethren have turned traitorous. The son of Nathan Bedlam comes out of hiding and dares to make noises of conquest!" He pounded his fist on the table. "For countless years, these lands have been ours! They shall remain ours!"

There were shouts of agreement.

"I have received information concerning the warlock Azran. He lives among us! He lives, yes, he lives in the domain of our brother Red!"

The lord of the Hell Plains started. His two companions eyed him suspiciously. He glared back at them.

Gold smiled. "Peace, Red! I accuse you of no treachery. The sorceror lives in a castle hidden from the sight of man, firedrake, or beast. Until now."

The emperor snapped his fingers. The dark figure stepped out, its face still hidden by the folds of its hood. From within the robe it drew out a large rolled parchment. This was placed on a table in the midst of the Dragon Kings. Unrolled, it proved to be an accurate map of the Dragonlands.

"There!" The Gold Dragon put a finger on a spot in the lower portion of the Hell Plains. The others studied it, Red most of all.

"There is nothing there! I and countless of my clans have been there often enough!" The crimson monarch fairly bristled. "It is merely volcanic land!"

"This is a castle of the old races."

The voice brought shivers to each of the Dragon Kings, even Gold. It was the sound of the grave, the touch of a wind from the underworld. No one kept their eyes on the stranger for more than a moment.

The emperor was first to recover. "This is Madrac. You need know no more save that he has little love for our enemies, as they would treat him no better than they would us. His studies unearthed the secret of the castle, and he urges us to hurry. You see, with one strike, we may rid ourselves of the last of the Bedlams!"

"Son and grandson are both within the castle walls?" Red bared his teeth in a very inhuman smile of satisfaction. Not only would honor be restored to him, his feats would be told for generations. All this could only give him the favor of his emperor. No doubt, the Dagora Forest would be his soon after.

The faceless Madrac spoke again. "You will need a sizable force, my lord Red. Azran counts the Seekers amongst his servants. Though they are reluctant slaves, they are deadly fighters."

"I look forward to the battle. I will summon the largest of my clans and crush him!"

"I meant no disrespect. Merely warned."

Gold looked to his brother. "Bring the corpses to me. They must be burned before all of us. Only then may we rest with the knowledge that the Bedlams are no more!" He rolled up the map and returned it to the warlock. Madrac drifted back into the shadows.

"Black has begun his assault on the City of Knowledge, hoping, obviously, to take it for himself. He is a fool! The Gryphon, half-breed that he is, is still more than a match for him! While both weaken each other, Kyrg will stay back, pretending to wait for Toma. Should Black somehow succeed, Kyrg will assure that it is my legions that occupy the city and libraries. By that time, brother Black's hordes of madmen will be depleted and his clans reduced in strength."

"What of Toma?" Storm, partially gray, partially yellow—at the moment—asked in curiosity.

"Mito Pica is the city that protected the grandhatchling of Nathan Bedlam during his growth. For that reason alone, it has forfeited its right to exist. Toma shall raze the city!"

Something that should never have been born cried out from the depths of Kivan Grath. Gold kept his face expressionless, but cursed to himself. The other three Dragon Kings looked about, openly startled by the eerie sounds. Madrac, half hidden, revealed no emotion at all.

The emperor improvised quickly. He leaned toward his brothers. "Know and remember this; I am ruler of the Dragon Kings! To disobey me is to suffer the consequences! To betray me is to die! The legions of Iron and Bronze discovered that!"

They visibly shuddered. Gold nodded, pleased. Let them

wonder about the unknown servants of their master. It would help to keep them under tight rein.

"You are dismissed! Brother Red. See to it that you do not fail! Great rewards await you if you succeed, but great pain will be your only prize if you should fail!"

"I understand, my lord!" The master of the Hell Plains departed last of the three, his mind contemplating the rich life of the Dagora Forest and what he would do when it was his.

Gold was now alone. Alone, save for the warlock Madrac.

The emperor turned to his ghostly companion. In his mind, the sorceror was the only one he could really trust. Madrac spoke as if destruction and death were sustenance for him. They were kindred spirits in many ways.

"I have not forgotten you, Madrac."

"I merely await your pleasure, King of Kings."

"You shall be well rewarded for your services." Gold did not mention that the warlock would be rewarded with death soon after the present crisis was over. Kindred spirits, perhaps, but that also made Madrac dangerous once the present crisis was over.

"The destruction of the Gryphon and these new Masters will suffice."

The dragon lord nodded. His mind turned to other matters. "I have much to think on. You are dismissed for now."

Madrac bowed and drifted into the blackness. The eerie cry of Gold's most loyal servant issued forth once more. Lost in thought, the emperor wandered off to feed his pet. The few torches in the chamber were dying out. Soon there would be total darkness.

In what little light remained, a shadow was formed. The shadow took on the shape of a cloaked and hooded figure. Madrac. Though servants of the Dragon Emperor lurked in the hidden recesses of the room, none detected the presence of the intruder. The warlock laughed, a laugh of death and horror, and, for the first time, pulled the cowl from his face. What he had of a face, that is.

He may have smiled. It was difficult to tell with the blurred features of Shade.

XII

"Kyrg just sits there. None of his force even received a scratch. I don't understand it, Lord Gryphon."

The lionbird turned to his companion, Blane. There had been a lull in the fighting. It was now a normal siege situation. The Lochivarites and their firedrake commanders were testing the durability of the city. The dragons obviously feared more attacks of the kind the Gryphon had used to destroy the initial aerial assault. That would change very soon if the lord of Penacles was unable to translate the words he'd read in the books. Why rhymes and poetry, of all things?

One consolation: the longer the firedrakes waited, the harder their human fanatics would be to control.

"Kyrg," he said, "awaits Duke Toma. Toma is, at present, destroying Mito Pica."

"What?" Blane dropped his helmet, which had been held under his arm. "Mito Pica? Can we do nothing?"

"Nothing. So many of the spells I thought useful are proving to be insufficient. Small wonder that the Purple Dragon was unable to kill Nathan Bedlam outright. Most who study the books think in terms of generalizations, not specifics. More and more, I am finding out that to receive what you really wish, you must be very precise. If not, the libraries will play games."

"Why has no one ever written down the spells in some simpler form? Surely, one of this city's rulers—"

"In three days, every copy of the page will disappear. Anyone who read it will forget what it said. Some sort of fail-safe, I would imagine."

The commander's scarred face became even uglier. "Bah! Magic! Give me a simple war!"

Looking out at the vast army of the enemy, the Gryphon shook his head. "There are no simple wars."

An aide stepped into the room behind them. When they did not turn to him, he cleared his throat nervously.

Blane looked at the man. "What is it?"

The aide blanched. The commander's visage had halted more than one man dead in his tracks. "Pardon, but I've come to speak to the Lord Gryphon concerning the Lady Gwen."

The lionbird became interested. "And?"

"I went to summon her, as you requested. I searched first in her room, and then in that of her missing companion. She was in neither."

"Indeed." The Gryphon was tugging at the hair under his beak. "What then?"

"I—I asked others to assist me. We searched several floors with no success. It was then that I discovered the truth."

"And that is?" Blane was growing impatient.

The soldier was white. "She talked to your spy before you yourself, Lord Gryphon. She heard that Mito Pica falls to the dragon forces of Toma. A servant overheard all this, but remained silent out of fear of the Lady's powers."

"Understandable. Go on."

"She flew into a rage. The spy shrugged and departed. Only the servant overheard her final words. She had planned to leave for Mito Pica!"

The growl of anger that escaped from the throat of the Gryphon caused both humans to step back. There was little reason in the mind of the lionbird at that moment. Only after several seconds was he able to calm himself down enough.

"Are we a sinking vessel, that our allies disappear one by one?" The words were more to himself. "Mito Pica is finished! What she seeks is most likely no more! She might die for her folly!"

Blane asked cautiously, "What does she seek?"

"Cabe Bedlam grew up near Mito Pica. Over a space of several generations. The why and how remain in question since no one knew of this until one of the Dragon Kings accidentally discovered him. The Lady no doubt believes that she can glean some information about his past that may enable her to rescue him from Azran. Thin hope at best, but she is acting more with emotion than logic. I should have feared as much.''

The commander from Zuu coughed hoarsely. ''Now what do we do?''

The Gryphon stared at the room. The Gray Mists had drifted into the city. Every room was dim, despite more lamps than usual in those areas used by the military.

''I've heard several men who have that same wretched cough you do. It now strikes me that this is all too familiar.''

''What is?''

''The Gray Mists are sapping our strength. We grow weaker while the Lochivarites inhale freely. I remain uninfected, but the rest of the city is in danger.'' He walked over to a window and peered out at the interior of Penacles. ''This will be a short siege. We must either break them in the next week or two or fall to them like sick infants.''

Blane managed to grin. ''I will gather my men—''

''No. It would be a slaughter. The key is to find the source of the Gray Mists. If only I—'' The Gryphon broke off. ''It could be! Blane! Please inform General Toos that I will be in the libraries for the next several hours!''

''What is it?''

''I may have mistaken fire for air!'' The lionbird rushed out of the room.

Behind him, Blane shrugged, coughed, and picked up his fallen helm. ''He claims the Gray Mists don't affect him! Sounds like they've addled his head, Zuu-kala help us all!''

The tapestry had been moved to one of the deeper, more secure areas of the palace. Though he fairly ran through the building, the Gryphon felt as if he were crawling along. It was only a hunch, and probably wrong at that. Still, it explained a lot, such as how Lochivar had gone from a clean, peaceful land to a dreary, ghostlike wasteland. It amazed him that the thought had never occurred to him in all these years.

This time, the libraries were located in the center of the city. The dead center. He wondered if this was some sort of safety factor.

He found himself standing in the corridor of one of the libraries without having even noticed the change in locations.

The gnome—or *a* gnome—waited patiently. This came as no surprise to the Gryphon, but what the little man held in his hands did. There, without having searched for it, was a blue book. It was open, and ancient script filled the two pages visible. The lionbird eyed the keeper of the tomes.

Without blinking, without hesitating, the gnome handed him the book. "To save you some much-needed time, Lord Gryphon."

A day had passed. Cabe was still in the chair. It was becoming painfully uncomfortable, but Azran's shock spell would have been much worse, no question about that. Still, it might have been easier if he had at least eaten. His father had apparently forgotten all about him.

Such was not the case now. With a trace of sulfur, Azran and his throne materialized no more than three feet away from Cabe. There was a smile on the black magician's face. It did not encourage his prisoner in the least.

"Well, my son, how are you feeling today?"

"Can I get out of this chair?"

"I suppose so."

Azran waved his hand. Cabe watched the area around him glitter and sparkle. When things returned to normal, he cautiously stood up. Every part of his body ached. He straightened up slowly—

—and leaped at Azran.

It is difficult to do anything while floating in the air. Cabe discovered this the hard way. His father frowned, whirled his finger, and watched the hapless victim spin around several times.

"I'm disappointed in you, Cabe. I really thought you might behave yourself." Azran's face darkened. "I can see that there is little hope in talking this out with you. Pity. I shall have to use more drastic means."

Cabe was unceremoniously dumped on the ground. The sinister warlock stroked the black half of his beard. This boy, he decided, was far too similar to Nathan.

"You know, yesterday, I found it difficult to face you. Family relations have never been my strong point, but I think you've heard about that already."

Equilibrium totally out of sync, Cabe tried desperately to separate the floor from his face. He was paying little attention to his father's words. Azran, lost in his thoughts, did not notice.

"Having tried again, I see no alternative but to introduce you to the darker side of the spectrum immediately. Once you've seen how much more efficient and satisfying it is, I doubt you'll ever want to turn away. I speak from experience." Azran's eyes glowed with a strange light.

Finally able to differentiate between up and down, Cabe pushed himself to his knees. Most of what his father was saying had escaped him, but one thing did sink in. Azran planned to turn him to the dark powers. He tried to stand up, his legs wobbling haphazardly. His head was still reeling from the spins.

"No!" The word came unbidden and in a voice that was his and not his.

The black-clad figure of his father was thrown backward, chair and all, against the stone wall. Only Azran's quick thinking saved the evil sorceror from a broken skull. Just before impact, he disappeared. Wood collided with stone. The chair fell to the floor, shattered into countless fragments.

Cabe collapsed.

Moments later, Azran reentered. Winds howled and lightening filled the room. A glowing shell encased him. He was crouched, ready for mortal combat. The crumpled form escaped his notice at first. Instead, Azran turned his head this way and that, looking for some new attack.

When time had passed and all remained quiet, the malevolent warlock finally calmed down enough to observe that his opponent was unconscious. The spells dropped almost instantly, much to the relief of several indescribable and quite agitated servants.

"My son—pfah! You're Nathan's, body and soul, and therefore of no use to me!"

Growling, Azran threw a bolt of pure force at the inert body. It glanced off, forming a new window in the far wall that it eventually struck. Puzzled, the warlock tried again. The resulting hole in the ceiling allowed several dark creatures immediate access to safer portions of the castle. Azran stood back and tugged at the silver half of his mustache. He knew that the boy had the potential for unheard of power, but that did not explain his use of abilities most adepts had to wait years to learn. The strike that had nearly ended Azran's career was no mere raw force. It was designed to nullify several defenses before reaching the target itself. The fact the he had escaped meant nothing save that, unlike some sorcerors, he always added a twist to his personal-defense spells. Only that had given him enough time to teleport away rather than shatter against the wall in an invisible and unbreakable magical grip.

It was very obvious that Nathan was responsible. The attack was as clear as a signature. The style was one that no one had ever attempted to copy. It required skill and costly power.

All this pondering, Azran realized, was getting him nowhere. His son was protected by the Turtle's Shell, a strong barrier that could be called up naturally. It would be a waste of time and energy trying to penetrate it. Besides, the boy—boy? After several generations?—was helpless. He could not leave unless the barrier was dropped, at which point escape would be impossible since Azran would set up spells that would strike immediately. No, Cabe was still a prisoner, despite his safety for the moment.

There was a flapping at the window facing out into the greatest expanse of the Hell Plains. One of the Seekers, behaving unusually. Azran turned his attention to the creature, permitting it entry with the pass of a hand. The avian flew through the window and landed, standing, on the floor. It kneeled before the warlock, the crest on its head bristling from excitement. Curious, Azran put a hand to its head.

Dragon pack. More than one, a divided army, in fact, with several groups coming from all directions. To—to the warlock's castle! Azran pulled his hand away. The Red Dragon was coming for him. Somehow the location of his stronghold was known. He had assumed the spells of the ancients powerful enough to hide him. That, it seemed, was not the case. Someone had informed the Dragon Kings. They now believed him unsuspecting and vulnerable. In both cases, he would prove them terribly wrong.

He dismissed the Seeker after ordering it to prepare its kind for battle. Whether the avians would prove equal to the task was questionable. They had the will and the power, but they lacked numbers. No, Azran decided, he would have to enter this battle and make short work of the Red Dragon. For that, he would need the sword.

The body nearby remained motionless. Satisfied that his son would not escape the spells he had cast around the Turtle Shell, the dark warlock departed for his inner sanctum. This battle would announce to the world that here was a force to be reckoned with. Here, Azran would be seen invincible.

Dreams of grandeur filling his head, he marched off. If—and only if—Azran had kept his mind, he might have seen the small glow of light that formed out of nothing in the middle of the room, no more than three feet away from Cabe. A spell of shunning deflected the various traps set for the figure on the ground. Then, as if unfolding from his very cloak, the shadowy sorceror called Shade stood surveying his surroundings.

A smile may have briefly touched his lips. As planned, the residents of the ancient castle were now caught up in preparations for battle. The Red Dragon's hordes would be in sight any minute now. Once the battle started in earnest, Shade would take Cabe and depart. Who would prove to be the victor was unimportant to him. Both the Dragon Kings and Azran would suffer a loss of strength, and that was more than satisfactory.

Shade bent to awaken Cabe. He was instantly repelled by the shell of pure force. The blink of an eye would have missed a rare, clear look of surprise on the hooded warlock's face. This was something unexpected. It now put both men in jeopardy. Shade would most likely survive, but he did not care much for the idea of suffering at Azran's hands. For Cabe, there would be no hope.

Somewhere outside and above, the cries of the Seekers as they caught sight of the enemy filled the air. Whether ordered to or not, they would defend the fortress to the death. There was a connection to this land that went deeper than any spell. To invade the home grounds of the avians was to invite destruction. Only Azran's quick thinking had saved him from a grisly fate. The dragon packs would not be so lucky.

A slight groan alerted Shade to the fact that Cabe was

regaining consciousness. He hoped reason would return just as quickly.

"Cabe!" Even a whisper seemed earthshaking.

Rubbing his head, Cabe forced his eyes open and looked bewilderingly at the strange cage of color around him. It was like a rainbow gone mad. Bright tones crisscrossed here and there, completely enclosing him. Turning, he was only barely able to focus on the figure next to him. When he realized who it was, he nearly tried to break his way through the shell. It was only a warning from Shade that prevented him throwing himself uselessly against the side.

"That is not the way to go about it, Cabe. You must release the spell."

"Release the spell? Azran—"

The shadowy warlock held up a gloved hand. "Azran is not responsible. The Turtle Shell is a purely defensive incantation. If it was invoked, it had to be from you, and you alone!"

"Az—"

"Silence! Say his name one too many times and he may notice, despite the coming battle!"

"What battle?"

Shade growled. "I'll tell you later! *If* you ever free yourself!"

Cabe decided against mentioning that he had no experience or training and could hardly be expected to release himself unless he could merely wish the shell away.

The Turtle Shell vanished.

Mystified, Cabe stood up. Though his legs wobbled, he was able to stay erect this time. "That's all I had to do?"

His companion hesitated before speaking. "Yes, that's all."

The fierce roars of inhuman warriors engaged in battle alerted both of them. The dragon packs of the master of the Hell Plains had met with the Seekers and Azran's other servants. Sounds that chilled the marrow were constant. Cabe had no intention of viewing the slaughter outside.

"Come!" Shade extended a hand.

A rip in the very air itself emerged from nowhere and spread until it was large enough for both to step through. The faceless warlock led the way. Cabe was tempted to touch the edge of the tear, but decided that he might be risking a limb. Suppose the gap closed while his hand was still in the room? The thought was not pretty.

They were in a place that was not a place. Shade halted only long enough to give Cabe a warning.

"We are in something quite close to what men might call damnation. You must hold tight and ignore anything that you hear! If we should lose one another, you may never find your way out!"

The two continued on. Cabe stared down at his feet, trying to see what they were walking on. It was like staring into nothing. A misty nonland. If he released his grip, he wondered, would he fall forever?

The voices touched him. Calling to him. Pleading to him. Laughing and crying. Not loud. Far worse. They were just above the lower limit of his hearing. Whispers from everywhere. Each one catching his attention and trying to distract him.

One sounded like the stentorian voice of Darkhorse. Cabe strained to hear it, but his guide chose that moment to tug him forward. The voice was lost as new ones took its place. He prayed he would not go mad before they returned to reality.

Forever. They had been walking forever, it seemed. Shade was quiet and unusually harsh. The voices were apparently affecting him as well. Possibly even more so, considering his curse. He had, no doubt, spent some time here.

"There!"

The voice of Shade broke through the whispering. Cabe squinted in the direction his hooded comrade was pointing. He saw a tiny, almost insignificant speck of light. Insignificant, until one realized that no other form of illumination existed save a slight glow that had accompanied the two travelers as they entered this nightmarish nonworld. With renewed enthusiasm, both men moved toward the speck.

It grew in strange leaps. Distance had no real meaning in this place. What was far away one moment was near the next, and so on. They nearly walked into the patch of light without expecting it.

Shade reached into the light with his free hand. A tear formed in the light. From behind his companion, Cabe caught a glimpse of some rocky landscape. Whatever land it was, it sparkled. Sparkled like a diamond.

They stepped through. Cabe was more than happy to sit down. Shade sealed the rip in reality and turned to the younger warlock. The expression on the cloaked sorceror's face was, of course, unreadable.

"We will rest here for the moment." He sat down across from Cabe. The ground was rocky and uneven, but both managed to find a satisfactory spot.

Now that things had calmed down, Cabe had a few questions to ask the other. "Simon—Shade, what happened to you? We thought you dead with the Seeker!"

"I am not easy to kill. Though the spell was strong, my personal defenses were able to save me. Barely. I was flung into the void between universes. You might say that I did die."

Cabe, remembering the shadowy warlock's curse, shuddered. "Thank the gods you didn't!"

Shade may have nodded slightly. "Yes. Thank the gods."

"Who was attacking Azran's stronghold?"

A definite laugh. "The Dragon Kings. I passed on information to them, knowing that they would provide me with the smoke screen I needed to free you. Most cooperative."

"How did you know where Azran was and that he had me?"

"Mine are powers far older than those now in play. It gives me certain advantages. Disadvantages, also."

Cabe did not press what was obviously a distasteful subject to his friend. "Darkhorse disappeared when you did."

His companion hesitated before answering. "I am afraid that Darkhorse may have been lost."

"Lost? How?"

"The void between universes is vast. Though the dread steed is one with that place, he can be banished to it forever. An eternity could pass without finding the proper way out. It may very well be that we have seen the last of him." Shade lowered his head.

Cabe wished he had known the creature better. Despite the

unholy appearance, he was sure the eternal's heart—if Darkhorse had one—was in the right place.

A slight movement caught his attention. The thing—it was too far away to see properly—was gone almost instantly. Whether it was animal or man was up for question. Cabe called to his companion, a low voice assuring that no one else would hear.

"Shade! Something is coming this way!"

The head of the hooded warlock came up slowly, as if nothing out of the normal had happened. "Can you describe it?"

Cabe shook his head. "It was large. Like a bear, but not quite so ungainly. Other than that, it was just a shape. Couldn't see clearly."

"We'd best be careful. I had little choice in locations."

"Why? Where are we?" Relief was giving ground to worry.

"The Legar Peninsula. Land of the Crystal Dragon."

Relief fled. The Crystal Dragon was one of the few Kings who did not deal with humans in any way. Of those, Ice hated mankind. Green had discourse only with the wood elves. Crystal—Crystal had no subjects save his clans. At least, that was the belief.

The thing was definitely not human. Cabe looked to Shade. The faceless sorceror was sitting quietly and apparently contemplating the nature of the multiverse. Before Cabe could say anything, though, Shade waggled a finger to silence him.

In quiet tones, the other whispered, "Let it get close. Trust me."

It would put his trust to the limit, Cabe decided, but he refrained from saying so. His companion may have smiled. The young warlock turned his attention back to the oncoming intruder.

It was gone.

He started to rise. Shade put an arm out to halt him. Cabe looked at him questioningly. In reply, the other pointed silently behind his younger comrade. Cabe whirled around.

An armadillo. An armadillo taller than a man, and standing upright. It was well protected by the thick outer skin and a pair of arms that ended in sharp, finger-length claws. Dusky brown, it was oddly tailless, a contrast to its otherwise similar appearance to the animal.

The creature glared back at him.

Shade stepped forward and began to emit strange hooting noises. The heavily armored monster eyed him patiently and, when the warlock had ceased, replied in the same sort of sounds, only much deeper. It then wandered off. Shade nodded and leaned toward Cabe.

"He says he will guide us to a better place. The patrols of the Dragon Kings come by here too often." There was a strange flatness to his voice.

"What is it?"

"A Quel. Once, they inhabited most of the Dragonrealms. Now, only the Legar Peninsula remains of what was once an empire rivaling the dragons themselves."

Cabe would have asked more, but the Quel returned abruptly. It was accompanied by another of its kind, nearly identical save that it was wider and slightly shorter. There was a look of malevolence in its alien eyes. Black as the void, it seemed to him.

Like the area around them, the Quel glistened brightly. Cabe first believed that it was natural, but then he was given a thin cloth cloak covered with small, sparkling diamonds. Merchants in Mito Pica or Penacles would have paid fortunes for it. The first Quel indicated that Cabe should put it on. Shade was wrapping a similar cloth over his hood and cloak. It was a wonder that the man did not die from the heat.

"What are these for?"

"The crystals bend and turn the light and, more important, spells. It also serves as camouflage. This way, the Quel blend into their surroundings. Even the Crystal Dragon cannot locate them. Being human, we need the cloths; the Quel carry their protection in their outer shell. They put them on during early growth. The cracks in the shell eventually cover much, but not all of each crystal."

The creature with the sinister eyes motioned angrily. It wanted them to move on. They hastened to obey. Cabe noticed that the other Quel had lined up behind him. He did not think it was to protect them from the Dragon Kings.

For such ponderous beings, they moved swiftly. Cabe and

Shade, physically and mentally weakened by their trip through the dark nonworld, were hard-pressed to keep the pace set. Neither human spoke, so as to conserve energy.

After traveling over countless and repetitive hills, by which time Cabe was more than half convinced that the Quel were purposely leading them in a circle, they came to a rather unassuming hole in a mound. The creature leading pointed at the hole and then at them. Its message was clear. Shade entered first. Cabe followed quickly.

It was a shock to discover that the tunnels and caverns of the Quel were far from the burrows the young warlock had assumed. Instead, it was only a short crawl before the first tunnel opened into a much wider one that was not only paved but also had walls smoother than any craftsman could have done. A little farther back, Cabe could see what he assumed was the edge of a large building in the cavern that opened up before them. He wondered how big the underworld dwellings of these armored creatures were.

Shade was becoming impatient. He started to pick up the pace, even catching up and passing the lead Quel. The great beastman stopped him with one armored, clawed hand. The shadowy sorceror slowed until he was back in his original spot in the group. When they reached the cavern city, all four paused.

Gwen's home had been partially natural rock, construction, and plant. It was a labor of legend, yet it paled before the sight that greeted Cabe. Here was a veritable metropolis cut from the earth and rock itself. Towers that began in the farthest depths rose until they met the high, flat ceiling of the cave. No castle or fortress was as tall as the nearest of the towers, but even this one seemed small in comparison to those farther inside. Gems glistened from every structure, a king's ransom on each. Oddly, though, there was no sign of life anywhere in the gleaming city.

The wider of the two Quel emitted a low hooting. His comrade answered rapidly. There was some disagreement. The taller wanted to head straight into the city; the other pointed to a path that ran along the cavern, opening often into passages in the rock itself. Shade angrily said something in the creatures' strange tongue. The wider of the two finally won. Cabe eyed the city wistfully, telling himself that he would no doubt see it later.

They walked on for what seemed forever. Cabe was amazed at the energy of the others; he was all for falling down and collapsing and had not eaten for a long time. Only pride, not to mention a little fear, kept him going. At some point, Shade, acting on some reserve of energy, took the lead. This time, the Quel did not protest.

These tunnels were worn and dusty, as if unused for some time. It brought up again the question of just how many of these monsters still lived. None had appeared in the city the few moments Cabe had viewed it, but that was hardly proof it was empty.

This particular tunnel opened up into another chamber, only a fraction of the volume of the one containing the city, but still huge. Man-sized lumps of crystal-encrusted rock dotted the cave walls by the thousands. It smelled of animals, a large number of animals. With a start, he noted that it was the same odor that clung to the two Quel.

"Where are we?"

He did not expect an answer, but Shade provided him with one. "The resting place of the Quel."

"This is where they keep their dead?"

"No, this is where they keep their race."

Cabe looked at him, but, as usual, it was pointless to try to read something from his companion. The faceless warlock pointed at the walls in explanation.

What he had thought ridges and lumps were, in actuality, thousands upon thousands of Quel, rolled up and clinging to the walls. Their crystal-specked shells were packed tightly together. Heads were barely visible, and limbs were not to be seen at all. Cabe could barely make out the fact that they were sleeping. Only a slight movement by each betrayed that fact.

"They sleep, Cabe Bedlam. Awaiting the time to rise once again to face their ancient foes, the dragons. Only a handful of sentinels remain awake for any one period. The rest will sleep until the spell that binds them is broken."

"How do you know all this?"

Shade laughed. The humor escaped Cabe. "Some memories remain, despite the deaths of countless past personalities. I studied long and hard in some lives, seeking these creatures even as Azran sought the castle of the ancients."

"How do we wake them? If they could be used against the Dragon Kings—"

"The power that causes them to slumber is far beyond the ability of our kind—until now. You, my friend, are the only one with the potential to do it."

The two Quel had been standing nearby, quietly patient while the humans talked. Finally, though, one issued a questioning hoot.

"What's that mean?" Cabe was having second thoughts; the Quel did not seem to be very gentle in nature. There was a predatory look in their long-muzzled faces, and the eyes of the wider one were narrowed, as if suspicious of the two warlocks.

"He is merely impatient. This is the closest they've come to breaking the spell. None of them expected their sorcerors to die in casting it. With my help, however, we can remedy their mistake."

Cabe was unsatisfied, but he had no idea why. "Tell me what to do."

"Excellent. Wait." Imitating the sounds of their guides, Shade conversed with the Quel. After some discussion, the taller one departed on some errand.

While they waited—for what, Cabe had no idea—Shade surveyed the room in what seemed to be outright admiration.

"This is a place of power. This is the only place it can be done." The words were barely a whisper; the hooded warlock was talking to himself, carried away by the moment.

Something about his comrade's behavior was puzzling Cabe. A nagging thought fought its way into his head. It was lost as Shade turned his attention back to him.

"Come! We have little time!"

The Quel remaining led them to a stone slab in the middle of the sleep chamber. It was horribly reminiscent of the sacrificial altars Cabe had heard some savage races used. Shade stroked the slab with what might have been passion. Involuntarily, Cabe backed away—

—and into the mountainous body of the other Quel. With

uncanny speed, the creature wrapped one arm around the hapless human. With the free hand, it placed an amulet around his neck. A bloodred jewel in the center of the piece began to pulsate.

Cabe cried out to the other warlock. "Shade—Simon! Help me!"

The shadowy wizard formerly called Simon turned—and chuckled. He bowed, flourishing his cloak. "Call me Madrac—this time!"

XIII

Mito Pica. Another name to add to the history of destruction.

The dragon hordes of Duke Toma tore through the unsuspecting city. The guards manning the walls died quickly as lumbering, unthinking minor drakes batted themselves against stone until they or the walls gave in.

There were always more minor drakes.

Wyverns, firedrakes, airdrakes—all wreaked havoc, maiming and killing those who fought or fled. The worst were those firedrakes who assumed human form; they did not kill with the ferociousness of wild beasts, but with the sadistic calculation of a thinking mind. Even the minor drakes and their kind steered clear.

There had been some resistance, and a small part of that still existed. Troops stationed deeper in the city had gained enough time to prepare themselves. The first wave of the horde to reach the barracks found only death. Unfortunately, numbers were on the side of the invaders. Those human commanders still remaining opted to retreat to the lands around and, if possible, make their way to Zuu, Wenslis, or Penacles, if that city had not fallen by then. The citizens of Mito Pica did as citizens of any region under attack would do. They fled for their lives if they were swift enough and died if they were slow. More civilians died than soldiers, but there are always more civilians to kill than there are soldiers. It is the nature of war.

It was into this that the Lady materialized.

Her powers were still not up to par. She was forced to make two stops before reaching the countryside near the dying city. The term *countryside* was a euphemism at best; most of the nearby land had been torn up under the claws, hooves, and feet of the participants. Many trees were uprooted. The Lady had spent a day scouting the area. She did not want to run into any patrols or, worse yet, Duke Toma himself. It was said that Toma was a strong warlock in his own right, a throwback to earlier days. Only the pattern of his egg kept him from joining the ranks of the Dragon Kings. Nevertheless, he was second only to them and, with the authority of Gold and the power he himself controlled, he could even command them at times.

Questioning the displaced had given her a vague idea of her destination. It was away from the city, closer to a village that had remained untouched by this slaughter. Toma was intelligent and devious, but he had erred this time. It was not Mito Pica that had raised Cabe—not directly—but rather this nameless village. Her luck now depended on how close the huntsman's home was to the village. If it was near, then it might have been passed up. If not . . .

A small group of firedrakes, shaped as men and mounted, appeared from nowhere. They were chasing three riders on horseback, a family. An old man and two younger people, perhaps a recently married pair or the man's children. They would not be able to outrace the fearsome steeds of the dragon men. Already, the gap between the groups was closing.

Gwen was protected. She had cast a spell of invisibility around her. If she ignored the situation, she would be safe, undetected by Toma's powers. If she interfered, she threatened her own chances.

She interfered.

The path being used led into a patch of trees that had survived the fighting. The Lady smiled. Plants were her friends, her willing servants. She talked to them, told them what she wanted and why. They thrilled at the idea of serving her.

The humans and their horses passed through unharmed.

The firedrakes were not so fortunate. The leader, confident that his prey was only moments from capture, pulled ahead of the rest. A stray branch struck him in the face; he brushed it aside. Another, stronger limb nearly knocked him off his mount. The firedrake barely ducked in time.

The third caught him in the throat even as he evaded the second.

With a satisfying crack, the leader fell from the saddle, his head at an awkward angle. There was no doubt that he was dead. One rider tried to avoid his fallen comrade. The enchanted drake under him tripped on a root that had not been above ground a moment before. The hapless rider was thrown to the ground, where he landed with a thud. He did not move.

Two of the remaining firedrakes dismounted. The others backed up, their half-shadowed eyes on the trees around them. Gwen called off her allies; she had already made her presence felt much too long. She hoped Toma was engaged in numerous matters and was not concentrating his powers.

The remaining riders picked up their fallen companions and dragged them out of the dangerous path. From the safety of her spell, the enchantress could see that the second victim was also dead. The two bodies were piled on the back of one of the two extra animals. The firedrakes had given up on their prey; just as well, for they would have never caught them after this long a delay. It was also obvious that none of them wanted to pass through the small, seemingly innocent grove of trees. The Lady smiled.

The sense of victory did not last long. From here on, she would have to go on foot. It would not do to go popping from place to place in search of a cabin that might or might not be there. Toma would most certainly be drawn to her then. Besides, she could easily miss her target that way.

Reinforcing her spell of invisibility, the Lady made her way through the desolation, destruction, and—she thanked Rheena, the goddess of the woods—the occasional piece of land that remained untouched by the horrors of Toma's butchers.

An hour passed. The land here was virtually untouched. Here and there, mangled brush showed the movement of some large force, but Gwen lacked the training to identify which side it had been. The path appeared to lead in the general direction she was headed. An ill feeling crept into her heart.

Twenty minutes later, she spotted something that was definitely man-made. That it was a cabin could not be verified; it had been demolished by raiders. She nearly stumbled over the dead form of a minor drake, its enchantment gone. No one could have mistaken it for a horse now. Or a dragon, for that matter. It was well burnt. Gwen touched the remains and detected something hauntingly familiar.

There was another form nearby. A third she discovered only a few feet from that. Both were firedrakes, killed while in their human forms. It was evident from the fact that their weapons were still sheathed that they had been caught unaware.

What had happened to the rest of the attackers? For that matter, where were the inhabitants of the cabin? Summoning to mind some of her more potent defensive spells, the Lady moved cautiously toward the wreckage of the building.

She found more traces of the firedrakes near what had once been the front door. One had actually been in the process of shape-shifting at the time of his death. Half-grown wings, arms that were too long, and clawed feet. These had not been burned. They had been frozen to death. Instantly.

More and more, the handiwork dregged memories from her subconscious.

A groan. She stiffened, expecting any second to be attacked by the rest of the marauders. A second groan wiped away that belief; this was a human voice. A dragon's voice would have been raspy, even hissing. This was more high-pitched, like a minstrel.

Stepping over what was once the floor base of the northern wall, Gwen entered the remains of the cabin. The moaning had quieted down now. She began to worry that she had arrived too late. Moving with less caution than before, the sorceress made her way to the originator of the groans.

He was buried under the rubble that had been the roof. She tugged at one of the beams. It would not budge. Reluctantly, she gestured with her left hand, knowing as she did that each new spell would draw the duke's attention to her more and more.

When the last of the wood had been lifted away and deposited nearby, the Lady eyed the figure at her feet. His face was turned away from her, but the woodland clothes and the curly hair reminded her of someone from her youth. She turned his head slowly, so as not to injure him. Fortunately, the neck was not broken.

She had been correct. His face was more than familiar. The name that went with the face was Hadeen. He was part elf. He was also an elemental. Nathan Bedlam would have trusted no one more than this half-elf. Some claimed that Hadeen was once the tutor of Nathan himself. It could easily have been true.

Hadeen's eyes fluttered open. For the briefest of times, he looked at her directly. A smile played across his marred face. He muttered something, but Gwen could not hear him. She leaned closer.

"Lady of the Amber, daughter of the wood goddess." As if satisfied with that statement, the half-elf expired.

She looked down at him with shock. So close! Toma had succeeded in destroying her one thin clue.

"Gwendolyn."

The enchantress jumped. The voice was that of Hadeen, but the limp body was not the source.

"Here, Gwendolyn."

A tall, strong oak shook its mighty headdress of green. The Lady nodded to herself; Hadeen was still one of the forest dwellers, despite his human side. That which was elf had chosen one of the trees for its final resting place; its essence helped the tree and the surrounding land thrive. In such a way were the spirits of the elves always with their people.

It was almost as if the tree smiled. "Thank Rheena you came before I died, Gwendolyn. If you hadn't, I would never have fought for semblance of personality. For a short time, I can communicate with you."

"What happened here, Hadeen? Where are the rest of this dragon force?"

The branches of the oak quivered in triumph. "Earth, air, fire, and water! An elemental will not be beaten easily in his own home! I caught the first with the cleansing flame. A tornado disposed of the next attackers; they should be somewhere in the eastern seas. Water, in the form of the numbing ice, gave several of the monsters a preview of the underworld. Earth swallowed most others. Regrettably, I was unable to shield myself during the entire time. One of those I burned was able to let loose a spell before expiring. It struck while my attention was elsewhere.''

The tree spirit was talking rapidly. It would not be long before consciousness gave way to the normal nature of the oak. After that, the Lady would have to deal with emotions. While she understood the way of the plants, the information she needed would be unattainable from a thing that thought by feeling, not by words.

''Hadeen—''

''There is no Hadeen; there is only the oak and the spirit that becomes one with it.''

She reworded her statement. ''That which was Hadeen, you cared for the young Cabe Bedlam, grandson of Nathan, your friend.''

''I did.''

''I seek him. I believe Azran has him. I would know—''

The disembodied voice cut her off. ''Hadeen knew of the treacherous son's stronghold. They who you seek are not there.''

Gwen could tell that the half-elf's spirit was incorporating itself with the very essence of the tree. She was running out of time, and now she didn't know where to look.

''Where is Cabe now?''

''He nears the beginning and the end. The ghost of two minds seeks his power, which is not his but theirs and theirs alone. If the power is passed, the Quel will wake.''

Frowning in frustration, the Lady tried again. ''Hadeen, listen—''

The voice struggled to pull what individuality remained back together. ''Gwendolyn. The faceless warlock now has Cabe. The scale is now tipped to evil where the shadow sorceror is concerned. Go to Talak. Await your lover of two ages there.''

''I don't—''

The spirit was becoming remote. ''The child was dying. Nathan wanted to assure that at least his grandson survived.

If he himself did, it would only be luck. He knew the Dragon Kings would win, but he hoped the seed would grow again."

She waited. At first, only the rustling of leaves in the wind answered her.

"Gwendolyn. Only the two who are one can succeed."

That was all. The half-elf Hadeen was gone. He had left behind more confusion than answers. Two who are one? She sighed. If time had permitted, she would have buried Hadeen's mortal body, but as it was, every extra second endangered her. The large number of spells in one small area was sure to attract Toma's attention, even if the loss of this force did not.

Something moved in the brush far to her right. She had dropped her spell to talk to Hadeen. Now, though invisible once more, Gwen sought the protection of the oak that now contained that which had been part of Hadeen. It was always possible that the firedrakes had some sort of enchantment that might counteract her spell.

A minor drake, in its true form, nosed through into sight. It did not care much for the foliage, being from the Tyber Mountains. The dragon tore up smaller trees and plants as it waddled toward the remains of the cabin. Two similar creatures followed close behind it. Hounds of the Dragon Kings.

She knew they could not smell her. Whether the wind was blowing or not had no bearing. Though she was no elf, the Lady was very much at home with the forests. She carried no scent that would mark her as human.

These, however, were not hounds in the normal sense. While two investigated the carnage, the original sniffed at the air, the direction it was headed too close for Gwen's tastes. It was homing in on her power. She knew that the Dragon Kings had been toying with the idea of a tracker capable of seeing the powers, but this was the first time she had seen that idea made into fact. It was not a pleasant discovery to make.

From the original path of the minor drakes came five armored figures. That they showed no fear of the trackers marked them as firedrakes even before they were close enough to identify visually. Four had swords drawn; the fifth was empty-handed. The enchantress noted him as the most dangerous. If he went unarmed, it was only because he had other abilities to protect him.

The dragon warriors poked around the cabin. The one without a weapon was evidently in command. He seemed more than interested in the corpse of Hadeen. Gwen tried to keep her breathing down. Three of the five firedrakes and the one tracker were all within only a few yards. Without the sorceror, she would have had no difficulty. His presence might delay her just long enough for one of the others to make a vital strike.

After searching the grounds, the firedrakes seemed satisfied that there were no survivors. With nothing to be gained, the sorceror decided it was time to depart. The warriors and two of the minor drakes obeyed without question; the third continued to stare toward the witch's hiding place. It did not move closer, but it also did not give up.

The sorceror stalked up to the animal and hit it solidly with the back of his hand. The thick, leathery hide of the tracker protected its wearer from pain, but the action was enough to stir it from its duty. The beast turned and lumbered toward its companions. The firedrake stood staring at the oak, as if sensing its true nature. One of the others called to him. The sorceror blinked, red, raging eyes looking directly at the cloaked enchantress, and shook his head. Gwen breathed a sigh of relief as he spun around and joined his fellows. Not until they were out of sight and sound did she step away from the tree.

It galled her to hide like some helpless animal, but secrecy was of the utmost importance. Hadeen had given her a jumble of disjointed pieces of information. Somehow she had to make sense of it all. She knew that Cabe faced danger. She also knew now that Shade had been added to their list of adversaries. Ever a two-sided coin. It would have been better to not involve the blurry warlock at all. His new identity would retain some memory, and his ancient powers would provide much of the rest.

Now that she was alone, all that remained was for her to visualize a materialization spot for her next hop. Talak was not far; it would require only one stop on the way. She prayed that her powers would be up to full soon. This sort of travel was far too untrustworthy for her tastes.

She remembered a dirt road that curved to the left. It was the only road to Mito Pica from the city near the Tyber Mountains. Even after all this time, Gwen was sure that it remained virtually unchanged. She pictured it in her mind and concentrated. The air shimmered around her.

The Lady vanished.

The Lady materialized. In a force sphere. A dragon warrior, clad in gold and wearing a helm almost as elaborate as that of the Kings, was seated before her. There was a goblet of wine in his left hand. He raised it in greeting.

"Welcome, Lady of the Amber!" Lord Toma smiled and sipped his wine.

It was too obvious.

Too dangerous, for that matter. It would mean confronting the Black Dragon himself. Only then could the Gray Mists be halted. The Black Dragon controlled the Gray Mists.

The Black Dragon was the Gray Mists.

The mistake was in making labels. Not all the Dragon Kings were firedrakes. The Ice Dragon was proof of that. Why, then, must the master of Lochivar be one? The answer was that he was not; he was an airdrake. The most powerful one of all. What other could spread his deathly presence over an entire land?

To destroy the Gray Mists, the Gryphon would have to destroy the Black Dragon.

No easy task. The lionbird was a veteran of countless battles, but even he had never taken on one of the Kings face-to-face. Nathan Bedlam was the only one who had ever succeeded, and it had cost him his life. Yet if the Gryphon failed to halt the choking numbness of the fog, Penacles would fall for certain.

He began seriously considering retirement from politics.

Closing the tome, the Gryphon handed it back to the librarian. The gnome took it cautiously, his eyes lit with excitement. When the ruler of the City of Knowledge departed, the short, squat man would pour over the pages his master had read. What was written was not so important as the fact that it was written. The gnome lived for books alone.

The libraries faded from the Gryphon's sight, but he paid it no mind. Plain and simple, he thought to himself. The book had given him his answer in plain and simple words. No tricks. No rhymes or riddles. Questioning the gnome had proved fruitless; the librarian claimed only that he knew that his master needed that particular tome. Where that idea had come from, the little man did not know or care. It was the way of the libraries.

He materialized in the palace not a moment too soon. From the sounds outside, it was evident that the Lochivarites had resumed their attack. Though he disliked the use of magic for the most part, time was of the essence. Gesturing quietly, he disappeared—

—and reappeared near the eastern walls. The violence nearly overwhelmed him. Black-clad figures were trying to scale the wall. Some of them made it to the top, only to be cut down by a defender. Countless dead littered the area outside the wall. The fanatics paid it no mind. They kept coming and coming, an endless wave that seemed ready to engulf all. It was hard to believe they were really human.

The casualty count was not one-sided. Those of the enemy who managed to scale the siege ladders to the top made their marks. Too many defenders were dying. Though ten times the number of the foe probably lay dead or wounded, their legions were far greater in size. In a war of attrition, Penacles would lose.

Where were these invaders coming from?

Airdrakes and firedrakes soared high above. Though they let loose with a volley now and then, their effectiveness had been curtailed by the accuracy of the archers. If those men fell . . .

"Lord Gryphon!"

A burly, well-armored boar of a man shoved into him. Both fell to the side. Seconds later, the spot on which the Gryphon had stood was bathed in flames. Archers manning a nearby tower made short work of the daring reptile. The firedrake fell to the ground, crushing several empty tents in the deserted bazaar nearby.

Grimacing more from the weight on top of him than from his near-death, the lord of Penacles grunted at the figure who had saved him.

"My thanks, Blane, but if you wish to make your actions count, I must request that you remove yourself before I die from lack of air."

The huge bear grinned. "Apologies, Lord Gryphon! When you appeared, the dragons took a sudden, unhealthy interest in you! Likely that they've been given orders to stop you at all costs!"

"Most likely. What happens here, Blane? Can we hold out?"

"I think so. The zombies are running out of ladders even if they aren't running out of no-minds to climb 'em! Gods! Where did they get all of them?"

"Would that I knew. Perhaps . . ." The Gryphon's words trailed off as he watched the hordes of Lochivar start to pull back. Penacles had survived another day.

"Perhaps what? Lord Gryphon?"

"Where is the general?"

"That fox? Out near the southern gate. Group of blackies tried to sneak around to the west side. Imagine he's mopped them up by now."

The Gryphon put his hands on Blane's shoulders. The commander shuddered involuntarily; the lionbird's claws could have easily torn through his neck. There was still something of the animal in the Gryphon's nature. That had already been proven.

"Blane. I believe I have the key to breaking this war before we all perish from fog or foe." As if on cue, the commander coughed hoarsely. "We don't have much time. I have to do it."

"Do"—cough—"what?"

"I know the source of the Gray Mists. It's the Black Dragon himself!"

Blane's eyes widened. "Then to destroy the mists, you have to kill the Black Dragon?"

The other nodded.

The commander turned red. "I suppose you think you're gonna go in there all by yourself and take care o' him! Insanity!"

"A large force would never make it. Humans would succumb to the mists the nearer they came to the Black Dragon.

Without Cabe, the Lady, or Shade, I have only myself to turn to."

"Suicide! I won't have it!"

The Gryphon pulled him forward by the collar of his uniform. Blane found his face perilously close to the predatory beak of the lionbird.

"You are not in the position to tell me what to do! Forgive me, Commander, but Penacles will not survive much longer! The Lochivarites nearly made it this time! Haven't you noticed how much slower the archers have become? We also lose far too many men with each renewal of the onslaught! I have no choice!"

He released the sweating soldier and turned to stare out in the general direction of the Black Dragon's lands. Dark masses were pouring toward that area, the remainder of the fanatics' armies. For the first time, the landscape did not appear so thoroughly covered by the hordes. The Lochivarites had sustained heavy casualties. That still left Black's clans, though. Many dragons had not yet entered the fray. It would not be long before they did.

There was also Kyrg to consider. No doubt he was waiting for both sides to weaken themselves, whereupon he would step in and attempt to capture the libraries in the name of the Dragon Emperor. How long would he wait?

Looking rather sheepish, Blane bowed before the Gryphon and presented him with his sword. "Apologies, lord, for my actions. Take my weapon. If you must face the Black Dragon, she'll be of good use to you."

The Gryphon smiled as best his avian mouth would allow him. "Rise, Commander." He studied the man. "Royal background?"

"Aye."

"Thought as much. Second or third son, no doubt. I've met your type before." Blane flushed. "Keep your sword. I'm sure it would serve me well for most needs, but few things can pierce the armor of a Dragon King. No, I will need something else."

"If his hide's so thick, you'll need magic. This would cut through anything normal."

The eyes of the Gryphon glittered. "Yes! I believe I have it! I shall let Azran's toy live up to its claim!"

If Blane had looked pale before, his countenance now took on that of a corpse. "The Horned Blade? It's said that Masters rather than Kings died on that accursed weapon!"

Grim, flat tones. "No tales that. At least three. It brought about the destruction of all they had planned. It gave the damned lizards several generations more! Azran has much to pay for; his creation will satisfy some small portion of that bill!"

Around them, survivors of the latest confrontation set about the task of locating the wounded, disposing of the dead, and removing the wreckage and rubble. There was an endless supply of each. The walls were becoming more and more sparsely manned. The Black Dragon was hastening lest Toma or Kyrg claim the prize before him.

Tearing his eyes away from the scene, the Gryphon turned once more to the commander from Zuu. "When Toos arrives, I want both of you to meet me in the stables. You'll receive your final orders then."

"You'll be needing supplies."

"I'll be carrying very little. I have to move swiftly if I hope to succeed at all."

Blane saluted. The Gryphon departed, his thoughts a raging, flooded river. The Horned Blade was a vile weapon; some said it could master the bearer. That was all supposition so far as the lionbird was concerned. Only three had ever held the hellish sword, the first two being Azran and the Brown Dragon. If they had been entranced, their actions had not shown it. The Gryphon wished he had had the foresight to question Cabe. Now it was too late.

Why was the weapon here? Azran would have wanted it. The lord of Penacles was not a believer in chance. Everything had a reason, especially this. No, he decided, the Horned Blade had been left for a reason. A trap? Perhaps. Why? Azran could not work on the assumption that someone would use it. Just as unlikely was the idea that the warlock's minions had betrayed him.

He eventually found himself at the door to his room. The two iron golems stared at him emotionlessly. At a slight nod, one of them opened the door. The Gryphon stepped inside.

Distrustful of the sword and unwilling to leave it in Cabe's room, he had ordered one of the golems to pick it up and deliver it here. That same creature now stood waiting, the ominous blade in its metallic hand pointed directly toward the lionbird. The Gryphon hoped that the sword had no control over unliving creatures.

He held out his empty palm. "Give me the weapon."

The golem grasped the blade in a way that would have left any man with one less hand. It held out the pummel to its master. Feathers and fur slightly ruffled, the Gryphon gripped the Horned Blade.

It tingled, but that was all. Strangely, he was almost disappointed. Almost. While the Gryphon enjoyed a challenge, he was not suicidal. Those who went fearlessly and wholeheartedly into battle lived rather short lives. Common sense dictated his actions. Up until now, anyway. He had to admit to himself that Blane was right; this mission could well be a disaster.

The Horned Blade was now in his right hand, though the lionbird was left-handed. Reaching down with his free hand, he removed his own sword and tossed it to the side. He then passed the sword to his left. A final motion placed the dark blade in his empty scabbard.

He would take only one of the emergency packs stored in the barracks of the palace guards. That and a sack of water would provide him with the sustenance he needed. The Gryphon prepared for a hunt; no animal would hunt on a full stomach. Despite his diplomatic ways, there would always be a part of him that belonged to the wild.

Bloody Styx and sister Hestia would pass near one another tonight. Not as terrible as nights when they met, but still a time to beware.

He laughed bitterly. When was there a night not to beware?

XIV

Madrac/Shade leaned over him. Though the warlock's face remained obscure, the aura of evil surrounding him was quite evident now. That Cabe had missed it earlier said much for the shadowy sorceror's power.

"Time is not quite right yet. we must wait 'til the beginning of the eleventh hour." He may have smiled. "That gives us some time to talk, if you wish."

Cabe glared at him.

"No? Not even questions? How about this? How did I know all about you and your situation, hmm? I believe you know that I retain only partial memories after each reincarnation."

Despite his anger, Cabe found himself listening.

"We are entering a new age, Bedlam. The rule of the Dragon Kings is dying. Decaying. Gold is an emperor who moves between calm reason and ungoverning paranoia. Most of his brethren are treacherous and bickering. They are no longer the cold, efficient masters of the lands. They have caught your grandfather's final weapon. They have been infected with the disease called humanity. In time, all but the lesser drakes will lose their right to be called true dragons."

"What do you mean?"

A low chuckle. "He talks! What I mean is this. Have you noticed how the firedrakes, especially the dukes and the Kings themselves, almost always parade around in their near-human forms?"

"They've always done so."

"Incorrect. The first Dragon Kings never shapeshifted. Only after they delved into the magic of humans did they begin to take on the forms of almost-men. The females found this easier, though they could not master much of the other spells. It became so common among the firedrakes that eventually the ability became inherent. At the same time, they weakened those abilities that had been theirs originally."

One of the Quel came near, a large ornate crystal in the creature's arms. Cabe pointedly ignored it. "What does this have to do with what you were talking about?"

"Everything!" The one who now called himself Madrac gestured at the endless rows of sleeping Quel. "Before the age of the Dragon Kings, this land was ruled by the beings you see before you. Their empire, at its height, was greater than that of the reptiles. As their might crumbled, the dragons entered the lands and grew. Powers shifted, some becoming dormant, others grasping more control."

He waved away the Quel who had brought the crystal. The armored monster hooted angrily, its huge clawed paws coming up in an obviously threatening attitude. Shade spoke back to it, his sounds higher, but no less angrier. The Quel finally gave in on whatever argument was taking place and backed away.

Shade turned back to his prisoner. "The Quel was anxious to get on with the ceremony. They don't understand that it must take place at a certain time." He leaned over and whispered to Cabe, though it was very likely that his nonhuman allies could not understand. "This will be a momentous time for all of us. For a short period, you will have power undreamed of. After that, the Quel will be released and I will achieve what has eluded me for untold years. Escape!"

Snapping his fingers, the warlock gestured to the creature. Cabe looked from one to the other. He did not like what was being done.

"What's going on?"

"The time draws near. We will proceed with the preliminaries in a moment. I fear I must cut my story short. Suffice it to say, the powers that control me are ones left from that ancient time. That which was dominant when Simon met you would prefer to leave this new world be, but that which now controls my actions awaits this new age. With the Dragon Kings waning in power, the Quel and the ancient ways will reestablish themselves and mankind will not take the reins of these lands. He will live only to serve."

"Like yourself?"

An open palm flashed across Cabe's face. There was anger in the other even though the features could reveal nothing.

"When the power takes control, I will be rid of this ridiculous curse! I will be Madrac! Only Madrac!" Shade glanced up. "But I'm afraid the rest will have to remain a mystery to you!" He laughed.

Insanity, Cabe thought to himself. From one madman to another! He turned his head and caught the sinister stare of the Quel. To confront the Dragon Kings was bad enough, but now people would have this threat hanging over them. He struggled to move, but to no avail.

Shade turned away from him. The hooded necromancer was uttering words that sounded hauntingly familiar to his captive, though he knew he had never heard the language before. Ominous tendrils of dark smoke materialized around Shade's head.

The Quel was staring at the smaller crystal on Cabe's chest. It had taken on a glow, barely noticeable at first, but increasing in intensity as the hour approached.

The cloaked figure was absorbed in his incantations. Cabe paid him no mind. His attention was riveted on the object on his chest. Everything else faded into insignificance.

As the eleventh hour neared, the crystal began to quiver. Worse yet, he could swear that it was slowly sinking into his chest. Yet there was no pain, no blood, just tingling.

The Quel shifted nervously. It was definitely unprepared for this incident. The long face turned to Shade, but the warlock was still occupied in his casting. The monster, more afraid of disturbing the ceremony, remained silent but eyed the sudden events with great trepidation.

Like some creature caught in quicksand, the gem sank deeper and deeper into Cabe's body. Horror was replaced by fascination—and something else. Cabe understood that this would not hurt him, but help him.

Looking the part of a wind-whipped specter, Shade moved swiftly in the midst of awakening powers, his hands darting to and fro, each movement adding to the swirling mists and things. The sleeping Quel shivered as one. Cabe's guard became distracted by the stirring of his people.

Something dark and nebulous formed in a far corner of the chamber. It was behind the creature that guarded, so only Cabe was aware of its presence. He, though, paid it little attention; the crystal demanded and received the vast majority of his awareness.

From within that ignored darkness, coming from eternity itself, laughter was emitted. It was low, almost beyond the hearing of any creature. Nevertheless, the Quel who stood shuddered and glanced about. It did not turn to the darkness.

Shade, however, did.

"Who laughs . . ." His eyes fixed on the hitherto unnoticed spot. Madrac cursed, glanced at Cabe, and began gesturing.

In one moment, it seemed the forces of all hells had been loosed. The laughter suddenly rose to great heights, cutting out most other sounds. The cowled warlock, alerted by senses far beyond the ordinary, unleashed his spell. It was not aimed at Cabe; rather, the powers were thrown at the darkness. The two forces met, fought for control. It was only a short battle. The darkness swallowed Shade's powerful spell as if it had consisted of nothing.

Through the blackness came a creature as dark and sinister as its home. Great hooves carved grooves into the rocky floor. Ice-blue eyes glared at those in its sight. The wild mane shook loose small particles of ebony night. The mouth was framed with a snarl, revealing very sharp and very unhorselike teeth.

Darkhorse leaped at Shade.

The Quel tried to block the rampaging form, but all that was accomplished was that the armored monster vanished into the void that was Darkhorse. The sleek equine shape was not even slowed. Warlock and eternal locked into combat.

Cabe was jarred from his fascination with the crystal by the appearance of his unearthly friend. He stood up, ignoring the sudden absence of his bonds. He only knew that there was incredible danger where two such powerful forces met.

Darkhorse kicked at the mage with his forehooves. What would have cracked mountains only jostled the shadowy sorceror. Shade rebalanced and threw a number of sharp black spears at the steed. Somehow the creature maneuvered around them, charging his opponent head-on as he did so.

"Cabe! Talak! Talak is your destination! Go!"

The eternal's words were not spoken, but rather came from Cabe's own mind. As if a puppet, his body moved swiftly toward the entrance to this chamber; behind him, he could hear the howls and explosions of powers unleashed. He had no desire to await the outcome.

Ignored in this was the crystal still buried deep in his chest. It had altered. The glow had changed color, and the gem was now as blue as the daytime sky and pulsating as well. Cabe did not realize it, but the more he exerted himself, the more the gem pulsated.

Whether it was magic or perhaps some hidden sense, something made Cabe duck. A huge, four-edged ax bit deeply into the rock on the level his head had been. The Quel holding it hooted angrily and pulled the weapon up for another swing.

Cabe was barely able to roll away as the armadillolike horror tried once more to separate his head from the rest of his body, while within the sleeping chamber, the battle of titans still reigned. The hapless young warlock now found himself contending with falling rock as well as his murderous adversary.

In an act of desperation, he extended his left hand at the Quel. Simultaneously, unintelligible words flowed from his mouth. The tips of his fingers glowed. The color matched that of the crystal.

The Quel stepped back for a better swing, his ax high in the air—unnaturally high. The ax bit deeply into the ceiling above, its hapless owner pulled from the ground. The rock, already loosened by the battle between Shade and Darkhorse, fell. A cave-in commenced. Cabe managed to leap forward; the Quel was not so lucky and was buried beneath tons of earth and rock.

Not willing to discover whether the creature was dead or not, Cabe continued his departure. His magic had saved him once again. Better yet, he felt more comfortable, more confident. The fact that he should not have known the spell never occurred to him. With no past training, he was unfamiliar with the route other magic-users were forced to take.

He ran past the city. No other Quel made an appearance. Were there only two? He could not believe himself that lucky.

Nevertheless, nothing impeded his progress. The entrance through which they had entered was only seconds away, and that caused him to think. Darkhorse had told him to flee to Talak, but Talak was far, very far, to the northeast.

Stepping out onto the surface, he scanned the area. The Legar Peninsula was misleadingly peaceful and beautiful. At any other time, it would have been fascinating to explore it, even barring the fact that it was controlled by the Crystal Dragon.

Night had fallen. Cabe disliked the thought of traveling by dark, but he could see no alternative. He had no light, and it was probably wiser not to carry one. In this area, a torch would stick out for miles. Cabe hoped that there were no large predators in the area, for this time he had no magic sword to save his skin. He would have to rely on his own powers and abilities.

By the stars that were visible, he determined the general direction he needed to go. The ground beneath his feet shook, reminding him of the fierce struggle taking place. With renewed effort, Cabe started off quickly from the mouth of the tunnel.

Seeing turned out to be little trouble. With both moons out, the lands fairly gleamed from their light. After a short time, he slowed his pace. This would not do. The battle between Darkhorse and Madrac/Shade might end at any moment. If the cowled sorceror proved triumphant, he would be close behind his intended victim within seconds. Cabe wished he could teleport or fly or summon something to carry him away. His powers, though, were apparently not ready for that stage yet.

No creature stirred. Were there no animals? It seemed strange. He had not even heard an insect or a night bird. Did the curse of the Barren Lands extend even farther than believed? To his knowledge, no one had ever mentioned traveling to this remote part of the Dragonrealms. That meant either that no one dared speak of it or no one had ever come back.

Time became a blur. Cabe remembered only running, then walking, and finally stumbling across the Legar Peninsula. At some point, he finally fell over, totally exhausted by his ordeal. He had paid no attention to the crystal in his chest; it was so much a part of him now. Nor did he know of the change in his hair, due partly to that gem. Not one trace of his original hair color remained. The silver had covered completely.

He slept through the night, waking only once, and that for just a moment. That which disturbed him might have been a movement of the earth. It might also have been the endless struggle between two immortals. At the time, Cabe couldn't have cared less. He was asleep again the next instant.

Though he had seen none, life did indeed abound on the peninsula. One or two small plant-eaters scurried by his motionless form. A bird flew past overhead. None of the dangerous animals, especially the hill wolves who dominated this area, came near. In fact, those that sought to suddenly changed their plans and hurried on to other hunting grounds, unaware that there had been any alteration. Each time, the crystal glowed brightly.

Morning came, and with it surprises. First and foremost was the wonderful smell of bacon turning crisp over an open fire. Second was the realization in Cabe's mind that he was no longer alone. With speed that surprised him almost as much as the other things did, Cabe rolled away from the figures nearby.

"Moves almost like elk, he does."

"Huh! Moves more like newborn elk, you mean. Will get grass stains over his pretty clothes, he will."

There were two of them. Having lived fairly close to the Dagora Forest, Cabe knew what they were even if he had never actually seen their kind before. It was impossible to mistake wood elves for anything else.

Both were short and thin and almost completely identical. They came no higher than Cabe's shoulder, although he had heard of taller ones who sometimes infiltrated and even intermarried with humans. These two, though, were definitely completely of the blood.

They were standing side by side. The one on the left grinned and said, "Has a bit of the People in him, he does. Can smell it, can't you?"

His twin nodded, albeit somewhat reluctantly. "Stinks much more of human, though, and something else."

Cabe decided to interrupt. "Who—?"

"Course he does! Must be the mage we seek."

"Excu—"

"Must be. Doesn't look to be much, does he?"

"I—"

"Looks can be deceiving. Still, you have a point, I think. Doesn't look like much of a mage."

Anger swelled to the breaking point. Something gave.

"He's a mage, he is!"

"Quiet! He might do it again, he might!"

"Why does he have to blow holes in the lovely countryside, though?"

"Quiet!" Cabe was barely holding back a second explosion.

The two wood elves became silent. Motionless, they might have been a pair of statues for some lord's gate. All they were to Cabe, though, were two great annoyances.

"Who are you?"

The one on the left: "Allanard."

The one on the right: "Morgyn."

Cabe folded his arms. "You were looking for me?"

Allanard rubbed his elbow and winced. Both elves wore identical clothing: simple woodland outfits colored green with small areas of brown here and there. The outfits blended in perfectly with the landscape around them.

"Are you Bedlam?"

"I am."

Morgyn nodded. "Can see it in the face, I can. The grandfather is in you." He made a face. "Your father too."

"Why are you looking for me? What do you want?"

Both of the elves started to laugh, but stopped when they caught sight of Cabe's face. Allanard smiled. "From you, we want nothing. This is a favor we do, it is. Favor for a half-blood relation and your grandfather, good Nathan."

Morgyn caught sight of the crystal. "Allanard, he's got a bloody gem poked in his chest, he does."

"Quiet!"

Cabe had not been listening. "Who is this half-blood relation? Why would he help me?"

"Why? He only watched you break the link with death and grow up! That's why! We're talkin' of the man who you thought was your father, we are!"

"My—"

"Hadeen was his name. He looked after you out of friendship to Nathan. There may be blood involved, too."

"Blood?" Cabe's face paled.

Allanard shook his head. Even his hair was tinted green. "We're talking relations here, we are. You might be our kin. That makes it doubly important for us to help you. Besides—" For the first time, bitterness edged its way into the merry voice. "—we owe the lizards for Hadeen."

Cabe did not catch the last part, his mind turning back to the danger beneath the earth. He hoped these two had good transportation. The more distance separating him from the Legar Peninsula, the better.

As if to emphasize his point, the ground quaked with unnatural fury.

Morgyn was thrown to the ground. "Has the nation of gnomes gone to war?"

Cabe regained his balance. "Worse! A wizard named Shade and a creature called Darkhorse fight somewhere below!"

The elves' mouths dropped. Allanard was the first to regain use of his tongue. "The black steed and the two-minded warlock at odds! Nothing was said of this! We must make haste, we must!"

"Where do we go? Do you have horses?"

"Horses? Are you not a mage and one of the blood as well?"

"That's debat—"

Allanard waved off any talk. "Swiftness we need, though I don't know if it's possible to escape the likes of those two should one come seeking you in evil! Morgyn! This is your specialty!"

"Aye, brother!"

The terrible combat beneath the surface was forgotten as Cabe watched in wonder. Morgyn took out a small piece of black chalk and was now outlining a shape in the air. Literally. Wherever he drew, a black line remained despite the fact that nothing supported it.

It took the young warlock some moments before he recognized the general shape of the drawing. It was definitely a bird, but it had to be one of the largest avians he had ever seen. If real, the creature would have been able to carry them all.

Morgyn finished the outline and then quickly added several details such as eyes and mouth. The last and oddest features were three man-sized seats on the back of the bird. When he was satisfied the bird was complete, Morgyn waved the piece of chalk and muttered in what had to be the elvin tongue.

A brownish mass filled in the drawing. The eyes of the bird blinked. The beak opened and closed, a pinkish tongue momentarily protruding from it. Massive wings were tested and found satisfying. The great condor turned its head and peered at its creator with one of the staring eyes.

All this in less than a minute.

Allanard looked at Cabe. "Well? What are you waiting for, the fuzzy-faced wizard to give you a boost up?"

Somewhat warily, Cabe climbed aboard the back of the bird and sat down in the middle seat, it being the largest of the three. The two wood elves took their places, and Morgyn tapped the condor lightly on the head. The young warlock looked aghast at him.

"Aren't there any reins?"

The elf patted his creation and smiled. "Now, what would we be needing reins for?"

The condor took off. Cabe held on for dear life. It irked him that Morgyn sat up front, only his legs holding him to the soaring bird. He was laughing, and so was Allanard. Both elves were at home with this type of transportation. Cabe would have been more satisfied with a bumpier but easier-to-handle vehicle such as a wagon.

The condor rose higher and higher. Cabe caught himself just as he started to look down. Allanard chuckled.

"You can look down, you can. Won't see nothin' but clouds this high up!" His emphasis of their altitude only wracked Cabe's nerves even more.

Morgyn's voice came from in front. "Heads up! We're goin' straight into a dark one!"

The warlock had only a minute of surprise before the gray cloud was smack in front of them. The condor flew in without a care. Much to Cabe's annoyance, the wood elves laughed heartily as they entered. They had, he decided, a particularly strange sense of humor.

Beads of moisture formed all over him, despite the fact that he was not in the least bit hot. There was an unusual smell in the air. Cabe finally recognized it as the odor left after a spring shower. It was clean and helped ease his nervousness a bit. Seconds later, they departed the rain cloud. All three of them were wet, but his companions were not bothered by it at all. The wind quickly dried them as they moved on.

The longer they traveled, the more accustomed Cabe became to such an odd mode of transportation. He even dared to look down now and then. It was the first of these glances that made him marvel at the speed they were moving.

Lest he lose his grip, he chose to speak to Morgyn rather than Allanard. "Is that the Dagora Forest below us?"

Morgyn looked down only momentarily. "Aye, that's home, right enough! When we've brought you to your destination, brother and I will return here!"

The lush forest, with its masses of greenery and ever-present wildlife, well hid the fact that it was the same forest through which Cabe had faced more than one peril. Somewhere, he knew, the Lady's manor lay.

"We've flown for no more than an hour! That's incredible!"

Allanard's chuckle reached him from behind. "Don't encourage him too much, Cabe Bedlam! You're liable to get us movin' so fast even I won't be able to hold on!"

His brother had turned to face the front once more. The condor increased its speed perceptively. Morgyn let out a quiet laugh.

A dark, green form flew up toward them from the forest. Even from the tremendous distance, Cabe could see that it was at least as huge as the condor. By its color and shape, he knew it had to be a dragon—at this height, most likely an airdrake.

He alerted the elves and pointed at the swiftly rising figure. It was set on an intercept course. Both elves watched it closely but did nothing to prevent a confrontation. Cabe released the hold he had with his left hand and held it, palm forward, in the direction of the airdrake. He was not quite sure what he was about to do, but was now at least confident that he would do something.

Allanard reached around him and swatted down the hand. He whispered in the warlock's ear. "Do nothing!"

The dragon's wings flapped hard as it lifted itself higher and higher. At one point, it let loose with a challenging roar. The condor pointedly ignored it. Cabe wondered if the bird was capable of reacting.

Some fifty yards or so from them, the drake halted. For a full half-minute, it hovered where it was, watching their movement. Then, as if totally uninterested, it tipped its body and dove with horrifying speed back toward the forest. It was out of sight almost instantly.

Cabe looked to his two companions, considering his position as best he could. Morgyn had resumed controlling the bird, but Allanard nodded to him.

"See? One must not be so hasty in proclaiming judgments, one must not."

Wishing he could turn around completely, Cabe twisted himself as much as was possible. "What do you mean? Why did that airdrake fly all the way up here and then depart without attacking?"

"Humans, even such as yourself, live near but not in the Dagora Forest. We live most of our entire lives there. Even still, we know little of our true monarch, the Green Dragon. When he commands, we obey, we do. When he says that you are to pass unharmed, even the strongest of drakes will not disobey."

"The Green Dragon allows us to pass?" Cabe had trouble believing that. Why would one of the Dragon Kings help him?

The elf shook his head. "Do not question good fortune, Cabe Bedlam, do not. More to the point, do not attempt to read the minds of the Dragon Kings. You may find yourself asking who your real friends and foes are."

Whether due to some joke of Morgyn's or some gust of wind, the condor dove abruptly. Cabe was forced to hold on tight. When the bird had leveled once more, the warlock did not resume his conversation with Allanard. He was too busy thinking about what had already been said.

Shade, Darkhorse, the Green Dragon, the Gryphon . . .

Whom did he trust?

Whom did he dare trust?

XV

Out in the midst of the Hell Plains, it was heard for the first time. Warlocks, witches, scholars—all those who dealt with the other realities heard or felt it. Had they been at the stronghold of Azran, they would have seen it in all its horror.

The hordes of the Red Dragon gazed upon it. Gazed upon it and died. Though servants of the dark sorceror died left and right, the firedrakes could not even so much as touch the master. Like the specter of Death, with his mighty scythe reaping steadily, Azran cut through their ranks with the Nameless.

Few dragons escaped, even though the warlock was only one man. With the sword screaming its bloodlust, he appeared here and there, striking opponents before they could even acknowledge his presence. The Nameless pulsated. Azran's face was totally devoid of all humanity. He laughed as he struck again and again.

Only the Red Dragon held his own. Summoning those powers he controlled, his true form swelled to mammoth proportions. A blaze of fire hotter than the core of the world covered all where it was aimed. Azran moved through it easily; he barely even felt the heat.

The lord of the Hell Plains summoned forth the substance of his very land. Though slightly less than his flame in intensity, the magma and steam overwhelmed through sheer abundance and force. The Dragon King cared little whether his clans died with the servants of Azran as long as he finally succeeded in destroying this wizard who was armed with Chaos itself.

The molten rock and earth slowed Azran only temporarily, and that was due mostly to the fact that he was forced to wade through it. The Nameless protected him from the effects, and before long, he was moving freely again. The boiling water from the geysers dampened him only slightly.

His magic failing him, the Red Dragon threw himself into battle. Great yard-long talons raked at the arrogant human; this attack Azran was forced to defend against. His deadly blade deflected the terrible claws, even slicing off the tip of one. No sooner had he fought off one massive paw then the other struck. The warlock was pushed back. Powerful though the Nameless was, it could not completely protect him from his own mortal frailties. Azran did not realize the contradiction this posted; though the source of the sword's power was the warlock himself, it was now much changed from his original intentions.

The crimson firedrake thrust its gaping maw at the momentarily imbalanced human. Azran was only barely able to meet him head-on. The Nameless swung screaming at the Dragon King. The great reptile snapped his head back out of reach, howling at the bloody gash now present along his nostrils. More angered than injured, the Red Dragon rose swiftly into the air, his tremendous bulk disappearing into the clouds with unbelievable speed.

Unperturbed, the black-clad warlock raised himself into the air and pursued his quarry. It mattered not that his stronghold was now in ruins and that most of his servants were either dead or dispersed. All that mattered now was the death of the other. Azran's face was the picture of berserker fury. It was the sword, not the man, who now dictated actions.

It should have been impossible for so huge a form to hide so completely among the clouds overlooking the carnage. Nevertheless, he could not see his adversary. That the Red

Dragon still lurked about was obvious; no Dragon King would run from battle, especially this one. Azran smiled. If hunt he must, hunt he would.

A shadow fell over him. Through its own volition, the Nameless arced upward, cutting deep into the thing above it. With an agonized cry, a drake who had survived the initial battle plummeted to the earth. The warlock grunted; he couldn't have cared less about such a minor creature. It was the ruler of this land he wanted.

Moisture and cool air calmed him down a bit. He became more aware of his precarious position. The dragon was a native of both land and air. Azran, on the other hand, flew occasionally, but was generally more satisfied land-bound. The crimson reptile knew how to move about in this aerial fog; the warlock had to make do with trial and error.

The more he regained control of himself, the more unsure he became. The Nameless, meanwhile, pulsated quietly and kept to itself. Its lack of evident power might have meant a thousand different things.

Silently, deadly, the Red Dragon chose that moment to strike. Its foreclaws were open to clutch, it jaws wide to crush. Azran was taken completely unaware.

The Nameless was not.

With renewed force, the sinister blade jerked its bearer around to confront the beast. Animal fury regained its hold over the sorceror's body. Laughing wildly, Azran flew straight toward the long, pointed fangs of the Dragon King. Neither would turn back now. The time for hiding was over.

Totally under the bewitching spell of his own creation, Azran soared faster and faster with no apparent intention of deviating from his suicidal course. The Red Dragon opened his maw to its limit; there was no way the human would be able to alter direction in time.

His reptilian teeth clamped together as the minute figure disappeared inside. The eyes of the firedrake gleamed with the joy of victory. That gleam was replaced almost immediately by a peculiar glazing, as if the creature were stunned by some thought.

No thought, though, ran through the mind of the Red Dragon unless, perhaps, there was realization of what had happened. The leviathan's body shuddered, only just realizing that it was dead. The hulking form twitched once more and then plunged earthward. As it did so, something burst through the back of the head. It was Azran; the sword had cut its way into and out of the skull. The swiftness of the weapon was such that there had been no time for the victim to react.

Covered with the indescribable remnants of his fallen opponent's skull, the warlock watched the bulky mass disappear below. Elation filled his very being. He had proved himself the master. Even his unlamented father had not succeeded in destroying a Dragon King and preserving his own life. Here Azran stood—or floated—nearly unscathed from a one-on-one fight with the deadliest of creatures.

He corrected that; it was obvious to him that he was now the deadliest.

Azran took in the deep breath of victory—not to mention the smell of his clothes and body in general. He coughed. So much for the sweet smell of success! He shrugged. It was a small price to pay for so satisfying a victory. He would clean himself up soon enough.

In his euphoria, he failed to take any notice of the Nameless itself. The demonic blade pulsated only slightly, yet it seemed to convey a feeling of newfound power. A power that would grow with each victory—

—regardless of who happened to bear it.

"And how arrre we today, sssorceressss?"

She almost expected a long, red ribbon of tongue, forked at the end, to shoot out from his mouth. There was something about Duke Toma that chilled her more than Kyrg or even the Dragon Kings had ever done. He was more the cold, inhuman reptile than any of the other dragons save the unthinking lesser drakes and their cousins. Here, Gwen decided, was what the first Kings had been like—save that Toma, by his birth, could never be one of them.

When she did not answer, the firedrake merely shrugged and smiled.

God! She could not help staring. Even his teeth were far more the sharp fangs of the dragon than his lords' were.

Toma walked slowly around the bubble, forcing his prisoner to try to rotate so as to keep the sinister warrior in view lest he pull some new trick. The dragon man was more than capable of such; his powers were at least as formidable as the Lady's—perhaps greater. Why, then, she asked herself for the hundredth time, had he always remained in the background? It was not like the Dragon Kings to waste a weapon of such potential.

The firedrake paused. As if reading her thoughts—it was highly likely he might be able to, even though Gwen always kept a shield up—Toma spoke.

"Has it occurred to you that a warrior of my . . . shall we say abilities . . . appears satisfied to serve those who are quite obviously his inferiors in power and leadership?"

"I assumed you were a craven coward at heart, like that sadist Kyrg."

The bubble became uncomfortably hot and severely stuffy. Gwen tried out a spell, but received only a headache for her actions. Her breathing became labored.

After watching her suffer for several moments, Toma casually waved a hand in her direction. Air circulation and temperature immediately returned to more tolerable conditions. The witch took in great gulps of fresh air and wiped the sweat from her brow.

This time, Toma did not smile, and the Lady saw that he did in fact have a serpent's tongue. He sat down in the only chair in his tent and poured himself a goblet of bloodred wine. By his slow movements, she knew that he was reminding her of her own thirst, something she had been unable to do anything about since her capture.

"You will avoid any such offensive outbursts in the near future, Lady of the Amber. They could prove quite breathtaking, at the very least." He took a long, teasing sip of the wine.

"You asked me a question. Yes, I have wondered. Why do you obey the Kings? Surely, even Gold is no match for you!"

Pleased by this comment, Toma poured some of the crimson liquid into another goblet. He passed a hand over it, causing it to vanish. Goblet and wine appeared almost immediately in one of Gwen's own hands. She forced herself to show restraint as she drank, lest the firedrake decide to take it from her in sport.

"Quite correctly put, milady! Still, I do not seek to unseat my father yet. His dreams are mine, though he swings from sanity to madness without warning. Only tradition prevents him from naming me as one of the successors. If one thing would unite the other Kings against him, it would be tradition." The duke spat as he spoke the last word; the ground sizzled where he had aimed.

"Surely, with your power—"

He raised a hand. "You are trying to determine the intensity of my abilities. I will tell you, quite freely, that it is insufficient to handle all of the Dragon Kings. That is why I have set about creating the basis for a new leadership!"

At first, the insinuations present in the remark passed over her head. Only after the words were allowed to sink in did she realize who and what she was dealing with. It altered much of what she had come to believe in the short time since her release from her crystal prison. They had all been fools, even the dreaded Kings, and—she felt a slight twinge of satisfaction on this point—the malevolent Azran had fallen so readily into the scheme of things.

"You. You started this chain of events! You've brought this new war upon the Dragonrealms!"

Reptilian eyes gleamed under the menacing dragonhelm that was and was not a part of the firedrake himself. He raised his goblet to her and drank. When he had finished, he smiled. It was more frightening than anything else he could have done.

"Yes! Through my agents, I stirred up several of the Kings. Blue was the easiest, the most pliant. Black was always harping about the Masters, although I must congratulate him for finding your companion, the young Bedlam hatchling. That was an unexpected bonus! It allowed me to twist Brown, who still held the Horned Blade. The fool! Call it foresight, but I knew the outcome of that meeting with the grandson of Nathan. Still, even if the boy had died, I would have played on the possibility that others might exist. I might have even released you, knowing full well that you would immediately set off to revive your legion of magic-users."

Toma's boasts were cut off by the appearance of a thing that was not exactly humanoid but close enough to make it a parody of men. It waited nervously for the duke to acknowledge it. Toma did so, barely nodding his head. The creature shuffled forward on legs that seemed uneven and much too short for the body. It handed its master a small, rolled-up piece of parchment. The item in hand, the firedrake dismissed his servant. Gwen noticed the eagerness of the thing to leave the presence of its lord.

For the first time, Duke Toma frowned in displeasure. He opened the parchment and studied its contents carefully. When that was done, the message was slowly lowered to the table bearing the wine. The firedrake stared into space, his mind temporarily occupied by the revelations he had just read. The Lady leaned forward, trying to scan the words from her magical cell. Whatever discomforted Toma was worth knowing about.

The duke noticed her straining to see the dispatch. He casually knocked it aside and out of her sight.

"Matters of which you can play no part, milady. I will deal with them should they prove troublesome. Now, then, where were we?"

Gwen did not answer him. Her mind was on the message. What had it said? Did it concern Cabe?

Dismissing her attempts to understand what he had read, Toma continued his tale of self-glory. "The Kings suffer from too much tradition. They believe that they and they alone command powers worthy for ruling." A laugh, disturbingly human, for once. "I sat among them, pretended to be one of them, even convinced one he had the power to resurrect his dying kingdom!"

A shapeshifter, too. More and more, the witch did not like what she was hearing. Even the Dragon Kings were confined to two forms. From what Toma was saying, he had taken on a third form as well.

"Does not this particular Dragon King ever suspect?"

"Hardly. The Crystal Dragon has never answered a summoning. Whether the rest of the lands destroy themselves does not concern him. He once told the council that he had duties far more important than bickering with his brethren.

What those duties were, no one has ever learned.'' He shrugged. ''It is unimportant.''

Unexpectantly, he rose. ''I have, up 'til now, supplied most of the conversation. While it has been interesting talking to someone other than ignorant rabble, I really should be receiving more information from you. That, sadly, must wait for a more attractive moment. If you will excuse me?''

Bowing in jest, Toma departed. The Lady watched him leave, curious. Not having been able to read the note, she could not know the concern that had suddenly sprung full-grown in the duke's head. The sphere in which she was imprisoned did not float randomly; spells locked it in one specific location.

Whether the commander of the imperial hordes would return quickly or not was uncertain. Nevertheless, Gwen had to take a chance. She had narrowed down the field quite a bit; somewhere there was a flaw in this spell that was holding her captive. One of the first things Nathan had taught her was that any magic-user could counter a spell merely by knowing where its inherent weak spot was. Even some of the most powerful spells could be canceled by apprentices if they could indentify the location.

Trouble was, the more complex the spell, the more difficult it was to find the weak spot unless one already knew where to look. That was one of the things that had made Nathan Bedlam so powerful; he plotted his spells carefully and made a thorough study of all others.

Her hands touched the bubble only lightly. It required a sensitive touch to find and move the various lines and colors that made up the basic ''physical'' components of the spell. What gestures or words were used did not matter so much. They would help, but she was confident that she could unbind the bubble without them.

Nothing. She lowered her hands to another spot. Still nothing. She shifted first to right, then to left. On the left, she felt a slight stirring. It was not much, but it was a sign. The fault was near.

Gwen wiped the sweat from her brow. She was so near! Pausing to catch her breath, she noticed now the real difference in temperature. Her breathing became labored. Immediately, the sorceress ceased all activity.

Something new was added this time. Slowly but consistently, her own body proved too great a burden to bear. She was forced to the smooth bottom of the bubble, her face pressed against its surface. The weight of several times normal threatened to crush her. Her only chance was to remain motionless.

In a flash, all was normal once more. Slightly sore, the Lady turned to face Duke Toma. He was shaking his head as a teacher would when scolding a troublesome student.

"The next time will be the final time, milady. Not that it would do you much good. While you were . . . lying down, I took the liberty of altering the nature of the bubble spell. I guarantee that you will not have enough free time to find the fault. We will be too busy traveling."

"Traveling? To Penacles?"

The firedrake looked at her, almost convincingly puzzled. "Penacles? Why should I wish to go there? It has nothing I want."

Now it was her turn to show puzzlement. "The libraries! The City of Knowledge . . ."

Toma shook his head. "City of Knowledge! By this time, the Gryphon has no doubt learned just how useful that knowledge really is. I have made a careful study of its past." He rubbed his leathery chin. "Do you know what I discovered? No ruler of Penacles has ever really been able to rely on the libraries themselves! It's all a lie, Lady of the Amber! A great hoax! The emperor, of course, does not believe that, and neither does the Black Dragon, who has always coveted the city. Kyrg, obedient fool that he is, was more than willing to take his forces there and wrestle the place from whoever survives. He expects me to meet him there, but I have already sent a message, changing his orders."

Gwen's eyes narrowed. "In what way?"

"He is to join in the assault on Penacles. Not right away, but soon."

It was what she had thought. Penacles could not possibly withstand the added onslaught of Duke Kyrg's imperial hordes. The firedrake had many faults, but his skill in leadership was near that of Toma himself. She suspected that none of the Black Dragon's commanders could even come close, which was why they had failed up to this point.

Something else struck her. There was always the chance that Kyrg, the master of the Gray Mists, and many of the other firedrakes in charge might be injured or killed. That would do well to cut down Toma's competition.

The dragon warrior waggled a finger at her. The bubble floated toward him without a sound or any means of propulsion. "Come with me."

As if she had a choice, she thought angrily.

The flaps of the tent spread widely apart as the bubble moved through. Once outside, the Lady was shocked to see that most of the firedrake's forces had already prepared for departure. They moved quickly and quietly, their inhuman speed cutting in half the time it would have taken many armies. She watched wagons being loaded and lesser drakes being hitched up. At that point, their new destination became evident. It was, after all, the only city to the north of Mito Pica.

She dared to interrupt Toma as he directed the efforts of his forces. "Why Talak, Duke Toma? Why turn back the way you came?"

The sphere glowed briefly with increased heat. It returned to normal only scant seconds later. The warlord studied her face, read her emotions. "I suppose there is no danger in telling you, since you are hardly in a position to do anything about it. My catalyst has served his purpose; to allow him to live might actually endanger my plans. Therefore, we return to Talak to remedy the situation. Cabe Bedlam will die before his powers are allowed to develop fully. His death will spell the end of any attempts to resurrect the Dragon Masters."

The Lady barely heard his last words. Cabe in Talak! How? Azran would not live so close to civilization. Therefore, as hard as it was to believe, Cabe had either escaped or was stolen from his treacherous father. There was still hope if the former was the truth.

Toma smiled coldly, his eyes gleaming. "I can assume, then, that you will be traveling with us? I should think you would be grateful at this chance to see your lover."

Her face reddened. "He's not my—"

The dragon warrior silenced her with a wave of his hand. "I will not discuss the idiosyncrasies of human behavior. We are ready to leave now. I think you will float slightly behind me, in case I should wish to talk to you."

He purposely turned his back to her. "Rest assured, I have the utmost confidence in my safety."

She did not argue the point.

Toma ordered his humanoid troops to mount up. The rest of his creatures were ordered forward. Those who seemed reluctant quickly felt the lash of the man-shaped firedrakes. Gwen wondered why the lower drakes did not rebel. They outnumbered their masters a hundred to one. She then remembered the duke's own words. The dragons as a whole were caught up in tradition. To turn on their rulers was unthinkable; only the royal factions would dare, but that was evidently something also considered tradition—save where a nonruling firedrake such as Toma was concerned.

It could also be that the dragons did not rebel because they were too stupid to. The witch decided that each notion was equal in validity. Without the Dragon Kings and their minions to steer them, most of the lesser drakes would be no more dangerous than the rogue wyverns and basilisks. Such threats were far easier to crush.

The army moved with amazing speed, considering the makeup of the bulk of its fighting force. Within an hour, the entire column was leaving what once had been the outskirts of Mito Pica. The Lady used this time to view what she could of the dying city.

Toma had based his camp on the eastern portion of the city. Because of this, she had not been able to see much of the actual destruction. The sounds and smells, though, created a vivid picture in her mind. If the bubble had not cut down her powers, she would have used farsight to discover the damage.

What the sorceress saw on departure was enough for her. Blackened buildings still smoked. Walls that had held countless foes back were shattered to dust. Gwen suspected that the warlord had had a major role in that portion of the battle.

She could imagine the faces of the city's spellcasters as their walls crumbled despite their best efforts.

She had assumed that Azran or Gold would be the greatest threat. She had been wrong. At the moment, the witch was now only a few feet away from the real cause.

The lands around the ruins were oddly untouched, save where some beast of war had gone rushing after a hapless victim. Even the nearby villages had remained unaffected. The duke had seen that Mito Pica—only Mito Pica—had fallen. Hadeen's cabin was the only exception she could think of.

The warlord was sending out a message to those who might defy him. Obey and you would live. Disobey—and disobedience in this case was rather loosely defined, she noticed—and you would suffer the consequences. Only a lack of information had saved the small village where Cabe had been raised from joining the city.

The dragon hordes pushed on. Gwen wondered what Talak would do when faced with the situation. Would they attempt to fight, or would they turn on Cabe in the hopes that they would be spared? From what she had gleaned of the ruler, Rennek IV or something, she did not think Nathan's grandson would receive a very courteous welcome.

Behind the swiftly moving forces of Duke Toma, the last smoking embers of Mito Pica burned out.

XVI

"Better eat, Cabe Bedlam, if you wish to keep your strength."

Cabe stared at the green mess in his wooden bowl—the same green mess that he had been fed for the past four days—and poured it slowly on the ground. He was convinced that the grass under the gruel died instantly.

"I'll pass, thank you. I've had more than enough of this . . . this . . . whatever! We've been here long enough! From what we've heard from passerbys, I don't think the Dragon Kings have any allies here."

Allanard swallowed a mouthful of food with great satisfaction. Cabe nearly turned the color of the wood elves' clothing. "The Dragon Kings have allies wherever humans are, if you'll be excusin' me for saying so. You may be the most abundant of the races, but you're also the most varied, you are."

The words brought Cabe's own father to mind. He nodded slowly. "Nevertheless, Darkhorse said to go to Talak. I trust him. Remember, he saved me from Shade."

Morgyn sighed. "The eternal's ways are his own. Mayhap he has some dark deed in mind."

Disgusted, the warlock rose. "You two can make excuses until the end of time, but I'm going in there. Thank you for your assistance in getting me here. I think I'll be okay from here on."

The two elves stood up, their faces the most sober he'd ever seen them. Allanard extended his hand. "Go with our blessings, Cabe Bedlam. It's not that we don't want to help you, but think of our people. We're not the fighters your kind are, we're not. If the Dragon Emperor thinks we actively move against him, there's no doubt that he'll order us crushed like Mito Pica, he will."

"The Green Dragon—"

"—may or may not do as his ruler orders. I'm sorry, I am. We just can't do anything else. As it is, we hope and pray that none of those thick-skinned flying sentries recognized us. Might very well find the hordes breathin' down our necks the moment we touch home."

The other elf also extended his hand. "Good luck, lad. Pleasure Knowin' you and your old man's old man."

Feeling somewhat guilty over his earlier words, Cabe took both proffered hands. "Sorry about what I said. Hope you have a safe journey back."

Allanard smiled grimly. "'Tis not us who have the hardest ride ahead."

Bidding them a final farewell, Cabe turned and headed

directly for the front gate. Behind him, he heard the sound of a large bird taking flight. He did not bother to look back.

Though darkness had fallen more than an hour before, people were still moving through the gate in both directions. Guards routinely checked them as they passed by. It did not appear that they made very thorough examinations.

Following a trader's wagon, he nonchalantly walked up to the first of the soldiers. The man's face nearly made Blane look handsome. Unlike the commander from Zuu, the guard struck Cabe as a rather unsavory sort of person. He decided to wait until he was inside before revealing his identity to anyone.

A hairy paw shoved him in the chest. "Here! Daydreamin' ain't any excuse to pass by inspection! Who are ya and why are ya travelin' empty-handed?"

Cabe became uneasy. He was sure his tale would go well above the soldier's head. If he had carried money, there would have been no problem. The warlock had seen this type several times while working as a serving man. He looked down at his clothes and came up with the only reasonable answer he could think of.

"I was by myself, coming here, when bandits ambushed me. I ran. Six-to-one odds I don't care for. Especially when they have bows." He was thankful that the gem was covered by his shirt. Allanard had suggested that a little magic could remove the article of clothing and replace it, more or less whole, over the crystal. After all, the elf stated, few people wandered around with gems in their chest, and it was more than likely that such a rock would only encourage the greed in many.

The guard nodded. "Yeah, we get that now and then. Be damned if I'm going out there to look for bandits, though. They tried that once. Lost seven men and never even caught one! Worse than wyverns!"

He waved a hand, dismissing Cabe and eyeing the next travelers, which included several young women. Thieves and their victims were dropped from his thoughts completely. The warlock let loose a deep breath and wandered through.

It dawned on him that he might have used his powers to enter the city secretly. Almost immediately, it also dawned on him that he might have ended up sticking out of a wall or landing in a well. For the time being, normal methods would do.

Like most cities, Talak was surrounded by a fairly non-decorative wall. Cabe knew, though, that such walls could prove to be little defense against the Dragon Kings. Penacles was fortunate in that the Purple Dragon, as paranoid as his brethren, had rebuilt the barrier completely. Ironically, it had probably saved the City of Knowledge more than anything else.

While the city itself could not boast such wealth as Mito Pica or Penacles, it still impressed him greatly. Much of this was due to the fact that, being far away from most human cities and too close to the imposing Tyber Mountains, Talak was forced to depend more upon itself. It had, therefore, acquired a style all its own.

Where most cities were filled with spires, Talak was a place of hundreds of ziggurats, ranging from small shops to imposing edifices that seemed like half-grown mountains. Banners flew everywhere, and orderly soldiers, much more professional than those at the gate, kept guard over the population. It would have proved even more awesome had not Cabe known that the firedrakes had come in, demanded, and received tremendous amounts of meat without any argument.

Darkhorse's suggestion to come here was becoming more and more questionable.

The bazaars were shut down for the most part. There was, however, much activity coming from the various taverns and inns that seemed to dominate the first streets one reached on entering the city. Some were quite elegant, and all of them were far beyond the penniless state he was presently in. Involuntarily, one of his hands went into the pouch that he had always carried his few meager coins in.

He blinked. His fingers caressed a coin of some sort. He quickly pulled it out and examined it. The lighting out in the street was not the best, but the glint of gold was quite obvious. That came as a surprise; Cabe could not recall where and when he might have picked up such a piece.

One would be enough to buy him food and a night's lodging, though it would have been nice to have a few more. He shrugged; no sense cutting down his luck. The fact that he had somehow gained a gold coin should be enough satisfaction. Perhaps, he thought, one of the two elves had slipped it in his pouch when he was asleep or occupied.

Cabe chose an inn and took a step toward it. The pouch clinked against his leg. He stopped. A tentative hand reached in, felt the round, metal shapes, and pulled out again as if bitten.

There were at least a dozen coins in there, and he did not doubt for an instant that they were all identical to the one in his hand. This was not the work of the elves. Rather, Cabe's own powers were becoming more and more active, obeying his every thought. He would have to be careful about daydreaming.

The inn he chose was a cut higher than the one he had worked in, even if the customers were not. He sat down and ordered some food and ale from the matronly serving woman. His table was away from most of the crowd, save for four men and two women behind him. Cabe did not bother to pay any attention to them.

The center of the place was brightly lit, and in that area of light was a band of minstrels that played tunes from every major city. As they played, a scantily clad young woman somehow managed to dance erotically, despite whatever the tune was. The warlock suspected that she could have danced without music at all and hardly anyone would have taken notice. As it was, they could barely be heard over the general din of the people.

His food came. Cabe attacked it with gusto. He noticed that it was almost completely vegetarian. The armies of Kyrg and Toma had stripped Talak of most of its meat. The city would probably send the rare trading party to Wenslis or perhaps buy from the farmlands to the west. Despite the absence of meat, however, Cabe found the meal more than satisfying.

Intent as he was on the devouring of his meal, he paid little attention to the increasing weight near his leg. At some point, he pushed the troublesome pouch so that it hung almost behind him. After that, he forgot about it completely.

That was soon remedied. There were shouts and grunts

from the people behind him. Someone bumped him from behind. Cabe turned around to find all six people on the floor, scrambling as best they could to round up the endless shower of coins falling from a tear in his pouch. Cabe had not turned off whatever spell he had inadvertently cast. He quickly fixed that, just by hoping, but the damage was already done.

Without thinking, he reached to retrieve some of the gold. One of the men, a bulky character with a tremendous beard and muscles to match it, looked up. Caught in the act of picking up what was obviously someone else's money, the initial greed gave way to panic. He reached forward, dropping several coins, and pulled Cabe down.

Cabe's chin came within an inch of the floor before it stopped for no particular reason at all. He did not have time to make note of it. The bearded one was trying to hammer him into the ground. Reflexes came into action and the warlock rolled away before the blow fell.

Still distrustful of his wild powers, Cabe decided to run rather than fight. Unfortunately, he had become disoriented, and he moved toward the kneeling figures rather than away. He tripped over the bearded one, who was still clutching his hand in pain, and fell face-first into one of the women, taking her down with him. By this time, others had seen the loose coins. The back half of the place was turning into a free-for-all.

Cabe found his head lying nestled between two soft mounds. He quickly extracted himself from the woman, who seemed more disappointed than hurt. Finding himself a clear spot, he crawled away from the growing mob.

His gaze fell almost immediately on two uniformed legs. The owner was a gigantic figure dressed in the garb of the city's army. The face was akin to a bulldog, and the soldier's attitude was no better. He was also standing in front of a group of several similarly dressed men—the town watch, who had just happened to be nearby.

The soldier literally picked up Cabe, but it was more to move him out of the way than anything else. Turning the hapless young man over to one of the other guards, he commenced a roundup of everyone presently engaged in fighting for the loose coins.

The work was done with quick efficiency. In only a few minutes, nearly all those involved were divided into two groups, one male, the other female. To Cabe's surprise, some of the soldiers in back were not really men; he learned later that Talak's army was about fifty-fifty in terms of men and women. It was actually quite an innovation. He knew of no other land that had even proposed the idea.

All that was forgotten as they were herded out of the inn. Cabe did not think to use his abilities; it was still too easy to think of himself as a normal person. Magic would only draw attention to him, and this close to the Tyber Mountains, that could prove dangerous.

The prisoners were all put into one holding cell. It was, in fact, the only cell in the place. The women had been taken to some other location.

Cabe settled down in the stained hay that covered most of the floor of the cell. If Talak followed the pattern of most cities, they would no doubt be released the next day, providing they could pay or knew where to obtain their fine. When that time came, he would carefully conjure up the exact amount.

Most of the other prisoners had settled down after the arrival of the newcomers. They were a mixed lot, including some particularly nasty-looking characters who appeared capable of every crime ever written up, but no one seemed in the mood to start trouble. Cabe closed his eyes to go to sleep.

"You!" The voice was rough and sounded of a man who had already drunken more than enough.

The warlock lifted his head. It was the bearded fighter, and with him were two of his companions; the fourth man was nowhere to be seen and might have escaped the town watch. These three, though, looked vicious enough without help from the other.

"Stand up!"

He stared at the drunken man. Surely, he wasn't planning on starting a fight here? The answer came swiftly as Beard reached down and pulled Cabe to his feet. It was becoming an annoying habit, the warlock decided.

"We're in here because of you, aren't we?" The last was aimed at his two companions, a short, weasel-faced character and a thin, dark-complexioned thug who had a mustache that drooped down past his shoulders.

"Thaz right," said Weasel. He was as drunk as the first.

Mustache merely nodded, grinned at Cabe murderously, and appeared in no way to be intoxicated. That made him the worst of the threesome.

"Hold him for me!" The bearded man waited until his companions had jumped Cabe from both sides so that he could not escape. Each had an arm pinned.

The burly man pulled back his fist for an all-out blow. He grunted as he swung for Cabe. Due in part to his drunken state, his fist hit his intended victim squarely in the chest.

That turned the grunt into an ear-piercing shriek. Not only had the Talakian used the same hand that had smacked against the floor of the inn, but he had also encountered a hard resistance on impact with Cabe's chest. The crunch that accompanied the scream was not from the gem. Beard had broken his hand this time. The warlock had felt nothing.

The cry was almost immediately answered by the guards. One unlocked the cell door and remained there, his eyes on the prisoners and his hand near his sword. Six others cut a path through to where Weasel and Mustache had hurriedly released their captive.

The captain of the guard looked them over. Cabe's attacker was on his knees, his face contorted into agony. The officer grunted and turned to Cabe.

"You look to be the center of this! What went on here?"

"He tried to j-jump me!" The words poured out quickly from Cabe's would-be assailant.

A boot struck the bearded man in the side, and he toppled over.

"I want an answer from you, I'll ask."

Catching the captain's attention again, Cabe looked him straight in the eyes. "It was my gold that they tried to take at the inn. For some reason, they blame me for their ending up here."

The soldier looked at him suspiciously. "Your gold?"

Cabe switched subjects. "Listen! I've got to see the King! Can you take me there?"

"Sure! Why not?" The captain suddenly smiled, something that did not improve his rather canine appearance.

"Wha—?" The warlock was taken aback. Was it this easy? Just ask?

He could hear more than one mutter of disbelief, and Mustache hissed angrily. The guard captain ordered his men to keep the other prisoners away. He turned back to Cabe.

"Follow me."

Confused but more than happy to escape his fellow inmates, Cabe did as he was told. The other soldiers looked at the commander with obvious curiosity, but no one dared question his actions. Within seconds, he was heading out the building with the captain and four escorts.

"You realize, of course, that I can only introduce you to the Master of Appointments. He'll determine whether you can have an audience with the king or not." He smiled again; it was very blank.

A spell, Cabe realized. He had accidentally placed the soldier under a spell. Eye contact, apparently. Something else to watch out for. If he was not careful, he might shoot off spells left and right without even noticing it.

After a long period of walking, they arrived at the gate of the largest of the ziggurats. This was the palace royal of the kings of Talak. Bright banners flew in the dim light of the Twins. Fanciful demons, imps, et cetera decorated the architecture here and there. An immense flower garden was barely visible to the right. Cabe wondered how the place might look in the daylight.

They were met at the gate by two elaborately dressed knights. One talked with the captain while the other kept an eye on Cabe, the obvious reason for the encounter. The conversation lasted only a minute, at the end of which the knight allowed the four to pass through.

Once inside the palace grounds, Cabe saw the archers and foot soldiers. Again, it was easy to see that the palace was heavily defended, and again, it was also disturbing that neither Toma nor Kyrg had been refused admittance.

They had to stop four times. Each time, the sentry on duty asked their reason for coming. Only the captain's reputation got them through. Cabe was thankful at not having to resort to another spell.

All of this just to see the Master of Appointments. Cabe might not even be allowed to see the king—unless, of course, he made them see his way. Remembering that rulers usually had court wizards or powers of their own, he felt no desire to make himself noticed.

The dog-faced guard leader knocked loudly on a thick, ancient wooden door. There was no sign proclaiming the function of this particular room, but Cabe trusted the knowledge of his guide. Under the circumstances, the man could not really lie.

"Enter." The voice was old and terribly scratchy. It reminded the warlock of an old priest who had passed through the village. Every spare moment had been spent trying to convince the young serving man that the holy man's gods were the only ones worth praying to. It was quite evident that he saw a potential priest in the young worker. Fortunately, guards from Mito Pica came chasing after him. It seemed that he also had a fondness for young males in general.

The door was opened, and the figure hunched behind the incredibly high desk stared down at them. Cadaverous, he picked up a quill with one bony hand and waited like one of the judges of the dead.

The captain spoke up. "Captain Enos Fontaine with one visitor to see the king!"

The Master of Appointments pulled out a pair of seeing lenses attached to one another. These he put over his eyes. Another innovation.

"His name?"

Everyone looked at Cabe. As best he could, Cabe answered him. "Cabe. Cabe . . . Bedlam."

Gray eyebrows arched. Other than that, the Master of Appointments revealed no other emotion. The guards were all muttering to themselves.

"Relation to Nathan Bedlam, the Dragon Master?"

"Uh . . . grandson."

"Indeed." The quill was dipped into ink and then applied to parchment. The Master wrote for several seconds before turning his attention back to the warlock. "What is the purpose of your audience?"

What was his purpose? Did he wish help to attack the Dragon Emperor? No, that was preposterous. What could he say? Darkhorse had told him to go to Talak; he'd said nothing about what to do after reaching the city. Cabe had made the assumption that the ruling powers should be told. Was he wrong?

The Master of Appointments was an incredibly old man who had seen and been involved with more than he had ever mentioned to the kings he had served in one station or another. Cabe's background and silence made him draw conclusions of his own.

He waved his hands at the guards. "You are dismissed! I will handle things from here on! Go!"

They were more than happy to do so. Cabe had scarcely drawn another breath before he found himself alone with this rather enigmatic man.

The official sat up high. "My name is Drayfitt. Once, long ago, I was apprentice to a warlock named Ishmir the Bird Master. That apprenticeship was cut off by the Turning War. Ishmir was convinced by Nathan Bedlam to join the struggle."

Drayfitt, Cabe mused, must have been a powerful apprentice to have survived all these generations.

The old man continued. "If you come seeking aid in a new campaign, I will tell you that you will receive none. Talak is a shell. I have watched it wither under the baleful eye of the Dragon Emperors. I have seen King Rennek reduced to a babbling madman. His son now occupies the throne. Melicard, though, is new to the running of a kingdom. He can ill afford entanglements with a new generation of Dragon Masters."

Cabe thought to say something, then realized he had no idea what.

The Master of Appointments watched him with sad, tired eyes. "This is our home, regardless of the presence of dragons in the Tyber Mountains. If we join in some mad campaign, we will feel the crushing paw."

He held out the parchment he had been writing on. Cabe could make no sense of the writing in the dim light.

"I have here your admittance to see King Melicard. If you wish to meet with him, then I will sign it. If not . . ."

There would be no use in seeing Talak's ruler, Cabe knew. Drayfitt was right. The city had nothing to gain but instant retribution if it was discovered helping the enemies of the Dragon Kings. Mito Pica had been much farther away, yet it had fallen to Toma because it was suspected of being Cabe's home during growth to manhood. How might Talak suffer for aiding him?

He shook his head. "I have no wish to see the king."

Drayfitt crumpled the parchment in his hand. "I will make no mention of your presence in this city. I only ask that you depart as soon as possible."

Cabe nodded. The Master of Appointments summoned the guards back. He turned his attention back to his desk, not glancing up once until Cabe was gone and the door was shut again.

The old man pulled out a tiny statuette, a bird in flight. He stroked it lovingly, sadly, thinking of his teacher, his brother.

Cabe wandered the streets of Talak for more than two hours. The darkness did not bother him. Nor did any of the more inhospitable citizens. His mood was dark, and his powers reflected it. He did not even notice the faint glow from the gem on his chest. It had become such a part of him that he no longer thought of it unless something happened that pointed it out to him.

Why was he here? What did Darkhorse hope to accomplish? He was not even certain whether the ethereal steed still existed in this dimension. Might Shade have been able to cast him out? The creature had claimed that Gwen had the power; Shade was surely at least as strong and skilled.

Tired, irritated, and seemingly eternally confused, Cabe wandered into the nearest inn and asked for a room. Without thinking, he reached into his pouch and pulled out a gold coin. He followed the bowing owner up to a rather dingy and poorly lit room.

When the man had gone, Cabe locked the door and fell onto the bed. At any other time, he would have searched such a bed for lice and bedbugs, so rotten was it. Though it strained under his weight, he merely rolled over and slowly slipped into a troubled sleep in which faces he knew danced just out of his reach. Only one of them was unfamiliar, and yet it really was not.

A face of power, much like his own in features.

Just beyond the horizon, less than a day's journey from Talak, the hordes of Duke Toma made camp.

XVII

They had nowhere to flee, and because of that they perished. The deadliest of warriors, whether male or female. Whether in human form or their natural shape. They died, and few would mourn them, even among their own kind.

The green wave of death stopped only when it reached the borders of the Barren Lands. Within it, the bodies and skeletons of the last of the Brown clans slowly added to the rich new soil. Animal life came quickly, as if magnetically drawn to the lush plant life.

The spell had been cast; the sacrifice, albeit unsuspecting, had been offered up.

The Barren Lands were Barren no longer.

Duke Toma took the lead as his army neared the city. The Lady was forced to ride alongside him, still trapped in the sorcerous bubble. She had accepted defeat where this prison was concerned, but she knew that there would come a time when the warlord released her from it. When that happened, he would pay, and pay dearly.

The firedrake had chosen early daylight for his arrival. He wanted the inhabitants just barely awake and only beginning their daily routine. Always best to catch your prey when it has just become occupied with something, he thought to himself. There was a human analogy about a man caught with one leg in his pants and the other out.

He turned to his captive. "Well, milady, we are nearly at our destination. Does not your heart beat faster at the thought of being so close to your companion?"

"I'd rather it was your heart that beat faster—until it exploded!"

"Such talk! Best that you practice your manners, Lady of the Amber. Such comments can only heat up your present difficulties." Toma raised the temperature of the bubble up just enough for Gwen to start sweating.

She forced herself to smile. "When will you tire of that little parlor trick? I used to use it reheat my meals when I was only an apprentice."

The duke stiffened. Gwen noticed the heat die down almost immediately. Her captor turned forward, his interest in the city increasing quite suddenly. This time, she did not have to force her smile. Toma was not immune to emotion.

As they neared the gate, the Lady was shocked and dismayed to find it opening wide to receive the firedrake. At the very most, she had expected Duke Toma to meet with the ruler of Talak through some intermediary. To enter the city itself, his army free to charge in should there be trouble, showed the power the Dragon Kings had over this city.

During normal periods, the gates would have been open to allow travelers in and out of Talak. Today, people were strangely absent. All movement had come to a halt. No one wanted to even breathe around the reptilian warlord. A single wrong movement could spell death and destruction for all.

The bulk of Toma's inhuman army remained outside of the city walls, much to the relief of the citizens. Only a personal guard, albeit sinister and capable in appearance, followed the duke in. His only other companion was the Lady, who scanned the crowds restlessly for some sign of Cabe. She wanted dearly to see him, but prayed he would not show himself. If he fell into the Dragon Kings' clutches, no hope would remain.

No less than the commanding general of Talak's army rode up to greet the warlord. He saluted sharply, as one would do to one's superior. Toma did not bother to return the salute. He was direct in his desires.

"You will take me to King Melicard immediately. Understood?"

The general, looking very much unlike a soldier at the moment, nodded nervously. "Yes, milord! Please follow me!"

As they resumed movement, Gwen could not resist asking a question. "Melicard is king? What has happened to Rennek IV? I understood he was king of Talak."

There was the faintest of humor in the dragon warrior's voice. "Rennek had the honor of dining with Kyrg before my half-brother made his way to Penacles. I assume that, being human, he was rather unsettled by the way we consume our meals."

It was enough to make even the sorceress pale.

They soon reached the tall ziggurat that was the palace. There was no need for the party to dismount and enter the grounds. Melicard, his features grim and only barely hiding his fear, waited for them outside the gate of his home. A half-dozen guards stood on either side of him, but Gwen doubted that they would be much help against the well-trained killers that made up Toma's protection. For that matter, with his skills, the firedrake did not really need his soldiers. They were there only for show.

"Hail to you, Duke Toma, First Commander of the Imperial Forces of the Dragon Emperor!" Melicard spoke with obvious distaste.

"Hail to you, King Melicard, who is hopefully a stronger man than his father."

The young king was visibly stung by these words. Though tall, athletic, and unquestionably handsome, he was barely into adulthood. Even Cabe seemed more experienced with life than this new ruler. The former prince had obviously led a somewhat sheltered life before his ascension to the throne.

Melicard choked back an angry response. He glanced with interest at Toma's prisoner and then asked the warlord, "What is it you wish of us? We have little in the way of meat at the moment, but we will do our best."

Toma dismissed the idea. "As long as there is one human in Talak, there is always meat. But that is not what I want. No, what I want has to do with my unwilling companion here."

"Who, if I may be so bold as to ask, have I the pleasure of addressing?" The young king had dared to speak to her directly.

"I am Lady Gwendolyn of the Manor. The Lady of the Amber."

The king's eyes widened; he had heard many stories of the enchantress, but he hardly expected to meet her in the flesh.

The warlord went on. "We seek a companion of this lady. He is a warlock. Young. A stranger in this city. His name is Cabe Bedlam. I want him before the end of the day."

It took some time for this to sink in. Melicard had just ascended to the throne. He had watched his father lose to madness, confronted a terrible dragon lord and a beautiful and legendary witch, and was now ordered to located a foreign warlock somewhere in his city before the sun set.

"How am I to find this warlock? Have you a description of him?"

Toma's description of the sorceror revealed only that he could be one of countless males in Talak. The king bit his lip, both because he hated the thought of turning over a fellow human being to the lizard and because he could see no way of locating this Cabe Bedlam before the time limit had expired.

As if reading the young ruler's mind, the duke made a suggestion. "Have your servants spread the order throughout the city. Make sure that no area is left untouched. I believe it is very likely that the one I seek will do your work for you."

Unsure of the logic, but unable to come up with any ideas of his own, Melicard bowed graciously to his inhuman visitor. "It shall be done immediately."

"For your people's sake, I would hope so. They will pay if you fail. I will leave just enough of them in one piece so that they may personally bring their frustrations out on you for having failed them." It was evident that the duke was a student of human psychology.

The king's voice was quivering slightly. "Will there be anything else?"

"Not at the moment. You will clear out one section of your palace for myself and my retinue. You will have meals delivered to those rooms." Toma smiled, showing his sharp, tearing teeth. "That should save you from any unpleasantness our eating habits may reveal."

With almost-evident relief, Melicard excused himself. The warlord turned to his unwilling guest. "I should think that before the day is through, your companion will walk up to the palace gate and turn himself in. Wouldn't you agree?"

She shook her fiery hair. "I think you underestimate his abilities. You may find him more than you can handle."

"My dear Lady of the Amber; I do not care how amazing his abilities are. I have you and this city in my claws. It is his nature that I rely on. It is his inherent goodness that will send him to me. Nothing else."

He turned his attention to his men, thus allowing Gwen to think on what she knew of Cabe. Duke Toma was correct; Cabe would not let any harm come to this city, not after what had happened to Mito Pica and what might be happening to Penacles.

She lowered her eyes in guilt. No doubt the Gryphon believed that she had abandoned his people. From what the Lady knew of the Lochivarites, they would swarm and swarm against the walls of the City of Knowledge until either they were wiped out—highly unlikely—or Penacles fell.

It was against everything Nathan had taught her to leave a people in danger. Nevertheless, she would have done it for him as she had done it for Cabe. For the same reasons, she suddenly realized.

Two things now confounded the Gryphon as he stumbled over a well-decayed tree. One was, of course, the source of the Black Dragon's inexhaustible man-supply. He intended to do something about that, too, providing, of course, that he survived his encounter with the Dragon King. The second item in question dealt with the master of the Gray Mists himself. The mists extended for mile upon mile, even advancing to the lionbird's own city. How, he wondered, was the Black Dragon capable of emitting so much of the mind-twisting fog?

His initial confidence in his idea and the knowledge from the libraries was evaporating. It was unusual for the tomes to ever read straightforward. He should have mistrusted it from the start.

His foot came loose from the bog with a noisy slurp. If anything, Lochivar's countryside had turned even more repulsive and gooey since his last visit. He wished he had wings like the creature whose name he wore. As it was, two small vestigial stumps were all he could lay claim to. Normally, he kept them hidden under his clothing. It was a sore spot with him.

As he took another step, the distant sound of water slapping against solid ground was picked up by his superior hearing. At first he wondered how deep the swamp was, but a much more reasonable idea soon caused him to disregard that line of thought.

Two-plus hours of slow, dragging steps brought him to confirmation of his idea. Somehow he had completely turned away from his original target. The water he heard was that of one of the eastern seas. The Gryphon had wandered all the way to the coast.

At least, he decided, the terrain had improved. Neither his animal nor human aspects cared very much for the quagmire he had just crossed. On solid ground, he could now move quietly and quickly.

There were several dim torchlights out by what he could only assume was the harbor. In the glow they stubbornly emitted despite the mists, he could see three large sailing ships and more than a dozen figures who could have been dragon warriors, Lochivarites, or anything else that even remotely resembled a human. Most were standing guard near the vessels, crafts of unusual configuration, if he saw them properly. Two or three were wandering toward a building away from the docks.

He picked up the footsteps of the guard well before the soldier was in sight. Once again, the advantage was his; by the way the man ignored him, the Gryphon could tell that his own eyesight was better in this soup than that of any of his human adversaries. He crouched low behind a gnarled tree that seemed to be attempting to grow sideways.

The guard paused some four or five feet from the tree and peered uselessly into the mists. The lionbird's eyes narrowed; this was no Lochivarite zombie. The man's actions indicated that even before his unfamiliar uniform became obvious. The sight was both curious and satisfying to the Gryphon. This soldier, he knew, might be taken alive. A Lochivarite would fight until one of them was dead.

In the soldier's hands was a spear that ended in a wicked barbed point. A broadsword hung at his side. The darkness made it impossible to read his face, especially since most of it was covered by some decorated helm. The slow, ungainly movements were important. The guard was tired. That might mean that he would be relieved soon. If so, it made the Gryphon's chances slimmer. Not that he had much choice.

He waited until the guard had turned back. Then, with a graceful leap reminiscent of his feline cousins, the Gryphon was on him.

It was almost more of a shock to him than it was to the soldier. Tired or not, the man had the strength of a bear. Fortunately, the lionbird had one hand over the guard's mouth. He wanted to end this quickly, before he lost that small victory. Yet the soldier had to remain alive.

Hissing into one of the man's ears, the Gryphon whispered, "Desist or I will extend my claws and shred your face!"

He was not sure whether the other would believe him. He might be able to do what he claimed. Then again, the guard might throw him off. When the guard's body relaxed, the Gryphon held back from the temptation to breathe a sigh of relief.

Pulling out the soldier's broadsword, he pushed the point against his prisoner. At the same time, he removed his hand. The guard did not seem inclined to act, though his head did move momentarily to the spear, which had been thrown some distance away in the struggle.

The Gryphon tapped him with the sword. "Turn around."

The prisoner did so. He was a hirsute man and looked more like a bear than the lionbird could have believe. The man muttered something that only faintly sounded like the Lands language used by all. It was coarse and sounded as if a dog had barked it. The word was recognizable, though.

He nodded. "Yes, I'm the Gryphon. As to who you are, that will have to wait. Do you know how far we are from the Black Dragon's lair?"

The man shook his head.

Putting the broadsword's tip to the guard's throat, the Gryphon asked the question again. This time, he received a better response. He was glad the man was so easy to read. The first answer had almost screamed its lack of any truth by way of the soldier's eyes and stiff movements.

He ordered the guard to kneel facing away from him. Taking a length of rope from around his waist, he cut it in two. One half was shaped into a noose. This was placed around the man's neck. The other went around the ankles, allowing the man to walk but not to run. The prisoner was then ordered to stand again.

Continuing to whisper, the Gryphon said, "I leave your hands free only to fool others. They will not see the rope around your legs, not in these mists. Try to yell, run, or fight, though, and I shall snap your neck before the first sound escapes your lips! Don't think for one moment that I don't have the strength to do so! Understood?"

The guard nodded cautiously. Satisfied, the lionbird prodded his captive along. He had debated throwing away the broadsword and using the Horned Blade, which was sheathed at his side, but decided that he did not care to draw undue attention to himself by utilizing the dark sword's powers too soon.

They walked for the space of a nearly an hour. The soldier made no attempt to lead him astray; evidently, he believed everything the Gryphon had said, especially concerning the noose. A good thing. Every word was true.

Three times they had to halt for patrols. These were Lochivarites. They stalked with mad determination through the blinding grayness. Fortunately, the Gryphon's sharp ears heard them just in time. It was more difficult than when he had listened for his captive; the Lochivarites were as silent as the wraiths they so closely resembled.

It dawned on him that the tremendous size of the fanatics' army was probably due to the steady flow of slaves and prisoners from the unknown ships: The uniform of his captive seemed vaguely familiar, but, try as he might, the lionbird could not place it. If there was time, he would question the man. Right now, silence was of the essence.

Visibility was almost nil. The Gryphon rested the tip of his borrowed broadsword on the back of his companion. He knew that the lair of the Black Dragon could only be a short distance away. He also knew that neither of them would find it if the fog got any thicker. Add to that the fact that his prisoner was now starting to cough and his own throat was just beginning to feel scratchy. He was not immune to the Gray Mists after all.

Something large and heavy ran by. From the hiss it let loose, the Gryphon knew he had at last reached his destination. He tugged slightly on the rope encircling his prisoner.

"Turn around," he ordered.

The man crumpled to the ground. Rubbing his hand, the lord of Penacles peered through the mist for a place to hide the unconscious guard. He finally dragged the body over to a large, weed-ridden thicket. The broadsword went in for good measure. From here on, he would have to trust in Azran's little toy.

Whether the enshrouding mists would work to his advantage remained to be seen. He knew that the Lochivarites could move fairly accurately through the fog, and he had little doubt that Black's clans were long accustomed to them as well. They would, however, give him some cover, and that would be all he could really ask for.

His feet moved without sound through the rocky landscape. The Gryphon thanked various deities for the fact that the lairs were on solid ground. It would have proven difficult to sneak up quietly in the swamps.

As he neared the cavern entrance, the dim light coming from six torches was just enough to reveal what awaited him there. A dozen firedrakes in human form sat astride the largest and meanest lesser drakes the lionbird had ever seen. They were constantly sniffing the air, and he gave thanks that the wind was blowing to him. Oddly, the mists continued to float in the direction of Penacles as if the air was calm. The Black Dragon's magic evidently allowed him to control his life-sapping mists.

Undaunted, the Gryphon felt his way to the side of the hill that made up the visible portion of the Black Dragon's home. Making sure that the Horned Blade was securely sheathed, he revealed fully his sharp claws and dug his hands into the rock. His feet found footholds few humans would have been able to use. Slowly at first and then more quickly as he gained confidence, the Gryphon made his way up.

Trying to ignore the thought that he made a very tempting target to anyone who spotted him, he scanned the hill above. The lionbird did not see what he was looking for and forced himself to move on farther. He cursed each second that delayed him, not just for his own sake but for the sakes of those who had chosen him to lead. There could be no failure on his part if the city was to survive.

One hand struck only air, causing the Gryphon to nearly lose his hold completely. Gingerly, he felt around the opening. Its width satisfied him. Caverns as large as the ones used by the Dragon Kings had to have ventilation shafts if air was to be able to circulate. Such a hole was rarely guarded since very few could reach them safely, much less fit inside. Only by twisting and turning would the Gryphon be able to do so. The thought of becoming trapped in the shaft did not faze him in the least. He would not allow it to happen.

Feet first, he lowered himself gently into the gap. The sheath had to be pushed against his leg in order for him to fit. When he was up to his waist, he lifted his arms and slid slowly downward into the heart of the hill.

It was not bad going. Long use had slowly eroded the sides, so that he sometimes even had to grab hold on both sides to prevent himself from falling too swiftly. His worst moment came when the shaft suddenly veered nearly ninety degrees. Only by contorting his body was he able to keep himself from becoming trapped at the turn.

The temperature had risen several degrees. The Gryphon hoped he had not chosen the shaft leading to the hatchery. If he survived the fall toward the magma pit, he would still have to contend with one or more angry dams. It would be a choice of being scalded to death or eaten. Even if he survived, the entire cavern system would be alerted.

Fortune was with him. The shaft ended in a minor chamber

that appeared to have seen little use in many years. The Gryphon estimated himself to be several levels below the surface. He was probably no more than two or three away from the main chamber where the master of the Gray Mists held the Dragon King version of court. The Horned Blade was pulled from its sheath. It pulsated in anticipation. The lionbird resisted a sudden urge to go charging through the tunnels. He would not allow the weapon to warp and dominate his thoughts.

The caverns were amazingly empty of any grayness at all. The lack of a mist did not concern him. If it made him more visible at this point, it did the same to his foes. He also found his strength increasing, but whether that was due to the clean air or the bewitching effect of the sword he carried was something he could not afford the time to think about.

He heard and felt the rumble that was the Black Dragon's voice long before he neared the main chamber. The king was angered. Now and then, there was a prolonged silence, as if someone else were speaking.

There had been no resistance or even any sign of a guard. While the Gryphon knew that the reptilian monarch had thrown the vast bulk of his forces into battle, he also knew the Dragon Kings. Black would never allow himself to be unprotected; he was one of the more paranoid of the tyrants.

Sword ready, the Gryphon stepped quietly toward his destination. The other voices became apparent; men or, like the Dragon Kings, shapeshifters. One could never be sure. As he had assumed, they were arguing. He moved closer to the source and found himself in a small side tunnel that allowed him a good view of events.

Both the men and the horrifying monarch they confronted had their profiles to him. Like the guard, they wore dark, furry armor, their heads covered by fierce wolfhelms. One of the men was speaking.

"I have said all that I may, milord! There will be no more for at least three seasons!"

The ebony leviathan twisted a massive head down to near the speaker's face. Hot, fetid fumes issued forth from both mouth and nostrils. For that matter, the Gryphon realized, smoke had been spouting from the Black Dragon before that.

A hiss. The long tongue slithered out momentarily. "I do not think you understand, D'Shay! Time is of the essence! Given another week, I would crush Penacles and the accursed misfit who rules there!"

D'Shay stroked the tip of his well-styled Vandyke. What features were visible were distinctly foxlike. "While that would greatly please us, I fear that I cannot supply you with the necessary prisoners. The ones you received should have been sufficient."

"Sufficient? You have never tried to bring down the walls of Penacles!" The statement was followed by a swift pulling away of the head in irritation.

"Nevertheless, we provided you with the manpower that you requested. We have yet to receive anything from your end of the bargain."

"When the City of Knowledge is mine, my brother's power will follow! Then, you will receive your landssss, warm-blood!"

"We have fulfilled our part; the rest is up to you."

The massive beast lifted his head to gaze up to the ceiling. He considered before making his next statement. There was what passed for a smile playing on his face. "I wonder . . . could it be that the great Aramites are finding their neighbors stronger than earlier believed?" The head swung down again. "Is that it, D'Shay? Have you come up against resistance to your empire's expansion?"

D'Shay's companion shifted in place uncomfortably, but he himself did not. "They have not seen their way to joining us, I must admit, but they are running out of time even quicker than you are. Within a year, we will have pushed them into the northern seas."

"I cannot wait a year!" It seemed as if the Black Dragon were about to crush his guests, but he held back. D'Shay ignored the display, if not the words.

"We have done what we could, milord. The rest is up to you."

"What of your sorcerors?"

"They cannot be spared. Nor can any of our troops."

The master of the Gray Mists spread his wings wide and lashed his tail back and forth. His eyes glittered angrily as he attempted to control his fury. "Then go! I shall crush Penacles without your assistance! Fear not; when I am done, you shall have your lands!"

The dark-clad speaker bowed. "That is all we need know. May I assume, then, that our conversation is at an end?"

"Pfah! What do you think, warm-blood?"

D'Shay nodded to his companion, and the two turned and walked out without ceremony. The Black Dragon watched them disappear, rage only barely held back. The mists continued to rise from his mouth and nostrils. A small jewel, dark blue and shining, was strapped to the mountrous neck.

There would be nó time better than now, the Gryphon realized. To wait any longer would only invite disaster. The Horned Blade throbbing, he leaped for the huge form of the Dragon King—

—and found himself held fast by some invisible web.

The airdrake turned his head slowly and confidently toward his prisoner. "I knew you would come! I did not know when, but I knew you would come! I have you!"

What a fool I am, the Gryphon cursed inwardly. Small wonder he had so few guards.

The entire bulk of the Dragon King's body filled the space before him. The lionbird hung helplessly in nothing, the deadly sword pulsating madly in his hand. Black laughed at him.

"I should summon back D'Shay! The pleasure of your death would no doubt give him incentive to replenish my thinning ranks! Then again, with your destruction, Penacles will fall for certain!"

The gaping maw moved toward him. In desperation, the Gryphon added all his will to that of the Horned Blade. It had tasted the blood of one Dragon King and thirsted for more. It would not be denied.

Arm and sword came free just before the jaws reached him. The blade sliced through the air. There was a harsh, guttural scream from the Black Dragon. The gigantic airdrake pulled back, red liquid dripping from within the mouth. The triumph and hate in his eyes had been replaced by a new emotion—fear. The Black Dragon backed away as his would-be victim freed himself and then stalked before him.

The Gray Mists had ceased to form. The Gryphon suspected that his cut had gone deep and that the blood was pouring into the beast himself. A monstrous hacking verified his notion. The Dragon King was in danger of drowning in his own life fluids.

The lord of Penacles knew better than to allow his admiration of the blade to get the better of him. To do so might very well put him under the weapon's entrancing powers. Besides, it had yet to prove that it could complete the task.

The reptile was still coughing up blood. The Gryphon caught sight of a huge gash in the back of the airdrake's mouth. The Horned Blade had cut without touching; its physical reach would not have been sufficient. Azran had been no fool. The warlock had found a way to fight without endangering himself more than necessary.

Still, the weapon had a way of overcoming such safety precautions. He did not doubt that it might try to pull him into the fray just for its own bloodlusting sake. Demon swords were known for that tendency.

The Black Dragon was only just recovering. The Gray Mists were strangely absent. At the drake's feet lay the shattered fragments of the jewel. The Gryphon came up with a number of quick hypotheses.

Several figures arrived from various entrances to the chamber. Among those first in were the mysterious D'Shay and his silent companion. The others were guards, both human and otherwise. The Gryphon was both irritated by their presence and eager to have more targets to strike out at. The latter thought was suppressed quickly as it smelled of the Horned Blade's desires.

D'Shay pulled out a menacing zweihander from what was definitely nowhere and was shouting out the lionbird's name along with a number of words that made little or no sense. His partner had out an equally deadly battle-ax. Soldiers and creatures filled every nearby exit. The Gryphon had lost any chance of escape, but he was determined to make his remaining moments count. Ignoring the others, he charged for the rising bulk of the Dragon King.

The screams and shouts that filled the room at that point were for the most part ignored by the Gryphon, as he assumed them to be concerning him. He did not hear the sound of steel cutting into stone, nor could he hear the roaring laugh until it finally managed to cut through his raging mind.

Between the two foes came a flash of ebony, a glimpse of the void. It wore the form of a horse, but it was easily much more. Both fell back from it, but only the Gryphon recognized it immediately for what it was. That made him back up even farther.

The ice-blue eyes targeted on him. "My Lord Gryphon! You are the one I seek!"

With that, the dark steed charged him.

"No!" He raised the sword to defend himself, uselessly, he knew, but the Horned Blade was still, cold. There was not even time to run as the specter touched him, pulling him—elsewhere.

Mocking laughter bid the inhabitants of the caverns goodbye. Through a portal that did not really exist, Darkhorse departed, returning once more to the Void.

XVIII

Light poked through the cracks of the shutter that covered the one window in Cabe's room. How long into the day it was, he could not say. His body still ached, and the only reason Cabe was awake now was the racket that echoed in his ears.

Someone was arguing outside the door.

Feeling oddly detached from everything, Cabe rose. He blinked, momentarily befuddled by the rather palatial settings that had only been there since shortly after his falling off into slumber. The original furniture, including the shoddy, motheaten bed, were gone.

As consciousness overwhelmed the last vestiges of sleep, Cabe smiled, for he remembered now—remembered everything. That he was not the same Cabe who had gone to sleep the night before did not occur to him. It was all natural to him now, even the reason for its being. The gem, once embedded in his chest, now lay on the plush blue carpet, shining like so much everyday quartz.

He picked up the gem and stared at it, thinking to himself how little Shade had truly understood what he was doing. The gem had served its purpose, unleashing the power that lay within, but not in the way the dark warlock had expected it. It had served as a focus, or perhaps a catalyst, for the power's own purpose, not Shade's. The deadly mage could not truly be blamed; how was he to know that Cabe's secret had a mind of its own?

Cabe let the crystal slip from his hand.

Memories of a time long past overlapped memories of the last few weeks. Cabe, the look on his face that of someone entirely different, muttered, "Azran!" and "Gwen!"

The door shook as something heavy rammed against it. The memories faded to the background. The altered Cabe made his way to the doorway and reached for the handle.

He opened the door and found himself facing six or seven men, the owner of the establishment among them. It took them several seconds to realize the door was open and even more to recover from the shock.

"Grab him!" The words rushed out from the owner.

To Cabe, the scene bordered on the hilarious. In their eagerness to jump him, the group acted as one. Unfortunately, the doorway was wide enough for only a single person. The two largest in the party became jammed and could not back out due to the zeal of their companions. After much struggling, they fell through, missing Cabe, who had wisely backed away. The rest of the party, save the man in the rear, tripped over the first ones.

Cabe watched with amusement as his would-be assaulters struggled to rise, each causing his companions to lose their footing. The single standing attacker pulled out a long dagger and tried to leap over his comrades. He succeeded, but a glance from the warlock kept him floating helplessly in the air.

With the one man under control, the young warlock turned

his attention to the others. He pinned each of them to the walls of his room and picked out the most fear-stricken of the bunch. The ruffian's face went pale as he was pulled close for questioning.

"Why have you attacked me? I did nothing."

Some small portion of courage returned to the hapless attacker. "Nothing? By Hestia, you've brought the wrath of the Dragon Kings down upon us!"

The quiet humor that had been an integral part of the new Cabe disappeared for the moment. "What do you mean?"

"That lizard, Duke Toma, says that he'll tear apart the city if you aren't handed over today!"

The mention of the warlord's name darkened even more the expression on the warlock's face. "I thought Toma was headed for Penacles. Why come here?"

"He says he wants you!" the man replied uselessly.

"And you thought to help me on my way there? Kind of you."

"What else could we do?"

Cabe nodded, remembering the Minister of Appointments' words. He could not blame them, not really. They had always lived under the fear the Dragon Emperor. Besides, what was one man where the life of an entire city was concerned?

Smiling grimly, he cautiously released his captives. They eyed him but did not move against him.

"Forget this ever happened. You can even share that"—He used a thumb to indicate the gem—"among the lot of you. I have no more use for it."

Without another word, he stepped toward the open doorway. Those standing closest to it gave him plenty of room. No one tried to jump him from behind, useless as that would have been. By the time he had departed the inn, his sense of humor had returned.

A few citizens watched him, but Cabe pushed aside all thoughts of action from their minds. He did not want any delays, not now, not after coming to grips with the reality of his situation. Not with the Dragon Kings threatening the lives of all.

As he strode purposely toward the front gate of the city, word of his approach spread ahead of him. By his manner and appearance, there could be no doubt of who he was. It was therefore not surprising when he was confronted by Talak's new king and several guards, all on horseback.

Melicard nodded. "Greetings to you, stranger. I take it that you are the warlock that scaly abomination desires?"

"I am Cabe Bedlam, yes."

The king studied the head of silver hair. "What a powerful sorceror you must be, Master Bedlam. Powerful enough to slay an army of shapeshifting vermin, I think."

Cabe gave him the ghost of a smile. "Perhaps. What do you want with me, my liege?"

"I wish to see those creatures dead! Kyrg is far away, but his master awaits your presence. The city will pay if you do not show!"

The warlock resumed walking. "Then I'd best be going."

Melicard maneuvered his steed in an effort to block Cabe's path. "Go? Will you attack them? Shall I summon my troops?"

Without pausing, Cabe stared the horse down. It moved away, trying to avoid his gaze. "No. It would only bring you the same fate it brought Pagras in the Turning War."

The king paused, his schooling bringing forth the meaning of the warlock's comment. Pagras lay to the east of of Talak. A strong, proud sister of his own kingdom, it had been reduced to ruins that had never been reinhabited save by wild animals.

"What will you do?"

"Give myself up."

Face reddening, the monarch practically screamed. "Give up! Are you a coward?"

Cabe did not look back. "I'm no fool, if that's what you mean, my liege."

Melicard made to follow, but his steed did not move. Not that it had no such desire, but because it could not make any headway. It was as if rider and mount had run up against a brick wall. He turned to his men. They were sitting on their horses, watching him. He became furious.

"Don't sit there gaping! After him!"

The commander hesitated before answering. "We—we have tried, my lord! Neither our animals nor we ourselves can move to aid you or catch the warlock!"

The young ruler slumped in his saddle. All the aggression had gone out of him. He sighed. It had been so much simpler when he'd merely been a prince. At least then he had not had to contend with sorcerors and dragon warriors.

Duke Toma found the palace irritating. It was too civilized, too elegant. The warlord was a born warrior and a powerful necromancer. His own caves reflected this. The heads of foes and animals decorated the walls. His personal laboratory took up nearly half of his dwellings. Here, much of the scenery consisted of paintings and sculptures and rich, varied furnishings. Only an occasional statue or suit of armor interested him for even the briefest of times. Even the fine meal he had just finished had failed to relax him. It was almost a waste of a superb, freshly killed ox. For all he remembered of it, it might as well have been cooked or something.

He pondered his adversary's movements. Nathan's grandwhelp had proven to be the fool in the deck, and those who played the games properly knew that the fool was no fool. It could topple opponents with even the strongest of positions. If only that cursed warlock, Shade, had not interfered. Whether good or evil in nature, the sorceror had clouded up Toma's knowledge of the young warlock for reasons of his own. Reasons that apparently had little to do with the situation in hand.

Finding himself near the ballroom where he had been forced to leave the enchantress—the sphere would not fit through the hallways, and he had had no desire to remove the spell—Toma opened the door and entered.

The Lady was sitting quietly in the bubble. Such a scene did not lull the firedrake into complacency. He knew that her mind, if not her body, had been working on the forces that held the spell together. He increased the temperature abruptly by several degrees and watched with sadistic pleasure as she shifted here and there in a futile attempt to escape being burned. When she had twisted around for several seconds, he returned the sphere to normal.

She glared at him. "One day you will suffer tenfold for that, oo—duke!"

The enchantress had stopped just short of calling him by the name of one of his very distant cousins, a swamp-dweller that built its den from its own excrement. Duke Toma smiled his cold smile as he nodded like an instructor pleased to see his pupil learn.

"If that word had escaped your lips, milady, the heat would have gone up much higher. I would not have killed you, as you have hostage value to me, but your suffering would have been greatly prolonged."

"How much longer must I live in this thing?"

"That depends on your companion. He has not revealed himself as yet. I'm more than half tempted to raze this city now."

"He might not be here. Have you thought of that?"

Toma bared his predator's teeth. "You and I both know he is in the general vicinity, milady. We are too well trained not to feel him, especially with the power he carries."

She smiled. "Knowing his power, you still think to stop him?"

"He is unskilled. Most of what he knows is only the instinctive part of sorcery. It will not save him when he is brought before the emperor."

A horn sounded. Toma hurried to the window and peered outside. Gwen wished dearly that she could push the rest of him through. The warlord pulled away from the window and turned back to his prisoner.

"Your companion has arrived! Come! I want you to be there to greet him!" He rushed out of the room. The Lady's spherical cell flew off after him, throwing its unwilling inhabitant against one of the sides. The enchantress muttered words normally reserved for use by the more unsavory elements of the city.

The duke swept past his aides, who had come to tell him the news. One was nearly bowled over by the bubble, something that gave Gwen at least momentary satisfaction. Moments after, both warlord and captive were outside the palace.

The object of everyone's attention was just entering the gate. Clad in a dark blue garment of perfect fit, his silver hair seeming to gleam, Cabe walked quietly toward the dragon warriors.

Toma frowned and muttered something the Lady could not hear. She could feel the pull of the darker part of the spectrum as the warlord made use of it. A slight reddish glow surrounded the firedrake commander.

"You will halt right there, Bedlam!"

Cabe stopped. He looked closely at the warlord's captive, shock and concern flashing across his features. Toma regained his confidence.

"Yessss, human! I have your female! A wiser move on my part than I imagined, now that I sssee you again!"

The young warlock barely contained himself. "You have me! Let her go!"

"I don't think so. Her presence assures me of your good behavior during our trip!"

"Trip? Where are we supposed to be going?"

The duke smiled, flashing his white, pointed teeth in dramatic triumph. "Where? Why, to the Tyber Mountains, of course! We mean to see an end to the line of Bedlam!"

"Aren't you forgetting my father?"

"Azran is the type to sit, trying to hatch insane plots. He will be little trouble as far as my plans are concerned."

This brought curiosity. "Your plans?"

"As I have already told your companion, much of the events of the recent past are due to my efforts." The tone was far from modest.

Cabe nodded. "I see. The misfit would be ruler. That explains much of the infighting of the Dragon Kings."

An almost human look of pleasure passed over Toma's face. "You grasp quite quickly! I instigated Brown and the others, either from behind the scenes or in the form of the Crystal Dragon." Pleasure gave way to mistrust. "You seem far more intelligent and informed than my spies indicated. Glad I am that I sought you out now other than later." To an aide he said, "Ready our mounts!"

The two eyed one another. "Am I to walk, Duke Toma? I have no horse."

"Much as I like that idea, I fear it would delay things far too much. I believe in speed foremost."

Uttering in a language long unused by any but those who trafficked in the arts, the warlord pointed at his adversary. A bubble like that holding Gwen surrounded Cabe, who studied it but said nothing.

"That is how you will travel to the halls of the emperor! You may discover from the Lady the advantages and disadvantages of this mode. I suggest you heed the disadvantages with more care than she has." Toma waved a hand, causing Cabe's globe to fly over to float next to the other.

The duke eyed them both. "An odd pair of paperweights. One of a kind, I'd imagine."

Toma turned his attention to organizing for departure. Gwen chose that moment to speak to Cabe, but he quieted her with a finger to his lips and a shake of his head. She looked on in confusion, wondering how he, being untrained, could take command. Cabe said nothing but made a signal to her before turning back to watch the dragon warriors act.

The signal did not reassure her. Rather, it only confused her further. She understood its meaning but not its origin. Only two people in the recent past had ever known that particular sign language. She was one, having studied it in a rotting old tome many, many years before. The other was the owner of that book, the man, the teacher, the lover. Only Nathan, who had recovered the tome from its centuries-old resting place, would have known the signal.

Preparations for leaving Talak did not require much time. The bulk of the army still waited outside the city and had not bothered to settle down yet. Duke Toma's retinue carried little in the way of supplies and equipment. Thus it was that the party neared the front gate only a half an hour after the confrontation.

The warlord looked around as he departed the city. "It seems that Melicard will not be seeing us off. Curious."

At mention of the young king, Cabe's head snapped up and his eyes closed momentarily. Gwen recognized his actions but pretended not to notice, though her puzzlement had increased. She dared a glance at Toma, hoping his mind and eyes were on other matters. Fortunately for both humans, he had already dropped the thought and was now concerned with moving his forces.

The massive bulk that was the dragon forces began to move, slowly at first, then picking up speed as the seconds passed. The duke, his retinue, and the two humans took their places at the front of the great column. Citizens of Talak lined the walls to watch them depart. Cabe glanced at the throngs and thought he could pick out Melicard. He could not see the young king's face, but he was fairly certain of his feelings.

Already the Tyber Mountains loomed overhead like so many titans of legend. Higher than the rest, Kivan Grath stood proud over his subjects and almost seemed to dare the puny creatures who would enter his domain. The closer the column came to the mountain range, the more imposing the Seeker of Gods appeared.

There were no animals along the path leading into the mountains, though Cabe spotted what looked to be the skull of a horse at one point. A few creatures flew lazily overhead, but their skins were leathery, marking them as servants and distant relations of the firedrakes.

No one spoke along the way. Toma was too deep in self-glorification; he was basking in the praise he believed his father would give him. There would be little opposition to his becoming one of the Dragon Kings, especially with most of the others dead. Once a King, he could openly restructure the empire so as to ensure its supremacy over the warm-bloods for millennia to come.

Lady Gwen watched the vanishing distance with much trepidation. To her mind, this was the stuff of nightmares. Here was a place she had known from her childhood as a bastion of evil, a land unfit for men. Her training under Nathan had not changed her image of the range; rather, it defined the form of the evil. She looked to Cabe for some reassurance, as she had his grandfather so many years ago, but he was absorbed in the study of his sphere and had his face away from her. She remained quiet, not wishing to accidentally catch the reptilian warlord's attention.

The sphere, Cabe had discovered, was a complex creation that constantly altered its general design. He suspected that his was far more advanced than that holding the Lady, since it seemed that the duke was more worried about his presence than that of the enchantress. Nevertheless, it was not difficult to identify the pattern of the changes. Cabe did not think for one minute that another magic-user would have been unable to do this, especially so quickly. All that concerned him was being able to escape in a hurry should the action prove necessary.

Satisfied that leaving would prove simple, he leaned against the side of the bubble and, much to Gwen's shock, closed his eyes. It would be best right now if he conserved his strength. Despite his new feelings of confidence in his abilities, the warlock knew that entering into the emperor's lair was even more dangerous than falling into a pit of venomous serpents while unconscious. He had no desire to arrive in anything other than peak condition. Fortunately, the sphere seemed to negate both hunger and thirst, so this would not be a problem.

Kivan Grath loomed far, far over their heads.

Because of the massive size of the army and the fact that its route was mostly upward, passage through the mountain range would take several hours. Gwen shivered, but not from the cold. She could feel as well as see the colors of the powers that dwelt here. She also sensed other forces, lesser, equal, and greater than those she knew, whether dark or light. They were older, far older, and filled with the touch of beings neither men nor dragon nor any creature she had ever encountered. Some emitted an indifference to all around them, while others felt almost benevolent. These the witch tried to contact, but with no result. Communication with such as these was beyond her.

It was probably fortunate, she decided. For there were also powers perverse in nature. Powers that seemed to want to crawl into her mind and twist her to their wills. She shunned away from any mental contact with these. A few probed, but apparently they lacked the strength to do anything else.

She noted that neither Toma nor Cabe appeared disturbed in the least by these specters of the ages. Cabe, though, had no reason for remaining so calm. The Lady knew from experience that apprentices and untrained magic-users were far more open to contact than those who had learned to shut their minds from intrusion. Yet her companion slept as if he were in his own bed. She grudgingly tacked it on as one more mystery about Nathan's grandson. She would live long enough, she hoped, to solve some of those mysteries.

But it was turning out to be all for naught, she realized. When first freed from the amber prison, Gwen had believed that this would be her chance to live up to Nathan's dreams and deliver the lands from the Dragon Kings. She had met Cabe and saw in him the beginnings of a warlock at least as powerful as her lover. Yet with the addition of Darkhorse, the Gryphon, and, yes, even Shade, the enchantress had come to believe in the realization of everything the Dragon Masters had planned.

Her face darkened. Once again, it was Azran who had destroyed the hopes of men. They could have held against the fanatics of Lochivar with their combined strength, even minus the enigmatic but tremendous powers of Shade. Azran, though, in his petty quest for domination over men and dragons, had kidnapped Cabe for reasons she still could not discern. It could not have been for fatherly concern; of that she was certain.

Neither she nor anyone at the front of the column noticed the single figure rushing through the air at a madman's speed. The intruder was coming up directly behind them, the tail of the army only scant minutes away from him. He seemed not the least bit worried about the tremendous size of the forces below. If anything, his pace increased.

A single scout, flying up for a routine check, spotted the figure. Curious and completely confident that no threat could exist in the Tyber Mountains, it flapped its leather wings and moved in for a closer scan.

At recognition, the scout gave out a startled squawk, but it was far too late. Grinning evilly and totally under the spell of his sword, Azran slashed at the air. Though far, far out of reach of the Nameless, the airdrake twitched and plummeted limply down the long distance toward the ground, a great gash across its throat.

Though the blood and lives of countless creatures had already been tasted by the warlock's devilish blade, it was not sated. Rather, its craving increased, and as it did, the hold over Azran solidified. The long, twisting, crowded column presented a target that could not be denied.

Azran dove, sword outthrust for assault against the hordes of the Dragon Emperor.

A cry rose up from the back end of the army. Duke Toma

and the Lady whirled around. Cabe was startled out of his slumber.

Gwen was the first to recognize the wielder of the sword, and nearly spat out the name. "Azran!"

Toma turned his beast so that he was facing the action, and glared. "Most of those in the rear are earth-bound or too stupid! They are also much too close together!" He stared at the marauding warlock intently. "Still, I did not think Azran would dare something such as this! I wonder . . ."

The whisper was only loud enough for Gwen to hear. "The sword! He's created another sword!"

She looked at Cabe, looked back at the berserker diving up and around and through the ranks of the Duke's army, and nodded. Even here, she could feel its malignant presence.

The warlord had come to the same conclusion. There was a frightening gleam in his burning red eyes as he watched. He had seen the Horned Blade, but Brown would allow no one else to touch it. Some of the other Kings had suspected that the lord of the Barren Lands was not totally himself. This did not bother Toma in the slightest. He considered the others much weaker than himself. If he could not have the one sword, then he would have this other one.

He could not rely on his forces; of that the duke was certain. Already, many were in panic. Other than the ruling members, there were few competent sorcerors among the intelligent clans. Thinking of that, Toma recalled that Red had gone out after the warlock. Evidently, the ranks of the Dragon Kings were now more depleted than ever before.

Glancing at his captives, the warlord ordered the two spheres to journey on. His father would see to their disposal and add more praise only when Toma showed him the new prize. With the enchanted blade, the duke's right to rule could not be challenged by any of the surviving kings.

The sudden flight of their bubblelike cells threw both magic-users wildly around. Gwen regained her balance first and looked to see how her companion was doing. Cabe rolled for a few seconds longer and then lay still, one hand on his head. He grinned at her. She could see little humor in their situation and let him know it without speaking.

To her surprise, he continued to smile and pointed up as if telling her to wait. The Lady watched him cautiously. This was not the man she had come to know; this was a completely different person, and one with so many alarmingly familiar expressions.

He caused all movement to cease, astounding her with his seemingly experienced control. The two spheres came to a halt, out of sight of Toma, but much too close to their intended destination. Cabe then placed his left hand on the inner surface of his own bubble and slowly ran it over the surface. Abruptly, he reached out with his right and touched another area, totally away from his original choice. With a slight hiss, the prison floated to the ground. As it landed, the entire sphere evaporated.

Cabe repeated the process with Gwen's cell, the time to do so twice as long since he was forced to walk around it and then had to rediscover its exact weak point. When the bubble had dissolved, the two dropped into each other's arms without thinking and remained that way for several moments.

With some awkwardness, he finally broke the embrace. "We have to move on."

They looked at their surroundings. The land dropped off quite abruptly in front of them. Though dwarfed by the nearby Kivan Grath, the mountain on which their ledge was located was still a leviathan in its own right. The ground below was a bleak and disquieting place, uninhabited by anything larger than a few pale-green bushes and one or two twisted firs. The mountainside was little better. The Tyber Mountains were as inhospitable as those who dwelled in them.

Gwen had lost all sense of direction. "How do we find our way out of here?"

"We don't. We have to go into the caverns inside Kivan Grath."

She went pale. "Into— Yes, you're right. We may never have another chance."

"It's not as bad as all that. If the Gold Dragon is expecting us, he'll be expecting us as prisoners, not free and willing fighters."

That relieved her. It also made her think. "Yes, that reminds me. How did you free us?" Her gaze demanded an answer.

Cabe shifted uncomfortably. "I'll explain later. I don't dare upset the balance between me now."

"What?"

He turned to face the Seeker of Gods. "We'd best get moving if we want to keep the element of surprise."

"Hold it! You mean you're going in there—" The Lady stopped short as Cabe turned away and marched on toward the lair of the Dragon Emperor. Furious, she hurried after him, praying to her patron goddess that she would give all the aid she was capable of giving—

—and doubting that it would be enough.

XIX

The city of Penacles was cautiously hopeful. The Gray Mists had thinned, enough so that sunlight easily cut through. Scouts were reporting great unrest among the remaining legions from Lochivar, and many of the fanatics were visibly exhausted, having been running on their addiction alone. To most of the citizenry, it meant victory.

To Blane, it meant that the worst was yet to come.

"What do you think?"

His words were directed at General Toos. The general, his foxlike features in profile, watched the enemy forces through his seeing lens. "I think that they are trying to organize for an attack. Every minute that they delay saps their strength and restores ours. Also, if they move swiftly, they might hope to catch the city while it still relaxes."

Blane nodded. "I've ordered all the men to stay alert for one more massive encounter. I think they'll be ready."

"They'd better be." Toos put down the seeing lens and looked squarely at his co-commander. "The Lochivarites are moving even now."

"Damn!"

"Indeed."

Blane was about to return to his soldiers when Toos stopped him with a raised hand. The general took up his lens again and turned so that he was facing more northerly. His attention became fixed on the large mass that had not moved since its arrival several days before.

It was moving now.

"Summon all able men—and women—Commander Blane."

"Why? What is it?"

"The sadist Kyrg is moving his inhuman army against us. Apparently, all the waiting is over. This is to be the final assault!"

Horns were already being sounded on all walls save the southern. The city returned to its deathly quiet, that most terrible sound of any war, in the expectation of horror.

Both commanders had gone to rejoin their men. Toos would be confronting the greater number, but Blane would be facing fresh, battle-hungry troops with a hatred for all that was human. His would be the near-impossible task. Fewer men lined the northern and western walls because the brunt of the attacks had always been on the eastern side. No doubt that was one of the reasons Kyrg was attacking now.

It might be that they knew the Gryphon was away. For all their abilities, neither commander could inspire the army the way the city's ruler could. The Gryphon had a force of spirit about him.

As one, the invading forces spread relentlessly toward Penacles. To the defenders, the tide seemed as endless as in the beginning. The landscape was covered by moving forms.

The frontmost Lochivarites came into range. Archers let fly with arrows, the air filling with a deadly rain as they did so. The first blow had been struck by the city, but the enemy would soon answer with violence of their own.

The shadowy form of what might have been a great ink-black steed materialized at the abrupt edge dividing the Legar Peninsula and what was once the Barren Lands, its eyes scanning the terrain for signs of unwanted strangers. Satisfied that all was safe and secure, Darkhorse raised his head and let loose with a roar that could never have come from a true animal.

From that which contained his essence and was also contained by him, a small speck appeared. It grew larger and larger, like a rash spreading over the creature's side. When it was large enough, it fell out rather than off of the steed and dropped to the ground with a fierce and angry grunt.

The Gryphon scrambled to his feet, the enchanted sword ready in one hand. He growled as any large cat might, save that it ended in a rather birdlike squawk. The Horned Blade went out before him as warning to the eternal.

If Darkhorse had been capable of rolling his eyes, it would have matched the tone of his stentorian voice quite well. "Please! I did not bring you here so that you could uselessly attempt to skewer me! Time is running out for all of us!"

Still cautious, the Gryphon lowered the blade only slightly. "What are you talking about, demon? Why have you taken me from what must be done to save my people?"

"Demon? Why— Never mind! I have need of your assistance! You and the sword, that is!"

"To what end?"

Darkhorse snorted in annoyance. "Ours—or at least yours, if I can't convince you! Only with your help can I banish Shade!"

"Banish Sh— He's alive?"

"As far as those terms can be used with one such as he! No longer does he go by the name Simon! Call him Madrac and place much of the emphasis on the first half of his new title!"

The tip of the sword went down, not without some objection from the weapon itself. "I feared as much. When we could find no trace after his battle with the Seeker, I was sure the worst had happened!"

"Well should you fear! This Madrac is the quickest and the strongest incarnation I have seen since knowing the warlock! I was barely able to contain him, and I do not know how much longer I can hold him! He remembers nearly all of his past lives, especially that concerning Cabe! If I had not broken free from the trap he set for me upon his reincarnation, the young warlock would have been used as a power source to free him from his curse!''

The Gryphon finally nodded. ''Better we should let the Dragon Kings maintain their tyranny. All right, but you must return me to Lochivar as soon as the deed is done!''

''There may be no need. Black will be unable to emit his horrid mists for some time, and he has lost the crystal that amplifed and controlled the mists that he had. It was a precarious idea to begin with and only served to weaken him physically and twist him mentally! He was no more master of his existence than his fanatic humans!'' His wild mane shook violently as he tossed his head. ''Come! Time is wasting!''

With that abrupt change in the conversation, Darkhorse reared, turned, and trotted quickly into the crystal lands. The lionbird sheathed his unwanted weapon and hurried after the eternal. He hoped the creature did not intend to lead him all the way along the outthrust piece of earth that the crystal Dragon claimed as his. He would be little use for anything, and he had no desire to be left alone in this most unknown of all the Dragonrealms save the northern wastes of the Ice Dragon.

Fortunately, or unfortunately, the ebony steed halted before what appeared to be a small crater that dropped far down into the depths of the inner world. The Gryphon came up from behind his guide and gazed down, both fur and feathers bristling in anger.

''You expect me to climb all the way down there? The sides are as smooth as glass!'' He paused at realization of what the statement could mean. ''Did one of you do this?''

''Shade. I can only feel that luck was with me on that one! Though I would not have died, there would have been great pain! The warlock knows me better than any other and now may call upon most of the memories of his past lives! I already know he recalls some of my weaknesses!''

The Gryphon could not imagine what weaknesses the spectral horse might have, and refrained from asking.

Darkhorse went on. ''As to climbing down there, you are correct! Even if it were possible, it would take you hours that cannot be afforded! That is why you will ride me!''

"Ride you?" There was no questioning his courage, but even the Gryphon was tempted to draw the line at the thought of climbing on top of this rather ethereal stallion. He dared not, though.

Mounting proved to be no more difficult than with a real horse, since the eternal had no desire to lose his passenger for any reason. Once balanced, the lionbird gave his wraith-like companion the go-ahead.

Darkhorse jumped into the hole and plummeted straight down.

The Gryphon had both arms wrapped around the massive neck. He had, in his folly, assumed that they would be flying down. Only now did he recall that Darkhorse, for all his power, was confined to the earth when in this dimension.

Four steel hooves struck the bottom with force that should have shattered each of the legs. Darkhorse pawed the ground for a moment, getting his bearings, then sped down one of the tunnels that riddled the earth. Glancing left and right as he held on, the Gryphon soon realized that these tunnels were not natural. There was that about them that spoke of a time before the dragons. A feeling of age. That calmed him; the inhabitants were, no doubt, long dead and of no concern.

With no warning whatsoever, Darkhorse came to a halt. The Gryphon blinked at the sight before his eyes and had to be reminded by his mount that there was still work to be done. Never tearing his gaze away, he leaped off and pulled out the Horned Blade, which pulsated in anticipation.

"What is that?"

A glob of constantly changing clay, a mass of liquidy blackness. It twisted and shaped itself without pause. The Gryphon grimaced as well as his face might allow. The nebulous form smelled as disgusting as it appeared.

"That is the prison I have created to hold the mad sorceror. It is of the essence that I contain and that contains me. No more did I dare unleash into this dimension, lest it tear the fabric of reality asunder."

"How do you know he's still in there?" The lord of Penacles could make out nothing that seemed human.

"I know."

"I see." He did not, but there was little sense in saying that.

Darkhorse stepped up. "The Horned Blade lacks the power to kill him unless it touches him directly in the heart. Therefore, banishment is all we can hope for. Were he his other side, Shade would want this."

"What do I do?"

"Thrust into the very midst of the mass. The sword will do the rest. I would have done this myself, but it would have meant my banishment as well."

The Gryphon, who had been readying himself to thrust, held up. "What?"

Eyes of frost gleamed. "Worry not. It is only because I am not completely attached to this plane. You are very much a part of this reality; I am of the void! Do it!"

Raising the demonic blade once more, the lionbird readied himself.

Who is it?

The words were not spoken but felt. The Gryphon turned and started to say something to Darkhorse, but the voice interrupted, this time with more determination.

Gryphon! Friend! Help me!

He stared at the glob in front of him. Could it be . . .

"Shade?"

It is you! Beware! Darkhorse plots evil!

"Evil? No, Shade—or rather, Madrac! I know about you!"

Madrac is dead! I am Benedict—this time.

"Benedict?" The sword hand wavered.

Darkhorse will unleash ancient evils that still live in this land! You must release me before he realizes!

The Gryphon wavered. He had little trust in the steed. Shade had always been a friend, as close as was possible for him, and an adviser as well. Yet he had always talked of his faith in Darkhorse, who understood the warlock more than anyone else could ever possibly.

"Why do you hesitate?" This was spoken in loud, commanding tones, even as a question.

He glanced at the eternal, unsure whether to trust or not.

Gryphon! In a moment of panic, the tone had changed. It was no longer the Shade he had known.

A hand burst forth from the blackness, grasping for something. Most of the arm continued out after it.

Darkhorse roared. "He's loose!"

Acting with a swiftness beyond the ken of man, the dark steed leaped forward. The black mass, including the arm, was swallowed up. Darkhorse stood alone, but he was wavering, as if part of him did not exist.

"Run the blade through my side!"

"Won't you be banished?"

"There is no choice! I cannot hold him like this and banish him at the same time! He would escape! No more explanations! Run me through!"

Without further hesitation, the Gryphon plunged the Horned Blade into that which was Darkhorse. There was a scream of pain, but it was not from the eternal. The lionbird released his hold on the sword and fell back as the tunnel shook with the violence of conflicting realities.

His form fading, Darkhorse laughed, though it was a laugh tinged with some other emotion. The phantom stallion looked longingly in the direction of the sky, and his voice was strained as he whispered, "Now we ride together forever, my one true friend!"

The walls and ceiling cracked, and the Gryphon feared he would be crushed under tons of earth. The tunnel held, though, for it had been designed to stand through the roughest of earthquakes.

Little remained of Darkhorse. With each passing second, he was less noticeable. Only the piercing blue eyes seemed to have any reality at all. They looked to the Gryphon only momentarily before vanishing with the rest of the shadowy figure. The laughter stayed only as an echo.

The quivering sword was the only evidence left of what had happened. The Gryphon dusted off the brown, dry dirt from his body and reached forward to pick it up. It fairly screamed in his mind. The power contained within had nearly doubled. Rather than risk loss of his freedom to the Horned Blade, he sheathed the weapon. Even then, it shook.

He had no intention of exploring these tunnels further. With Darkhorse gone, the place took on a new feeling, one of a waking evil. The ebony steed's presence had either masked it or kept it under control. Whatever the case, he knew that it would not be safe to stay here much longer.

* * *

The tunnel system held little difficulty for him. Like the animals that composed his namesake, his hunting and tracking skills were always on a level far above that of men. Timewise, it turned out to be much longer than he had originally estimated. Darkhorse had been going very fast.

At the bottom of the hole, the Gryphon stared up in dismay. The sides were almost like glass. He could make out very little in the way of foot- and handholds. Still, he realized, his only other option was to turn back. Better to chance a broken neck.

Sharp, ivory talons dug into earth baked rock-hard. He contemplated using the Horned Blade, but it would be much too awkward and he did not want to rely on the sword any more than he had to. Pulling the paw free, he reached high above his head and gouged out another hole. In this way, he proceeded slowly but steadily toward the top.

Some two or three lengths from the surface, he had his worst moment. The earth here was softer and gave way more than he would have liked. Stretching his one arm up, the Gryphon suddenly felt his other paw slip away from the wall, the loose dirt in his grip all that was left of his handhold. Only quick action saved him. As he slipped, the lionbird shifted his body and managed to reach his previous hold. He teetered somewhat, but this one did not give way. The rest of the journey was made much more cautiously. At the top, he fell to the ground and took several deep breaths.

When he was finally able to look up once again, his eyes widened. His head cocked to one side. The horizon was tinged in green. The Gryphon had not looked at it earlier. He stumbled toward the lush vegetation, half interested and half concerned.

His first good view of the landscape before him confirmed what he had guessed. These were the Barren Lands. *Were* was the correct term. If any place contradicted its own name, it was this untamed but peaceful meadow. There were birds in abundance. Trees dotted the meadow here and there, though there was a forest off to the northeast. Now and then, movement in the brush told him of wildlife, most likely rabbits and other small animals.

Fascinated, the lionbird wandered into the fields. There was such a change to this land. It was more beautiful than it had been those many years ago, before the Turning War.

His foot hit something hard. He pushed away the tall grass and discovered a broadsword half buried in the earth. It was decorated with serpents, identifying it as a weapon of a firedrake warrior. The Gryphon tried to pull it out, but the ground would not yield its prize. He finally gave in and resumed his journey.

The next discovery shook him. From a distance, he had been unable to identify the objects. Only up close did he know them to be the bones of a fully grown dragon. The skeleton, what was left of it, was fully entangled in the innocent-looking grass that spread as far as the eye could see. The back of the firedrake was broken, and much of it was already buried beneath the soil. It had been completely stripped of flesh.

Now that he knew what to look for, he came across several more during his travels. The most disturbing was the find consisting of five armored warriors, two still astride their minor drake steeds, smothered by the greenery. All were quickly in the process of returning their basics to the earth and would be gone before the coming of winter. Each corpse bore the mark of the Brown clans.

Having heard the tale of Cabe's struggle with the Brown Dragon, the Gryphon did not have to ask what had happened. It was not encouraging. He did not care much for magic, even that which he himself had. The sword at his side weighed on him with more than physical discomfort. Right now, though, he dared not leave the Horned Blade anywhere. It must not fall into the hands of a weaker mind.

A trembling in his stomach reminded him of the fact that he had not eaten in quite a long time. The Gryphon pondered the danger of seeking food in such a place. None of the animals appeared in danger, though they most certainly had done their best to decrease the amount of plant life. Would he be attacked as the dragons had been if he dared to steal some fruit or killed one of the rabbits? The westernmost border of his kingdom was several days' journey. He could not hope to complete the entire distance without food. Despite his hunger, no attempt at hunting was made. It would not do to end up like the hapless clans of Brown.

The riders appeared only moments later.

Six they were. The Gryphon's bird-of-prey eyesight identified them even from afar. There was no mistaking the glint of sunlight on armor or the faces covered mostly by helmets. The mounts were not horses but minor drakes. Here, in the middle of nowhere, there was little reason for dragon warriors to disguise their cousins, though they usually did so out of pure force of habit, a trait picked up with enthusiasm from the warm-bloods they despised so much.

The grass was tall and wild. That would hide him from the warriors, though their mounts might be trained to sniff out a foe. As of yet, the Gryphon's hand made no movement toward the devilish sword by his side. He would rely on the Horned Blade only if necessary.

They were riding with purpose, but they had not seen him. Their path would take them quite near his hiding place, and the wind was blowing his scent in their direction. Cautiously and quietly, the lionbird made his way to safer ground. He had no desire for battle; the delay would cost Penacles and his friends even more time. Time that could not be spared.

The leader of the pack was decked in an elaborately ornate dragonhelm. He rode purposefully toward the very spot the Gryphon had chosen. There was no question as to the rider's identity; the sense of power that flowed out before him, magnified by his oneness with the plant kingdom, marked him as the keeper of the Dagora Forest, the Green Dragon himself.

The Gryphon drew Azran's terrible toy, though it would also alert the Dragon King to his presence as if a beacon had been lit.

All six riders pulled up abruptly. After a brief pause, the leader moved slowly forward. With eyes fire-red, he stared straight at the hidden figure.

"Stay your foul tooth, Lord Gryphon! I come to speak, not to hunt warm-bloods!"

It seemed pointless to remain in the high grass when they all knew where he was. The Horned Blade ready, the lionbird rose to confront the reptilian monarch.

"What would a Dragon King have to say to me? I do not

surrender to words." He kept his words low and monotone to underscore his disbelief and contempt.

Some of the warriors stirred uneasily. The Green Dragon raised a four-digited hand to silence them. "I am not asking for surrender. Rather, I seek an alliance."

The thought was so unbelievable that the Gryphon almost jerked his head back in shock. Fortunately, he was able to hold his composure and revealed no more than a slight widening of his eyes.

"An alliance? With a Dragon King? Why?"

The burning orbs dimmed as a look of weariness overtook the firedrake. "I am a realist, Lord Gryphon. The Kings are a thing of the past. The Age of Mankind is upon us. I would have it that some of my kind survive rather than fall to a rightfully vengeful race of humans! No longer will I follow the folly of the emperor and my brethren!"

The sword tip pointed directly at the Dragon King's throat. "A sudden change of heart. Why should I believe you?"

"If you want proof, consider this. Bedlam's grandhatchling was forced to travel over the Dagora Forest on his way toward Talak—"

The Gryphon interrupted. "Talak?"

"Talak. I did not intercept him, even though I had standing orders to do so. As a matter of fact, it was I who provided him with the transportation."

It might be true. The Gryphon could not recall any tales of evil concerning the Green Dragon. The master of the Dagora Forest was one of the few Kings who did not interfere with his subjects' lives if at all possible. He generally remained neutral, allowing nature and its children to take their own courses.

"Assuming that I take your word, what do you propose?"

"The greatest threat to your rebellion does not come from my brethren. I know this. We have one in our midst who is a master of the darker side of the spectrum, though he himself cannot rule."

"Toma? I've heard the stories—"

The Green Dragon let out a hiss. "They are not stories, warm-blood! I have watched and studied. There is reason to believe Toma has been among us at our councils, cloaked by the form of a Dragon King!'' He did not have to elaborate on that point. A firedrake that could metamorphose into more than one form would have to have tremendous control over the powers.

Absorbing every word spoken, the Gryphon studied the Dragon King closely. ''I think much of your newfound enthusiasm comes from a greater fear that Toma may rule. Humans you could fight, if necessary. Toma, though, would probably kill you when he was sure you were no longer needed.'' One of the warriors reached for his weapon. ''I wouldn't do that unless you desire a new monarch!''

The hand moved away.

The Green Dragon leaned forward. ''If that is not enough, then I shall also tell you that Azran is also loose and destroying all he finds. I need not tell you what rule under one such as he would be like! If the information I have is correct, he may be a bigger danger than Toma!''

''What information?'' The Gryphon's first thoughts concerned Cabe and the Lady.

In answer, the other pointed to the ebony demonsword in the lionbird's grip. ''You bear the Horned Blade, Azran's curse. Rumor has it that he carries a new one that makes this look no more deadly than a hunter's knife.''

The weapon pulsated, as if angered at this insult. The Gryphon, meanwhile, was rapidly trying to assess the possibilities of the warlock's creating such a fiendish device. Unfortunately, the odds were good. Azran had skills far beyond most of his kind. It would explain his lack of action all those years.

He sighed, a strange half-purr, half-squawk. ''All right. I'll take your word—for now!''

''How kind. How fortunate, also. Know this last bit: I am one of the Lady's patrons, though I lacked the power to break Azran's wretched spell. I will permit no harm to come to her.''

''Do you know where she is?'' The Gryphon did not bother to ask about Cabe; he was positive that the two were together.

He was correct. The Green Dragon pointed to the northeast. ''There. In the Tyber Mountains. Everything nears a conclusion.''

"I assume that you have something in mind, seeing as you've come far from your own territories."

"I have. These lands, though, are not out of my territory; they are now part of it. . . . Unless you wish to make a claim?"

Thinking back to the scattered remains of Brown's clans, the Gryphon shook his head.

"I thought not. Very well, I shall explain what I have in mind."

The Green Dragon's features twisted into a predatory smile.

XX

The bronze gate was a fitting entrance to what, for all practical purposes, was a visit to the underworld. Its incredible age was apparent from the first, a relic from a time long before even the Dragon Kings. That age did not prevent it from being a very real barrier to the two magic-users.

Gwen looked up the entire height of the door. "Now what? Toma was ready to send us here unattended. There must be a way in."

"How about knocking?"

She wasn't able to decide whether he was joking or simply at a loss. She chose the latter as he suddenly reached forward and banged hard. The noise overwhelmed all else.

They both waited for a tide of devilish creatures and indescribable things to come rushing out at them. Nothing at all happened, however, save that the massive gate swung slowly open. No one stood by. All that could be seen was a vast darkness.

With little other choice, the two entered. Almost instinctively, the Lady surrounded herself with a soft green glow. It allowed her to see while not spreading unwanted light. To others, it would be nonexistent. She extended it so as to cover Cabe as well.

Above them, things that should not exist fluttered here and there, disturbed by the two beings they dared not face. These were lesser servants, the spies and messengers. Cabe shifted their sense of reality in a way he did not understand. The shadows quieted, no longer noticing that there were intruders.

In the dim glow of the few lit torches, something stirred up ahead. The enchantress sought it out with the glow, stretching it before them. A mockery of shape, just close enough to be considered humanoid, tried to shamble away from light it felt rather than perceived. It was not designed for speed, though, and Gwen was able to expel it from this dimension before it could escape to the cracks and corridors that lined the caverns.

Cabe grabbed hold of the hand that was nearest to him, squeezed it, and leaned over to whisper. "We're there, aren't we?"

She felt it as he had, and nodded agreement. There could be no hiding a place of such power as the master chamber of the Dragon Emperor.

Again, there was the feeling of age beyond belief as they entered the chamber. Ominous guardians of stone peered down at them, some recognizable, some hopefully only the products of nightmares. How many ages had passed since this place had first been carved out was questionable. Those who had built it were surely no longer known to this world.

Seated in the midst of all was the huge, savage figure of the Golden Dragon.

"Welcome, Bedlam. It hasss been a meeting too long put off. Decadessss too long."

The great wings spread wide, almost touching the walls to each side. The Dragon Emperor stood on his hind legs, foreclaws at the ready, his head near the ceiling. He roared his amusement.

Gwen could not help but step back in open fear. Even the new Cabe appeared daunted, his body shivering momentarily.

"Well? Have you nothing to ssssay, Dragon Masssster?"

Cabe's companion looked at him. "He thinks you're Nathan!"

"Thinks? Enchantress, you of all should know your lover, despite his new appearance! Perhaps this will help!"

There was a pulling on the darkest parts of the spectrum.

Cabe felt something cover him, but there was no attempt to harm him. He allowed it to complete.

A gasp arose from the Lady. The warlock looked down at himself, mildly interested in the blue robe and hood that he now wore. He turned to Gwen. Her mouth was open and she was pale from shock. Cabe smiled to reassure her.

Then he turned back to the beast. "Right and wrong."

The huge, gaping maw was rushing down at him. Cabe pushed Gwen aside and jumped back, barely clearing the massive head. Grunting, the dragon pulled back.

The powers were twisted as Cabe's towering adversary unleashed his strength. Golden the reptile might be, but his sorcery was of the darkest kind. As he fended off a crushing wall of pure force, the warlock realized that everyone had underestimated the Dragon Emperor.

The Lady joined him, melding her power with his. The great leviathan was forced back onto his throne. He roared and let loose with a sea of flame. Cabe shielded them both, but the heat was nearly unbearable. They lost the momentum they had just gained. The dragon moved in once again, adding physical threat to his magical attack.

Claws raked at both humans. The tip of one caught Cabe on his arm, but it did not cut. In reply, the warlock released a burst of light, which both startled and blinded the firedrake. Roaring angrily, the monster swung wildly with his claws in the hopes of catching one of his opponents off guard. Cabe and his companion were forced to back up against a wall.

The Gold Dragon's vision cleared. He spied the two tiny humans and gave them the smile of his kind just before attacking head-on. Two or three statues that had stood for countless ages tumbled over as he passed. The two magic-users readied themselves.

The ploy was so unexpected, it almost succeeded. The shift was so sudden, it might have seemed instantaneous. From enraged gargantuan to battle-ready warrior in the blink of an eye. A gauntleted hand reached for Cabe's throat even as he was casting a spell against the beast that was no longer there. The enchantress was shoved aside by the hand that carried a gleaming, sharp sword.

Cold laughter filled Cabe's ears as the Dragon King thrust

forward with his blade. The warlock barely twisted aside and was only cut superficially, though that hurt more than enough. Fiery orbs glared angrily from under the dragonhelm as the firedrake tried once again.

Though he managed to shove the sword tip away, Cabe was running short of breath, and the hand on his throat threatened to snap his neck. It made concentration almost impossible, yet he had to try.

He reached forth and pulled the brightest colors to him. When they had melded together, Cabe thrust the pure power into the Gold Dragon's mind and prayed his own neck would not snap first.

The reptilian warrior shuddered. He was trying to cast out the attack, but it was too unusual and too deeply entrenched. Mouth open, fangs gleaming, the Dragon Emperor put both hands to his head and fell half to the ground. The eyes lost all appearance of sanity. The twisted mind of the Gold Dragon could not tolerate the flood. Cabe remained where he was, one hand massaging his throat as he regained his breath.

Writhing, the Gold Dragon dropped. His face was frozen in a silent scream. Only with the greatest of efforts was he able to call out. The words, though, made little sense to Cabe.

Something shrieked in anger. Out of one of the many passageways that dotted the chamber came a creature only remotely resembling a dragon. Its head was too large for its body, and it had spindly arms of little use for anything. The face was partially covered by what seemed to be whiskers that drooped straight down.

The Lady covered it with darkness. It howled even more loudly, and the darkness dissipated. Cabe surrounded it with a field of cold. The thing fought with astonishing strength. There was a tug on the minds of both magic-users, but the misty cold held.

Fear-struck, the monstrosity turned. The move caught Cabe off guard, and the creature freed itself. It loped off into the endless caverns, burrowing into and beneath Kivan Grath. The Gold Dragon collapsed into a semiconscious state with its departure.

Cabe rubbed the sweat from his face. "What was that?"

"A Jabberwock. Rare and deadly. A mutation that may

occur only once in a hundred generations, if that often. I once studied an ancient tale concerning one."

"Is it dangerous?"

"If it had seen us clearly, we would have burst into flames."

He cocked an eyebrow. "Burst?"

"Unless you're a snowman, you contain some amount of heat. Don't ask me how, but the Jabberwock's gaze will increase the intensity of that heat at least a thousandfold! Poof! Spontaneous combustion!"

"What about the scream?"

"Probably to disorient its victim. I know I have a terrible headache now."

He nodded, his face becoming more and more that of another man, though it still retained just as much of his original features. When Gwen started to say something, he turned his attention to the quivering form at their feet.

"I find it hard to believe that it's all over so quickly." He shook his head.

"He almost had you."

"A brilliant idea. Caught us both by surprise."

The Lady nodded suspiciously. "Yes, but you recovered quite nicely. As if you'd been well trained." She paused, eyes moist. "How, Nathan? How and why did you come back?"

The warlock turned to her, smiling grimly. It was Nathan . . . yet it was also Cabe. "As I said to our scaly friend, you're right and wrong."

"I don't—"

"I am Nathan, as both of you suspected, but I am very much Cabe. Even more so, in fact. Call part of me an angel on Cabe's shoulder. That's more than I meant it to be."

"Meant it to be?"

Eyes half closed. Memories that pained. "You know most of this, but I'll say it all. Three weeks before the assault on Penacles and what I thought was the knowledge leading to victory, I—Nathan, anyway—discovered the birth of a son to Azran's woman at that time. What her name was, I don't know. She died in childbirth."

His form shivered, as one part was only just now realizing

what it had lost. "The child was dying, due mostly to neglect. His only chance was a spell that had been located some years back in a pile of old manuscripts. There would be one chance and one chance only."

Images passed briefly through Gwen's mind. Of Nathan carrying the small bundle and locking himself into his study, allowing no one, not even the woman he loved, to enter. Of the mage days later, emerging haggard and drawn, bearing the same bundle and summoning a spectral servant to transport him away because he no longer had the strength. Finally, the memory of Nathan preparing for battle, still pale. If he had not saved the child . . .

Cabe nodded. "The Turning War might have gone differently. Selfishness, however, is a human trait. I—that is, Nathan—would not allow his own grandson to die! There was a chance, too, a chance that something might be preserved from all of this should the battle go awry. So Nathan, out of both love and duty, gave more than half his life-force—his soul's essence—to his grandson. Until now, I—he didn't realize what that would mean. You know the rest better than we remember." The warlock frowned, the mixture of personal pronouns only one sign of his deep confusion over his true personality.

"Hadeen took care of Cabe—you—and pretended to be your father. Nathan and he must have foreseen a day such as this."

"Perhaps. So much of it's muddled in my head. . . . But that's unimportant for now." Cabe straightened and scanned the area. "We've still got things to take care of."

The sounds of inhuman movement had built up steadily, though neither had noticed until this moment. The warlock motioned for silence. Summoning forth the powers, he looked where mortal vision could not pass.

"We have nothing to fear from the denizens of these caverns. They are few now, know their master is defeated, and are fleeing to the safety of this twisting mountain range. Without him, they have no courage." He stared at the form near his feet. The Emperor of the Dragon Kings lay still, only his breathing relaying evidence of life.

Gwen wrinkled her face in disgust. "Azran and the firedrake Toma must still be engaged in struggle outside, though. Would that they would kill one another."

"I doubt very much whether Toma can defeat Azran. This new sword bears a blacker taint than the Horned Blade, if such a thing is possible. I doubt very much whether he even controls his own mind anymore."

The Lady paled.

Cabe turned toward one of the countless passages sinking into the land. "We've one more thing to do."

Gwen jerked her head around. "What?"

"Somewhere down there is the hatchery."

She put her hands on her hips. "Somewhere down there is a beast that just needs to see us to kill us!"

He smiled grimly. "Would you rather take the chance of fighting a whole new generation of Dragon Kings someday in the future?"

"That depends on whether we have a future or not! What about him?" She pointed to the still motionless body of the Gold Dragon.

"Leave him. I doubt whether he's capable of even standing." There was almost a sadness in his voice, as if Cabe would have preferred a different conclusion to their fight.

Reluctantly, she moved to join him. When they stood face-to-face before one of the tunnels, she impulsively put her arms around him and kissed him. When eventually they separated, she looked deeply into his eyes.

"Before anything else happens, I want you to know that I love you, whoever you may be."

"I'm still the same man who's been in awe of you since I broke through the amber. I just know the truth about myself now."

"Yes, that's one of the things I mean to talk to you about. How you just happened to come to know yourself in the nick of time."

He chuckled as he led her into the passageway. "Good planning and dumb luck!"

The caverns seemed determined to run forever, possibly to the bottom of the world, if not the deepest of the hells. The fetid smell of generation upon generation of dragons sometimes threatened to suffocate them. Irritated at her own stupidity, the Lady finally covered them both with a sense-altering spell that made the tunnels smell strangely of lilacs. Cabe said nothing but smiled at the touch.

They encountered only one warrior. Every species has its scavengers, and the firedrakes were no different. This one was bent over a precious hoard left by a dead or fleeing relative. What the scavenger planned to do with it after it had all been gathered together was unknown, for he pulled out a wicked ax and charged the two.

Cabe had no patience left for delays. The dragon warrior froze in midstream. His form twisted and shrank, and the reptilian features became dominant though he was no longer a drake of any kind. The tiny lizard scurried along its mindless way, the warlock not even pausing to watch it depart.

There was no sign of the Jabberwock. To keep such a beast hidden from the eyes of the Kings, Gold would have secured it deep. Few creatures visited the lower tunnels. It was rumored that things of past ages still roamed down there.

That they had originally taken the wrong passageway was obvious. The hatchery would normally be located higher than this and nearer to underground volcanic activity. Now, though, they sensed a rise in the temperature. Their path would, after all, lead them near their destination. It was the loss of time that concerned Cabe. Azran and Toma could not be expected to battle forever.

The sudden appearance of the hatchery entranceway was not so surprising as the burnt and torn corpse of a firedrake warrior lying just outside of it. Gingerly, they stepped up to it and then peered around into the room.

Blazing red eyes met theirs.

The old dam who guarded the young was far too massive to leave the hatchery. She was almost as large as Gold had been and much more savage-looking. Cabe suspected she could not shape-shift. It would be important if they had to run.

"Sssstep no farther, warm-blood! I have already protected the children from one ssscavenger, and he wasss one of my own kind!" Beneath her massive wings she sheltered a number of firedrakes, three of which were clearly marked as new

Kings. There were even a few lesser drakes, who stood in front, hissing at the strangers. They were too small to be anything more than an annoyance.

Both humans looked at one another, and then Cabe slowly stepped inside. He was instantly bathed in flames.

When the fire had ceased and the smoke had cleared, he raised both hands in a gesture of peace. "We will not harm the children. I seek only to take them elsewhere. They will be fed and well educated."

"To be used asss ssslaves by your kind!"

He shook his head. "No. I will give them every right we give our own children. At least then, they will have a chance to live in peace. Nothing remains for them here but death."

The dam raised her wrinkled head and glared sharply at the small figure. "I will raissse them asss I have raisssed countlesssss othersss!"

"With what? There will be no more food! The Gold Dragon is defeated; what remained of his clans have fled in the face of the battle between Duke Toma and the warlock Azran!"

"Toma will feed the young! He—"

"—cannot win! Why else would the others flee? His army is already decimated! Would you have the warlock come for the children next?"

That struck a chord. The dam shivered. It was as if a human nanny had just been told that her charges would be fed to a wild animal. There was pain in her eyes, but she at last relented.

"Take them!" She unfolded the wings and shoved them forward. They waddled around uncertainly until she crooned to them in a startlingly sweet voice. Even the young minor drakes obeyed her, although they continued to hiss at the two humans.

"I trussst you for sssome reasssson, warm-blood. You appear honorable, sssomething lacking from most of your kind, and mine asss well lately." She folded her massive wings around her head as if to go to sleep. "Leave me now."

"What will you do now?"

She lifted her head momentarily to peer at him with one eye. It was older than it had first appeared. "My function isss no longer necessssary. The other dams fled. I, though, I will ssssleep. A very long sssleep, I think."

The dam refused to say more. With one last look at her charges, she covered herself again. The two humans said nothing and started herding the various young into the tunnels.

Pushing a wandering firedrake back into the bunch, Gwen muttered, "What do we do now? I wasn't planning on playing nursemaid!"

Cabe stopped. He listened for something that his companion could not hear. The dragon young stirred nervously. She was annoyed that they had some inkling of what Cabe was doing while she herself did not.

"I'm afraid you'll have to play nursemaid a little longer."

She started to say something but never had the chance. Surprise was with the warlock. With skill that spoke of years of training, he encircled everyone but himself in a blue transparent sphere. The last thing he saw was the look of indignation on the Lady's face. He only smiled sadly.

The sphere winked out.

This time, the voice was loud enough for all to hear. It echoed through the tunnels, carried along by a wave of power so that it would reach anywhere. Cabe had not had to hear it even the first time. He could only feel too well the presence of the other. It was as much of him as anything else could be. Nevertheless, he listened to it a dozen times before taking a step.

"Cabe! My son! Come to your father!"

XXI

With almost childlike glee, Azran chopped apart one of the ancient stone monitors decorating the chamber. The Nameless sliced through without touching. Fragments flew here and there.

Once again, Azran shouted, his spell carrying his voice to the deep tunnels beyond. Still his impertinent son did not answer! In sudden anger, he destroyed a relief upon one of the walls, shattering through two feet of stone as he did so.

Writhing at his side, Duke Toma looked on in a mixture of hatred and fascination. The bonds that held him were not physical. Azran was taking special care with this, his greatest of prizes so far. The dragon warlord had come very close to nearly overpowering the sorceror despite the presence of the sword. His mind was fuzzy as to exactly why he was keeping this one prisoner. When he tried to remember, the warlock experienced a severe headache.

The demonsword glowed brightly at those times.

It was a vast disappointment to find the emperor of all dragons lying on the ground like some helpless babe. Even the sword had not bothered with him. The condition of Gold was, however, definite proof that Cabe had been through here. Therefore, it was only a matter of time before the two of them met.

The Nameless pulsated hungrily. Even the hordes of Duke Toma had not been sufficient to appease it. Besides, many had escaped during the battle with the warlord.

One part of Azran's mind had an almost overwhelming desire to go charging through the mazes, but the slightly saner part knew the risk that meant. The point was made moot, however, by the arrival of the warlock's greatest desire.

The figure who stepped from the passageways startled him. The robe was more than familiar, and the physical resemblance was so close as to leave a great distaste in his mouth.

"Greetings, Azran."

He growled, almost giving in to the sword's impulse to leap forward and cut down this . . . this . . .

"You do little to endear yourself to me by wearing that outfit, my son!"

A smile. All too familiar. "I have no intention of endearing myself to you. At least, not until I've brought you back to reality."

Toma was dropped to the ground unceremoniously. The firedrake watched both warlocks closely, knowing all too well that his fate most likely depended upon which of them won.

Azran's voice dripped with evil intent. "You should show more respect for your elders, my son. I shall have to reprimand you."

Cabe's eyes turned a misty gray. "You were always an arrogant child, Azran. Nothing moved you. I was negligent; you should have been punished long ago."

Despite its hold on the mind and body of Azran, the Nameless almost fell from his grasp. The face was dead as comprehension slowly seeped its way into the twisted mind of Nathan's son and Cabe's father. Almost was the battle won there. Almost.

The dark warlock recovered. Arrogance had given way to pure hatred and . . . a hint of fear.

"Father." He whispered, the word sounding like the blackest curse of the hells. The grip on the mind-numbing sword tightened frantically.

Cabe sighed. It was a twofold sigh. That which was Nathan sighed for a family torn asunder, while Cabe himself sighed for the coming of more useless bloodshed. Both parts came to an agreement.

"There has been enough blood. This will be decided another way." He gestured quickly, catching Azran by surprise.

A moment later, the chamber was minus two warlocks.

"Where are we?"

The scream was Azran's, but the question had its origins in the blade in his hand. It pulsated unevenly, caught in a situation it could not comprehend completely.

Cabe/Nathan spread his arms out solemnly. "This is nowhere. This is that commonly called 'the Void.' The existing equivalent of death, some say."

The Nameless was brandished. "Take us back!"

"No. One way or another, this shall be decided here and now."

"I can kill you so easily!" The sword flew this way and that as if cutting up some imaginary foe.

That which was Nathan consulted with Cabe. How to separate what was still Azran from what was really the Nameless was debatable. The demonsword was his creation; much of it was the warlock himself.

"Azran, my . . . son, do you remember your departure from my keep?"

The face changed. The memories took dominance. "Of course! You were sending me far! Never trusted me the way you trusted Dayn! Couldn't teach me this or that because I always reached too far, wanted to learn both sides!"

"Especially the darker side."

"Of course. Far more efficient. I tried to tell you that." Azran smiled a childlike smile of satisfaction.

"You've done amazing things with it."

The Nameless quivered. "I've done things few other sorcerors could even imagine! I proved you wrong! There is no danger!"

"Not even from something like the blade in your hand?"

"This? Do you like it, father? I've dubbed it the Nameless. Shall I tell you why?"

Cabe/Nathan shuddered. "I think I know why."

Like a young child seeking praise from his father, Azran went on. "You should have seen it, father! Nothing could withstand its power! It slew the Red Dragon! It destroyed two armies, even defeated the lizards' best warlock! Nothing can stop it!"

"Not even you."

That took Azran aback. "What?"

"Are you certain that you can control it? How do I know it doesn't actually control you?"

The Nameless pulsated wildly. Azran's face emptied of almost all emotion. "Of course I control the sword. I created it just as I created the Horned Blade, only much better."

That which was Cabe asked, What are you doing?

Sword and sorceror must be separated if we hope to win!

A new tactic had to be applied. "I never meant to alienate you, Azran."

The demonweapon's control diminished as emotion surged through the sinister warlock. "You hated me! Dayn was always your favorite! Dayn did everything right! Dayn was so perfect! I showed both of you!"

Sadness crept into Cabe/Nathan's voice. "Dayn looked down at you, then? He taunted you?"

A pause. "No. No, Dayn never did."

"He showed off in front of you? He laughed at your attempts?"

Childlike, sulking. "No."

"Did he never help you, try to teach you when I no longer had the time?"

"He—he taught me many of the beginners' spells. Tried to encourage me when you were gone."

"That's why you killed him."

". . . Killed him." The Nameless wavered in his grasp. It had yet to learn how to control shifting emotions. Azran's change had left it unprepared.

Or, Cabe/Nathan pondered, is it more of its creator than we imagined? Is it that it cannot cope with what we say any better than Azran?

"What about your instructors? Did they prove haughty, disciplinarian?"

Eyes widened in anger. "Yes! Always pushing! Never letting up on me!"

"It is the way of magic. They often told me how strong you were and the potential you had. If not for their training, you would have never survived your delving into the darker side of the spectrum."

Pride. "I did it all myself!"

"Did you? Did you never use the wards they taught you nor incantations of preserving they'd made you memorize for countless hours? I have studied both sides, you know."

This time, there was only silence.

"Why did you kill them?"

Just barely was Cabe/Nathan able to avoid the spell fired off by Azran. The silence had been twofold; the warlock had retreated to some inner part of his mind, confused, while the Nameless had taken the opportunity to regain control of the host body.

A nebulous green cloud floated away into the eternal emptiness of the Void. Cabe pointed at Azran before the possessed warlock could attempt any further attacks. The sorceror floated helplessly, his arms pinned to his sides and his form surrounded by a blue glow.

Too close, that which was Nathan said. Thank you for watching, Cabe.

It's my body too.

Azran struggled, though his face was totally impassive. It was not complete control. The sword was losing once again, but each battle brought it closer to total domination of the body.

What now?

Good question.

The bound warlock blinked. He struggled until it was obvious that the bonds would hold him.

"Father?"

Cabe/Nathan could not hold back the surprise. "Yes, Azran?"

"I—I'm sorry about Dayn . . . and about my instructors, too."

"Good." Neither Cabe nor his grandfather knew what to make of this. If it was a trick of the Nameless, it was an abrupt change in strategy. If it was Azran, it could very well still be a trick. Either that, or the demonsword had taken its toll on whatever sanity had remained.

Caution slipped ever so slightly.

"Father!" Azran vanished.

Cabe whirled around. Despite the vast emptiness, there was no sign of the other. Nor did a glance using other senses locate any trace. Azran was far, far away.

Can't we just leave him here?

With the combined abilities of sword and host, they would find a way out. It might be to our plane of existence or to another. Neither is acceptable unless we control Azran. Pause. We were so close! I'm afraid he finally lost his struggle with the sword.

So what do we do?

Drift.

Drift?

Which is exactly what Cabe did. With a slight boost from his powers, he pushed off into the blankness of the Void.

Much later, if time could be reckoned in a place such as this, they were still searching. Around them, the nothingness went on forever.

Neither personality had spoken much during the flight. The

Void was not a place conducive to conversation. It was more to ease the growing tension that Nathan spoke to Cabe.

I am saddened by Shade. I knew him once when he was a good man, though he later changed in a way similar to that of the recent past. It is a more terrible curse than most think.

What happened in the underground city? Why did the crystal placed on me by that Quel help us? I know that was not Shade's intention.

Though he understands much that we do not, Shade had never come across the type of spell I used. He did not know that his catalyst would function as well with my magics. We can thank him; you would still be unprepared if not for that. I meant for you to grow up in a much quieter environment.

What does that mean? Cabe was curious about his long childhood.

The spell required an . . . incubation period. Hadeen watched over you for many years while you slept. When all was done, you were released. Only then would you start to grow. I'd hoped by then that things would be more peaceful. My mistake. It cost Hadeen and almost cost you.

A small, alien object floated by. Cabe broke off the internal conversation to look at it. He had come across things now and then. So far they had been artifacts similar to this.

The Void is as near to the center of the multiverse as is possible for anything other than Chaos itself. You will see debris now and then. Gates exist everywhere.

If that is true, why is it not more crowded?

The Void is endless. It is not bound by the laws of Order, nor is it bound by the randomness of Chaos.

What is it?

The Void. It is a thing totally of itself.

Darkhorse comes from here.

There are a few native creatures from the peripherals. They would be just as lost as we if thrown into the midst of this place. We are anchored firmly to one location. The only other means is to find a gate. That could take anywhere from a second to all eternity.

Cabe developed a sweat.

Something!

Both parts cried out in unision, an action that gave Cabe's

body a massive but swiftly fading headache. He squinted, trying to make out the figure in the distance. It did not look like Azran. In fact, it did not look human at all once it became more visible.

What is it?

The thing had four arms and an almost owlish face. It was clad in a shimmering robe of silver and was most definitely dead.

A traveler from some other plane or universe. Either dead when he entered or unable to withstand the shock. It happens.

The creature was a dusky brown and well over six feet in height. Cabe wondered what its home might have been like and why it had come here. He watched it drift away and thought about how precarious his own position was.

Interesting that we should run across so many objects.

Why?

One could go for centuries without sighting a single thing. We must be near a focal point.

Focal point?

An area—if one can use the term—containing two or more gates, thus the larger number of items or people one runs across. We must find Azran before he falls through or finds one of those gates!

Adding a little to his speed, Cabe moved in the opposite direction of the floating corpse.

There!

Cabe's arm shot up to point at a small speck slightly to his right. He veered toward it, moving cautiously. It was humanoid, though one appendage seemed much longer than the others and somewhat distorted. On closer examination, the appendage proved to be a sword clutched in a hand.

Azran.

He was drifting limply. Despite the awkward angle of the rest of his body, his sword arm looked ready.

Move closer, Cabe.

Closer?

Closer, but below!

He did so. The sight he saw shocked both personalities. Azran's face was a twisted, maddened picture of horror. The eyes stared blankly into the Void. Glancing at the Nameless, Cabe noted that the demonsword was vibrating only faintly.

Extreme shock.

From what?

The Void is dangerous for those unprepared. Nathan would say no more.

What now?

A sigh. We take my son and your father back with us.

And the sword?

Unless we decide to cut off his hand, we'll have to take it with us.

Cabe could feel almost nothing from the Nameless. It had apparently exhausted itself in the attempt to escape. The decision was to return to the caverns and then to a place of safety where warlock and blade could be dealt with with minimal risk.

Taking one last look, which showed him nothing, of course, Cabe tugged mentally at his link. Both sorcerors vanished from the Void.

Disorientation.

Holding his head, Cabe first stumbled and then tipped forward. He was alone in his head. The sudden emptiness only made him even dizzier. Everything was swimming. Barely visible to his eyes was a crevice in front of him. The warlock twisted as he fell, avoiding the deadly fall.

His new view was no better. Azran, his face still frozen in shock, stood near him, arm raised.

Pulsating violently, the Nameless swept down in triumph.

A blur of white blocked the way. The demonsword was forced to twist in an attempt to block the attack on its host body. It failed. An ebony blade cut through Azran's chest, spilling out his life and sending the body into convulsions.

The two swords met. The Nameless shattered its adversary into several fragments, but was knocked free from a grip that was by now almost nonexistent anyway. It bounced oddly, at angles that defied logic, and fell into the crevice. It was out of sight almost immediately.

Cabe looked up at his savior. The Gryphon stared at him with his avian eyes.

"If it's all the same to you, warlock, I would dearly like to go home."

XXII

Cabe stared down at the limp, twisted body. He was alone in his mind. Nathan was gone permanently, it seemed, either from the machinations of the Nameless or through some choice of his own. The knowledge and skill were still there, for they were as much a part of Cabe as anything else. Still, even that did not seem like enough at this moment.

"I wanted to stop the bloodshed."

"It was out of your hands. I saw Azran. There was nothing left in him but the sword itself. He was only a tool." The Gryphon tossed away the hilt, all that remained of Azran's other devilish blade. "I'm sorry."

The warlock had turned away, his thoughts now on the Nameless. He peered down the crevice, trying to discern the presence of the demonsword, but other powers, their origins and uses long forgotten, interfered with any real chance of finding it. Cabe stood up and frowned. It would be futile to search.

He sighed, hoping the Nameless was lost forever. "I'd hoped to contain the parasite, but it's beyond my powers to find it down there."

The Gryphon was eyeing him intently in his avian manner. His visage failed to mask the curiosity the lionbird was feeling. There was a difference in Cabe that he was interested in knowing much more about.

Cabe surveyed the chamber. Two other problems immediately became evident.

Both Toma and the maddened emperor were missing.

When asked, the Gryphon answered, "There was nothing in this chamber when I appeared. I hid, assuming you and the Lady to be here somewhere. When you and Azran materialized together and I saw that sword ready to strike, I charged."

"None too soon. Thank you."

"If I may ask, where is the Lady?"

Sudden realization flashed over Cabe's face. "I teleported her and several dragon young back to Penacles! You're here! Does that mean—"

The Gryphon cut him off. "I cannot explain now, but I've made a deal with the Green Dragon. But I had no time to discover how badly off the city is. He may arrive too late. It was enough trouble for him to teleport me here."

"Then I may have just sent Gwen into the heart of destruction!" He began gesturing. "We've no time to lose!"

His companion had just enough time to shout a protest before they disappeared.

They materialized in the midst of chaos.

Soldiers were everywhere. They were all running. Some were dragon warriors, many were human. They did not fight one another. Rather, they chased after a common foe.

These, the two realized with a start, were the forces of Penacles and the Green Dragon. The objects of their pursuit were the remnants of the Lochivarite horde and the few living members of Duke Kyrg's own army.

The Gray Mists were nowhere to be seen. The Lochivarites, ragged and worn, stumbled away. Kyrg's firedrakes, vastly outnumbered by those of the keeper of the Dagora Forest, tried to make a stand, but were only minutes from being completely overwhelmed.

An unfamiliar banner, held by one of a number of riders, went by. Belatedly, Cabe recognized it as the flag of Mito Pica. Survivors of the overrun city, here to make sure that their city would not be so soon forgotten by the servants of the Dragon Kings. They were particularly bloodthirsty, having little left to go back to.

The Gryphon chuckled. It came out as something resembling a cough. "Never trust a Dragon King! While he made deals with me, his army was already on its way here along with other reinforcements!"

Cabe nodded, his mind only partially on the advancing soldiers. He was looking at the walls of the city and finding that portions were missing. What little he could see of the inside told him that the enemy had managed to break through at some point in time.

He tapped the Gryphon on the shoulder. "Hold tight. We're going inside the city."

"Wha—

—aaat?"

A closer view proved no more comforting. A path of destruction led purposely toward the palace. Many buildings to the far left and right had not even been touched. The attackers had come with only one thing in mind: capture of the libraries. The Gryphon would have liked to tell them how foolish they had been.

Nervous, Cabe gave no warning whatsoever for the next jump.

"It's about time you arrived!"

The Gryphon inspected his palace for damage while he waited for the two to separate. There were a few cracks in the walls and stains on the floor. Here and there, bodies of fallen warriors from both sides lay sprawled in death. One of the golems was scattered about and another was missing an arm and was covered with dents. The lack of real damage indicated that fighting had been sporadic by this point.

Gwen was the first to speak. "I was afraid Azran had killed you!"

"No. He's dead. The Gryphon had to kill him."

She looked down. "I'm sorry for you, but not for him."

"I understand. Another thing." He took a deep breath before continuing. "From here on, it's only Cabe."

A pause. "That's fine. Nathan and I—that's a thing of the past. I realized that when I thought Azran might have killed you."

They kissed again.

The lord of Penacles cleared his throat. "Excuse me, both of you, but I was wondering if the Lady might know the extent of the damage."

The tones of the lionbird's voice only caused their faces to redden further. After that, Gwen became quiet.

"That bad?"

"The northern and eastern walls need heavy rebuilding. So does the northern corner of the west wall. Have you seen the trail leading here?"

They nodded.

"Most of the carnage was reserved to that path. Fortunately, that means a great many of the people were unharmed. Casualties are high among the army, though."

"I shall see that their families will be cared for. No one will suffer while I rule. Have you seen General Toos or Commander Blane? I'd like to talk to them."

Gwen took time before answering. Both Cabe and the Gryphon shifted anxiously.

"Toos is in control of the mopping up. Blane . . . Blane died defending the libraries."

Cabe shook his head in sadness. The lionbird hissed. They had not known the commander from Zuu for very long, but he had always been friendly and helpful. Without his assistance, the city would have surely fallen.

"How?"

"That lizard Kyrg chose himself a squad of handpicked murderers. They tore through the streets with only one destination in mind. Blane apparently managed to gather his own men and halt them. They took heavy losses, and a few managed to get inside. I don't know what they planned to do if they succeeded in finding the libraries."

"Kyrg believes in crushing all opposition to his goal whether he can attain it or not." The Gryphon's tones spoke of nothing but contempt for the firedrake warlord.

"Blane and the few remaining men with him battled it out with Kyrg here. The commander personally put an end to the lizard before going down from an ax."

That was it, then. The tragic part in their minds was that so many had died fighting over a thing that few could even understand. How much use would the Dragon Kings have gained from it? In the end, it had done little to save the Purple Dragon, and he had studied it far longer than any. Even the Gryphon had gleaned nothing much in all the years he had ruled, though that had been more than a human life span.

The libraries were of secondary importance now. Their secrets would still be waiting long after the dead had been buried.

The Gryphon summoned a servant and ordered food. "Come tomorrow, we will begin rebuilding this city. For now, I think we could all do with a little rest."

Neither argued with him.

Thanks to a preservation spell, the bodies of Blane and the rest of the dead from Zuu were carted off to their homeland. Survivors of the band and escorts from Penacles rode along to protect them from damage. Also with the caravan were dukes of the Green Dragon who had vowed to openly take the side of humanity from here on. That alone would slow Toma's plans should the firedrake attempt to garner support from his kind.

The dead of Penacles were burned, as ritual had always stated. The Gryphon placed honors on each of the dead, whether warrior or civilian. Cabe went about the task of easing the rebuilding the city, while Gwen helped with healing and food. Both were only human and had their limits; they assisted but could not wipe out the problems.

When not helping the people, most of their time was occupied with teaching the young turned over to them by the dragon dam. The firedrakes proved as capable and as unruly as human children. The minor drakes were no more intelligent than dogs or horses, and were eventually turned over to the stables. A request quickly followed for the building of a separate stable, as the regular animals were having trouble sleeping so near to the predators.

The Green Dragon gave suggestions but declined when asked to take over the training. It was his feeling that the young should be raised as human as possible. Only that way could his kind have a chance of surviving in the world to come.

Scouts reported that the Gray Mists had completely vanished from Lochivar, along with the Black Dragon and the few fanatics and drakes left to him. The Gryphon looked into explorations across the eastern seas. Something nagged him about the sinister, wolfhelmed agents from the lands beyond. Something he felt he should know. Much of his past was shadowed even to him.

Through some encouragement by the Lady Gwen, Cabe finally summoned the Sunlancer bow. It was now evident that his subconscious, perhaps through Nathan, had been responsible for his narrow escape from the Brown Dragon. The bow was the final legacy of Nathan. To Cabe, it meant that he was prepared to follow the path of his grandfather. That pleased him almost as much as the presence of the woman at his side.

Overlooking his kingdom, the lionbird was interrupted by the two magic-users. He knew why they were here. They were looking for a chance to get away for a short time. By themselves. The Gryphon laughed quietly. It was the least he could give them. The city could run on its own.

Cabe offered his hand. "Have a minute?"

"I believe affairs of state can wait while I talk to two good friends."

The two smiled at him. Cabe paused before going on. "We were wondering if you could spare us for a while. We'd like some time to ourselves."

The Gryphon stroked his chin as if in thought. "The food supply has stabilized. The treatment centers are starting to empty out. The walls are seventy-five percent completed. I think I can spare you for a day—" The look on their faces reminded him of children who had just missed dessert. "—or even a month or so."

They both thanked him at once. Cabe was shaking his hand and patting him on the back. Gwen pulled his head down slightly and kissed him on one side of his beak, an action that ruffled both fur and feathers more than he would admit. He quickly excused himself and turned back to the task of running a city.

Outside the Gryphon's room, they kissed again.

Cabe grinned. "So. Where do we go?"

"I thought the manor would be a good place. I'd like to restore it to what it once was."

He pretended to grimace. "I thought this was supposed to be a holiday!"

Gwen held him in a long embrace before replying, "It will be."

A sudden, terrible chill ran through both mind and body.

When it had passed, Cabe was frowning. "What was that?"

Though she still shivered at the memory, Gwen rejected any unhappiness. "I don't know and I don't care. Not now, anyway. We are going to enjoy ourselves and rest for a change. After that . . ."

"After that?"

"After that," she held him close, "we'll just have to save the Dragonrealms again. That's all."

This time, nothing disturbed their embrace.

Authors Guild Backinprint.com Editions are fiction and nonfiction works that were originally brought to the reading public by established United States publishers but have fallen out of print. The economics of traditional publishing methods force tens of thousands of works out of print each year, eventually claiming many, if not most, award-winning and one-time best-selling titles. With improvements in print-on-demand technology, authors and their estates, in cooperation with the Authors Guild, are making some of these works available again to readers in quality paperback editions. Authors Guild Backinprint.com Editions may be found at nearly all online bookstores and are also available from traditional booksellers. For further information or to purchase any Backinprint.com title please visit www.backinprint.com.

Except as noted on their copyright pages, Authors Guild Backinprint.com Editions are presented in their original form. Some authors have chosen to revise or update their works with new information. The Authors Guild is not the editor or publisher of these works and is not responsible for any of the content of these editions.

The Authors Guild is the nation's largest society of published book authors. Since 1912 it has been the leading writers' advocate for fair compensation, effective copyright protection, and free expression. Further information is available at www.authorsguild.org.

Please direct inquiries about the Authors Guild and Backinprint.com Editions to the Authors Guild offices in New York City, or e-mail staff@backinprint.com.

Printed in the United States
69185LVS00001B/20